PRAISE FOR TH

THE SECRETS (

'Perfect for fans of Sarah Addison Allen or Mary Stewart.'
— Lisa Redmond, *Lisa Reads Books*

'I thoroughly enjoyed *The Secrets of Ghosts*. It was just as magical and just as enjoyable as *The Language of Spells* and I am soooooo glad Sarah Painter decided to go back to Pendleford . . . I really do love magical fiction and I think Sarah Painter is one of the best at giving you a realistic look at magic and all that comes with it.'
— Leah, *Chick Lit Reviews*

'An enjoyable, escapist read, light hearted romance and a bit of paranormal whodunnit.'
— Jeannie Zelos, *Book Reviews*

THE LANGUAGE OF SPELLS

'Sarah Painter is a talented new writer, and her debut is a charming, romantic and intriguing story, with a little touch of magic. It had me enchanted.'
— Clodagh Murphy, author of *The Disengagement Ring*

'This really was a fantastic debut novel . . . I honestly could not put it down. 9/10'
— *Laura's Little Book Blog*

'Utterly enchanting.'
— Lisa D., *The Madwoman in the Attic*

'This is a little gem of a book, and every time I had to put it down I was sad because I just wanted to continue reading and get it finished because it was that enjoyable! *The Language of Spells* is a really great novel so do pick it up, it's well worth your time!'
— Leah, *Chick Lit Reviews*

IN THE
LIGHT
OF WHAT WE
SEE

ALSO BY SARAH PAINTER

The Language of Spells
The Secrets of Ghosts

Sarah Painter

IN THE
LIGHT
OF WHAT WE
SEE

LAKE UNION
PUBLISHING

The characters and events portrayed in this book are fictitious. Any similarity to real persons, living or dead, is coincidental and not intended by the author.

Text copyright © 2016 by Sarah Painter

Published by Lake Union Publishing, Seattle

www.apub.com

ISBN-13: 9781477849965
ISBN-10: 1477849963

Cover design by Lisa Horton

Printed in the United States of America

In loving memory of
Betty Phyllis Violet Le Grys
1916–2014

MINA

Sometimes you just know you are in for a rough ride. There are plenty of signs: it's raining; the bread has gone mouldy and you forgot to buy milk; the car won't start even after you paid the shifty-eyed mechanic seven hundred big ones. For women, the biggest portent is supposedly written in the follicles. A Bad Hair Day. You wash it, you blow-dry it, you brush it and spray on enough lacquer to immobilise a small army. A long hard look in the mirror reveals the awful truth: you still look like a scarecrow.

I don't mind the rain and I don't even own a hair dryer, but a day that begins with a ghost-bird is never going to be good.

The small bird was hovering just below the snowy peaks of the Artex ceiling. I drew the duvet up under my chin and watched as it fluttered from one corner to another. Mark was asleep next to me, one arm flung above his head. Oblivious. I could see every detail of the bird, from the bright yellow wing feathers to the flash of blue-grey on its crown. But I knew it wasn't real. If it had been, it would've been dive-bombing the window, hitting itself against the glass in a frenzy of panic. Instead, it fluttered across the room and landed on the chest of drawers I used as a dressing table. The bird sat amongst the perfume bottles, the tubs of moisturiser and eyeshadow, and the piles of discarded jewellery, and looked straight at the bed. Its eyes were bright and so alive. Very slowly it cocked its head as if considering me. Then it was gone.

Moments later Mark stirred. 'Christ alive, don't tell me it's morning.' He had a hand over his face and moved his fingers apart to peer out with a single bloodshot eye. He'd been sinking whisky with his pals from the hospital and had rolled into bed sometime after two.

'You're going to be late,' I said.

Mark swore and rolled away from me and out of bed. He went next door to the tiny bathroom. I heard the water running.

I stared at the place where the bird had disappeared and wondered why, if I was going to start seeing birds again, it had been a siskin. Mum's favourite.

Mark came out of the shower, a towel around his waist and his sandy hair black with moisture. I jumped out of bed and dressed quickly, escaping when he tried to grab me for a kiss. 'No time for that.'

I put the kettle on, dropped instant coffee into mugs and tried to ignore the siskin, which was now sitting on the window ledge, looking at me through the grimy glass.

Mark was still sleepy but he caught me by the sink, pushed me back against the counter and kissed me good morning. I wrapped my arms around him; it was like hugging a small land mass. I tried to relax, to let the reassuring bulk of him soothe my jumpy nerves, but could hear a small *thunk-thunk* noise. The tapping of a tiny beak against glass. Logic told me that I shouldn't be able to hear it over the sound of the kettle boiling, that the noise must, therefore, be inside my own head. It wasn't a comforting conclusion.

'You okay, babe?' The harsh lines on Mark's forehead deepened.

I smiled for him and picked up the kettle, my hand shaking. Mark reached around me with a wet cloth, wiping away coffee granules and the puddle of water, and snatched his mug to finish stirring it himself.

I turned my back to the window and concentrated on ignoring the bird.

'Did you hear me?' The frown lines in Mark's face seemed permanently etched there these days. I had no experience of long-term relationships, and no sense of whether this confusion and distance between us was normal; whether the tightness in my chest when he spoke was a symptom of a proper adult partnership, or of something else.

He ran some cold water into his mug and took a long drink. 'I booked the table for eight tonight. That still okay?'

I nodded.

'You'll be on time?'

'Eight o'clock and not a minute later,' I said, and crossed back through the living room to get dressed, turning away to hide my sudden annoyance.

The phone rang and I called to Mark to leave it. 'No time.'

Pat's voice, undiluted by distance or technology, stopped me with my head halfway into my jumper.

'This is a message for whoever is squatting in Mina Morgan's flat. If you could call the undertakers and have her remains sent home to her family, we would be very grateful.'

I was frozen, unable to move in case Pat sensed my presence. Mark was walking towards the phone and I shook my head violently.

'If she isn't dead, perhaps you could ask her why she hasn't had the common decency to call home in over four weeks.'

The machine clicked off, only for the phone to ring again immediately after.

'Babe,' Mark said. 'You know she won't give up.' He didn't care if he was late. As far as he was concerned, family obligations came first. That I still hadn't introduced him to my aunt and uncle was one of the many bones of contention in our relationship.

'No time. We've got to go.' I was snatching things up now; grabbing my bag, coat and phone with the kind of mania reserved for emergencies. 'Can't be late.'

'Babe.'

It was one word. One word filled with oceans of disappointment. Mark had known me for two years and he still didn't have a clue: it would take more than that to make me change my mind.

Romulus and Remus have a lot to answer for. In stories about twins, one is usually good and the other evil. My aunt Pat is the bad sort. My mother, on the other hand, spent every spare second of her life making dreamcatchers. Instead of shell, catgut and brown feathers, she used ribbon and lace and fake pink Birds of Paradise that sit on the bottom of the hoops, their jewelled eyes pretty and sightless. They still clutter up Pat's house and I've got several packed into boxes. My mother also pulled off the coup of not living past her twenty-first birthday. It's much easier to be the good twin if you're also the dead one. Ask any saint.

My aunt Pat, on the other hand, has a different skill set. She is an expert in not seeing things. If it's nasty or ugly or simply in the wrong place, she'll move it until it sits according to her inner sense of order. If that isn't possible, she'll simply refuse to see it. She makes over the world, shaping it to her will, until it looks immaculate and smells like bleach and lavender air freshener.

By the time I was seventeen I smelled of Jack Daniel's and desperation, so when I left home I vowed not to go back.

One of the many problems with Mark sleeping over was that it was ridiculous for us not to leave for work together. I turned up the heater in my battered old Peugeot and stuck a cassette in to play. I liked the fact that nobody else used cassette tapes any more, but I especially liked that it annoyed the hell out of Mark. He had surround sound, an iPod dock and heated seats in his car. I dropped him off at the end of the road. Too close to the hospital for my liking, but far enough away to irritate Mark and to kick off one of our well-worn arguments. 'This is ridiculous, you know.' He grabbed his briefcase from the back seat and aimed a kiss at my cheek.

'I know,' I said and, before he could launch into the hundred and one reasons we should tell the people at work we were sleeping together (as if it was any of their business), I pulled away from the kerb, forcing him to slam the door shut hurriedly. My whole body breathed out and I punched up the volume on the tape deck. After I'd parked and locked the car and walked into the hospital, I'd calmed down somewhat. I hadn't seen any more ghost-birds either, and was able to half convince myself that I'd just not been properly awake earlier.

I knew that the birds weren't real and I also knew that they were not really harbingers of doom. I had a couple of undergraduate psychology modules on my CV and I wasn't a fool. I knew that they were more likely manifestations of an inner trauma or a sign that I was developing schizophrenia than psychic ability. I knew that I had connected one bad event to the sighting of a ghost-bird in the manner of a child connecting dots. I knew that human beings are predisposed to see patterns, to ascribe cause and effect, and that cognitive bias means that we subconsciously discount data that doesn't support our hypotheses; in other words, all the times I had seen ghost-birds and something bad hadn't happened.

The point being, I knew that precognition didn't exist and that thinking of ghost-birds as bad omens was ridiculous superstition. At the same time, I believed in them wholeheartedly.

I was no crazier than the next person and I knew the difference between reality and a figment, but I also knew – deep in the marrow of my bones – that something dreadful was going to happen.

GRACE

August 1938

Grace touched the bluebird brooch on her lapel and tried very hard not to think about what would happen if the woman on the other side of the desk sent her home.

'You look very young,' Matron Clark said. 'I won't have any silliness.'

Grace smothered the urge to smile. She felt as far from being silly as was possible.

Matron looked her up and down, slowly, as if assessing a cow for market. 'You're wearing decent shoes, at least.'

Grace looked down at her brown leather brogues. She decided not to say they were the only pair she owned.

'Always look at shoes,' Matron said. 'At least you come from a family with common sense. That's something.'

'I'm very sensible,' Grace said, and the urge to smile disappeared. A sensible girl. She'd lost the right to that description.

Matron looked as if she'd like to snort if such a thing were not beneath her. Instead she said, 'Mmm,' and looked down at a piece of paper.

'I'm a hard worker,' Grace said. She'd already given the matron her letters of recommendation. She didn't know where her mother had procured them, only that it had been part of the hurried organisation of the past two weeks.

Matron looked up and smiled thinly. 'I would hope so. The problem is this: every girl who comes to see me says the very same thing.' She stared at Grace without blinking.

Grace kept quiet. She was trying not to think about her mother that morning, trying to hold on to the numbness she'd been feeling. Saying goodbye just inside the front door, her mother had reached out a hand and, for a moment, Grace thought she might be about to hug her, but the hand had floated upwards and patted her mother's hair instead.

After a moment of contemplative silence, Matron Clark gave a tiny shake of her head. Her dark brown hair, swept in an improbable wing above her high forehead, didn't so much as tremble.

Grace felt the punch of disappointment. She would have to go home. And then what?

'You had better not let me down,' Matron said, sliding a piece of paper across the table. 'Sign at the bottom and report for duty Monday morning sharp.'

'What?'

'It's pardon, Nurse, never "what".' Matron Clark shook her head as if already regretting her decision. 'Once you've signed you may stay in the nurses' home. It's irregular, but your mother has indicated that you are to begin immediately.'

Grace nodded and managed to sign her name although her fingers were suddenly trembling.

Outside the office, she stood alone in the green-painted hallway. She felt as if she could take root there so she forced herself to choose a direction and begin walking. Almost immediately she was waylaid by a nurse in a stiffly starched uniform. 'New recruit?' she said, looking at Grace's suitcase. 'Outside and to the left. Nurses' home has its own entrance.'

There were gardens filled with vegetable plots behind the hospital. Grace noted a couple of sagging sheds and a beautiful glasshouse, the kind you expected to see attached to a grand house. There was a white shape moving inside, like an enormous butterfly or a ghost, which Grace assumed was a nurse in full uniform tending to her tomatoes.

There was another entrance, not grand like the one at the front of the building. The servants' entrance, her mother would've said, and inside that, endless brown-painted corridors with nobody in them. Grace walked briskly up and down, reading the occasional plaque fixed to a closed door and every sign she could find. Eventually another human being appeared, a nurse in cape and cap, walking regally towards Grace.

'Excuse me, I'm looking for the nurses' bedrooms?'

The nurse sighed, as if Grace had asked her to swing from a trapeze or whittle a likeness of the king from a stick. 'I'll show you.'

They walked down another corridor, this one painted a sickly pale green. There were more nurses here. One slowed and nodded at Grace's escort. 'Aren't you off?'

'Supposed to be,' she said, indicating Grace. 'Found a lost lamb.'

'If it's not one thing, it's another,' the second nurse said, frowning. She had very black hair, just visible underneath her starched cap.

Grace was hot with shame and the fear that her saviour would decide to abandon her.

'That way,' the nurse said, pointing to a door and rushing off.

There was a black metal sign above it with white writing that read: 'Private. Nursing quarters'. Underneath, stuck with drawing pins, there was a sheet of paper: 'No unauthorised persons at any time. Nurses must abide by curfew'. It was signed by W. S. Bennett.

Grace pushed on the door, half expecting it to be locked, and it swung open. Inside a windowless corridor was bathed in bluish light. Two nurses, dressed in travelling capes, appeared from a side door. 'Excuse me,' Grace managed to say as they swept past. 'Where are the bedrooms?'

The nurses stopped walking. One had a pleasant round face and laughing eyes, and the other, shorter one, had a dark look. 'New girl, I suppose,' she said. 'Poor you.' Round Face turned down the corners of her mouth in sympathy. 'I suppose you've signed your papers?'

Grace nodded.

The dark girl blew out her cheeks. 'Nothing to be done, then. Rooming list is down the hall. Good luck.'

Grace found her room number from the list. Until she saw her name neatly printed on the paper, she'd almost expected to discover that it was a joke. Or that she'd misunderstood the matron and she hadn't, in fact, been offered a position at all. It seemed so unlikely that she was soon going to be wearing a uniform. That she could ever be as confident as the nurses she'd just met was unthinkable to her.

The room was a double. Two iron-framed beds, two nightstands, one wardrobe. Grace's trunk stood in the middle of the floor. She set about unpacking and was just about to push the empty trunk underneath her bed when the door banged open.

'You're new. Hullo.'

Grace straightened up. 'Yes. I'm—'

'You can't do that.' The nurse gestured to the trunk. 'A porter will take it to the luggage room.'

Grace had been looking forward to using it for extra storage. 'Why can't I keep it here?'

The girl swept into the room and began unpinning her cap. 'I'm Evie. Last girl I roomed with was a terrible drip. You're not planning on crying yourself to sleep every night, are you?'

'No,' Grace said. It sounded bald, put like that, and her voice held a note of challenge. The short silence that followed didn't feel entirely friendly. She added: 'At least, I don't think so.'

'Good,' Evie said. 'It's hard enough to kip down in this place as it is.' She put her cap on top of her nightstand and began struggling out of her long apron and pinstripe dress.

Grace quickly looked away. She nudged her trunk with her foot, trying not to blush.

'Has anyone showed you around yet?'

'No.' Grace nudged the trunk a little more, then risked a glance at her room-mate. She was down to her slip and was fussing with her fringe, trying to pin a single roller in it.

'Come on, then,' she said.

'But—'

'What?' Evie had pulled on a silk dressing gown and slippers.

Grace didn't know how to say 'You don't have your clothes on' without sounding rude, so she closed her mouth.

Outside the room, doors banged and footsteps echoed. 'Night shift are having breakfast, then it's the sisters, and then us sorry lot get our grub.'

'Does Matron Clark eat with us?' Grace asked.

'No fear.' Evie shook her head.

'Nurse Jones.' A square-ish woman wearing sister's uniform and a thunderous expression bore down upon them. 'This is not a doss house.

'No, Sister,' Evie said, sounding contrite. 'It's just the new girl was desperate to be shown around and no one had had the time yet and I'd only got a few minutes . . .'

10

'I don't care if you had but a single second, you should've used it to dress yourself properly. Go back to your room at once.'

'Yes, Sister Bennett.' Evie rolled her eyes as she turned away, which the sister pretended not to notice.

She turned to Grace. 'Follow me,' she said curtly. 'I will show you the dining hall.'

As they walked, Sister Bennett waxed lyrical on the many failings of Evie and how they typified the shoddy calibre of young nurses today. Grace was so busy trying to make polite noises at the appropriate points that she completely forgot to pay attention to the way they were going and the warren of corridors and hallways remained a mystery to her.

She couldn't eat at supper and escaped to the relative sanctuary of her room as soon as possible. It was all too much, too strange. Apart from when she'd been in hospital with flu, she'd never stayed away from home before and, much as she didn't want to disappoint Evie, she felt like howling into her pillow.

Evie was sitting up in bed, reading a magazine. She looked momentarily shifty when Grace walked in and then relaxed.

'Thank goodness it's you,' she said.

Grace felt a spark of warmth.

'I thought you might've been Matron doing a spot check.'

'Does she do that?' Grace sat on her narrow bed and unlaced her shoes.

'Oh, yes. We're treated like bloody prisoners here.' A small hip flask appeared above her bedclothes and Evie took a ladylike sip. 'We're grown women, got the power of life or death, and we're treated like naughty schoolgirls. It's ridiculous.'

Grace looked nervously at the door. She felt as if the swear word might've travelled, through some miraculous intervention, directly to the ears of her mother. Or the matron.

'I don't suppose you want any of this?' Evie screwed the lid back on to the flask and stashed it in the pocket of her dressing gown, which was hanging over the end of her bed. 'It'd help you sleep.'

'No, thank you.' Grace began undressing for bed. She suddenly felt too tired even to care that she was doing so in plain view of a stranger.

'Thought not. You've got "good girl" stamped all over.'

Grace felt sick. Not good enough.

'You'll probably even like it here.'

MINA

At work, I peered at the scan images on my monitor, my hair swinging forward and tickling my cheek. I pulled it back into a ponytail using one of the bands I kept around my wrist. The contrast agent had done its job and the images were excellent; the glowing white area in the right hemisphere of the axial MRI was as clear as daylight. Not a good prognosis for the poor owner of the brain, of course, but I was glad to see the new scanning technique I'd pushed through the department was working well. I rubbed the back of my neck and began adding my notes to the patient file.

The door to the lab banged open and Mark strode in. He was incapable of walking in any other manner and, once upon a time, I'd found it unbearably attractive. He was so tall and solid that he didn't really need his exquisitely tailored suit or Italian leather shoes to give out an air of authority and ownership. As always he stood too close to my chair and I shifted a little to increase the distance between us.

'Everything all right?'

'Fine,' I said. 'Busy.'

'Good, good.' He rubbed his hands together. Mark Fairchild was head of radiology and medical physics but he'd left behind the practical, scientific milieu long ago for management spreadsheets and finance meetings.

After a moment, I said: 'Did you need something?' I shared an office with two other physicists, Parveen and Paul, and they bent over their work, pretending not to listen.

Mark shook his head. He looked around the room, as if coming out of a daze. He raised a hand in a half-salute and left. I let out a slow breath.

'You in trouble again?' Paul said.

'Must be.' I forced a laugh.

'Checking up on you,' Parveen said.

Paul and I looked at her in surprise. Parveen rarely joined in the banter. She was a good British-Bangladeshi girl. Well, that's what I assumed. She spoke so little, I would have to admit that I had no idea what she was really like. She could've been a raving, drug-taking nymphomaniac in her spare time. But she came to the hospital, worked industriously, turned down all invitations to social engagements, and went home at six on the dot every day. I had the vague feeling that she lived with her parents, but if pressed would have to admit that could be a terrible stereotypical assumption.

Parveen nodded, a tiny smile tugging at the corners of her lips. 'Yes, you'd better watch out. If you're in trouble, perhaps he'll call you into his office and put you over his knee.' She waggled her eyebrows suggestively and I nearly fell off my chair.

Paul burst out laughing. 'Filthy,' he said, approvingly, and turned back to his work.

And there you had it: you couldn't rely on what you thought you knew about people. They were changeable. They refused to follow rules. I looked back at the MRI scan instead, with its area of abnormal white. It was deadly, yes, but reliably so. I had always loved certainty. Right or wrong. Yes or no. Subjects at school that involved 'discussing' or 'interpreting' were the work of the devil to me, and it was no surprise to my teachers when I took all the sciences. After my PhD I'd been tempted to stay in the department, researching for the rest of my working life, but there had been another impulse. To help. To feel worthwhile in some way.

No, that was a lie. I clicked the icon to pull up the next patient file. I wanted to be good. To balance the scales. If people asked, 'What do you do?' and you replied that you were a doctor, helping to diagnose and treat cancer, then you had to be a good person. Had to be.

⁓

After work I declined a half-hearted invitation to drinks and went straight home. I acted on autopilot, and a casual observer would have had no reason to think that I wasn't getting ready for my dinner date. Right up until the last moment when I needed to leave. And didn't. Instead I sat on the sofa and took off my shoes.

Part of me wanted to switch on the television and drink wine and just pretend everything wasn't happening, to split up with Mark by default rather than action, but the other part of me still seemed to retain some shred of moral fibre. I thought about him, sitting alone in the restaurant, and about the time I broke up with someone by leaving town in the middle of the night. I knew I didn't love the man, but he had been good to me and hadn't deserved that. Looking at the clock, I knew I'd left it too late and that Mark would probably already be en route. I pressed call on my mobile and crossed my fingers for the answer machine.

'Are you running late? That's okay, I'll have a drink in the bar.'

He sounded so happy, so confident, and I was going to shatter something. I might have known that it was broken but he hadn't. I hated myself. I hated this.

'I'm not coming.' The words of a lie, something about feeling unwell or being too tired, sprang forward but I closed my lips against them. I forced myself to be honest. 'I'm sorry. Things haven't been right for a while now—'

'What are you talking about?'

'I think we need to take a break.'

'Don't be stupid,' Mark said, his voice flat. 'I'll see you at the restaurant in half an hour.' And he hung up.

That was typical Mark, of course. In the early days, his confidence, his utter certainty about us, had drawn me to him. The first time I'd realised I liked him was at a Friday night drinks thing. A group had gone out after work and I'd been swept along. I remember talking to Paul but feeling Mark watching me from the next table. When I'd got up to leave, he'd followed. Outside a light drizzle was falling and he'd opened a golf umbrella. I remember thinking how laughable that was, how boring and grown up, putting him so far away from my type as to belong to another species. I'd always gone for long-haired bad boys with personal hygiene issues and marijuana habits, not a man twelve years older than me, who liked classical music and watching cricket.

'I think we should get to know each other better,' he'd said, angling the umbrella to shelter me. 'Let me buy you dinner?'

'When?' I was playing for time, trying to work out a good way to turn down my boss.

'Now. I get the feeling you'll talk yourself out of it otherwise.'

'You'd be right,' I said. 'You're my boss. Isn't there some kind of law against it?' And, with those words, I'd personally guaranteed I'd be going home with him that night. I was aware that my pathetic rebellious phase should've ended before I'd hit twenty-five, but my libido hadn't received the memo. Looking up at him that night, slightly drunk on gin and tonic, I'd thought, *Fuck it*. A one-night stand with my boss. Naughty, but fun. What harm could it do? Yes, I was an idiot.

By nine o'clock I'd ignored seven calls from Mark's mobile and was sitting on the sofa in a state of agitated paralysis. I knew that the grown-up, humane thing to do would be to go and talk to the man I had been sleeping with for the past eighteen months, but my brain had shut down. I'd always been good at keeping everything separate and tightly controlled and my brain kept helpfully partitioning off this little drama, enabling me to wonder whether there was anything on the telly.

I hated myself so I did the thing I always did when I felt low and listened to Geraint's voice. I clicked through to the answer machine on my phone, to the one saved message.

'Mina?'

That first enunciation always hit my stomach. I swallowed as his voice carried on. I'd listened to the message so many times I could recite it, but it never lost its power for me. Horror mixed with comfort. Guilt mixed with love.

'Mina? You've got to call me back. Right now. Or, like, five minutes ago—'

A hesitation. An audible breath. Then, 'I'm in trouble.'

I leaned back on the sofa and pressed my palms against my eyelids.

I didn't want to think about the last time I'd seen Ger, so I was glad when a different memory jumped to the forefront. It was from before I'd moved to Brighton. I was still at University College Hospital and living with Alex. She was the perfect flatmate. We shared a predilection for alcohol and had similarly sluttish standards of housekeeping. Alex's only fault was a preference for Welsh men. She had the idea that they were the sexiest, the most desirable. Men with the brooding looks of Richard Burton and the lilting poetry of Dylan Thomas. Alex wanted one. As soon as I'd moved to London, I'd shrugged off my Welshness like an old cardigan. I avoided the ex-pats and lost my accent. I purged my vocabulary, stripping out the Swansea and replacing it with the flattened vowels of the modern Londoner. Much against my better judgement, I agreed to go with her to a Welsh pub on St David's Day.

'Prime hunting ground,' Alex said.

The place was packed and I stood in a corner to avoid getting lager spilled down my back. I liked leaning against the wall and settled in to watch the crowd. Alex was roving the bar, popping back every so often to gulp down a drink and shout a few words into my ear.

The pub played Stereophonics, Catatonia and Tom Jones on a loop, pausing only for a round of the National Anthem. The words were printed on some specially produced Happy Hour menus: **Mae Hen Wlad Fy Nhadau** in bold lettering above a list of cocktails with names like Red Dragon and Leek Breath.

Alex appeared again. She gestured into the crowd, yelling something. She turned to me and leaned in close. 'I'm going to talk to him.' Alex's breath was a hundred per cent proof and it left dampness on my cheek.

I couldn't be bothered to shout above the noise, so I nodded, waving my hands to indicate enthusiasm, permission . . . whatever, in short, she was looking for.

Alex turned and fought her way through the crush. I drank.

A stocky man, who looked like a parody of a rugby player – short neck and solid muscles – tried to pick me up. 'All right, love?'

'No, thanks.'

'What?' he yelled, trying to be heard above 'What's New, Pussycat?'.

18

I gave up on verbal communication, shook my head.

'Cunt.' The rugby player enunciated the word so it was clear for me to lip read, and turned to the next nearest female.

I drank some more.

Later, after I'd thrown up in a toilet cubicle so dirty vomit almost improved it, my mobile rang. By way of greeting, Geraint sang 'London Calling' by the Clash. It was the first time I'd heard his voice in over six months.

'Hello, Ger.' I tucked the phone under my chin while I washed my hands.

'I'm on the train.'

'Okay,' I said, waiting for the other shoe.

'I'm visiting you. Today. I didn't know London was so far, though. It's taking for ever. I should've brought another book.'

'Where are you?'

'No idea. There's a man taking a piss on the platform. Does that help?'

'Not really.'

Ger had taken his fine brain and gone to crack codes at GCHQ in Cheltenham. If he'd come from his flat, I knew the route he'd have taken. 'The train terminates at Paddington,' I said. 'Call me when you get there.'

'God, I love train terminology. Terminates. Alight. Conductor—'

'Call me,' I said. 'I'll come and meet you.'

In the end, he'd got himself into a taxi and I met him outside the bar. 'I'm not going in there,' he announced, executing a body-swerve and going into a nearby hotel instead.

I trailed back in to tell Alex I was leaving. She was sandwiched in a group of men, sitting so close that they seemed to form one multi-limbed beast. 'I'm going home,' I shouted over the music. 'Will you be okay?'

Alex held out her hands and I pulled her upright. 'I'll come with,' she said, leaning close and spraying spittle into my face.

I didn't want to introduce her to Geraint, but I was caught. I shrugged and turned away. I left Alex shouting goodbye and letting one of the boyos write his phone number on her arm.

I waited outside and gulped soupy city air, shoving the panic down. What did it matter if my flatmate met my brother? It was just one drink.

The hotel bar was standard issue and filled with suits.

Geraint sat in one corner. He was wearing a hoodie underneath his coat and I couldn't tell if he'd lost weight.

He stood up and gave me a quick hug.

Alex bounded over like an excited puppy. 'I'm Mina's flatmate Alex,' she said, showing her teeth. Ger smiled in his lazy way and I felt Alex's attention go up a notch. I turned away, unable to watch, and went to the bar for an overpriced round of drinks. She was in full flow by the time I got to the table. Ger was lolling, one arm stretched along the back of the padded seating, the other hand toying with a lighter. Alex was telling him an involved story about the people at her work. He gave me a quick, private smile, while Alex was rooting in her bag for her mobile, and I felt a rush of love for him.

'What do you do?' Alex asked, finally finishing the saga of Francis-in-accounting.

'If he told you, he'd have to kill you,' I said, just to see Ger smile again.

Alex leaned forwards and I watched my brother check out her breasts. It wasn't his fault; they were practically resting on the table and I knew full well that Alex was doing it deliberately, but I was still irritated. More so by the end of the next round when I returned from the toilets to find him with his tongue in Alex's mouth, one hand underneath her top, in a move I'd seen him make many times before.

Alex was often flirty but not usually the kind to go from 'hello' to public snogging in such a short space of time, but Ger had that effect on women. I banged my bag down on the table, instantly soaking the bottom in spilled vodka tonic. Ger pulled back, looking slightly sheepish but mainly pleased with himself. I fought the sudden urge to swing my bag at his head.

'It's getting late. Shall we call it a night, yeah?' Alex said. She looked at me but I saw her hand on Ger's leg and I wasn't fooled. The question was not for my benefit.

'Fine.' I rooted in my bag for my Oyster card, just to avoid watching them. Alex's hand on Ger's leg, his hand curled around her shoulder.

Outside, Alex was on the kerb, flagging down a taxi. 'It's not that late, we should get the tube.' I waved my Oyster card. As always, I didn't have much money and I'd blown my budget on drinks in the hotel. Ger threw an arm around me and pulled me in for a hug. He knew I was being pissy. One hug. A wry smile. The laser focus of his gaze and a few jokes during the ride back to the flat, and he was forgiven. Which, of course, he also knew.

The next evening, Alex had come in from work and disappeared into the bathroom. Geraint had gone by then, of course, off on whatever errand or secret meeting or highly technical course he'd been sent on by his work. Alex didn't know this and exited the bathroom in a cloud of perfumed steam. I was going to let her down gently but then she closed her bedroom door and put our getting ready to go out mix on really loudly and I decided not to disturb her. I pottered around in the tiny kitchen, fixing myself some pasta and drinking a bottle of beer. When Alex emerged looking, it must be said, smoking hot in a black silky top and jeans so tight she could've saved herself some cash and simply painted her legs dark blue, I raised my bottle.

'You want one of these?'

'I'll wait, thanks.' Alex smiled but I knew it wasn't for me. It was a secret smile. A smile of anticipation and excitement. Alex was my friend and I resented her happiness. Which was petty and selfish of me, especially considering how short-lived I knew it was going to be. Ger was even worse than me at relationships. Once he started working on something (and he was always working on something), he forgot everything else. I could've warned Alex, of course, but I knew there was no point. I'd watched this dance a hundred times.

Ger came back to sleep that night. He'd missed the drinks and dinner Alex had planned and dressed up for, but was in time for a nightcap. He charmed her just enough to make sure he wasn't going to be sleeping on the sofa while I sat, hunched and goblin-like, unable to enjoy their light-hearted flirting and equally unable to tear myself away.

Alex was sitting with her feet tucked up on the sofa, one arm stretched along the cushions to play with the back of Ger's neck. I was trying not to stare, but I could feel her fingertips as if they were on my skin. Alex had drunk a fair amount while waiting for Ger to show up and now her eyes were bright and unfocused. She was joking around, clearly finding herself adorable. 'You two,' she pointed at us in turn, 'are so similar. It's creepy.'

'We're not,' I said, automatically. It wasn't exactly the first time somebody had made this observation. Ger's shoulder-length hair was tied back in a low ponytail but it was still dark and straight, just like mine.

Our olive complexions were the same, and our string-bean shape.

'Even your ears are the same, it's weird. Look at them.' Alex was close to Ger's ear, examining and comparing.

'They are not,' I said, touching my ear lobe self-consciously.

'Exactly the same shape and colour. And your eyes. If I squint at you,' Alex scrunched up her eyes, 'you could be Ger.'

'I could not,' I said, mildly offended.

'Are you, like, identical twins?'

I waited a beat, giving Ger a chance to weigh in. He could be cutting to the terminally stupid, but he just took a swig of beer.

'No,' I said, carefully. 'We're not identical.' After a beat, I added, 'He's a man.'

'Yeah, I know,' Alex said. 'But apart from that.'

'Do you have difficulty with the word identical?'

'What do you mean?' She stopped squinting and started frowning.

'Not a thing.' I waved my hand at her and got up from the sofa. I hadn't decided to get another drink until I had the bottle in my hand and was prising the top off with a novelty Simpsons opener.

Back in the living room, Alex and Geraint were kissing deeply. He was leaning on her in a way that looked more drunk than erotic, but then I probably wasn't the best judge.

'I'm going to bed,' I said.

Ger pulled away from Alex, wiped his mouth with one hand and then proceeded to salute me with it. 'See you bright and early,' he said.

'Are we busy?'

He nodded. 'Very.'

'What?' Alex had caught the scent of intimacy from us.

'Nothing,' Ger and I said at the same time.

I was a little dizzy from the booze and as I lay in bed, the room gently spinning and music playing through my head-phones to make absolutely sure I wouldn't hear my brother's sex noises, I felt utterly relaxed. Much as I hated all that twin-cliché crap, I did feel different when he was close. I felt safe. Like I was part of a smooth whole thing, not a broken half, my jagged edges exposed to the air.

⁓

I don't know how long I'd been sitting there, thinking about Geraint, but it was late and it had gone dark. I heaved myself off the sofa and moved around the flat, closing curtains and turning on lamps. I loved my flat. It was small, but it had been recently renovated and the bathroom was the nicest I'd ever had. The living room had a bay window at the front and French doors at the back, which led down some steps into the little rectangular yard. Pat had always told me never to rent a ground-floor flat, but my building had steps leading from the pavement up to the front door, so I never had people walking directly outside my window.

Besides, ignoring Pat was a habit I couldn't seem to shake.

I was just arranging the cushions on the sofa and considering calling it a night, when I heard a noise. A dull thumping and a bit of a low moan, like the soundtrack to a zombie film. I picked up my phone and dialled two nines, then carried it with me as I headed in the direction of the sound. The French windows. I wished I hadn't just pulled my thick door curtain across as now I had to move it back to see outside. I knew it would be a cat or a dog or the branch of a tree but I had to check. I forced my hand to twitch the material aside. It was Mark I saw. I recognised him instantly, which was the only thing that stopped me from screaming.

He was leaning against the glass and I was frightened he would come right through it. I thought about the shattering glass and a worried neighbour banging on the wall, maybe even calling the police, and I opened the door.

'I had to see you,' Mark said. He ran a hand over his face and stumbled into the living room, trailing dirt from the garden on to my floor.

'You can't be here,' I said. I crossed my arms and tried to block the way to the sofa, thinking that if I could prevent him from sitting down, he'd be more likely to leave quickly.

It was like trying to block a linebacker. He lurched past me and on to the sofa, sitting down heavily. 'Why didn't you come?'

'I told you,' I said. 'I'm sorry, but this thing, us, it's over.'

'Because of today?'

He looked bewildered but I just felt annoyed. 'That's part of it. You've never respected my feelings about that. You're always coming to see me at work. People have been talking—'

'So let them,' he said. 'I don't see what the problem is.'

'I know.' I took a deep breath. I had always kept things separate. Neat. When this thing had started with Mark, I'd made it clear that no one in our department could know and he'd readily agreed. 'But you knew the deal,' I said.

'The deal?' Mark's face flushed red. 'Is that how you see us?'

'It's just a word.'

'It speaks volumes,' he said. 'I'm a transaction. A tasteless little bit of business, conducted out of hours and strictly in private.'

He no longer looked pathetic.

'I'll call the police if you don't leave,' I said, going to pick up the phone.

'You won't.' Mark stretched out on the sofa, patting the cushions, seemingly calm again. 'You don't like drama. Come and sit down. Let's talk. You know we're going to have to at some point. May as well be now.'

'You're drunk.' I tried to make my voice sound reasonable, not like I wanted a fight. 'We should talk tomorrow. Go for coffee.'

'I've been drinking,' Mark agreed. 'But I'm not drunk.' He held his fingers a small distance apart. 'Only had a little.'

'Can you hear yourself?' I said, giving up on reasonable for the time being. 'You are the textbook definition of drunk. Complete with the unshakable idea that you are somehow adorable in your inebriated state, which, for the record, you are not.'

'I love it when you talk like that.' Mark was definitely leering now. Not a promising development.

'Like what?' I edged towards the kitchenette. My mobile phone was on the counter. I would pick it up and telephone the police and let them deal with this.

'All uptight and schoolmarmish. It's hot.'

'I'm serious.' I tried to make my tone as serious as possible without being 'marmish'. 'If you don't leave, I'll call the police.'

'All right, all right.' Mark lurched to his feet and I stepped back. He paused, a look of hurt crossing his face, then held up his hands in surrender. 'I'll go.'

'Thank you.'

'Will you take me home?' His shoulders slumped. 'I'm so tired. And I'm very, very sad.' He glanced up. 'You've broken my heart, Meen.'

I hated it when he shortened my name, but he did look pathetic: leaning forward, his head bent. And I owed him something, that was true. Some kindness.

'Okay,' I said. 'But this isn't the time for us to talk, remember? We'll do that when you're sober. We can meet up again, I promise.'

'Right.' Mark nodded.

He continued with the sad but calm act all the way out of the flat, through the building and while we got into my ancient Peugeot. Once on the road, however, with the crappy windscreen wipers working overtime to clear the pouring rain, he stopped behaving.

'I just want to know what I've done wrong.'

'You haven't done anything,' I said, concentrating on the road ahead. Thankfully, it was quiet, because the visibility was bloody awful.

He was wheedling now. 'Because if I've done something, you can tell me and I won't do it any more. Like, I'll back off at work. We can keep things private, I don't mind.'

'You do mind, though,' I said, drawn into the old argument despite my best intentions. 'And that's a problem.' *One of many.*

'So it is something I've done? We can work on stuff.' Mark was relentless; his voice had taken on the patronising edge that had always made me grind my teeth. 'That's what people do in relationships, they work on things.'

I wanted to say 'I don't love you and we can't work on that' but I didn't want to be cruel. Or, more accurately, I didn't want to set him off. Mark was an incredibly calm and reasonable man sober, but he was a belligerent drunk at the best of times. And this was not the best of times.

I tried ignoring him, concentrating on the road while he tried to pinpoint areas we could improve. 'I know it's not the sex,' he said. Irritatingly, that was true.

'I'm not talking about this now. It's late. I'm tired and—' I stopped myself from saying 'you're drunk' again.

He was quiet for a moment. Then: 'Is there someone else?'

'No,' I said, changing lanes to avoid some flooding. 'I barely have time to see you. How on earth would I have time for another relationship?'

Mark's voice was tight and angry. 'So it's a matter of scheduling, not inclination?'

'That's not what I—'

'So why, Meen? Why are you doing this to us?'

'We're not talking about this now,' I said, peering through the rain-soaked windscreen. 'And don't call me "Meen".'

'You're very controlling, you know? Why not now? Why do *you* get to make all the decisions?' He was slurring his words again and I realised the moments of almost-sobriety had been an act. 'You say we can't be seen together at work. You say we have to be a secret. You say I can't move in. You say I can't meet your family. You say we're splitting up. What about what *I* say?'

I felt the familiar coldness inside. I knew that I should feel something else. We had been together for over a year and there had been plenty of good times. Mark was loving and attentive and extremely competent in the sack. *There you go again*, I thought, nudging the wipers into overdrive in an attempt to improve visibility. *'Extremely competent'. Who thinks like that? What is* wrong *with me?*

Mark was still ranting, but I had the feeling he was going to start quietly crying or something awful like that. Instead, his mood went in the other direction. He grabbed my arm. 'Listen to me, for fuck's sake! Why won't you listen? Why won't you bloody hear me?'

The car lurched sickeningly to the right and I hauled the steering wheel back to correct it before it veered into the central reservation.

I opened my mouth to tell him to stop being an idiot but I didn't have a chance; he grabbed the wheel with both hands and yanked it sharply. I tried to stop it from turning, but it was too sudden and he was too strong. I braked, lights blazing in the rear-view mirror, and then the car was sliding on the wet surface of the road. It was spinning, the back wheels veering to the left. Panic was present in me, but I didn't really feel it. The outside world was a blur of smeared headlights and terrifying blanks, but at the same time it felt curious, rather than urgent. I seemed to be outside myself somehow, aware of the terror and the adrenaline but from a distance, as if I was observing the car spinning, rather than trapped inside. It was slower, more balletic, than I'd ever imagined a car crash to be. I marvelled that there was time to see the headlights of the oncoming cars getting brighter and bigger and closer. At once, they were so close they were blinding, my eyes filled with a burning white. In the next moment there was nothing, only blackness.

GRACE

At breakfast the next day there were twenty or so tired faces, all of them complete strangers to Grace except for Evie, who was yawning so widely her jaw cracked. Grace had never eaten breakfast with anybody other than her mother and father. She forced herself to walk into the room and take a place at one of the large tables. A couple of the nurses gave her quick smiles, but most were too busy concentrating on their meal. They seemed to move as one, grabbing food and shovelling it into waiting mouths. Grace had never seen such appetites before. She took a spoonful of her porridge and found she couldn't swallow. The mass of it sat on her tongue, congealed and peculiar, until she spat it back on to her spoon as discreetly as she could.

A girl opposite stuck a hand across the table for her to shake. 'Barnes,' she said. She had wide, cow-like eyes and pink cheeks.

'Nice to meet you—'

'You going to finish that?' Barnes indicated Grace's bowl.

Grace pushed it across the table.

Sister Bennett appeared at seven-fifteen sharp and stood at the head of the table. She carried a notebook and read out each nurse's name, followed by the name of a ward. Since Grace hadn't the slightest idea what any of the ward names meant, she had no particular care except for one desperate wish. She wasn't at all sure that she believed in God any more but she sent a prayer up anyway: *Please don't send me to midwifery.*

'Nurse Kemp, Princess Mary Ward.'

'Bad luck,' Evie said, nudging her.

'What is it?' Grace hoped her voice didn't betray her dread.

'Private. You'll be nothing but a skivvy.'

Grace let her breath whoosh out.

The private ward turned out to be a series of single rooms leading off a central passage but, according to the sister in charge, it might as well have been a suite at the Savoy. Only cleaner. Grace was supposed to scrub the floor in each room, before starting on the morning drinks. She couldn't get all of the patients' names straight and who had warm milk, hot water or sugared tea. There was a list in the kitchen, of course, but by the time she'd found the relevant room, been stopped and asked what she was doing by a nurse, then answered a buzzer from room twelve in which the resident wanted her curtains opened a fraction of an inch, and told a wandering patient, Mr Greene, to go back to bed for the seventh time, she had mixed up everything on the tray. She ended up giving milk to Mrs Aniston, who couldn't tolerate it but didn't say a word until the doctor did his rounds, when she promptly threw up all over her bed.

Grace was shouted at by the ward sister more times that first day than she had ever been before in her life and it took every ounce of her courage not to burst into tears. She was on her hands and knees scrubbing a stubborn patch of floor in an empty room when the sister swept in and told her to look lively. A new patient was being brought in and, the sister couldn't stop a thrilling note from creeping into her voice, he was a 'wounded officer'.

Grace helped to make the bed and then a trolley bearing a sheeted shape appeared. The porter who wheeled the trolley was a cheerful man, who had joked with Grace earlier, but in front of Sister he confined their interaction to a stiff 'Over here, please' and 'Right you are, Nurse'.

'Run along, Nurse,' Sister said as soon as the patient was settled into bed, so Grace had only the briefest peek at the officer before rushing off to mess up the afternoon drinks. When Evie asked her later what he looked like, she could only say he 'didn't look well'.

Evie snorted. 'You're no use.'

Grace tried again, grubbing up the memory and trying to see the details. Dark brown hair, messy from lying in bed. Eyes that seemed too big somehow. A thin face, drawn in pain. 'He had nice eyes,' she said.

It was after lights out and they were whispering. Grace heard Evie shift in her bed, the springs complaining. 'Did he have nice hands, too? Officers always have nice hands. It's the breeding.'

'I didn't look,' Grace said.

'Look tomorrow. You'll see.'

The next day, Grace did look. Burrows, properly known as Captain Burrows, had his teeth clenched as the doctor checked his wounds. It was Grace's job to assist. To hold the dish for the dirty swabs and dressings to be dropped into, and the dish of clean hot water, and to swish the curtains for the doctor to make his entrance and exit. She was also in charge of holding the patient still, but that was hardly needed. Captain Burrows clenched his teeth, fingers curled around the edge of his top blanket so hard that his knuckles stood out bright white like a row of dice.

After the doctor had stepped out, the sister no doubt leading him to her room for a reviving cup of tea and a slice of cake, Grace tried to make the man more comfortable. She felt shy as she gripped his shoulders to hoist him further up the bed and had to keep reminding herself that he wasn't Captain Burrows while he was in here, nor was he a nice-looking man with interestingly shaped lips, he was a patient. Once she'd heaved him upright and plumped his pillows and held a glass of water to those interesting lips, Grace felt nurse-like once again. The urge to blush had thankfully gone. She busied herself tidying away the spare cotton wool and straightening the top sheet.

'What's your name?'

Grace didn't look at him straight away and even when she did she focused on his left eyebrow, not trusting herself to take in all of his face at once. 'Kemp.'

'Don't you have a first name?'

Grace couldn't stop the quick smile that escaped. 'Nurse.'

There was a pause. Grace stared at her hands, still resting on the edge of his blanket, which suddenly seemed like an intimate thing to be doing. Touching his bedclothes, straightening them like a mother would with her child's or a wife with her husband's.

'Kemp, then. Get my cigarettes, would you?'

'You've got a chest wound,' she said. 'It might make you cough.'

'Rot,' Burrows said, but his voice was mild. Grace risked a quick glance. His head was tipped back against the pillow and his eyes were shut. Grace was free to look at him for longer. She could see a patch under his chin that had not been shaved properly; the peak of his Adam's apple, which gave her a strange feeling in her stomach.

'So, what did you do to end up in here?'

Grace almost jumped out of her skin. 'What do you mean?'

Burrows waved a hand. 'This place. It's just like the army, so I'm quite at home, but I can't see why anybody else would choose it.' He smiled faintly. 'Not that I'm not grateful, you understand.'

Grace concentrated on her swabs. It was peculiar to be spoken to in this manner. As if she were of the same rank in life as he.

Perhaps that was another facet of him that disappeared when he put on the stiff khaki uniform. Or perhaps he was just very nice.

She risked a glance at him, using her trick of looking at his hairline instead of his whole face. 'It was this or teaching.'

There was a silence and she risked another glance. He was watching her with a thoughtful expression on his face. 'I bet you're good with children.'

'What happened to you?' Grace said, to change the subject. His face clouded and she could've kicked herself. 'Sorry. I'm a clot. I didn't mean to—'

'Quite all right. I just assumed you'd know. Nurse and all.'

'I'm hardly a nurse. Still training.' She glanced over her shoulder, suddenly fearful. 'Please don't let Sister know I told you that or I'll be for it.'

He put a finger to his lips and Grace found herself staring at them all over again. Burrows closed his eyes, as if the conversation had exhausted him. Grace turned to leave but she still caught his words, quiet though they were.

'Funny you said training. That's what got me.'

Grace turned back.

'Explosives training,' he said, opening his eyes. They were grey, fringed with very dark lashes. 'New recruits to the regiment. One of the chaps fumbled it. I went to him but it was too late and, well . . .' Burrows gestured downwards.

Grace wished, more than anything, that she could take back her admission. Why had she told him she was in training? He must be furious. Worse, he was probably frightened that she would make a mistake. 'I won't hurt you,' she said.

Burrows raised his eyebrows. 'It wasn't his fault. Just an accident, could've happened to anyone.'

'You're very forgiving,' Grace said. Perhaps he was a religious man.

Burrows shook his head. 'I think he's paid enough.'

It took Grace a moment to realise what Burrows meant. 'Oh,' she said. 'I'm sorry.'

'Not your fault either.' He smiled very slightly, clearly with some effort. 'One expects to get hurt during battle, but it's rather embarrassing to be laid up in this way.'

'I'm glad there isn't a battle,' Grace said. 'And I heard Chamberlain say there won't be one.' She surprised herself by speaking her mind.

'Ah,' Burrows said, his smile sad now. 'If you'd known as many leaders as I have, you wouldn't set so much store by their words. It's actions that count. Every single time.'

'You're frightening me,' Grace said, feeling suddenly stupid and a little sick.

'Really?' he said. 'You don't seem the sort. Besides, aren't nurses supposed to be made of iron?'

'Perhaps,' Grace said, conscious that she was letting herself down again, enjoying the conversation too much. She was supposed to be made of iron. She wasn't supposed to be flesh and blood and breath that quickened. 'Maybe one day.'

MINA

The pain was everywhere and everything. It was impossible to separate a 'me' from it. After a while, it receded just enough to allow thought and I thought: *Help me*. I don't think I said anything but, for a moment, I sensed a presence nearby. There was a change in the air. I could smell something different and I heard a voice. A woman's voice, calm, and a man's voice further away. Deep and unhappy. An edge of worry in the voice that I saw as a red line running across the blackness behind my eyes. The red line fractured, became a web of red lines, crazy paving.

Then more blackness.

I knew something unhelpful must have happened to my skull, but I put that thought aside for the time being. It was too scary. My mind shied away like a horse refusing a jump. I tried to wiggle my toes and felt them move against something smooth and cool, then tried my fingers, and my arms. Not paralysed then. Just really, really fucking sore. It felt good to swear, even just in my own mind. For a moment I wondered if it was in my own mind. I might have sworn out loud or I might be on stage in the Royal Opera House, suffering from stage fright so severe it had rendered me temporarily blind, or I could be . . .

Blackness.

The next time I woke up I opened my eyes straight away. I was done with this no man's land shit and I wanted to re-enter the world. The light was still too bright but I forced myself to keep at it and gradually, with a lot of blinking and more blinding head pain, I found I could see. So, I wasn't blind either. A knot of tension that I didn't know I'd been holding on to slid undone.

I was in hospital. That much was made abundantly clear by the metal-framed bed and the cluster of machines. It was hushed and the curtains were drawn so I couldn't tell if I was in a ward or a small room or what.

My head felt enormous. It felt like it had been replaced with a big glass pumpkin. I wanted to move it from side to side, just to prove that I could, but even the thought of movement hurt. A big glass pumpkin filled with pain. I imagined raising myself up a little, trying to sit, and that was enough to make the pain explode until I thought I would throw up. I took a few deep breaths and became acutely aware that every other part of my body appeared to be hurt, too. This was bad.

The curtain swung open and a nurse walked in. She smiled in that professionally warm way that nurses do. 'You're awake. How are you feeling, honey?'

I opened my mouth to say 'Wonderful, I'm thinking of running a marathon before lunch', but just a wisp of breath and the hint of a strangled croak came out. I swallowed and tried again.

'It's okay, have a sip of this.' The nurse slipped a hand underneath my neck and raised my head, bringing a cup of water to my lips. The pain bloomed anew and I wanted to punch her. Then the liquid eased into my mouth and down my throat and I wanted to hug her. Perhaps getting my head bashed in had given me multiple personality disorder. I wanted to ask her if it was normal for a person in my situation to be full of rage, but I didn't trust myself to speak and, besides that, I didn't really want an answer. If it was 'no' then I was most likely just a horrible person.

I must have fallen asleep – or lost consciousness, or whatever – as the nurse disappeared and some of the machinery was different, or moved. A big thing that had gone 'beep' in a reassuringly regular way was further from the bed and wasn't making any sounds at all. The curtains had been pulled back, too, and I could see that I was in Intensive Care. The light that I had thought blinding was actually quite dim and there were what seemed like hundreds of medical people doing important-looking things with instruments.

One of these peeled away from a bed further up the room and walked towards me. I kept my head turned and watched him approach. He looked too young to be a doctor, which made me feel old, then I panicked as I realised I wasn't sure of my age. I was hyperventilating a little bit by the time he was looming over me, another professional smile hovering in my sight line.

'Hello, Mina. I'm Dr Adams. You're in the hospital.'

Tell me something I don't know. Like, at this moment, literally *anything* else.

'You've suffered a serious head injury and have been unconscious for quite a while. We're really glad to see you awake.' He shone a little light in my eyes as he spoke, holding my eyelids open as if I was a plastic doll.

He smiled with more warmth. 'How's the pain?'

'Painful,' I managed. 'And I can't sit up.'

'I wouldn't try just yet,' he said, looking serious again. 'You've been through a lot. It's best to take things slowly.'

'I want to,' I said, realising that I sounded like a toddler.

He reached out as if to touch my shoulder, then hesitated. 'I can help you sit up, but it'd probably really hurt. If you wait another day or so, it'll hurt less. It's your call.'

'Sit up now,' I said.

'I'll give you a little dose and then we'll give it a go.' He fiddled with the tube that led into a shunt in the back of my hand. I felt a tiny rush of something and then the edges of my vision went black, swiftly followed by the rest. Tricksy bastard, I thought, before slipping into unconsciousness. Again.

⟨⟩

More time passed before I could stay awake for any length of it. Eventually I was well enough to sit up. Then it was like someone was hammering spikes into my skull and I couldn't manage it for long. Today I was feeling marginally better. I was sitting up, pillows arranged behind me by the smiling West Indian nurse, and the pain in my head had receded enough to allow me to think at least a little. I managed to ask the question that had been forming for what felt like days. I licked my dry lips. 'What happened to me?'

'You don't remember?' The nurse wheeled a table so that it sat over the bed. She poured a plastic cup of water and slid it towards me. I turned my concentration to my arm and hand, willing them to obey me, not to shake or to miss the cup the way they had earlier when I'd misjudged and swiped it on to the floor. Not this time.

By the time I had the cup to my lips and was drinking sweet liquid, the nurse had gone and it wasn't until I'd successfully drunk without dribbling and replaced the cup on the table that I remembered I'd had a question to ask. Frankly, it was frightening. One thing you could say about me: I was a brain. Top-of-my-class type in school, at least until my rebellious phase began, and after all that,

I'd gone to the local college, done the A-levels I'd missed and gone to university to do . . . Something. I had a momentary blank on what, exactly, I'd done for my degree and that was terrifying so I skipped over it. I knew I'd worked hard, though, refused all distractions. I also knew that it had been easy for me. Something I'd always counted on, taken for granted, really, was my intelligence and now it appeared to be on the fritz.

The curtain swished but instead of a nurse or doctor, it was a man in a cheap suit. My old instincts kicked in. I knew he was police before he flashed his warrant card. 'Nothing to worry about, routine visit,' he said. Perhaps he was aiming for avuncular, but he had a shiny face and the look of a man who was anticipating his lunchtime pint a little too much. I didn't like him, but then that was nothing unusual. As I spent more time conscious, my sense of self had returned and I remembered that I wasn't a very nice person.

He flipped open a small notebook. 'You've been here for seven days, correct?'

A week? Now that surprised me. I felt sick. A week spent mostly unconscious. That didn't seem good. I hadn't asked about my injury or injuries and nobody had told me. Which, now I came to think of it, was a bit odd. Wasn't that the kind of thing doctors and nurses did? Although maybe not when you were seriously hurt. Perhaps the rules were different then. Seriously hurt. I tried to swallow the lump that formed in my throat.

'Do you remember what happened before you were brought here?'

I thought better of shaking my head and said 'no' instead. It came out in a whisper making me sound like a proper ill person. Like a plucky heroine in a made-for-television movie. Damaged but still beautiful. Hah!

'You had an accident. Do you remember that?'

'No,' I said, my voice stronger now, with shock. Which was stupid. Of course I was in an accident. What else could've happened? It was obvious, which was why I was spooked. Why hadn't I been thinking about this stuff already? Why hadn't I been wondering? And why the fuck couldn't I remember anything?

'It was a car accident. Do you remember driving your car?'

'No.'

'You don't remember where you were going?'

'No.'

He sucked his teeth and scribbled something in his little book. I realised he didn't believe me.

'I don't,' I said.

'Okay, what's the last thing you do remember?'

'Before waking up here?'

He nodded. Show off.

I thought. Nothing. Blank screen. I began to panic. That couldn't be right. I ran through some facts. My name was Mina Morgan. I worked as a medical physicist. Fuck. I worked in a hospital.

'Where am I?'

The policeman frowned. 'In hospital, love. You're in hospital.'

'Which one?'

His frown cleared. 'Royal Sussex.'

Yep, that sounded familiar. I worked in the Royal Sussex. I remembered the big scanning machines of the radiotherapy department, downstairs in the basement. I pictured my job title, written on my business cards, the NHS logo in the right-hand corner.

The nurse came in. 'I said two minutes.' She didn't look at me, angling her substantial body between my bed and the policeman. I felt a rush of affection for her. I needed a moment to process what he'd just told me. I was in the Royal Sussex. My place of work. Where people knew me and I usually projected professionalism. My job in the hospital was important and I was proud of it. I signed off on treatment plans, which went to the oncology consultants. And now I was flat on my back with a messed-up head. Like some kind of victim.

'This is just routine,' the policeman was saying. 'I need to confirm the circumstances of the incident for my report.'

'You'll have to come back later,' my saviour-in-nurse-form said.

The policeman heaved a sigh. He took out a business card and put it on the table. 'Call me if she gets her memory back. I'll try to pop by in a week or so, but it'll depend. Workload, you know?'

He was trying for solidarity with my nurse now, but she wasn't having any of it.

After she'd shooed him out, she came back in. Natalie? I tried to focus on her name badge.

'Don't worry, honey, it'll come back to you when you're ready for it. Sometimes our minds just protect us for a little while.'

I didn't like the idea that my mind was doing this deliberately. Conspiring against me. 'I really can't remember,' I said. Suddenly, it seemed important that she should believe me.

'Makes no difference to me, honey. If I judged people who came in here, I couldn't do my job.' She poured me another cup of water. 'Besides, I didn't want him tiring you out, not when your sweetie is waiting to see you, too.'

'My sweetie?'

'Shall I show him in?' Maybe-Natalie's eyes were bright. A romantic then. I was back in the afternoon movie. I knew how this went. My amnesia would be magically healed by a kiss from my loving boyfriend or, I felt a lurch in my stomach, my husband. I looked at my hands. No rings. No telltale tan line on my wedding finger. Boyfriend then. I had a boyfriend. I tried to summon a picture, a name, anything.

'Okay,' I said, exhausted by the effort of wracking my poor bruised brain. I'd just meet the guy.

As soon as he walked up to the bed I recognised him. Mark. It was Mark. My boss in the radiology department for three years. My lover for the last year and a half. I was so relieved to have remembered something, to recognise somebody, that I didn't even have to fake being pleased to see him.

'Hello, you.' He leaned over and hesitated, as if working out where to kiss me. I wondered how bad I looked. He settled a little to the left of my lips and I caught a whiff of his familiar smell. Paco Rabanne aftershave. Soap. Mark. 'I'm sorry I wasn't here when you first woke up. They said I had to wait. Not being family.'

'Hello,' I said. 'No grapes?'

Mark's eyes crinkled. 'I wasn't sure if you were back on solids yet.' He indicated the drip in my arm.

'It's tradition,' I said. 'Plus, I was allowed a vanilla yoghurt this morning so I'm fully expecting beef bourguignon and a glass of red this evening.'

Mark looked around for a chair. I patted the bed. 'No chairs. They're not kidding about government cuts.'

Mark sat at the end of the bed, below my feet. There was plenty of room so I added 'short' to the list of things I knew about myself. 'How are you feeling?'

I paused, wondering which of my pains to mention first. 'Confused,' I said, finally. 'I don't know what happened. I don't know how I ended up in here. And my head is killing me.' This last bit wasn't true. Not any more. It hurt, yes, but compared to the nauseating, all-encompassing pain of the first few days, it was nothing. It had hurt so badly I'd thought I was dying. It had hurt so much I'd wanted to die.

'You must've hit it pretty badly when you crashed.'

'I don't remember.' An awful thought struck me then, made worse by the guilt that it had only just occurred to me. 'Did I hurt anyone else? What did I crash into?'

'Central reservation on the dual carriageway but no one else was involved. Miraculous, really.'

I sank back against the pillows. 'Thank God.'

'You really don't remember anything?'

'No.' I still wasn't up to head shaking. So I just said it again, for emphasis. 'No. I don't remember getting into my car; I don't remember where I was going. A policeman was just here and I told him the same.'

'Hey.' Mark leaned forwards, patted my hand through the blankets. 'It's okay. It's not your fault.'

'We don't know that, though, do we? I can't remember so who knows what I was doing? I could've hurt someone.'

'You hurt yourself. You just need to get better. Don't be upset.'

'I'm not upset,' I said, then realised that my face was wet. There were fat drops of moisture landing on my chest. I reached for a tissue from the box on the table and my head exploded. When I woke up next I was flat on my back again, Mark was gone and it was as dark as it ever got in hospital.

I was angry with myself. With my weakness. I'd wanted to be with Mark for longer. I'd wanted to look at his face and enjoy the act of recognising it, remembering it. I kept probing the gaps in my memory like I was checking out missing teeth with my tongue.

I was thirsty, too. I knew that if I struggled to sit up on my own, there was a good chance I'd black out again. Part of me wanted to, actually; it might be a relief to get back to sleep so instantly. On the other hand, I was sick of being at the mercy of my bad head. I was sick of not knowing what had happened to me. I was sick of lying down, trapped with my own broken thoughts.

The curtain next to my bed fluttered, as if there was a breeze. I waited a moment, expecting Maybe-Natalie or one of the other nurses to appear. When they didn't, I turned my head away, trying to find a cool spot on the pillow and, perhaps, get comfortable enough to slide back to sleep.

Instead I very nearly screamed. A figure was standing next to my bed. At first I thought it was a girl – she was very slight – but as I looked more closely, I realised she was a young woman. She had light brown hair that was severely tied back and a neat little fringe that was curled inwards, like it had been set with tongs. I didn't feel like screaming any more. She had such a pleasant face, a pale oval set with soft brown eyes and a pretty mouth. She was wearing a costume of some kind, but before my brain could begin to catalogue it, she gave me a half-smile that was so sad, I felt tears pricking my eyes. I was about to ask if she'd help me to sit up – which was odd as I wasn't in the habit of asking complete strangers for help – when she disappeared.

Now that I was awake for longer periods, Dr Adams decided I was strong enough to be given the rundown of my injuries. He said my right knee was the worst – something I could've told him – and talked about the posterior cruciate ligament and how lucky I was that the fracture of my patella wasn't worse. He declined to elaborate on my ongoing memory-scramble, giving me platitudes about time and relaxation and post-traumatic stress and how lucky I was to have come out of the coma. Now that the pain of the knee itself was more manageable, I had begun to feel the other injuries. I lifted the bed sheet and stared at the soft white dressing that covered my left leg from thigh to ankle. My right knee – the bad one – was in plaster but below that was another dressing, strapped into place with tape, and below that, mottled red skin. As soon as I looked at it, it began to throb and itch, as if showing off under the new attention. 'What happened?'

The nurse tilted her head. 'In the accident, lovey. You still don't remember?'

I shrugged a tiny bit. Just to show I didn't. 'Dr Adams said that my knee probably got broken hitting the dashboard. That looks disgusting.'

'Looked worse when you came in,' she said. 'It's healing really well underneath those. You'll have the dressings off in no time.'

'It hurts,' I said. Although that didn't feel true any more. Not now I had the fresh memory of the pain in my head to compare it with. 'Well, it's a bit sore. Tingly.'

The nurse smiled widely. 'That's the first time I've heard second-degree burns described as tingly. I'm going to miss you.'

'I'm going home?'

'No, bless you. New ward. Medical or ortho, depending on where has the space.'

'I don't want to move,' I said. 'I like it here.'

'It's a good thing you're well enough to leave the ICU. That's cause for celebration. I'll see if I can't find us a cake.'

My stomach turned over at the thought.

'When will I remember?'

'I don't know that, lovey.'

'But on average. People like me. How long before they remember?'

'I've never had one like you.'

I thought she was being kind, saying what I'd want to hear. That I was a unique little snowflake and our nurse–patient bond was special. The sort of nonsense that probably worked on most of the pathetic creatures she dealt with, made them feel cared for and safe. It worked on me too, of course, but I didn't have the energy to be annoyed about it.

After she'd left and I was alone with the tingling in my legs that now seemed to contain the memory of heat, I saw the young woman appear again. This time I saw her emerge from the curtain, coalescing from folds in the fabric into a recognisable figure. I blinked several times but she didn't disappear.

Then Mark swished aside the curtain, displacing the folds of fabric, and she was gone again.

'How are you feeling?' He was being excessively cheery. Hearty almost. I curled my hands into fists, digging my nails into my palms.

'Have you heard the good news?' I sat up a little. 'I'm being moved to medical. Or ortho, whatever that is. Somewhere that isn't Intensive Care, at any rate.'

'That's great,' Mark said. He leaned down and kissed me and I fought the sudden urge to flinch away. I didn't know what it was about him, but I seemed really jumpy whenever he came near. I looked at his suit, the skin of his neck and the way his hair grew up from his forehead. He had a bit of a widow's peak and his forehead, already high, was extenuated. The strangeness disappeared and he appeared dear to me. There was something vulnerable about the downward droop of his eyes.

'I'm so proud of you,' he said, taking off his raincoat and sitting down.

At once the warm feeling disappeared. In my sudden irritation he seemed older. I couldn't force a smile so I told him my knee was hurting. He jumped up and went to find a nurse.

I wished I knew what was wrong with me. Mark was my boyfriend. That didn't sound right. He was my partner. My lover. Why wasn't I happy to see him? That wasn't true. I was happy, but then, within minutes or seconds, I wanted him to leave. Had I always been like this?

He appeared again. 'She says you're not due more painkillers for another hour. Sorry.'

'That's okay. Thanks for trying.'

Mark had a funny expression on his face.

'What?' I said. 'What did I say?'

'Nothing.' He shook his head. 'You're being very calm, that's all.'

'Am I not usually?' I hated the thought that I'd changed.

'Not as such, no.'

'I remember things,' I began. 'But some of them I'm not so sure I'm pleased to remember.'

Mark was suddenly pale. He glanced away and I wondered why I'd upset him.

I sighed in frustration. 'I wish I could remember properly. Everything is so fragmented. And sometimes it feels like maybe I wasn't very nice.'

'You weren't,' Mark said, colour returning to his cheeks.

'Oh.' The sick feeling in my stomach got worse.

'I don't mean that in a bad way. But "nice" is a bit of a wishy-washy word.' Mark smiled faintly. 'You weren't wishy-washy.'

'Not like now. I'm very wishy-washy now.' I didn't add that I felt insubstantial. Like I would run away down the plug hole if I had a bath.

'You could never be that,' he said.

ᘒ

The next day I dismissed my disappearing woman as another fun trick of serious head injury. A little something to go with the excruciating pain and memory loss. A nurse I didn't recognise arrived with my doctor. I looked more closely at him today and identified laughter lines and a certain coarseness to the skin along his jaw. Not as young as I'd first feared. Maybe even a little older than I was. Which I'd remembered. Twenty-nine. 'I'm very pleased with you,' he said, flashing his eye crinkles. 'I think we can move you out of the ICU this afternoon.'

'Yay,' I said. 'When can I go home?'

He gave a short laugh as if I'd tried to make a joke and, although it wasn't funny, he was giving me marks for trying.

'I'm serious,' I said. 'When can I go home?'

The eye crinkles disappeared. 'Not for a while. You are lucky to be alive, you know.'

'I thought they only said that on the telly.'

'I say it all the time. Especially when it's true.'

'Okay.' I considered risking a small nod, then decided I was too chicken. Plus, if I passed out, he might reconsider my move out of critical care.

'You must've hit your head pretty hard in the accident,' Dr Adams said. 'There was inter-cranial pressure, which is what caused you to fall unconscious. We drained the excess fluid with a shunt, but we didn't know how much damage had occurred until you woke up.'

My mouth was flooded with saliva and I swallowed hard. That didn't sound good but there was something more worrying on my mind. 'Had I been drinking? I don't remember what happened, why I crashed the car.'

'Definitely not. No drugs – prescription or otherwise – either.'

'Thank you,' I said and meant it.

After Dr Adams had scribbled some notes on my chart and rushed away to something more important, the nurse fussed with my IV for a bit. 'You'll most likely be in trauma orthopaedics. Or general med if there isn't a space in orthopaedics.'

I turned my head and tried not to think about the needle in my arm. The metal that was piercing a vein. I knew I should be braver, being lucky to be alive and all that, but it gave me the dry heaves.

Later, after I'd wowed the nurses with my ability to sit up, lift a cup of water, and feed myself glutinous mushroom soup without either throwing up, passing out or crying, I was moved to a less critical ward. I didn't catch the name, but something like 'ortho', so I wasn't surprised when I found myself in a large ward full of uncomfortable souls with either a leg hoisted high or their arms sticking out at funny angles in comedy casts. I was immensely grateful that I only had one leg immobilised and that it didn't require a pulley-system of any kind.

I wasn't ready to make social chit-chat, so I asked for my curtains to be pulled. I lay and stared at the wall until visiting hours started. I heard the main door open and people arriving. Parents and partners, friends and their kids. Who brought kids to a hospital? My curtain billowed as a set of feet tramped past and I imagined the family they belonged to. I caught rough accents and was filling in a paunchy dad with a gold sovereign ring, a mum with a slicked back ponytail and too-small jeans, and a sullen ten-year-old head to toe in Nike, when my curtain swished and an enormous flower arrangement appeared. The flowers were beautiful, cascading out of a pale green box. The kind of hand-tied artisan bouquet provided by upmarket florists. Mark put them on the tiny locker by the bed and leaned over to kiss me. I turned my head a little so that the kiss landed on my lips. I wanted contact. I wanted to remind myself of my boyfriend. Of my feelings. I desperately wanted to feel like myself again. It was a nice kiss. His lips were soft but not sloppy. It was familiar and that was enough to make me want to throw myself into his arms.

'Still no grapes,' I said to hide my sudden attack of feelings. I didn't do feelings. I was remembering more and more about myself and I knew that the weepy mess Mark had visited before was not the real me. Or, at least, not the old me.

'You look better.' He sat on the chair by the bed. Now that I wasn't hooked up to a bank of space-age machines, there was room for one.

'Since my head isn't as sore, I can feel all the other pains. I feel like I've been boxing.' My chest hurt, my back hurt, my legs ached, my left hip pulsed. I wiggled my toes; the only things that seemed to be working properly. 'I've got physio today. Walking, I think.' An irritatingly cheerful woman had been to see me that morning, talking about mobilisation until I felt I could run down the ward just to get away from her.

'That's good,' Mark said.

'Is it?' I didn't say the thing I was thinking which was this: *what if I can't walk?* What if my motor skills were banjaxed along with my memory? Was this the training montage part of my lifetime movie in which I stumbled along behind a Zimmer frame, drooling, while a peppy nurse shouted encouragement?

'Everyone misses you at work.'

'That's nice.' I tried to picture my work. The people. All I got were fuzzy black-and-white images and it took me a second to realise I was thinking about X-rays. I swallowed back the panic. The doctor said that it would take time for my brain to get back to normal. I had to trust that it would. That this strange lag in my thought processes, the disconnect, and the gaps in my memory, would magically heal.

Mark put his hand on mine. 'I miss you.'

'I'm right here,' I said, even though I knew what he meant. I missed me, too.

'Everything's fine at the flat.'

'Good,' I said, still thinking about the strange landscape of my mind. The blind alleys, the twisted steps that led nowhere, the blank areas that were filled with fog. I knew there was terrain there – complex, beautiful terrain with mountains and valleys and cities – but it was hidden.

'I'm even keeping on top of the washing up.'

I focused on Mark and realised that he was looking at me with an intensity that seemed at odds with the subject matter. Maybe I'd been a real bitch about the dishes?

'I don't know how long I'll be in here,' I said.

Mark reached for my hand. He looked relieved, as if he'd been expecting me to say something else. 'It doesn't matter. I'm not going anywhere and when you're ready, you can come home.'

I tried to smile. I wanted to go home. I wanted to go back to my flat. Our flat. Like so many things, I couldn't picture it, but I knew I wanted to go there. I took a deep breath that hurt my ribs. 'Tell me about it,' I said.

'The flat?'

'I can't bloody remember anything. It's driving me mental. Can you describe it?'

Mark was holding my good hand with both of his. It was lost inside them, and the warmth and the contact were anchoring me. It felt nice.

'It's on Grove Street.' He raised his eyebrows a little and I shook my head.

'It's on the ground floor, which isn't ideal from a safety point of view but as soon as you saw it had a garden you wouldn't listen to me.'

'A garden?'

'Tiny strip of muddy grass and the bins.' He smiled. 'You keep saying you're going to grow stuff but the evidence has yet to appear.'

'I'm probably biding my time,' I said. 'You can't rush gardening, everyone knows that.'

'The front door is a bit scabby, to be honest, and the shared entrance hall, but the inside of the flat is nice. There's a living room and a kitchen and a bedroom. And a bathroom, of course.'

'Can you be more specific? This could be anywhere.'

'Sorry, right.' Mark started to stroke the top of my hand with his thumb and it made me want to pull away. I didn't, though, as I didn't want to stop him talking.

'The walls are all painted white but you've got loads of stuff hanging up. Art and postcards and these weird crochet flowers on a string. The sofa is purple velvet with little turned wooden legs. You got it on eBay for a hundred and fifty quid and didn't stop talking about it for a week.'

'Okay. Good.' I couldn't pull up an image of my sofa. A memory. But I inserted a picture of the kind of purple sofa I would like to find going cheap on eBay and used that. 'What else?'

'The television is ancient and the screen's too small. It's rubbish.'

'What else?'

'There's a big stripy rug in the living room. All different colours. There's a pink stain in the middle, which you hide with the coffee table.'

'Red wine?'

'From your housewarming, I think. I didn't know you very well then.' Mark shifted slightly. 'The bedroom is a bit small. There isn't really enough storage space.'

'Romantic,' I said.

Mark smiled. 'I was going to describe the bed but I suddenly felt a bit weird.' He lowered his voice, leaned closer. 'Anyone could be listening.'

'I don't care,' I said. 'What's it like?'

'Comfortable.'

'Wow. We really have been together for ages, haven't we?'

Mark laughed and patted my hand. 'Plenty of time for that once you're better.'

Suddenly, I was irritated and wanted him to go. Thankfully, a nurse arrived and swished the curtains back. 'Sorry,' she said. 'I need to take your blood pressure.'

'I'll come back later.' Mark was out of the chair and kissing me goodbye.

'You don't have to run off,' the nurse said, but he'd already picked up his jacket and was halfway to the door.

The nurse wound the pressure cuff around the upper part of the arm he'd just released. It was an automatic machine and she left as soon as it had begun. I hated that machine. I didn't trust it to stop inflating, thought it might go on and on until my arm was compressed to the diameter of a drinking straw.

I was grateful for the distraction, though. I was annoyed with myself for being irritated with Mark. He was the only person I knew in the world. I needed him. The thought made my stomach lurch. A memory leaped up from my subconscious; my aunt Pat shaking her head, saying, 'You'd rather fall flat on your face than accept a hand to hold you up.' Pat. Long, long grey hair, always up in a gigantic bun. Firm fringe, frowning eyes. Married to Uncle Dylan. Waxed jacket, crinkly eyes, long walks. So I couldn't remember the last year or more, but I'd remembered Pat and Dylan. That was something.

I thanked God I hadn't listed them as my emergency contacts on any forms and, as far as I could remember, hadn't told Mark about them. The last thing I wanted was for them to worry. No, that wasn't true. That would be the altruistic thought. The truth was this: I didn't want to see them. I didn't want them to see me lying in this stupid bed, with my head caved in and my memory fucked up, and for Pat to purse her lips and say 'I told you so' without even having to open her mouth. I couldn't picture Dylan in a place like this, not even to visit. He belonged on the Gower coastal path, above rocky coves and beneath a blue sky, dotted with razorbills. No, I was going to deal with this on my own. I'd tell them later, once I was well again.

GRACE

Grace waited outside the closed door of Matron's office, trembling all over and with a sick, faint feeling. She ran her thumb over the shape of her bluebird pin hidden in the pocket of her dress, trying to draw comfort from its familiar shape. The sharp points of its wings, the smoothness of the enamel.

All the juniors dreaded being sent here. They swapped stories of standing on the rag rug in front of Matron's desk and of being struck mute, paralysed by the ice in her voice and the coldness of her words. Even the indomitable Evie had been a little red around the eyes after she'd been hauled up for coming into the home late.

It wasn't that Matron shouted. After all, they were used to shouting; the ward sisters issued every order at a high rate of decibels. It was the gimlet stare. And the knowledge that with one movement of her fountain pen, Matron could place a black mark on their hospital record. A stain that would stay for ever. A stain that would affect their chances of securing a position after their training or, perhaps, stop them from graduating altogether. If there was one thing that was worse than the thought of nursing for the rest of their born days, it was the thought that they wouldn't get to wear the uniform of staff nurses or to bellow at terrified juniors. In short, to have scrubbed all of those blasted bedpans for nothing.

There was a noise from inside the office which might have been a 'come in' but Grace was glad she didn't enter when, a moment later, the door opened of its own accord and the director of the hospital swept out. He didn't so much as glance in her direction.

The door was still open and she caught a terrifying glimpse of Matron, behind her desk. A giant insect in a starched cap. 'Nurse Kemp.'

Grace stepped into the room, concentrating on putting one foot in front of the other. She could feel the sweat prickling all over her skin and, in one horrible moment, thought she might've forgotten how to breathe.

'I've had a report from Sister Bennett.'

Grace looked in the direction of the voice, but terror rendered Matron invisible to her. It was as if she'd been snipped out of reality with a pair of scissors. Grace curled her hands, digging her fingernails into her palms in an attempt to regain some focus.

'It seems,' Matron continued, 'that you've been behaving inappropriately with one of the private patients.'

Grace looked up. The shock of the accusation and its complete unfairness made her speak up. 'No, Matron. That's not—'

'Are you questioning Sister's honesty?' Matron's thin voice stretched until it almost disappeared.

'No, Matron,' Grace said, after a beat. 'But—'

'You have been witnessed conversing with Captain Burrows in a way which does not befit your position in this hospital. I warned you before you came here, Nurse Kemp, I will not have any silliness in my hospital.'

Grace felt dread descend. This was it. She was going to be sent home. The other girls might fear a black mark on their hospital record, but Grace feared the end of it. If she was sent home in disgrace she may as well do away with herself. Evie had told her about a girl who couldn't hack the training. She'd drunk a bottle of bleach and the morning nurse found her stiff as a board with dried vomit all over her bed. With that realisation, a kind of clarity came back to Grace. However wretched she felt she did not want that. She straightened her spine. 'I'm sorry, Matron, it won't happen again.'

'See that it doesn't,' Matron said.

Miraculously, that seemed to be the end of it.

Back outside in the deserted hallway, Matron's office door carefully and quietly closed behind her, Grace took a deep, shuddering breath. She felt as if she'd stepped away from a cliff edge.

It wasn't a surprise to her the next morning when she checked the rota sheet and discovered that she'd been moved to another ward. The unfairness of it burned, but a small part of her was relieved. She hadn't done anything inappropriate with Captain Burrows but she had liked him. Her behaviour might have been strictly professional, but her thoughts hadn't been so scrupulous. She thought his face was handsome and his manners pleasing. He had an intelligent light in his eyes which ignited feelings in her, and that was not something she sought or welcomed. She was making a life for herself at the hospital. An ordered life of hard work and self-sacrifice. She didn't want reminders that she hadn't always been Nurse Kemp. She didn't want to give her traitorous heart the slightest reason to beat faster.

That night, as she and Evie got undressed, rubbing their aching feet, Evie surprised her by saying, 'I heard you were on the rug. '

'I had to see Matron.' Grace climbed into bed, marvelling at how wonderful the thin mattress felt after a day on her feet.

Evie was looking at her with an assessing look. 'Not as dull as I first thought. Good show.'

'I don't know what you mean,' Grace said, rolling over to face the wall. 'I shan't be doing that again.'

MINA

O nce I was awake enough to notice details, I became slightly obsessed with the peculiarities of my ward. The windows were set high up the walls so that the inmates could only glimpse the lower part of them, seeing a tantalising slice of trees and sky through the glass. It was in the Edwardian part of the hospital and, despite the fresh paint and modern equipment, there was something undeniably shabby about it. I had spent hours mining for memories of my life and could picture my shiny modern office in the therapeutic radiology department; it felt unreal that the two places could belong in the same building.

The ward flooring was the same industrial-grade linoleum that ran through the rest of the hospital, but it was a speckled grey-pink with a faded stripe of black that ran around the middle of the room, past the end of the beds. I couldn't stop looking at that pattern and imagining it as a kind of track, as if in the old days the nurses had run on wheels that needed a special surface. I liked to imagine them gliding along that strip, never deviating, calling to the patients six feet away in their beds: 'Now, Mr Jones, just sit up yourself there, you know I can't help you'; 'Mrs Smith, if I throw this bedpan, be sure and catch it'.

There was a rhythm to the days that I found comforting. Every detail – the sucking sound of the door to the corridor or the clatter of trays on the food trolley, even being woken up because Queenie in the bed opposite needed her blood pressure taken at regular intervals – created a soothing backdrop. It was half past four when the trolley came round with our evening meal. I'd asked why so early and the care assistant explained that she wouldn't get round all the wards before half five if she didn't start then.

The smell emanating from the tower of covered trays was not promising. I sat up and tried to feel hungry. While I was working on that, I tried to feel properly grateful for being alive and for being able to eat in the usual way and not through a tube fixed in my stomach like the woman in the bed by the window. There was a blanket rucked up at the bottom of the bed but I didn't have the strength to straighten it. It was printed with the words Royal Sussex Trust but, because of the way it was lying, the letters 'sex' were visible uppermost and alone. Someone really should've thought of that before they ordered the blankets.

'Here you go, love.' A tray appeared on my table. It was still swung out to one side and I knew I couldn't move it myself. The woman had already moved on, her wide back to me. I addressed the swathe of dark blue polyester. 'Excuse me? Could you just—'

She swivelled the table around on its castors with a quick movement, not even bothering to turn around. As a result the table ended up halfway down the bed. I managed to grab the edge and inch it back. Just as I was contemplating lifting the metal cover and releasing the dubious odour of my meal, a movement caught my eye.

It was a tiny brown-feathered bird, sitting calmly on the rumpled blanket at the bottom of the bed. It regarded me, head on one side. I blinked, expecting it to disappear, part of me hoping that it wouldn't. It felt utterly familiar and I wasn't alarmed in the slightest. That in itself should have been cause for concern, but I couldn't make myself feel anything except relief. The small bird, sitting so still, was a reminder that I was still me. It felt like the most normal thing I had experienced since waking up in hospital. The bird hopped to the edge of the bed and then flew to the curtain track that ran above my bed. It flew to the door and then back to the rail. The door, the rail. Back and forth. And I remembered something else about my birds: they appeared in order to tell me something.

I pushed the tray table away. I wanted to say 'I can't follow you', but I remembered, just in time, that I was effectively in public. The bird kept going. The orderly finished clashing food trays and pushed her trolley out of sight, into the next ward. I realised that I was sitting forward, my legs bent and ready for action. I felt a rush of adrenaline. I pushed the sheet down and dragged my legs over the side. The bird flew down, hovered for a moment in front of my face and then flew to the door again. I ignored the pain in my head, the sickness in my stomach, and edged my backside off the bed, my feet planted on the floor. I reached down for the catheter bag that was hanging on the side of the bed and hooked it on to the stand the nurses used when they helped me walk to the shower room. I was sweating by now, nausea rolling in waves through my body. I shuffled a few steps, making it past the end of my bed and halfway to the door. My head throbbed and the edges of my vision grew dark, like my eyes were closing up. I felt my knees sag and the horrible sensation of the catheter tube tugging at my insides as I slumped down.

An arm gripped under my elbow and hoisted me back up. 'What are you doing? Come on. Back to bed.'

I turned obediently, desperate to be lying down again, for the pain in my head to go, for everything to stop hurting. As I turned I saw the bird. It wasn't on the door, enticing me to the corridor and freedom, it was on the nurses' desk. The one I couldn't see from my bed. It fluttered from the surface of the desk on to the telephone.

As soon as I saw it I remembered something. Geraint had called me. He'd left a message on my mobile. I didn't know when the memory came from, but it was clear and I was certain it was real. I could feel the phone held to my face, pressing into my cheek as I listened to the message. At once I could hear his voice, the breathless panic, the little catch before he said my name. Like he'd been running or was trying not to cry. I examined the memory for clues but there was nothing else: I had no idea whether it had happened the day before my life became a long-running episode of *ER*, or whether it was months old.

The nurse propelling me back to bed was talking. I realised there was an expectant pause but since I had no idea what had come before it, I didn't say anything. Geraint. How could I have forgotten my twin brother? What else had been shaken loose in the accident? I pictured Ger's face. His long limbs and skinny torso. Sitting in his bedroom and listening to music, shouting at me to shut his door and leave him alone. That was a long time ago, when he was a teenager. When we lived at home together. I dug my fingernails into my palm. I had to stay in the here and now. I wanted to shake my stupid head and make it cooperate. I couldn't be woolly and useless. I had to help Geraint. He needed me.

'I have to use the phone,' I said. 'Please.'

'I'll bring it to you. You don't need to get out of bed for that.'

'I know,' I said. I was acutely aware of how vulnerable I was, how much I relied on these people to help me. What if I'd annoyed this nurse so much she didn't bring me the telephone? Refused me privileges. It was possible I was mixing hospital up with prison, but the black edges of panic were advancing, condensing my vision into a single bullet hole of light. 'Sorry,' I said, as meekly as I could manage. It sounded exceptionally convincing even to my own ears, which was one of the advantages of being so banged up. To my knowledge, I'd never pulled off meek before.

'No harm done,' the nurse said. She had greasy brown hair pulled back into a tight, shiny ponytail, and enlarged pores spread out from the creases either side of her hooked nose. Her large features were sort of crammed on to her face, jostling for space, but when she helped me back into bed and immediately fetched the phone, and – praise be – left it within reach, she took on a beautiful glow.

I dialled the number, miraculously available in the front of my mind. Just as if it had been waiting for me there, waiting for me to remember that I had a brother and that he was in trouble. I listened to the ringing, but no matter how hard I willed Ger to pick up the phone, it remained unanswered. I imagined the click, the sound of his voice saying 'Yes?' The way it would lift at the end of the word. I imagined each detail so perfectly that I could almost believe I'd heard it happen. Except for the ringing that began to sound like it was taunting me.

I had just replaced the receiver when Mark appeared. No flowers this time. 'You look better.' He kissed me quickly, sat in the armchair next to the bed. He was freshly shaved and I could see a tiny nick on his throat. I imagined him dabbing at the spot of blood with a bit of tissue or his flannel, the sting of it when he doused his skin with aftershave. That line of thought made me think of something . . . Something I couldn't quite get hold of and that annoyed me, so I pushed the jumble to one side and focused on Mark. He was frowning at the telephone table.

His expression was intense and it disturbed me. Actually, it frightened me, but that was silly, an overreaction. I tried to make conversation, to distract myself from my sudden panic and to derail whatever Mark was thinking that made him look so severe. 'I can't believe they still make these.'

'What?' Mark's frown deepened. It made him look ten years older. 'Did someone call you?'

'No. Payphones. Look.' I lifted the receiver again. 'See how clunky it is. I'd forgotten how heavy these things are.' I weighed the receiver in my hand, feeling the unfamiliar curves, so different from my mobile. My touchscreen mobile. With its leather case that flipped open like a book. It was a memory, clear and crisp. 'Where's my phone?'

Mark sat forward in his chair. 'You don't have one.'

'I don't have a mobile phone? Everyone has a mobile phone.' I gestured down the ward. 'Even Queenie has one and she's homeless.' And I remembered listening to a message from my twin brother on my mobile. I felt utter certainty that Mark was lying to me and my stomach dropped.

He took my hand, stroking the palm with his thumb in a way that made me want to snatch it away. 'You said they were unnecessary.'

'No.' I thought about shaking my head, to emphasise the point. I could picture Mark's face. Not now, but in the past. I had a sudden, blindingly clear memory of him. 'You said that. You said it was a waste and a sign of disposable consumer culture. We had a fight about it.'

Mark let go of my hand. 'I don't remember that.'

'It definitely happened.'

'Don't upset yourself. Things are going to be muddled for a while. Remember what the doctor said.'

'I'm not confused.' I paused to consider. 'Not about this anyway. I had a phone. It had a swipey screen.' I was sure I was right; I'd liked that phone. I could almost feel it in my hand.

'Parveen has one,' Mark said. 'You said it was annoying.'

At once, I wasn't so certain. I had said swipey screens were annoying. Maybe I was thinking of someone else's phone. Maybe I'd played with Parveen's phone and had got mixed up.

'Who were you trying to call anyway?'

I lay back and closed my eyes, wincing slightly as if my head was hurting me, hoping to buy a few seconds to think. I didn't know why, but my instinct was to lie.

'Was it your aunt?'

I opened my eyes in surprise.

'Pat? If you give me her number, I can call her. Let her know what's happened.'

'No.' I struggled to sit forward.

'It's no problem. I can look in your address book, if you like. If you can't remember. I know where you keep it.'

'No,' I said again, as firmly as I could. 'Don't.'

Mark looked satisfied. 'Whatever you think best.'

'I don't want to worry them. I'm fine.'

He held his hands up. 'I said okay.'

I struggled to get hold of my thoughts. He hadn't mentioned Geraint, which meant he probably didn't know about him. I looked at the man in the suit sitting on the visitor's chair and tried to remember. I'd liked him enough to tell him about Pat and I had remembered enough about my essential personality to be pretty certain that I wasn't very free with that kind of information. He knew that I had an aunt and he hadn't mentioned a mum or a dad, so I guess he knew about them, too. I was trying to work out a puzzle but there were too many pieces missing and no picture on the box.

෧⌇

When my physical therapy appointment rolled around, the physio turned out not to be a perky woman with a high ponytail, but a blond and irritatingly fit man. He looked like a Viking. The kind of person who gets their five-a-day and, after doing their gruelling daily exercise, plays rugby for fun. As I raised myself painfully to my feet, fighting the urge to pass out, I found his aura of glowing health insulting. His presence was a personal affront to every sick person in the room.

The Viking's name was Simon and I soon realised that his golden exterior, friendly smile and gentle northern accent were all a lie. He was a sadist. I didn't notice at first as I was so delighted to have made it to a standing position without fainting. Wave after wave of dizziness rolled over me but I prevailed. I felt amazing. If I'd been steadier on my feet, I'd have punched the air. As it was I tried to sit back down on the bed.

'Up, up, up,' Simon said. 'Again.'

I didn't know why he was speaking to me as if I were a child, but I gave him my best raised eyebrow and said, politely enough: 'No, thank you. I'm fine.'

He laughed as if I'd made a joke and took hold of my hands. 'Upsy-daisy.'

Okay. Now I knew I would have to get better, so that I could kick him in the nuts.

Before I really knew what was happening, I was shuffling towards the Viking, holding his hands as he walked backwards in front of me. Humiliating didn't even begin to cover it.

After a few steps I felt as if I was going to be sick. I wanted to tell him this, but my head was pounding so hard that I'd lost the power of speech.

I think I must've blacked out because I had no memory of getting back into bed or of the Viking leaving. I came to for long enough to realise that I was alone and horizontal and then I went to sleep.

After three days with him I had to grudgingly admit that I'd improved. He didn't make me use a Zimmer frame, for which I was pathetically grateful, and I could shuffle down the ward and the adjoining corridor with him walking beside me, making chit-chat. That was the worst part: the conversation. I felt rusty and ill-equipped. All of my usual defences and linguistic ease had been stripped away by the accident and I felt pale and naked. It was as if I had too few layers between me and the outside world, and it terrified me.

'Sorry?' I said, realising that the Viking had been speaking for a while and had now stopped, probably expecting a suitable response.

'Nothing. It's okay.' He was unbearably gentle in his speech. It slayed me. 'You're doing really well,' he said. 'We'll go to the end today.'

I was feeling stronger and steadier. I did feel lucky that I could walk, hadn't needed to relearn it, but at the same time I felt rather fraudulent about my recovery, as if I'd just been pretending to be unconscious all those days. Despite the agonising pain in my head and back, I felt that I should be worse off, that I was somehow cheating by tottering down the hall with increased vitality. 'This is a waste of your time, I expect,' I said, surprising myself.

'Not at all.' He smiled at me. 'It's my job.'

'You don't look like a physio.' I didn't know why I was making small talk; I'd never been any good at it. In the next moment I realised the answer: I was lonely. Too many hours lying in bed alone, too few visiting hours with Mark and, even then, a nagging feeling of separation. Being severed from so many of my memories made me feel isolated and off-balance.

The Viking hadn't answered, which was fair enough. What could he say to a vacuous comment like that? He noticed that I was listing to one side and took my arm very gently.

'I used to swim,' the Viking said as we turned at the end of the corridor. The way he spoke let me know that he didn't mean he got his ten-metre badge in the local baths.

'I used to walk,' I said, and tried to smile properly, like a normal human being.

He rewarded me with a squeeze of my upper arm.

I was feeling good about all of this progress, so it was something of a blow to realise that the young woman was back again. The one in the white apron, who didn't look quite real.

She smiled thinly, not showing any teeth. I ignored her. I wasn't going to have anything to do with flights of my imagination. I was having quite enough difficulty as it was without adding hallucinations into the mix.

'Are you okay, Mina?' The Viking's perfect face was creased into a question mark.

I nodded. I was fine. I wasn't seeing people who weren't there. It wasn't happening.

I once read a book by one of those popular psychologist types that described all the different kinds of hallucinations people suffered from after brain injuries, strokes, going blind, that kind of thing. I had a feeling it was very comforting on the subject of seeing things that weren't really there, so I decided I wasn't going to panic and ask the Viking to have me admitted to the loony bin just yet.

'Mina?'

Besides, I'd been seeing birds that weren't real for years and years, I wasn't about to panic over a ghost-woman. I was just obviously the over-imaginative type. Highly strung. The Viking was still peering at me, concern etched on his face. I smiled in a determined fashion. 'I'm tired,' I said. 'And everything hurts.'

At once his frown smoothed away. This, his expression said, was entirely normal. Business as usual.

'Just a little further.'

'Has anybody ever punched you?' I said, conversationally, as I limped back towards the bed.

'Loads of times.' His voice was cheerful and I couldn't help smiling even as I collapsed back into bed. The woman was still there. She stayed even after Simon had walked away to find his next victim. 'I'm going to sleep,' I said out loud.

'Good for you, love,' Queenie said.

The woman didn't move or change expression. She had a kind face, though, and I didn't feel scared. 'Goodbye,' I said, trying to sound firm, but not mean. The woman stared back and I watched her until my eyes got too heavy and I had to sleep.

GRACE

For the first few months of training, Grace was so utterly exhausted that the thought of doing anything in her off-duty other than lying on her bed was impossible. Her idea of a big treat was to wait for Evie to leave the room so that she could enjoy the release of a quiet weeping session. Gradually, though, she became accustomed to the hard work and the days took shape for her. There was a rhythm to the routine that was comforting and it lulled Grace into a kind of stupor.

Eventually, it dawned on her that nurses were allowed to leave the hospital and, once she'd surfaced from the black waters of exhaustion, she felt a desperate urge to do so. There was precious little leave, one day a month, and then only if Sister or Matron didn't decide to cancel it, but there was off-duty time. For a day nurse, this meant a couple of hours in the evening and a half-day every week. The others made the most of it, walking down into town in groups of two or three, arms linked and spirits high. They went to sit on the seafront or to paddle in the sea, and to the cafés in town for slap-up feasts and cream cakes. The more daring and energetic went to dances in the evening. Although Sister Bennett disapproved it wasn't against the rules and there wasn't a thing she could do about it.

Grace was sitting on her bed, rubbing her aching feet and watching Evie get ready. The shyness she'd felt in her first week had rubbed away, and now Grace handed Evie her brassiere and did up the snaps on the back of her dress.

They had to be in the nurses' accommodation by ten o'clock. It didn't matter that they were living away from their parents, doing a job and earning a wage, those were the rules and if the house sister or the porter on the gate caught anyone breaking them, she would be up in front of Matron. 'It's like prison,' Evie complained regularly. 'We're kept in a cage.'

'It's to protect us,' Grace said, parroting what the house sister had said on her first day.

'I don't think *you* need protecting,' Evie said, her voice turning nasty. 'I'm sure your morals are in no danger. I bet you've never sinned in your life.'

Grace didn't say anything, just got undressed and climbed into bed. She pretended to read while Evie finished getting ready. When she left for her evening, a dance at the pavilion, she said, 'Don't wait up,' her voice full of life and the promise of fun. Grace turned her face away and stared at the wall until she heard the door close.

It was almost quarter to eleven when Evie climbed through the bedroom window. If Sister caught her, she'd be in Matron's office before her feet even touched the ground. Grace had thought about closing the window tight, leaving Evie to wander the grounds until she got caught, but knew she wouldn't do it. Evie was tactless and self-involved and she'd hurt Grace's feelings, but she didn't deserve that. Besides, they were like siblings, united against parents. Us and them. At least Grace assumed that's how it was for siblings. She'd only ever read about them in books.

The juniors, at any rate, looked out for one another as much as possible, one watching out for the senior nurses and the ward sister, while the others hid in the kitchen stuffing down leftover cake from the tea round or slices of bread and marge when they'd been sent too late to the dinner hall and there'd been nothing left except some steamed currant pudding, which was solid when fresh, but pretty much unchewable after it had been left on the side for three hours.

Grace pretended to be asleep. She heard the soft sound of Evie's feet on the floor, the whisper-quiet movements as she undressed quickly and got into bed. Evie never took her make-up off when she came in this late and she wore black eyeliner. In the morning she'd look more like a patient than a nurse until she'd been to the bathroom to wash it off.

Grace kept still and waited for Evie's breathing to become deep and regular. She was holding her own breath – she couldn't relax until Evie was safely asleep. After a moment, the small snuffles of Evie's breathing became more ragged. Grace strained, listening. After another moment she realised that Evie was crying.

'Are you all right?' Grace whispered.

She heard the click of Evie's throat as she swallowed. Then, 'Not really.'

'Did something happen?'

There was another pause and, just when Grace had decided that Evie wasn't going to answer, she said: 'A bit homesick. Silly, really. I didn't like it much when I was there.'

Her voice was stronger, more like daytime Evie. Lipstick Evie.

Grace felt the silence between them expand and soften until it was a bubble that held them both. She wriggled over to the very edge of her bed and reached out across the strip of floor between them. Her fingers couldn't reach Evie and she was about to say something instead. Something comforting, she hoped, when she felt the tip of Evie's fingers touch her own.

The next day, Evie acted as though nothing had happened. When Grace said, 'Are you all right?' Evie tilted her head back and said, 'Of course, darling,' in a cold tone.

At breakfast Evie didn't sit with Grace, as she usually did, and when Grace bagged ten minutes of off-duty in the smoking room, Evie stood up from the prized position by the radiator, passed her half-finished cigarette to the nearest nurse and left.

By the end of her shift, Grace had decided to leave Evie to it. Whatever mood she'd got herself into, Grace was sure she'd come out of it again in her own sweet time. Evie wasn't the sort to stay down for long.

For all her flouting of the rules and her glamorous ways, Evie was a born nurse. Grace envied her easy manner with the patients. While Grace crept around, waiting to be found out at any moment, for a patient to scream 'imposter' at her with stiffly pointed finger, Evie wore the demeanour of an old hand. It didn't matter that she was just twenty years old, the same age as Grace; she spoke to the patients as if she'd been a nurse since before they were born. The old dears and the grandfathers, the young soldiers and the children, were all treated with the same authoritative, slightly cross manner. And they all adored her for it.

'What do you mean, you need a bottle?' she'd say, marching past the end of a bed. 'It's not time and I've got better things to do.' Evie wasn't cruel. She'd fetch the bottle for the man in question to relieve himself or she'd plump pillows or pass a handkerchief or whatever was required, but always with a sharp word, and an air of harassed efficiency.

The adults were respectful and apologetic to her face, but joshed with one another behind her back in clearly affectionate tones. 'Oh, no,' Grace heard one man say, 'we've got Jones, again. Mind you, don't need any nursing today or we'll all be for it.'

The children found her hilarious. The sterner her face became, the harsher her tone, the more they giggled or gazed adoringly at her frowning face. 'Tommy Wilkins, have you been scratching your spots again? If you take these mittens off I'll stick them on with glue. Don't turn those big blue eyes on me, it won't do you a bit of good.' She'd turn and walk away, leaving Tommy Wilkins convulsing with laughter.

They called her 'Patch', which Evie pretended not to realise was short for 'Cross Patch', and when Grace was on the children's ward with her, the constant refrain was 'Patch do it' or, from the politer children, a plaintive 'Patch, please'.

Off duty, Evie was a riot. While the rest of the girls were drooping from exhaustion she seemed to tap a never-ending source of energy. She was out more often than she was in and she regaled them all with tales of adoring men and stolen kisses and showed off the gifts she was given – soft leather gloves, silk stockings, a cashmere scarf in buttery yellow.

Evie knew all the latest songs and dances, too. She would perform in the common room, projecting fearlessly in a voice that wasn't always exactly in tune, and striking outrageous poses. She would put a hand on her hip and throw coy glances over one shoulder. They were exaggerated and ridiculous, but they gave Grace a funny feeling in her stomach.

ᕲᖇ

Sister Bennett walked at a bracing clip down the ward and began bellowing at Grace while still ten feet away, as was her style. 'There's been an accident at the factory and we're to get ready for casualties. They said we're to take at least six. We'll need to shift some patients into this ward to make room downstairs.'

Grace wanted to explain that she was about to go off-duty, but she knew that it wouldn't do any good. You were only grudgingly allowed to take your off-duty. It was a privilege, if you could be spared, not a right. Still, Grace was dead on her feet and didn't know how she was going to stay awake for another hour, let alone a whole night.

When the casualties came in, the men went to another ward and Grace's got seven women. One had bruises and a broken arm and was complaining that a brick had come flying at her.

'Did the building fall down?' Grace asked as she helped the patient into a more comfortable position.

Sister Bennett gave her a withering look. 'Focus on your job, Nurse. This is no time for idle gossip.'

Grace didn't think asking about the accident that had brought the casualties into her care was 'idle' but she wasn't about to contradict the sister. Besides, her superior had already stepped away to the other end of the ward and disappeared behind screens, no doubt to do something highly medical and efficient.

Grace looked away from her patient, feeling overwhelmed and uncertain before the number of people clamouring for attention. The excitement had woken up all of the existing patients and there were various requests for information, medication and, from the gastrics, cries for milky drinks.

One of the women from the factory was moaning loudly, almost rhythmically. Another, not so badly hurt, was asking anyone who'd listen to 'keep her quiet, for gawd's sake'. Grace didn't know who she was supposed to attend to first and everyone was so busy.

Sister Bennett, arms full of bandages, slowed down long enough to say, 'It's the quiet ones you've got to watch,' and that bit of attention and advice was just enough to unstick whatever glue had been in her gears. She followed the sister to the bed of a young woman, not much more than a girl. Half of her face was pale but pretty, and the other half an angry red mess. The shock of it brought the raw taste of vomit into Grace's throat and she turned away to take a deep breath.

'Don't you dare!' Sister Bennett wheeled around and whispered harshly into Grace's ear, 'Don't you bloody dare.'

The shock of hearing the sister swear was enough to snap her out of the sudden nausea. Grace swallowed down the sick and turned back to the patient. Sister Bennett was right. It didn't matter how she felt. She had to be Nurse Kemp. Not Grace. Not even human.

'You're all right,' Sister Bennett was saying briskly, as if the girl was complaining of a splinter in her hand. The girl's good eye had rolled upwards, tears leaking from one corner. Her mouth was open, dragged wide on the good side as if she was screaming, although not a sound came out. It was eerie and horrifying, but Grace concentrated on her training. She needed gauze for the burns. Morphia for the pain.

'Fetch hot water bottles,' Sister Bennett said and Grace did as she was told.

'Shock is the first biggest danger,' said the sister, packing the hot water bottles around the girl. 'We've got to bring her body temperature back up . . . and please don't say it!' She held her hand up. 'Not a word about blinking ironic, I don't want to hear it.'

As they worked, the morphia seemed to be taking effect and when the girl's remaining eyelid was closed and her chest was rising and falling steadily, they moved on to the next casualty. It wasn't until later that Grace let the horror wash over her. The girl was a corpse-in-waiting. If the shock didn't take her, then infection would. The burns were too extensive for her to survive.

Grace worked for hours, on different casualties and in different parts of the ward. She fetched and carried and washed wounds and bandaged limbs. All the while, held in the space just behind her eyes, she carried the image of that first young woman. Later, when her shift had finally ended and the sister had raised her chin slightly and said, 'I suppose you'd better go off-duty,' in that grudging way she had, Grace expected to stumble towards her room and the hard narrow bed that had become like paradise.

She didn't look for Evie, expecting that she was still in the dog-house, although the last six hours had erased a lot of Grace's worry over that. She was just too tired and too sad to think about Evie's bad mood.

Instead of heading out into the crisp, cool night air and crossing the quad to the nurses' home, Grace's legs carried her in the opposite direction, down towards the end of the ward. She was too tired to argue with them and she found herself next to the burn patient's bed.

She was asleep, at least. The doctor had been in to see her and topped up her morphia for good measure. Grace stood beside the bed and watched the rise and fall of the thin blanket that covered her chest. Underneath, the sheet rose in a tent over the legs. Covering them, without touching. Her mother had always greased a burn. When Grace had been at home she'd never questioned it, why would she? She wondered if she'd dare correct her mother next time she went home. The thought pierced her. Grace hadn't seen her parents for three months. She didn't know when she would be welcome back. She was paying a penance with no clear rules or boundaries. When she'd left she'd had the vague notion that she would come home in a crisp uniform, her navy cape swirling about her shoulders and her cap just so. They'd open their arms to this fine young vision and all would be forgotten. By them, at least.

So, the woman in the bed didn't have grease on her burns, and she had a drug that dulled her pain and she was in a scrupulously clean bed, but there was absolutely nothing else they could do for her. It was all in the waiting, as Sister Bennett would say. 'We watch 'em, that's all. Some of them live and some of them die and we just watch.'

Grace felt tears pricking at her eyes and she swallowed hard. She couldn't cry here, on the ward. Just then, she heard footsteps, felt someone arrive next to her. Before she could find something to do, some excuse for drooping next to the patient's bed, she felt a sharp dig in her ribs. It was Evie.

'Buck up, old stick,' she said. 'We'll go for a cream cake at the Blackbird tomorrow. Just think about that. You and me and a plate of buns the size of Brighton Pavilion.'

Grace felt the tears recede. The Blackbird Tearoom was lovely and just the thought of their cream cakes made her mouth water. She nudged Evie in return and they walked back to their room, arms linked.

MINA

On my third day on the ward, I was just telling the three (non-existent) siskins perched on the end of my bed to bog off, when Dr Adams paid me a visit. I must've been feeling better because I noticed how nice he looked when he smiled. His blue eyes sparked alive and he was in possession of what could definitely be called a cheeky grin. I've always been a sucker for a lovable rogue, someone with an optimistic, cheerful disposition. Opposites attract and all that. He grabbed my chart and flopped down into the chair next to my bed in a most informal manner. 'You're looking better.'

I felt a bit flustered by the reactivation of my hormones and, consequently, sounded even frostier than usual in my reply. 'I would be a great deal better if you'd let me go home.'

He just smiled at me, though, his lips twisting up on one side in a way that gave me interesting feelings in my stomach. I decided that I was overreacting because I'd been under a kind of sensory deprivation. I was surrounded by geriatrics and the very ill, plus mainly female nursing staff dressed in navy polyester. That explained my reaction to the closest thing to an eligible man in the vicinity. It was an accident of circumstance. 'I'm serious,' I said. 'This place is making me ill.'

'I think the head trauma had a little to do with it.' He held up finger and thumb a small distance apart and I tried hard not to notice how nice his hands were. Knotty knuckles, long-ish fingers. It was a short step to imagining what those hands would feel like on my own skin.

'You're a sarky bastard for a doctor,' I said, trying to ignore my inappropriate thoughts. 'Aren't you supposed to be all soothing and full of platitudes?'

'I'm not your doctor any more. You are now under the capable care of,' he glanced at the chart, 'Manjiri Kanthe. I don't know Dr Kanthe, but I've heard good things about her. You're in safe hands.'

'So what are you doing here?'

'Just checking up on my miracle.'

'Still miraculous,' I said. I stretched out my arms and waved my hands to demonstrate my superior motor skills and knocked over the glass of orange squash. The liquid spread across table but the lip that ran around the edge mostly saved the bedding. It's always surprising how much liquid a glass contains when you spill it.

Dr Adams sprang up and returned with a roll of blue paper towels, which he used to mop up the mess.

I hate the way women are always saying 'sorry' but I had to force myself not to apologise. It was my table after all. My disgust-ing orange squash. My bed.

'Shall I get you a replacement?'

'No,' I said. 'Thank you.'

'So, what do you do when you're not in here?'

Chit-chat. Interesting. He only had to glance at my file to see that I worked in the hospital. We might even have crossed paths before, although I would've thought I'd have remembered his face. 'I'm an international spy.'

He smiled. 'You're not a fan of small talk, then.'

'I prefer telling stories,' I said. 'It's more fun.'

His smile widened, but I was suddenly depressed by how easy the game was. Make a frosty joke or two, don't smile too much. Act a little distant, even when trapped in a hospital bed, and men lift their heads and sniff the wind. I felt tired of it all. And I'd just remembered that I had a boyfriend. A partner. A live-in partner. Mark. I said his name in my mind again, just to remind myself. To try and cement it there. The good thing about the distance game is this: it's extremely easy to sabotage. You can call time whenever you want. So I did.

'When will I get my memory back?'

Dr Adams snapped into professionalism. 'It's impossible to say. The timing in these cases . . .'

I swallowed. 'But it will happen? Everything will come back?'

'The odds are overwhelmingly in your favour. People with post-traumatic amnesia almost always regain their entire memory function.'

'Almost.' I closed my eyes. 'Why does that word seem suddenly very big?'

He didn't answer and I kept my eyes shut. I expected him to leave but he said something that threw me.

'Who were you talking to?'

My eyes wanted to open, instinctively, but I kept them shut. 'What do you mean?'

'Just now.' I felt him move closer, heard the rustling sound of paper.

'Myself,' I said promptly. I opened my eyes and looked him square in the face. I wasn't going to tell him that I was hallucinating. That way talking therapy and psychotropic drugs lay.

'I see.' Dr Adams indicated the chair next to my bed. 'May I?'

'Knock yourself out.' It sounded a little more aggressive than I'd intended so I attempted another smile.

'You needn't worry, by the way. If you're seeing things. Hearing things. Hallucinations are very common after a head trauma.'

'Hmm?' I widened my eyes, trying to look interested but in a detached, 'this has nothing to do with me' kind of way.

'Are you experiencing anything like that?'

'No,' I said promptly.

'Well, as I say, it's completely normal. There was a case of a man who, after waking up from a coma, had olfactory hallucinations. Potatoes roasting, rotten eggs, lemon, that kind of thing.'

'And you call that normal?'

'I'm not sure there is a normal.' Dr Adams used his direct stare. The one that he probably used to get people to admit they'd snorted coke when they arrived in A&E.

'Well, I'm not hallucinating. Unless you're not really here, of course.'

He smiled, very gently. 'You can trust me, Mina. I'm here to help.'

'That's nice.' I smiled blandly. I wasn't about to tell him that I was seeing the ghost of a nurse, or that I'd had hallucinations before I ever had my accident. I wasn't stupid. 'Do you know when I can go home?'

'Not for a few days at least,' he said. 'I know it's frustrating for you.'

'I'm so bored,' I said. 'I might start hallucinating just to liven things up.' Actually, that was probably the answer. I had conjured the nurse out of my imagination because of the boredom. I felt hugely relieved by this explanation.

৵৩

I hadn't had the best night's sleep when an unwelcome visitor appeared. Parveen. Having kept a strict separation between all the different areas of my life, having my laboratory buddy take a seat next to my bed was a new experience and not a comfortable one. She'd brought a helium balloon with 'Get Well Soon' on it in pink letters and a bunch of yellow chrysanthemums from the shop downstairs. Chrysanthemums have a bad reputation but I quite like them. Still, it felt odd. The kind of gift you'd get someone when they'd had a baby or something. Cheerful and innocent. Although, maybe that's what she'd expected to find. If she'd heard about the amnesia, maybe she expected a whole new Mina. A shiny new girl, who clapped her hands for balloons. I all but snarled in my attempt to disabuse her of any such notion. 'They never have enough vases around here,' I said, pointing at the flowers. 'They'll die.'

'Ah-ha,' Parveen said, and bent down to delve in her tapestry rucksack, producing a clear glass vase and a pair of scissors. She trimmed and arranged the flowers, filled the vase with water and put it on the locker at my side, next to the ones from Mark, which were already wilting.

She sat back on the visitor's chair and folded her hands neatly in her lap. After a long silence, in which Parveen regarded me, I said: 'Aren't you going to talk?'

'You always said you hated small talk,' she said. 'Which kind of makes it difficult in situations like this.'

I couldn't stop myself from smiling. 'How's work?'

Parveen smiled back and then launched into a description of everything I'd missed. I hated to admit it, but it was nice. Dispatches from reality. Apparently Paul was working as slowly as usual and a funding application had been approved. Parveen assured me that I'd been instrumental in completing the application and that I should feel especially good about this bit of news. As I couldn't remember a bloody thing about it, I didn't.

My cognitive impairment made the conversation a strange and disorientating process; some snippets of information were like keys, opening doors to things I knew, but hadn't been able to see, while others just led to blank walls. I had no idea what was new information, old memories coming back or just plain wrong.

Parveen began to talk about Mark. I knew that I wouldn't have told anybody about our relationship, but it was still a relief when she confirmed this by the way she spoke about him. Every day was a fresh opportunity for unwanted surprise and confusion and it was nice to know that my sense of self wasn't entirely compromised. There was silence and Parveen was looking at me, waiting. I had let her run on and had drifted away. Maybe even closed my eyes.

'Sorry,' I said. 'I missed that last bit.'

'They said you'd be very tired.' Parveen fiddled with the zip on her bag.

'Lying in bed is surprisingly knackering,' I said. 'So, we've covered work. How are things with you?'

Her hands went still on the zip. Her eyebrows lowered and I thought for a moment that she was angry. Then she smiled and said: 'You've never asked me that before.'

'I'm a bit of a grumpy bitch, by all accounts.'

Parveen tried, and failed, to hide a smile. 'I wouldn't say that.' Her black hair was cut just too long to be called a bob and she had a metallic red hair clip on one side. I had a memory of her niceness and of being irritated by it. Thinking it was fake, the way I automatically did with anything pleasant.

'Mark,' I began, a strange urge to connect to another human being bursting out. I was going to say 'Mark's my boyfriend' but that seemed ridiculous. The man was so old. That thought surprised me. He wasn't old. He was forty-one, but very well maintained, and it wasn't as if I was exactly a babe in arms. I felt ancient. Correction. I had felt ancient. I realised that despite being laid up

85

in bed and every bone in my body aching, I felt younger than I had in years. I felt reborn. I winced inwardly. I should watch that crap. Being a bit nicer was one thing, joining a religious cult was quite another.

'He's been lost,' Parveen said, surprising me. 'He keeps wandering around the department.'

'Doesn't he always?' I said. It was a genuine question. My memories were still so sparse, I just had fragments – inklings, really – of what constituted normal life and routine. I was hungry for hard facts.

'He misses you,' Parveen said.

And then I realised. 'You know about us.'

She bit her lip. 'Sorry.'

'That's okay.' Another wall down. 'Does Paul?'

'I don't think so. We haven't spoken about it and he's kind of oblivious. You know?'

'Good.' I felt surprisingly calm about Parveen knowing one of my big secrets, but I didn't relish the thought of being the subject of office gossip.

'How did you—' I stopped, waved my hand. 'It doesn't matter.'

'Before you started, we had a PhD student. She was in the department for a few months and she and Mark went out a few times.'

I kept my face carefully neutral, waiting for this to hurt in some way. It didn't.

'He kept hanging around the lab. Had the same expression. Happy.' Parveen shrugged. 'When he started it again I figured it was you. I mean, it wasn't me and I doubted it was Paul.'

'I didn't realise it was so obvious,' I said.

'It's none of my business.' Parveen shifted slightly, suddenly looking like she was about to get up and leave. I didn't want her to go. This day was just full of fucking surprises.

'Thank you,' I said. 'For visiting. It's been really weird. I have these . . . gaps. I remember lots of stuff but I've got no idea what I haven't remembered because, well, I can't remember. It's frustrating and I really—' I broke off, wiped my cheeks with my hands. They were dry, thank God.

'We miss you in the department,' Parveen said. 'We're all hoping you'll be back soon.'

'You see, that's another thing,' I said, happy to be on more familiar ground. 'Either that's a gap in my memory or I've got false memory syndrome or brain damage or something.'

'Well, obviously,' Parveen said. 'You know you've got brain damage. I mean, you must've looked at your chart?'

'I meant, my memories don't tell me that the department would have warm and fuzzy feelings about me. But here you are. I'm surprised, that's all.' I paused, another thought hitting me. 'Please don't be offended, but had we become friends or something? Have I forgotten?'

'No,' Parveen said, her lips compressed. 'We've never been friends. Just colleagues.'

'Okay.' I felt a funny mixture of relief and hurt. Relief that my memory wasn't hiding a best mate from me, hurt at her emphatic tone of voice.

'Maybe it's the grit in the oyster,' Parveen said. 'In the department. I miss the grit. Plus,' she was smiling now, 'you made me look really nice just by comparison. It's harder to maintain that on my own.'

I was surprised into laughing and Parveen's smile grew wider, her eyes bright and suddenly beautiful.

'Can you tell me more?' I hated needing people, I hated needing full stop, but this situation was forcing it upon me. I was the Grand Canyon of need and it terrified me.

'Like what?'

'Just describe a day in the office. Anything. I want to match things up.' *Please.*

Parveen nodded and began.

Sometime later, I opened my eyes and realised that I'd drifted off. Parveen was gathering her stuff together, moving quietly as if not to wake me. 'Sorry.'

'That's okay,' she said. 'I stayed too long. Tired you out.'

'Will you visit again?'

Parveen hesitated.

'I know we're not friends and there's no obligation. But I'd like it.'

She gave a quick smile. 'Maybe. If I've got time.'

'Fair enough,' I said. 'Can I ask you something before you go? It's about Mark.'

Parveen stiffened. 'He's my boss.'

'I know. It's just—' I didn't want to ask the question, felt vulnerable even thinking it, but there was a niggle in the back of my mind that wouldn't go away. 'You know, you said that Mark seemed happier. Have I?'

Parveen gave me a look of pure panic.

'It's okay,' I said. 'Don't worry. I shouldn't have asked.'

'Not really. To be honest, you always seemed kind of tense around him,' she said. 'But, like I say, I don't really know you and I certainly don't know anything about your relationship.' She stood up and I felt panic that she was leaving. Parveen felt like a real link to my old self, more real even than Mark. Which was odd.

'Can you get something for me? I'll pay you.' As I spoke I realised that I didn't know if I had any money. I didn't know where my clothes or handbag were.

'Okay,' Parveen said. She seemed relieved that I'd moved away from questions about emotion and feelings. I didn't blame her.

'I mean, I will definitely pay you back. I don't know where my stuff is right at this moment, but I will—'

'It's fine,' she said. 'I know where to find you.'

I sank back, grateful. 'I'm not about to skip the country.'

She nodded. 'Your skipping days are over.' As if realising that this might be a little too mean, even for the uneasy teasing truce we'd struck up, she said quickly, 'Temporarily.'

I smiled widely to show I wasn't upset and made my request while she was still feeling guilty: 'A cheap mobile. Pay as you go with some money loaded.'

'A phone?'

'I know there's a payphone but I have to ask to use it.'

'Fair enough,' Parveen said. 'Isn't it against the rules, though?'

'I'm a maverick,' I said.

'And a layabout.' Parveen was pulling on her jacket. 'You'd better hurry up and get back to work. Stop skiving.'

I wanted to remind her about the phone, ask her when she was planning to bring it. Just the possibility of it had made me want it more urgently. 'Thank you for coming,' I said, instead. 'It is so good to see you.'

Parveen gave me another arch look, shaking her head very slightly. She waited, as if expecting me to say something else, said, ''Bye, then,' and left.

෧ඏ

Parveen was as good as her word. I was having one of my monster sleeps. The ones which embraced me so tightly that I didn't know anything about anything for twelve hours straight. When I woke up I wasn't groggy as usual; I felt tingly and alive. Sharp. The smell of the hospital was freshly antiseptic, like someone had just sloshed bleach around the room, and even the muted colours of the walls and curtains seemed bright. There was a starling on my nightstand. It was regarding me with that classic bird look of inquisitive stupidity. Both bright and blank. Despite my neurons firing on all cylinders it took me a moment to realise that the starling was standing on something. A box. A mobile phone box.

I managed to sit up in double-quick time, ignoring the pains that ran up my spine, sending spikes into my skull. A nurse I didn't recognise was at the bed opposite, chatting to Queenie. Every word seemed amplified and I hoped this new clarity would go away as quickly as it had arrived. Either that or I'd have to ask Parveen to bring me sunglasses and some earmuffs, too.

I unpacked the phone and switched it on. The nurse gave me a disapproving glance but she didn't come over and tell me I couldn't use it. I guessed they had mostly given up enforcing that hospital rule. For a moment I was intensely glad for the overworked and under-organised National Health nursing. The phone was far fancier than I'd imagined. It had a touchscreen and icons for internet and email, as well as text and calls, and Parveen had put the SIM card and battery in ready for me. I was so grateful that I forgot to be annoyed by her presumption that I wouldn't be able to do it for myself. I typed in Geraint's number and listened to it ring. Eventually, on maybe the twentieth try, I was forced to put the phone away in my bedside locker. A nurse arrived to take my blood pressure and she was followed by someone else, who wanted to check my leg. By the time they'd finished, it was breakfast followed by Simon the Viking.

❧

Now that I had remembered Geraint and his phone call and I had the means of calling him back, I could hardly think of anything else. Simon made me do the most excruciating exercises, flexing my shattered knee until I thought I would pass out, but all the time my thoughts ran on an endless loop. It was The Geraint Show twenty-four/seven. I was remembering all kinds of things and each memory seemed to lead on to another. The time when we were children and he cut my hair. I had a clear memory of us standing in the hallway and looking at ourselves in the big mirror. I could see both of our faces: Ger's dark-eyed and serious, from the neck up; mine barely visible. I was too short so just my eyes, forehead and my jagged new fringe were showing. I don't remember Pat going spare over the haircut or Geraint actually doing the cutting, just that moment in which we stood side by side and admired his handiwork.

Another memory: Auntie Pat was doing something mysterious with a big pot on the stove and the kitchen was filled with steam. I was sitting on the floor and she was singing. Geraint was drawing on the window with his finger and I felt intensely jealous that he'd thought of it first and had dibs.

Another: sitting in our favourite corner of our regular. Geraint was explaining something to do with prime numbers and I was watching the barman with the ponytail and nice arms. Another time in a club, when Ger was with some girl. We were seventeen or eighteen. She worked in Boots and told him she could get hold of out-of-date medicines and they kissed for hours. I couldn't stop watching them. The memory of fascination and disgust and a weird kind of jealousy was so vivid, I found it hard to believe I was remembering something from years ago and not the week before.

'You're quiet today,' Simon said.

'Apart from all the screaming,' I said.

He nodded. 'But you usually insult me more. You off your game?'

He was smiling but his eyes were soft with concern. It made me want to cry, which made me want to be sick. I hated this mushy feeling, it was like I was dissolving. I forced a smile in return and made it brittle. 'Just thinking of some good ones for next time.'

After Simon had gone, I sank my head back on the pillow and closed my eyes. Geraint had always been highly strung. He'd get obsessed with things and forget everything else while he pursued them. He could forget to answer people, to wash, to eat. Just when you'd be starting to think things were getting really serious, the obsession would peak. He'd solve the equation, or finish building the computer, or master the clarinet, and would appear, hair brushed, ravenous, at the breakfast table. He was like an explorer, going on long voyages of discovery, pushing himself to the brink of mental and physical exhaustion and then returning just in time for tea. If any of us said we'd been worried (we'd said it before, of course, but he hadn't been listening), he'd turn his insufferably confident expression on us and say, offhandedly, 'I had it all under control.'

Drugs were a bad idea.

We smoked a little weed, did a few mushrooms, and that was it. One time, Geraint tried speed, something that any idiot could've told him was not a good mix with his personality type. He thought he was chewing gum and bit his cheeks and tongue bloody and, by the end of the night, was sitting on the ledge of his open bedroom window while I begged him to come inside.

Afterwards, maybe the next day, I tried to talk to him about it. He laughed in my face. 'This is serious,' I said. 'You can't take that again. You could've fallen out of the window. You could've really hurt yourself.'

Ger rolled a cigarette and told me to stop acting maternal. He said it didn't suit me.

I reached into the bedside cabinet and retrieved the phone. My back was hurting so I lay flat and held the phone above my face. I pressed the buttons and listened to Geraint's phone ring and ring.

GRACE

When Grace was fifteen, their neighbour Bridget had taken her to see a gypsy fortune teller. It was their little secret; Grace's mother would've gone spare, but Bridget said it was vital for every young girl to have her palm read. Grace spent the morning before they went in a state of anxious excitement. She'd read an adventure story once that featured gypsies. They lived in brightly painted caravans and had tiny bells sewn into their clothes, tinkling as they walked.

The woman had lived in an ordinary semi-detached on Lowden Avenue and Grace was both relieved and disappointed when she opened the door in a navy wrap-over just like the one her mother's housekeeper wore to do the cleaning.

Madame Clara had ushered them through to the kitchen. It was smaller than Grace's mother's kitchen but had the same deep sink and water heater bolted to the wall. While Grace's mother had smartly painted green cupboards, Madame Clara's were tired-looking and mismatched. There were gingham curtains hanging underneath the sink and plant pots lined up along the windowsill.

'Please, sit,' Madame Clara said, gesturing to the small table tucked against the wall.

There was a crystal ball on the table. Grace blinked but it remained just as real as ever, planted next to the salt and pepper set on the flowered oilcloth. Madame Clara pulled the yellow blind down at the window, bathing the room in a warm glow, and lit a white candle. The candle was a tall dinner one stuck into what looked like a wooden egg cup. All in all, it wasn't what Grace had been expecting.

'Give me your hand.' Madame Clara held out her hand for Grace's.

'Go on,' Bridget said, nudging her.

As soon as Grace's fingers grazed the older woman's, she felt a spark. She pulled her hand back. She smiled a nervous apology. 'Static electricity. It always happens in the summer.'

'You've got powerful energy,' Madame Clara said. Grace didn't believe her for a second. She was always getting little shocks from static electricity. There was nothing mystical about it.

Clara reached for Grace's hand and, once again, the static sparked between them. 'Ouch,' Clara said, sticking her fingers in her mouth. She looked at Grace appraisingly for a moment and then said: 'Tea leaves.'

While the kettle was boiling, Clara and Bridget chatted. Bridget spilled every detail of her life and, seemingly, every thought that had passed through her mind since waking up that morning. When she came to have her reading done, Clara would have plenty to choose from. Grace was wondering how much Clara charged and whether it would be a good way to make pocket money, assuming of course that Grace's mother didn't kill her flat dead for even considering such a low-class idea, when she saw something odd. Madame Clara had crossed the kitchen to make the tea and when her back was turned, Grace saw a shadow. It was square in the middle of Clara's back. Grace looked around to see what was casting it, but there was nothing. She looked again and the shadow was still there, and when Clara moved the shadow moved with her. Grace blinked. She stared at the place Clara had been standing, trying to see the shadow against the sink or the cupboard, but it wasn't there.

Clara put the pot of tea on the table, making 'uh-huh' noises while Bridget rattled on, nineteen to the dozen.

'May I have a glass of water?' Grace said. She felt sick and the skin on her arms was raised in goose pimples. Bridget shot her an old-fashioned look, but Clara nodded and went to the sink. There it was. A large black shadow, its edges clearly defined and unmistakable. It was an asymmetrical oval, the topmost point jutting up between Clara's shoulder blades and finishing just above her square waist.

'There's something on your back,' Grace said. She couldn't help herself.

'What's got into you today?' Bridget said, frowning.

Clara turned around. She was pale. 'I beg your pardon?'

'Sorry,' Grace said, fighting embarrassment and ingrained reticence. 'There's a dark shape on your back. Is it a stain?' Grace knew it wasn't, but she had to see it again.

'I'm so sorry,' Bridget said to Clara. She reached out and tapped Grace smartly on the back of her hand. 'Don't be so rude, young lady.'

Clara didn't answer, she was twisting her neck, trying to look over her own shoulder. 'I can't see anything. I can't see . . .'

'Here,' Bridget stood up. 'I'll look. Perhaps the dye has been fading in your pinny. That happens, especially with the dark colours. Don't you find?'

Clara joined her in the middle of the kitchen, presenting her back to Bridget for inspection.

'There's nothing there,' Bridget said. She gave Grace another look. This one was harder to read. Confusion mixed with irritation.

Clara's face was frightened, though. 'What does it look like?' She twisted again, showing her back to Grace. 'What do you see?'

Grace looked at the black oval. It seemed to be moving slightly, undulating with the shifts in Clara's position. It was a shadow but it looked alive somehow. Shapes stretched out on either side of the oval like the wings of a bird, the tips of its feathers brushing her shoulders. Grace closed her eyes. 'Nothing. There's nothing there. It was just a trick of the light. Sorry.'

Clara sat back down, grasping Grace's hand. She felt the jolt of static electricity again and saw Clara wince, but the woman held on tight. Too tight. 'What did you see? Tell me?'

'Nothing,' Grace said, truly frightened now. 'Nothing. I swear.'

❧

Three months later, Grace was eating porridge at her mother's dining table when Bridget dropped in for an early visit. She was in a lather and wouldn't join the family at the table. She and Grace's mother were closeted in the kitchen and when Bridget was fit for company, her eyes were red. She played nervously with a sodden handkerchief. 'You remember my friend Clara, don't you?'

Grace nodded, her breakfast porridge making a sudden bid for freedom, back from her stomach and up her throat.

'She's in hospital.' Bridget paused and when she spoke again her voice was barely a whisper. 'Cancer.'

'I'm sorry to hear that,' Grace managed. She thanked the heavens for ingrained politeness, for the socially acceptable platitudes that sprang to her lips. She didn't know if this was why Mother had always been so strict about manners, but they did give you a road map, something to follow when you felt as if you were dissolving from fear and uncertainty.

Bridget, however, was staring at Grace with a piercing gaze. As if she was waiting for the girl to say something else.

Two weeks later Clara was dead, and, from then on, whenever Grace saw shadows that shouldn't be there, she looked resolutely in the opposite direction. Even when one appeared on her own body, a shaky black circle on her stomach, she pretended it wasn't there. She used every ounce of willpower to ignore it, never allowing her gaze to stray towards her middle, until it was too late.

MINA

When I was a kid, I thought X-rays were magical, that those wobbly black-and-white images were brought about by some strange alchemy. Working in radiology, I used multiple-imaging techniques as tools for diagnosis and research, and X-rays were the least impressive of the lot. They should have become routine to me, but I never lost the feeling that they were dispatches from the unknown. I knew the science, of course, but there was a part of me that had never really stopped believing they were something else, something other than the effect of electromagnetic radiation on photographic paper. There was something ghostly, something otherworldly, about the blurry white shapes glowing on the dark background. They revealed and concealed in equal measure. They had revolutionised medicine, given us the ability to see inside ourselves without cutting, but they gave an incomplete view. A shadow on an X-ray might be an artefact, a mistake in the developing process, or it might be a tumour that was going to kill your patient within the next seventy-two hours.

I was sitting up in bed, waiting for my breakfast and thinking about my brother. I was trying to remember whether I should be worried about Ger, or whether I was merging memories and feelings from the past. I had an inkling that it was myself I should be worrying for, a horrible sense of dread that had wound itself around my insides, but that could be the depression. Dr Adams kept on reassuring me that every thought, every feeling, every down-in-the-dumps day, every bleak view, was normal and to be expected. It made me feel worse. Not only did I still feel like crap, but I also felt like a walking (or, more accurately, lying) cliché. I didn't want to be a collection of symptoms. I wanted to be a person. I wanted to be me again.

I closed my eyes and ran through the things I was certain of. My name, my age, my address. I still couldn't picture my flat. I had an image of a purple sofa, the one that Mark had told me about, but I had no idea if it was a memory or just my imagination. I remembered my office at work, Parveen, Paul and Mark. I remembered starting at the hospital and the early months of my relationship with Mark. I'd never been out with anybody so grown-up and sorted, and I remembered how much I'd loved the novelty of a man who organised proper dates and trips away. Then things got hazy.

Further back was easier. If I let my mind wander, memories from childhood were crystal clear, just waiting. Memories I didn't think I'd visited in a long time. Memories I hadn't wanted to visit. When I left the peninsula, I left it. The way most people leave childhood, by shoving it into an unloved corner of the mind and forgetting about it until psychotherapy or hard drugs or, apparently, head trauma, dragged it kicking and screaming into the light.

Today I was at the giant's grave. A Neolithic burial ground made of stones. It was sixty feet long and twenty wide, low stone walls with a grassy roof. I was sitting on the edge with a friend. I don't remember what we were talking about, or which of our rambling walks had taken us there. I just remember the quiet in the clearing, the line of trees in my sight line. I remember the

Opal Fruits I was sucking, and that I was letting the chewy sweet spread out and lie on the roof of my mouth to give maximum sweet-eating time.

And then, with the visceral memory of the sugar syrup running down the back of my throat, I remembered something else. We'd been warned not to go walking on our own. A girl had been found in the woods and it had been in the paper. My friend's dad was in the police and she said that he'd told her the girl had been interfered with. I didn't really know what the phrase meant and I never knew the girl, but I dreamed about her for weeks. I'd seen a bird before the news had broken. Every day while I was waiting at the stop for the school bus there had been three wagtails. They sat inside the bus shelter, in a neat little row, their tails unnaturally still and sombre. When I got on to the bus they flew inside and perched on the rail of the seat in front of mine. Every morning I had my wagtail shadows and every night I dreamed of a girl, about my age, sleeping in the woods. Her clothes were torn and dirty and her leg didn't look right. She had fairy music playing in her ears and her eyes were wide open.

After my physio session with the Viking I lay back, exhausted, feeling the burning pain in my knee and spine and feeling something that might have been gratitude. Contentment even. It was wrong, I knew. I was in hospital, with a long recovery ahead. My mind was playing hide-and-seek with my memories and I was still avoiding calling Pat and Dylan to tell them where I was. I had rationalised that I needed to get much better first, so that I didn't worry them, but that wasn't the whole truth. It was habit. I might have lost half my mind, but I remembered that much. I knew I wasn't a good daughter.

The gratitude fled and I was left with the more familiar feelings of guilt and panic. How could I be feeling sneakily happy? I hadn't reached Geraint yet. I didn't know what was wrong and I needed to help him. True, it would have to be help that could be offered from the confines of a hospital bed, but I had at least to try.

I reached for the mobile, hidden in my nightstand drawer, and pressed redial. As I listened to it ring, I tried to remember when I'd last seen Ger. Had he been worried then? The fear I remembered hearing in his voice . . . Was that a new thing? An ongoing issue?

Frustratingly, my mind delivered nothing recent, nothing helpful. I switched the phone off and hid it again. I didn't want Mark to see it and for us to have an argument about it. He seemed so protective of me and would want to know where I had got it and who I was calling. I didn't have time to worry about what that said about my relationship with him, because the action of holding the phone had brought another memory flashing back.

Another phone call from Ger. I didn't know how recently it had been, how close to my accident, but I remembered that he'd asked me to meet him. He'd said he couldn't talk on the phone and I'd felt a jolt of anxiety that he'd taken something that had made him paranoid. Of course, he'd always had a flair for the dramatic and I'd comforted myself with that. I was sure he was fine.

I had driven to meet him, I remembered that, which meant it had to have been in the last three or four years. Before then, I didn't have a car. I probed the memory, trying to extract every detail, until I could relive it.

The air was cool and clear. High above, geese drew giant arrows in the morning sky. I was nervy, expecting to see something untoward out of the corner of my eye. A bird on my dashboard, perhaps, or one sitting calmly on the bonnet of the car while I cruised the motorway. Something that suggested Ger was about to drop some unwanted bombshell. I didn't know why I felt so anxious, only that it wasn't unusual, that worrying about Geraint had become habitual.

I arrived before Ger and found a table at the back of the café. I sat facing the door and straightened up every time the door opened. He was twenty-five minutes late, which was standard Geraint-time, and I watched him walk in and look around. He spotted me and smiled the usual tight-lipped Geraint smile. I did a half-wave and watched him walk over. He was wearing a coat over a hooded sweatshirt. I studied his face, trying to work out if he was more than usually gaunt. Ger caught me looking and the corners of his mouth pulled down.

'Sorry,' I said.

Geraint slid into the seat opposite. 'Is that man looking at me?' He addressed the sugar bowl.

'Which man?' I moved my head to look behind him.

'Don't look,' he said. 'Jesus.'

I stopped. 'No. Nobody is looking at you. Except the waitress. She's probably planning out the name of your first born.'

Geraint smiled and leaned back in his chair, visibly relaxing. 'Long time no see.'

'Yep.' I was about to ask him what was so urgent but he beat me to it.

'So what have you done this time?'

'What do you mean?'

'Pat's going mental; she called me, like, three times yesterday.'

'Oh, her.' I took the lid off the pot and jiggled the teabags with a spoon. 'Do you want some?'

He nodded. 'Black.'

'I know.' I concentrated on pouring the tea. Ger watched the ritual and then wrapped his fingers around the cup. His hands looked ridiculously large on the end of his narrow wrists and they were so thin that every knot stood out. They were an anatomical drawing of a pair of hands. No X-ray needed.

'So.' I decided to get it over with. 'What does she say I've done this time?'

'The usual,' Ger said. 'Broken her heart.'

'Is that all?' I was shooting for funny, but Ger didn't smile. I changed tack. 'Did you lose your phone?'

'What?'

'New number. Your texts were freaking me out. You should've signed them.'

'I did.'

'Just the last one.' I smiled. 'I was beginning to think I had a stalker.'

Geraint sat forward so fast his knees banged the underside of the table. 'You, too?'

'No,' I said, worried by the sudden intensity in his voice. 'Not really. I was joking.'

'Oh.' He shook his head slightly as if dislodging something. 'I've been working a lot. I thought—' He stopped abruptly. 'It's nothing. I'm sure it's nothing. But I got a new phone.'

'Okay.' I paused. 'So, what did you need me for? You sounded really freaked out in that message. I've driven all this way—' I stopped. 'It wasn't because of Pat, was it? Because that's all I need. If she wants to talk to me, she can call me. It's not fair to go through you.'

'She says you don't answer when she calls. She thinks you screen her.'

I shrugged. 'Of course I screen. Everyone screens.'

'But you don't call her back.'

'I do,' I said. 'Usually. Not always super-quickly, but I do call eventually.'

'Well, if you could do it a bit more often she'll stop hassling me to pass on messages.' He had his work bag with him, a giant khaki messenger bag with a slogan that read 'To err is human, but to really fuck things up you need a computer' on the side. He started rummaging about in one of the pockets, pulling out handfuls of data sticks until he found the one he was looking for.

'What's that?'

'Picture. Don't save it to your computer. Just open the file from the stick. Then get rid of it.'

'What's going on?'

'Probably nothing. I'm imagining things. Most likely.'

'You got me to drive all the way here so that you could give me this.' I waved the stick at him. 'You ever heard of email? The postal service?'

'This is safer. Don't save it to your computer, mind.'

'Fine.' I was annoyed now. 'I heard you the first time.'

Ger pulled a face.

'Why don't you just tell me?'

Geraint shook his head again. 'This is better. Honestly. You won't believe me if I try to tell you . . . Just look at it.'

'Fine.' I took the stick and shoved it into the pocket of my jeans. I found his secrecy infuriating but I didn't want to fight with Ger. So I asked him about his current obsession and settled in for the long haul, drinking tea and letting his description of particle systems wash over me. Ger became animated. His hands were still, cradling the warm cup, but energy radiated from him. It wasn't as if he smiled much, but he seemed happy, totally focused and in the moment. Zen.

'What?' Ger was frowning at me and I realised I was half smiling.

'Zen and the art of particle systems,' I said. I smiled properly at him, the familiar rush of love and concern and frustration.

I asked after Katya, his live-in girlfriend of the moment. Ger had never had any trouble finding a girlfriend. He attracted the kind of woman who wanted to save a man, to look after him, and that was fine with me. In my opinion, he needed looking after and wouldn't let me close enough to do it.

He shrugged, looking deep into his tea.

'Oh, no, Ger.'

'It's fine. It was never serious.'

'She moved from Russia to be with you.'

Ger looked blankly at me. 'She was studying.'

'I thought she worked in the Co-op?'

'Yeah . . . She did that, too. She was out a lot, anyway.'

I could see the goodbye scene as clearly as if I'd been there. Katya frustrated and tearful, Ger oblivious. When he was deep into his work he didn't hear you. Katya could've been talking to him for days and he might not have even noticed. She could've been hanging from a sex swing stark naked and it wouldn't have made any difference.

We said goodbye outside on the street. The temperature had dropped again and I hunched my shoulders up inside my jacket. Geraint grabbed me for a quick, unexpected hug and for a moment we clung together. I breathed in the smell of his hoodie and tried not to notice how skinny he felt.

'Are you sure you're okay?' I said, and watched him brush off the comment like it was an irritating insect.

'You need to call Pat,' he told me.

'I will.'

'Today,' Ger said, mock seriously.

'Could you run interference? Tell her I'm away on a research trip. That I'll call her in a couple of weeks.'

'That'll never do it. I'll tell her I split up with Katya.'

Pat went through phases of worrying about us each in turn, never at the same time. When it was Geraint's turn for the laser beam of her focus, I'd call her, lie for him, distract her. It was the perfect system.

'Be good.' Geraint gave me his crooked smile and turned away. I watched him lope across the road and disappear down a side street before I turned away myself.

The sun was low in the sky, shining into my eyes on the drive home. After a while it dipped to the horizon, blazing red through a line of black trees. It looked like the wood was on fire. I tried hard not to picture Geraint alone in his flat, lit from the glow of his computer screen.

☙

The data stick from Geraint turned out to have one, very blurry photograph on it. I stared at the picture, trying to work out what was so terrible that he couldn't have just emailed it to me. After several minutes of squinting and using the zoom function, I worked out that it was a person. Probably a man, but that was far from certain. No matter how much I looked, though, I couldn't see anything shocking or incriminating.

I knew that I should call Geraint, check that he was okay, but I didn't. I didn't want to talk about the picture, to find out that he had constructed some kind of story to go along with it. I didn't want to think that he was getting anxious or paranoid, the way he used to when he was little or when he drank too much caffeine and stopped sleeping. I wanted to pretend that everything was fine. That he was fine. So I did.

I managed to bury my worries over Geraint and the incident I had privately labelled 'the nothing picture'. It was easy. Life was busy. Between working on my degree, reading books and watching films and living the single life with nights in clubs and the occasional one-night stand, time passed at a rate I would've found alarming had I been paying more attention. Then I had a phone call from a number I didn't recognise. It was Katya. 'I'm worried about your brother. I didn't know who else to call.'

'Are you still an item?' I was surprised.

'No. Not for ages. I care for him, though.'

Geraint had that effect on people. He treated them like total crap and they came away caring. When I was feeling resentful and childish I hated that. If I made one little mistake it felt like the whole world was coming down on me.

'I think you should go and see him. He needs you.'

'I can't just drop everything here.' I was thinking about my dissertation viva and the flat-hunting I still hadn't begun. And I was annoyed with her for presuming to know what my brother needed better than I did. 'Why don't you pop in and see him? You still live in Cheltenham, right?'

'I can't,' Katya said, her voice cracking a little. 'It's too painful. I thought I could be his friend, but I can't.'

'Okay, fine.' I knew that I sounded narky and that it wasn't fair. I forced myself to thank her for calling me, for her concern.

'Has he said anything. About me?'

I closed my eyes. How many more times was I going to have to clear up the emotional wreckage from Geraint's life? 'No,' I said. 'I'm sorry, you know what he's like.'

'He was so keen to start with,' she said.

'He just got distracted. It's nothing personal.' I was about to add 'He does this all the time', but I managed to stop myself. I was working on not being cruel.

'But he asked me to move in, why did he do that if he didn't want me around?'

That was just Geraint, I wanted to tell her. He was very efficient. He put in the exact amount of energy – no more and no less – required to get the result he wanted. Then, once his attention had wandered, he didn't expend any further time. 'I don't know how to put this, but it would've been a logical decision. He probably thought it made sense for you to be in the flat.' Then he wouldn't have to waste time and energy travelling to see you.

'Your brother is a sociopath,' Katya said.

'No. He's just busy,' I said, defending him even though I'd just been thinking the same thing.

I could hear snuffling noises. Katya was crying, now, and the horrible part of me was glad. It meant the excruciating phone call was almost over. 'I'm truly sorry,' I said, trying to sound like a normal, caring human being. 'He's always been this way and I swear he liked you. He didn't mean to hurt you.'

'He wasn't eating,' she said, and I could practically hear her wringing her hands. 'I just thought I should let someone know. He doesn't deserve my help, but—'

'Thank you,' I said, again. 'I'll take care of it.'

But I didn't. I called and didn't get an answer, but I didn't go and visit. I emailed and sent text messages and, eventually, got a terse reply: *Working. Tired.* Like I said, when Geraint didn't want to engage, nothing on this planet could make him do so. At least that's what I told myself as I threw myself into my own work.

GRACE

It was December and ice had formed on the inside of the windows in the nurses' quarters. Grace barely noticed as she had reached a pitch of tiredness that no longer felt like being properly alive. She fell into bed at night, her feet and calves on fire and the rest of her body already asleep, and woke up only with the morning nurse shaking her shoulder and shouting into her face, 'Nurse! You'll be late for breakfast.'

Looking back on these months, Grace wasn't at all sure what had stopped her from simply turning over and refusing to leave the scratchy warmth of her single bed. Knee-jerk obedience, she supposed. She'd been trained to do as she was told by her parents and by school and the habit was ingrained. It was this habit of obedience that made her body rise to a sitting position, her still-aching feet finding the cold floor. Still, though, she wondered at how she'd carried on. Her eyes burned from tiredness before the day had begun, not recovered from the days before. She stood in the sluice, running water over bedpans, or pushed the tea trolley down the ward, or hefted sheets in the laundry, or any of the other menial, dogsbody tasks that occupied her in her position as the ward junior, the lowest of the low, and felt that at any moment she would simply fall down dead. But she didn't. She hadn't.

Grace walked as fast as she could from the sluice to the women's ward. She buttoned her cuffs as she went, her numb fingers struggling to fix the fiddly little buttons. Some of the other juniors complained about the cuffs, very quietly of course. Characteristically, Evie had ranted about them just the night before. How silly it was that they had to take them on and off all day long. How ridiculous they were at all. 'They're simply not practical,' she'd said, daringly smoking, even though smoking in the bedrooms was strictly forbidden. Along with most other things.

But Grace liked the cuffs. Without them, she was just a girl in a dress. Up to her elbows in soapy water and getting everything wrong, as she had at home. When she put the cuffs on, she felt transformed.

Over the months, Grace had grown accustomed to the patients and their bodies. In addition to cleaning floors and bed frames, wrestling with dirty sheets for the laundry and slicing endless rounds of bread, she was slapping poultices on to chests, washing backs and smearing cream on to bedsores. When a man old enough to be her grandfather called for her to look at his whatsit, she didn't even consider blushing.

'It's awful sore,' he said. He had a thick Scots brogue, which Grace had difficulty understanding, although she tried. Nurse Barnes just shook her head at him and shouted, 'Can't understand a word, duck.' He had a heavily pitted complexion and red-rimmed eyes now turned beseechingly upwards as he held the covers away from himself. Grace peered at the whatsit, coddled gently on a bed of cotton wool, and wished, for a single, exhausted moment, that she could swap places with the strange male part. A bed of cotton wool seemed like heaven and Grace suddenly realised why the pictures of it always involved fluffy white clouds. Soft puffy clouds to rest upon, to drift blissfully asleep on . . .

'Nurse?' The man, whose name wasn't Jock, though everybody called him that just the same, looked more worried than ever and Grace realised that her silence was being misinterpreted. 'It looks fine, Jock,' she said.

He replaced the covers, wincing elaborately as they made contact. Grace put her hands on her hips. 'Is it truly that bad?'

Jock nodded his head mutely.

Grace turned on her heel. 'I'll tell the sister and she can take a look.'

There was no time for Jock's whatsit, however, as the rounds were due and the frenzy that preceded the grand visitation of the doctor was in full swing. Cabinets that had been dusted only that morning were re-dusted, beds were straightened and sheets and blankets were tucked in with such ferocity that patients had difficulty breathing, let alone moving. The ward sister always barked orders with increasing fury up until the moment the doors opened and the great man arrived, when her voice turned to honey, and cuffs were most certainly on.

'Can't stop, Jock,' Grace said, tucking his sheets in as loosely as she dared.

'Nurse!' The ward sister's sandpaper voice seemed alarmingly close and Grace spun around to face her. 'I do hope the pans and bottles are properly put away.'

'Yes, Sister,' Grace said.

'I won't have slovenliness on my ward,' the sister began, but before she could list all of the other things she absolutely would not tolerate and the accompanying litany of Grace's deficiencies, footsteps began echoing down the ward from the outside corridor. Sister pulled herself to her full height and waddled off in the direction of the doors.

'Hair,' Barnes hissed. Grace's hair had a tendency to resist tidiness and bits kept escaping throughout the day. She was for ever tucking stray strands back underneath her cap. She'd barely finished when the doors swung inwards and Dr Palmer arrived. As always, he was followed by a scurrying retinue of students and nurses. As he paraded around the ward, stopping at each bed and holding court, Grace dug her fingernails into her palm and prayed that he was satisfied. Any criticism of the ward was viewed as a direct attack on the ward sister and her ability to maintain order within her domain. When she discovered who was responsible it would result in the culprit – invariably a junior nurse – being sent to Matron's office the following morning.

Dr Palmer stopped at Jock's bed and inclined his head, listening. Jock was speaking and Grace had the sinking feeling that he was complaining about his whatsit. She held her breath as she stood to attention on the other side of the ward. She could hear Jock's voice rising and falling. He spoke in the deferential and diffident way of male patients to the doctors, to be sure, but he could be complaining nonetheless. Finally, the sister peeled back the bedclothes and Dr Palmer leaned forward, his head on one side, as though assessing a work of art, or a steak he was considering eating for supper.

Jock pointed at Grace and she felt a clammy sweat break out on her neck. By the time the procession had made its way around the ward to the point at which she was standing, Grace felt as if she might faint. All work ceased on the ward while the doctor was in residence so she couldn't rush off to busy herself with something. Couldn't hide in the bathroom or the sluice.

'Ah,' Dr Palmer said. 'Nurse Kemp, is it?'

'Yes, Doctor,' Grace said, her voice barely a whisper.

'Do ensure that man has zinc oxide applied.' And he winked at her. So quickly Grace thought she must have imagined it. No doctor would do anything as vulgar and familiar as wink. Especially not in the middle of rounds, with the ward sister on his left looking like she wanted to throttle someone and quickly.

'Coo,' Barnes said, once the esteemed party had left, the ward sister had exhausted herself shouting and retired to her room for a cup of tea, and they were back in the safety of the sluice. 'He's a bit of all right.'

'Dr Palmer?' Grace still felt sick.

'I should say.' Barnes fanned herself with her hand. 'He could be an actor.' Barnes was stockily built and had a permanently red face. She said that hospital life was making her fat, all the bread and marge and not enough fresh air, but Grace thought she looked well on it. Sturdy. Curvy. There was a nurse called Davies, who was so thin she looked like she would break at any moment. When you saw her lifting a patient you couldn't help but hold your breath, waiting for the crack as the birdlike bones in her arm simply snapped under the pressure.

'I hadn't noticed,' Grace said.

'Ooh, yes. He's gorgeous,' Barnes said. 'Lovely pink lips.' And she cackled.

'I don't like him,' Grace said, and Barnes looked at her as if she'd gone out of her mind. As if that had anything to do with anything.

Grace closed her lips tight. Barnes was right, of course. It didn't matter whether Grace liked him or not. In her experience, it didn't matter what she liked or what she didn't. At once, she wanted to cry and she turned away to tidy the linen cupboard, determined to hide her red eyes from Barnes.

Grace had been a good baby; Mother said that she had slept like a little angel and always smiled at people when they peered into the pram. Then she'd been a good girl. She'd kept her clothes neat and washed her face morning and night. She said please and thank you and did as she was told. She'd been good even when a friend of her father's didn't seem to be quite the thing. She'd been polite all the while he had been quite the opposite, although – during – her clothes hadn't remained quite as neat as usual.

Later, when her stomach began to push against the waistband of her cotton circle skirt, and her chest hurt inside the strict confines of her clothes, her combination painfully digging in, she stopped being a good girl. Just like that.

The very best thing about being a nurse, Grace thought, was that it was beyond all of those labels. Grace wasn't naughty or nice any more; she wasn't even a person. She was a nurse. However frightened or repulsed or tired she felt, she rejoiced inside her starched cocoon. Maybe one day, she'd emerge from it. A woman. A lady. Or, more likely, she'd remain Nurse Kemp for ever and ever, and that was just fine, too.

Grace wanted to be like Sister Gilbert. She had never married and, if she hadn't been a nurse, she'd have been called a spinster. She would've been something to be pitied, but as Sister Gilbert she was beyond all of that. She'd risen to a higher state of being. Sister Gilbert was so good at her job, so experienced and capable, that even the doctors inclined their leonine heads to listen to her. As if her words were worth listening to, almost as if she were a man.

Grace followed the sister, mimicking the graceful way she moved around the ward. She was lightning fast but never seemed to hurry. She moved smoothly, as if on castors rather than clumpy feet and legs. She had a serene expression, like a nun, as if nothing in this mortal world could ever surprise or alarm her. Grace watched the way she spoke to people and tried to emulate her gentle, commanding tone. She studied hard for the exams and listened in the lessons, fighting her desperate tiredness and ignoring Evie's attempts to distract her. She, Grace Kemp, was going to be a nurse. She was going to work so hard that nobody could ever be disappointed in her again.

MINA

I gripped the mobile phone and willed it to ring. If Geraint would just call and say 'Hey' or, more likely, 'Stop ringing me all the fucking time, I'm busy', then I'd be able to relax, to concentrate on the stuff that Mark (annoyingly) kept saying I should be concentrating on – getting better.

Dr Adams said the same, to be fair, although it irritated me less coming from him as at least he was medically trained. When he'd scheduled my hydrotherapy session he'd mentioned counselling to help me deal with the trauma of the accident. He'd even used the words 'holistic approach to recovery'. I'd given him my dead-eyed stare and said, 'I don't have any trauma from the accident. I can't remember the accident.'

He'd matched my stare with an impressive one of his own and said, crisply, 'Point. Proved.'

I closed my eyes and tried – again – to think about the accident. It was ridiculous that I couldn't remember something so huge and, besides, the stubborn part of me wanted to prove Dr Adams wrong.

Memories were shining threads in the dark and I followed them one by one. Mostly they merged into another thread, like the tangle in one of those mazes you got in puzzle books, but sometimes they ended with an image or a vignette. Moments from my past, my personality, nuggets of knowledge. I had to follow them patiently, though. If I tugged to try and pull the memory closer, the thread just snapped.

A nurse bustled in, pulling my curtains back and leaving them half open in a way that I knew was going to bother me. Then she gave me something else to worry about, by taking the dressing off my leg, along with what felt like a layer of skin.

'That's looking good.' She wagged a finger at me as if I were a toddler. 'Now, no scratching.'

I bit back a sharp retort and focused, instead, on not thinking about the mess of my lower leg and how badly scarred it would be. I'd never considered myself especially vain, but I didn't want to draw looks of disgust or, worse, sympathy, every time I wore skirt.

'Can you close the curtains?' I asked the nurse as she moved away.

'You don't want to block out this lovely sunshine,' she said and I considered throwing something at her back.

Then I had to stop myself from yelping out loud. My hallucination had returned. She was leaning over the end of the bed, peering at my burns and giving me an excellent view of her white cap. I could even see the hairgrips holding the edge of the material. I twitched the blanket over my legs and glared at her, wondering whether getting annoyed by a figment of my imagination was more or less futile than with the real-life nursing staff.

She pursed her lips and reached out as if she wanted to move the blanket. I tensed, not sure I could cope with the sight of a ghostly hand moving through the fabric, but she stopped and smiled at me. She was so pretty it made me forget that she was a hallucination. There was something warm and very real about her expression. Calm poured through my body, making me almost drowsy.

She produced something from the pocket in the front of her apron and moved it just above the bed sheet. It was a small metal train with flaking red paint, so detailed that I couldn't believe it wasn't really there. She smiled at me encouragingly, holding out the train as if I was supposed to take a turn. I reached out a finger to touch the train and the vision disappeared. There was nobody there. I took a deep breath and tried not to feel abandoned. The train had stirred a memory, though: Christmas shopping with Mark. We were in the toy department of John Lewis and I was trying to pretend I cared about gifts for his nieces and nephews. I winced as I remembered my off-hand tone as Mark showed me toys and books and asked my opinion.

Later, we'd gone to a pub for a reviving drink and Mark had asked me relentless questions about my family. We'd argued, of course, when I wouldn't answer him to his satisfaction. 'I have ways of finding out,' he had said then. His face was flushed with emotion and from the warmth of the pub. 'You're not as bloody mysterious as you like to make out.'

His words made me feel sick. Then and now. I wasn't trying to be mysterious. I wasn't playing games. I just felt like everything was safer if things stayed in their correct zones: work, boyfriend, family.

I explored my memories of Pat, Dylan and Geraint and tried to recall when we'd last been all together. Every time I thought of us as a group, my mind flickered to an early Christmas when Geraint and I got matching Aran sweaters in itchy wool. Or the Easter when Pat organised an egg hunt, but the weather was unseasonably warm and the eggs so well hidden that we spent days finding the misshapen melted chunks of chocolate.

I couldn't bring forward memories from after I'd left home. Not of my family, anyway. I assume I spoke to them, visited home, wrote emails, but I couldn't conjure up a single specific incident. I could remember university; my friends and the shared houses I'd lived in. All those new and exciting experiences. Perhaps it was just a symptom of the self-involved selfishness of youth. Family receded as you launched from the nest, spreading your wings and, hopefully, flying.

What was more worrying was that I couldn't remember the time after university either. I tried to remember my birthday last year. Or job hunting, which I knew I must've done to get work at the hospital, but it was another terrifying blank.

I clung to the things that I knew; I was twenty-nine, I'd completed a PhD in the research department at UCL, which meant maybe three or four years after that in the hospital job. Parveen had programmed her number into the mobile and I texted her. *How long have I been working in radiology?* It felt good. Proactive.

A message came back quickly.

3 yrs. Are you bored?

I replied:

Thanks. Yes. Very.

Another text:

Me, too. At least you're in bed.

I smiled. It seemed I had to have a car crash and a coma in order to make friends. I knew that I'd never taken the easy path, but even I had to admit this was a bit extreme. Still, I was grateful.

⚬⚬

When Mark came in to visit, I asked him how things were at work. I'd been planning to tell him about Parveen, to show off my new social skills, but once he was in front of me I just clammed up. No matter how good my mood, as soon as Mark appeared it seemed to turn black. I liked the idea of him, but once the reality showed up my chest got tight and I couldn't shake the feeling that something was wrong between us.

After he'd talked about his day for a while, I used a gap in the narrative to ask: 'Could you bring in my laptop?'

Mark frowned. 'What for?'

'Just stuff. You know, email, internet.'

He shook his head. 'I don't think that's a good idea. If you're getting bored I can bring you some more books. Do you want any magazines?'

'No, thank you,' I said between gritted teeth. 'Why don't you think it's a good idea?'

'I don't want you stressed.'

'I'm not stressed,' I said, consciously unclenching my fists. 'I just want a bit of normality.'

'If it means that much to you, I'll speak to your doctor.'

His tone of patronising solicitude made me want to punch things. Instead I forced myself to smile. 'That would be great. Thanks.'

'Now,' Mark said, chipper again. He produced a slim box from his jacket pocket. 'How about a game of dominoes?'

∽

The next day, after Mark had visited with no mention of my laptop, Dr Adams appeared. The curtains were pulled around the beds, creating little bedrooms, and it felt strangely intimate. He threw himself into the chair and ran a hand through his hair. 'Well, that was a boatload of crap.'

My senses kicked up. It was ridiculously pleasing to be spoken to like a normal human being, not a patient. 'Bad shift?'

He shook his head. 'Normal shift, stupid bloody meeting.' He tipped his head against the high back of the chair. 'God, I hate SM.'

The phrase jogged something loose. Parveen and Paul complaining about senior management, calling them 'S and M' and making a whip-crack sound. Paul laughing with his mouth wide, showing his crooked bottom teeth . . .

Dr Adams glanced at me. 'Senior Management. Bunch of—' He broke off, colour flooding his cheeks. 'Christ. Sorry. Ignore me.'

'That's all right, vent away,' I said. 'I remember management problems. Sadly, even a coma isn't enough to erase those.'

'I guess they're the same in every department. I know they've got a difficult job and that there are budgets to be balanced and so on. If only they weren't such . . .'

'Arseholes,' I said, conveniently and deliberately forgetting that I'd been sleeping with my manager for over a year.

Dr Adams smiled and told me a little about the meeting he'd just had. Something strange happened as he spoke, though; bits of my old life came back. I remembered Paul buying himself a Danish pastry every Friday and eating it slowly at his desk, spreading a wide circle of flaky crumbs. I remembered going out for a drink with a girl who'd worked in the department for a few months, and that Mark had shown up halfway through the night, sitting down at our table and being weirdly grumpy. I couldn't remember why – or whether we'd had a fight that day – but I remembered the awkwardness of the moment with such force that I felt myself blushing.

I pushed the memory away and tried to concentrate on Dr Adams. After a while, the details were running into one another, so I just lay back and enjoyed listening to his voice.

'Sorry,' he said. 'I shouldn't be burdening you with this. And it's dull. How are things with you? Are you in pain?'

I opened my eyes. 'I'm fine. Bored. Frustrated. But, as you've just reminded me, that's not the preserve of the hospitalised, so thank you. At least I'm out of meetings for the foreseeable.'

'Always a silver lining.'

'You know, it's pretty easy to have a car accident if you ever get desperate.'

He was suddenly alert. 'Have you remembered something?'

'Nothing important,' I said. 'But I am going crazy'.

The alert look intensified and I realised I'd misjudged my tone. 'Not crazy with a capital "c", not "in need of sedation" crazy. Bored crazy. Sick of being sick crazy.'

'Do you need more books?'

I glanced at the teetering pile of paperbacks and shook my head. 'I've actually got a project in mind. I think I must be missing work or something, but I need something to do. I asked Mark to get my laptop and he said he was going to speak to you about it.'

He shook his head. 'Not yet.'

'He's worried that I'll overdo it, set back my recovery.'

'I don't think that's likely,' Dr Adams said. 'What sort of project are we talking about?'

I felt self-conscious. Which was silly given that the man in front of me had probably seen me naked – a singularly unhelpful thought.

'Mina?'

'I want to research the history of the hospital. I know it sounds daft but I can't believe how little I know about this place. I mean, I've been coming here every day for years and now I'm sleeping here and it's just kind of made me wonder about it.' *And I keep seeing a nurse in old-fashioned uniform and I'm wondering if she might be a real person.*

'The history of the hospital.' He didn't sound like he believed a word I was saying. He probably thought I wanted my laptop to watch kitten videos and I was just too embarrassed to admit it.

'I'm so tired of trying to remember things about my own life I thought that if I concentrated on something else, maybe things would just pop back into place. You said I should relax and I've been trying but I can't relax just lying around doing nothing. I know that sounds counter-intuitive—'

'It doesn't, actually.' He pointed to himself. 'Classic over-achiever reporting for duty.'

I smiled encouragingly. 'I know you've got a million things to do, but I'd really appreciate it if you could get my laptop. If you ask Parveen in my department, she might go to my flat and get it, or perhaps . . .'

'Have you got your keys? I'm happy to pick it up for you.'

'That's really kind. I would ask Mark—' I began, but he cut across me.

'One condition,' he said. 'You stop calling me Dr Adams.'

'I'll call you "God" if you get me my laptop.' I blushed as soon as the words were out.

He was smiling in a slow, easy way that was completely inappropriate, and intensely attractive. 'Stephen will do.'

'Stephen,' I said, glad when my voice didn't waver.

After he'd gone I kept thinking of that smile and smiling myself.

∽

Stephen Adams was as good as his word. He appeared the next afternoon with a laptop that I recognised as my own and a large paperback. 'History of the hospital,' he said, waving it. 'I can't believe someone actually spent a good chunk of their life researching and writing about this place, but their loss is your gain.' He flipped to the front page of the book and frowned at it. 'It's self-published, mind, so that might actually be "their loss, your loss".'

'And the tree's loss. Don't forget the tree,' I said, reaching for it. It was a thick book and I could see the telltale sign of photos included throughout – thick, grey-edged paper.

'I was thinking about what you mentioned,' he said. 'I brought you some files from your office. Nothing you need to worry about, everything is being completely covered by your department, but I thought it might help you to look at familiar things.'

'Thank you.' I was touched.

He put the files on to my table, moving the plastic jug of black-currant squash to do so.

'Thank you . . .' His voice trailed off, leaving a significant gap, his eyebrows raised.

'Thank you . . . very much?'

'Stephen. Thank you, Stephen.'

'I can't be expected to remember every little thing,' I said, pointing to my head. 'Coma patient. I get a free pass.'

'You're not in a coma now,' Stephen said, smiling a little. 'You're my miracle patient.'

'That's nice,' I said. My fingers were itching to open the files, to look through my new book.

'I've got to go,' Stephen said. He ran a hand through his hair, sweeping his fringe away from an impossibly high forehead. 'I can visit later, though, after my shift.' He hesitated. 'If you'd like.'

'Great,' I said, wondering how many photos there'd be, whether I'd open to a group shot of nurses and see my appearing/disappearing woman smiling back at me. Proof I wasn't completely insane.

'Later, then.'

As soon as Stephen had gone, I opened the book and began flipping through it. I was vibrating with excitement and hope. Black-and-white images of the hospital and grounds, nurses and doctors and men in old-fashioned suits, blurred together. I closed the book and my eyes, trying to calm myself enough to take things in properly. I wanted to giggle or clap my hands or something equally inane. Anything to release this sudden rush of energy.

Instead I hauled my laptop closer and opened that, savouring the rush of normality that switching it on gave me. I realised that I had more than a distraction here – I had the key to my past life. Perhaps I'd even kept a diary.

∽

When Mark came in before dinner (swede boiled until soft and scooped into a perfect round, beef casserole which was surprisingly edible, and a low-fat strawberry yoghurt), he was chipper. In fact, he was verging on giddy. Rather than being happy for him, his good mood made my own disappear. I finished my dinner with grim determination, concentrating on chasing every last morsel around the plate and not looking at him.

'I've got news,' he said once I'd pushed my tray away.

'Can you bring me something to eat tomorrow? I'm so sick of hospital food. I'd kill for a burger.'

Mark looked irritated at the interruption and I felt the devil rise up in me. I knew I wasn't being very nice, but I was powerless to stop. 'One of those gourmet ones from a gastro pub. A hundred and ten per cent pure steak, with cheese and relish, and loads of chips. Good crispy ones. Do you remember the skin-on ones we had from that place . . . what was it called?' As I talked, the reason for the words changed. They weren't just to annoy him any more, they were a delaying tactic. I was frightened of what he was going to say.

Luckily, Mark was distracted by something. The edge of my purple laptop case poking out at an angle on the shelf of my bedside cabinet. 'Who brought that?'

'Stephen,' I said. 'Dr Adams.'

'First-name terms now?' Mark's face was twisted. 'What the fuck was he thinking? You need to be resting. Not working. I know what you're like. Give you a computer and you'll be logging on to your work account, answering emails, trying to keep up.'

'I asked him about it,' I said, my voice stuttering a little. 'I thought maybe you'd forgotten.'

'Of course I hadn't forgotten. I was trying to protect you.'

I couldn't understand why Mark was so angry about this, but my heart was racing. *You're okay. You're in a hospital.* I swallowed hard, and forced myself to speak. 'What's so terrible—'

'Have you used it, yet?'

'Not really. I can't get into my email account or my private files.' I tried to smile, to show how little any of this meant, how it wasn't upsetting me or putting back my recovery or anything. 'Can't remember my password.'

Mark hesitated and he seemed to be deciding whether to find this funny or not. The moment stretched out. I had the feeling I was missing something important, but I didn't know what and I was too scared to ask. Finally, Mark smiled. His expression was calm and his voice was warm and jokey, like he hadn't been furious moments before. 'Well, that's a shame. You'll have to wait to read all the exciting staff memos.'

I smiled, too, relieved that the argument seemed to be over. My heart was still thudding, though, and my head began to throb.

Mark straightened the laptop. Without the corner poking out I wouldn't be able to catch hold of it, but I didn't say anything. Without my passwords, it was pretty useless anyway.

'Now,' Mark said, sitting forward in his chair and clasping my hand in both of his. 'My news. I've found us a house.'

His words didn't make any sense. I thought: *When I get out of here I'm going home. To my flat. With the purple sofa that I don't remember and my white walls.*

'You're going to love it.' He was still speaking, his gaze not meeting mine. If I didn't know better, I would've thought he was nervous. He let go of my hand in order to reach into the carrier bag I had assumed contained magazines and newspapers, and pulled out some stapled sheets of A4. Glossy paper, estate agent's details.

The house on the front was beautiful. It was an end terrace and the street name was one I knew well. A road I'd walked down, peeking covetously at the tall town houses behind the neat black railings. Big windows with the original sash and casements, expensive front doors painted in Farrow & Ball green or confident red. The brickwork was creamy white, like so many of the properties in Brighton, and before I glanced down at the next image – a location shot – I knew that I'd see the sliver of blue sea.

It was beautiful. Perfect. And the numbers beneath the picture were laughable.

'I can't afford this,' I said. I didn't say 'We can't afford this', because that seemed irrelevant. I wasn't moving in with Mark, let alone buying a house with him. Especially since I'd need a never-ending supply of kidneys to keep up with the mortgage payments.

'We can,' Mark said, sitting forward. 'Together we absolutely can.'

'You can, you mean.' I kept my voice flat, trying to signal that the conversation was over.

'It's nice inside, look.' Mark flipped open the brochure, which was lying on my lap like a dead seagull.

'Really spacious. Four bedrooms.'

Despite myself, I looked down. A kitchen with cream-painted wooden units and a range cooker. There were big windows and glass doors leading out to the garden, like the Big Girl version of my flat. A long garden with a gazebo type thing at the back. A bedroom with the beautiful bay window seen in the street view. High ceilings, pale walls, pretty mouldings . . . even, I had to take a deep breath, original fucking fireplaces. Yes, I wanted it. Of course I did. If I won the lottery, I'd buy it in a heartbeat. I pushed the property details off my lap and on to the floor.

'It really is doable, I promise,' Mark was saying. 'I've run the figures. I can't wait for you to see the place, I just know you're going to fall in love with it. We're going to be so happy there.'

'Wait a minute.' And the penny dropped, with a resounding clang. 'You've already bought it.'

'I had to,' he said. 'It was a steal. There were loads of people interested and I only got a first viewing as a favour. I know John, that's the agent, from way back. School, actually. I've had him keeping a lookout for me for a while, now, and then this came up. You were in here.' He spread his hands. 'What else was I supposed to do?'

'You've been house hunting while I've been here. In hospital.' I was trying to process the conversation, but the words refused to make sense. He was talking about being a cash-buyer, money from a flat he'd sold in London last year and how he'd been waiting for the right thing to put his cash into, but how the sums didn't mean anything, that it was ours.

'I wanted to surprise you.'

I wanted to slap him. 'Congratulations,' I said, in lieu of violence.

'I didn't want to bother you with the details or any of the stress. And I wanted to make you happy,' Mark said. 'This'll be a new start for us.'

'Did we need a new start?' I had realised something over the last few days: before the accident, maybe for a long time, I had been desperately unhappy. I wasn't sure if that was despite or because of my relationship with Mark. All I felt when I looked at him was a kind of exasperated confusion. The knee-jerk relief of recognising someone had eased off and what was left didn't feel anything like love. Although, I would be the first to admit, I was no expert.

'Perhaps.' Mark looked guarded again. He took my hand and began stroking my palm with his thumb. Parts of my hand appeared to be linked to nerves elsewhere in my body and I felt my libido unfurling, my senses waking up. Suddenly, I wanted Mark's mouth on mine, I wanted to feel the lust building, his man smell to obliterate the antiseptic of the hospital and my own stale, sick odour. Like I said, I was no expert. I leaned forwards and, mirroring my movement, Mark moved inwards. I tilted my head and his lips met mine.

I kissed him and kissed him. I wanted to hold on to the spark of sensation I'd felt, the prickle of feeling in places other than my spine and neck and head. I mashed my lips against his and willed myself to feel like a whole person. It didn't take long before my back was hurting too badly and I had to lean into my pillows again. I opened my eyes as I did so and caught sight of a movement behind Mark. It was a sign of my years of seeing things that I didn't shout in surprise. The woman in the white apron was standing a few paces behind him, staring at the back of his head with an expression of extreme antipathy.

'Is that a yes?' Mark said, looking delighted with developments.

'I don't know,' I said, turning my gaze resolutely away from the apparition. 'I will come and see it, though.'

He smiled as if I was putting on a show of being stubborn, as if he'd already won. 'Fair enough.'

'Tell me about our problems,' I said. I didn't want to wander into argument territory again, not so soon after the laptop skirmish, but I had to ask. 'Why do we need a new start?'

Mark took my hand, gazed into my eyes. It was difficult not to glance over his shoulder to check if the woman was still there, but I managed it. 'You've always been very independent.'

That sounded right.

'And it took a long time for you to trust me, to let me into your life. I stayed the course because I knew we had something special.'

I sucked my tongue to the roof of my mouth to stop myself from smirking. The phrase 'something special' made me want to laugh. Or shudder.

'I think I'd started to hold back, too, to protect myself.' Mark hesitated, glancing down as if this was all too painful.

I nodded to show I understood and wished I felt something other than cool detachment. What was wrong with me? Had I always been this much of a cold bitch or was it the head injury?

'You wanted us to move in together but I didn't feel able to make the full commitment. That's why I kept my own place. It's been more like I've been bunking with you and you weren't happy about that, said it showed I had one foot out of the door.' He reached down and opened the flap of his leather bag, pulled out a sheaf of paper. 'You were flat hunting for us, but I wouldn't talk about it. I'm sorry. I think I was punishing you.'

The details were of flats to buy in Brighton. Two-bedroomed places of the kind I thought were completely out of my price range. I stared at the photographs, the lists of phrases 'gas central heating', 'double glazing', 'single entrance', and tried to remember them. I must've picked them up from estate agents or, more likely, registered online and had them delivered.

'It was causing problems but I was too proud to admit that I felt the same way.' Mark was leaning forwards. He was the picture of an earnest lover. The lowered brow, the shining emotion in his eyes, the quiet tone of his voice. I computed all of the signs and understood the effect, but couldn't shake the feeling that he was playing a part. Nothing seemed real to me any more. Not the other women in the neighbouring beds, not the nurse who came at regular intervals to torture me with the blood pressure cuff, not the man I had apparently been plotting to buy a flat with.

'I got over it,' Mark was saying. He gave a small smile. 'Apparently almost losing the love of your life in a car accident makes things very clear. I knew I didn't want to waste any more time being scared or resentful and I thought this house was the perfect way to show you that I'd changed.'

It all made sense. The mixed feelings I'd been having were explained by the fact that we'd been arguing. I'd been trying to get him to commit and now he had. Everything was solved. I was going to get out of hospital and move into my dream home with Mark. I knew I should be happy and I tried to arrange my face into an appropriate expression. If it hadn't been for the nurse hovering behind Mark and shaking her head, I think I might've managed it.

'I wish you'd say something,' he said.

I wished I had something to say. I tried to form a sentence in my mind, something appropriate and conciliatory, but not too definite. I needed time to think.

'Say you'll come home with me,' Mark pressed. 'To our house.'

I wanted to go home very badly. I wanted to have a home and a place in the world that wasn't this ward. I wanted to make Mark smile a real smile, to make somebody happy for a change. 'Okay,' I said, and pushed down the urge to throw up. Hard. The nurse shook her head and disappeared.

GRACE

When Grace had woken up the day after she had lost her baby, there had been a moment before she'd remembered. It lasted for a fraction of a second, just one tiny moment in time, and it had been blissful. Then everything had come back and she knew the flickering life was gone. She knew she ought to be glad. Mother was glad. 'It's for the best,' she'd said over and over while she mopped up blood. Grace hadn't expected to go into hospital, but she had thought Mother might call the doctor. She had refused, though. Shaking her head as if Grace was asking for the impossible. 'Can't afford that,' she'd said, but Grace didn't think she'd meant it in the financial sense. 'Mrs Lewis is coming. Hush now.'

When Mrs Lewis had arrived and taken in the scene her lips had gone very thin and white but she'd rolled up her sleeves and got to work. After she'd checked Grace 'down below', she'd inspected her stomach. She couldn't have missed the livid bruising or the place where his boot had split the skin along her ribs, but she didn't say anything.

Grace closed her eyes and felt the tears leaking out, running over her cheeks. She knew that her condition had been what made

Father so angry, caused him to lose control like that. She knew she was no longer a good girl, and that she had come within a hair's breadth of bringing almost unimaginable shame on their family. She knew that, barring her doing anything so stupid again, he would never touch her. He never had before; it had always been Mother who'd administered discipline. Smacks and slaps and harsh words. Grace also knew that if there ever were a next time, he'd kill her.

This was a lucky escape. The baby that was going to ruin her life was no longer inside her. It had been cleared away by a grim-faced Mrs Lewis. It hadn't even been a baby, not yet. Mrs Lewis had whispered that it was just a beginning, just the idea of a baby, not a real child at all. Nothing to be sad about. 'Lucky escape, my girl,' she said, wrapping the thing in a bundle with an old towel and some newspaper. 'If my girl had come home like this, she'd have ended up in the workhouse.'

Grace knew that the workhouse was worse than death, but she knew that would not have been her fate. Not in her family. Not when appearances were so important. She didn't believe Mrs Lewis. Not that she was better off; there was nothing lucky about this. No matter that she hadn't asked to have life started inside her, she'd felt it. She'd never resented the little thing, she'd imagined it swimming and flipping like a little fish.

And, staring at the blank white ceiling, Grace had known: her life was already ruined. The damage had been done. Her father had gone to work already, she'd heard the front door close. She knew he'd come home and they'd eat dinner around the table as normal. She might be excused to stay in bed upstairs tonight, but certainly not tomorrow. No malingering in this house.

Something was broken inside her, Grace knew, with the certainty brought by pain and fear. Something had snapped and would never be repaired.

She had been brought up to believe that she would be a wife and mother. Her own mother had been hazy on the details of the second condition, but Grace knew that it was something that happened when you got old enough. Married at nineteen or twenty, first son or daughter a year after the wedding. The bit in between was a mystery. It had something to do with love, but Grace didn't think that could be the whole story. She knew plenty of married people, her cousin Mary for one, who didn't seem to have very much of the stuff but still produced children with predictable regularity. Mary had a grim little bowl of hair that looked as if her husband cut it for her with blunt scissors, and a slash of fuchsia pink lipstick which came off on her protruding front teeth as she spoke. There didn't seem to be anything like love in their household. Lots of mess. Lots of noise. Endless nappies on the washing line and big circles around Mary's eyes that got darker every year.

Grace had so dreaded being put with the women and their babies that she'd quite forgotten that it would involve nursing. She had been resolute in her refusal to think about the midwifery or children's wards, a shutter coming smartly down in her mind whenever she contemplated words like 'post-partum' or 'infant nutrition'. The lessons on midwifery (which everyone cheerfully referred to as 'midders') had passed for her in a haze but, to be fair, most of Grace's lessons did. All lectures and study time occurred during their precious off-duty time and it was hard to stay awake, let alone take in the information.

Grace stared at the printed list, the tiny black letters dancing over the paper, and willed them into a different order. Some other arrangement which would result in her going to the men's side of the hospital or to surgery or even to infectious diseases. Anywhere else.

'Bad luck,' Barnes said, looking over her shoulder. 'The sister on children's is a horror.'

Grace's spirits drooped lower still. 'What kind?' Some sisters were mad keen on cleanliness, most of them shouted, but the very worst crept around, hoping to catch you doing something you shouldn't like eating or sitting down.

'Creeper,' Barnes said, giving a theatrical shudder.

The children's ward was in the recently built new wing. The walls were shiny with fresh paint and the floor had new linoleum that some bright spark had laid in a pattern. The main floor colour was speckled grey, but there was a thick line of black which ran six feet in, around the bottom edge of the beds. Sister Harris shook her head when she saw Grace. 'Juniors get sloppier by the week. Fix your cap, Nurse.'

'Yes, Sister.' Grace tried to keep her eyes cast down respectfully, but this seemed to engage Sister Harris further. 'Look at me when I'm speaking.'

Grace lifted her chin and stared at the spot where the sister's cap met her forehead.

'You can start by polishing the floor. And mind nobody steps on the black. It leaves footprints.'

'Yes, Sister.'

There was a side room attached to the ward intended for pre-delivery women but which, due to a recent local epidemic, held a number of polio cases. It also had the dreaded black lino, but Grace was mindless with gratitude that she hadn't been sent to the nursery with the crying babies. On her hands and knees, she rubbed at the black linoleum and tried to bring it to a shine. Sister Harris had already rejected one portion, telling her it was still scuffed where a child had had the audacity to step on it.

Grace wanted to ask how they were all expected to avoid the black line, given that it ran around the ward and had to be crossed to reach a patient's bedside. Not to mention how sick and injured children were meant to remember to hop over it when they were out of bed.

'They shouldn't be out of bed. A child who is well enough to be out of bed is well enough to go home.'

'Hello?' A boy's voice, high and wavering.

'I'm just doing the floor,' Grace called up. 'Don't be alarmed.'

She stood up, rubbing the small of her back with one hand, and looked properly at the boy. He had infantile paralysis and one arm was immobilised in plaster, bracketed to hold it up in the air. It was supposed to aid healing for a reason that escaped Grace. Sometimes she had the sneaking suspicion that the doctors were making things up as they went along.

'Would you mind handing me my train?' The boy, Billy, pointed at his bedclothes. 'It got away from me.'

Grace located the small metal engine. It had once been red, but the paint was mostly flaked away. Billy held it up to his eyes, rubbed his thumb over it and smiled. 'Thank you.'

'You have lovely manners,' Grace said. Hospital had been an eye-opener in terms of people's language. Of the way even small children could speak.

'Mam says I'm going to need them,' Billy said. 'Because I won't have legs. Won't be able to walk, I mean.'

'It's too soon to say that.'

Billy's expression changed and Grace wondered if she'd said the wrong thing, when he whispered, 'She's coming.'

Grace ducked back down to the floor just as Sister Harris swept past.

Once the sister was safely at the opposite end of the ward and fully engaged in giving another junior a thorough dressing down, Grace rose from the floor. She adjusted Billy's pillows. 'Comfy?'

'Thank you,' he said. He held up his train. 'Do you want a go?'

'Please.' Grace took the train and ran it carefully over the lumps made by his legs. She felt awkward. Out of practice. Not just at playing make-believe but at being a person.

'When's visiting?' Billy reclaimed his train and spoke to it, not looking at Grace.

'Three o'clock. Not long to go.' She opened her mouth to ask if his parents were coming and then shut it again. What if they weren't?

'Mam might be in today. She's hoping to finish early, she said.'

'That's good. Cross fingers.'

Billy crossed his, expression serious. Held them up for Grace to inspect. She crossed hers and held them up, too.

'So this is where you've been hiding.' Dr Palmer's voice acted like a bucket of freezing water being emptied over Grace. She managed to stop herself from physically jumping into the air, but she had a horrible feeling that her flinch had been obvious.

He pulled the screens closed and walked uncomfortably close, backing Grace towards the wall. 'I was just seeing to Billy,' she said, hoping to draw his attention to the child in the bed.

Palmer seemed oblivious to anybody else but her. He put one hand on the wall next to her, casually, as if he were just leaning there for a moment, but something about it frightened Grace.

'On the skive, I'll bet. I know what you young nurses are like.'

Grace couldn't reply, felt sick with nerves. His hand darted forward, like a fish and adjusted her cap. 'Sloppy,' he said. His tone was gentle. Playful, almost.

Grace was paralysed. Her forehead burned where his fingers had brushed it.

'Quiet, though. That's good.' Dr Palmer was smiling as if making a joke but Grace knew it wasn't a real one.

'Dr Palmer.' The screen moved aside and Sister Harris appeared.

Grace felt her stomach fall to her feet even though she hadn't been doing anything wrong. Despite her terror of the ward sister, though, she felt relieved. Saved.

She didn't dare look at the boy in the bed, didn't think she could stand to see the expression on his young face. Would it be frightened or disgusted?

'Don't let Nurse Kemp detain you,' Sister said to the doctor. 'There are three patients waiting for linseed wraps and if her past performance is anything to go by she'll need extra time to redo them at least once. Isn't that right, Nurse?'

'Yes, Sister. Thank you, Sister.'

'After that, you'd better go to the dinner hall, although Lord knows I can't spare even a useless lump like you.'

'Yes, Sister. Thank you, Sister.' As Grace stumbled out of the sluice and into the ward, she had the feeling that she'd escaped from something, although she wasn't sure exactly what. One thing seemed clear: she would have to be more careful. It wasn't until she was halfway down the ward that she realised she still had Billy's toy train clutched in her hand and would have to return it to him later. The metal edges of the engine had dug into her palm leaving deep red grooves.

MINA

After bringing me the mobile, Parveen visited a few more times and always managed to make it seem casual, as if we really were friends.

'Just visiting my phone,' she said. 'Checking you're not mistreating him.'

'It's a boy?' I struggled to sit up and Parveen tucked a pillow behind my back while continuing her treatise on gadget gender. 'All mobiles are male. iPods are female. Not sure about tablets.'

I liked seeing her. She was an envoy from the outside world. I loved hearing about life in the department – sometimes Parveen would mention a person or event and I'd find the memory waiting for me. It made me feel hopeful for the future. Like I'd be able to slot back into my old life.

There would be changes, though. Friendship for one. Parveen talked about restaurants and bars we were going to visit once I was well; we planned days on the beach and yoga classes. I thought she was still just being kind and that these things would never actually happen. Either that, or my old reclusive personality would reassert itself. But it was nice talking about these things. I was daydreaming, trying on a new life for size.

The one subject that was awkward was Mark. I didn't like to talk about him because I still felt conflicted and confused, but as soon as I realised that Parveen didn't really approve of our relationship I felt closer to Mark out of loyalty.

She had brought tea and chocolate brownies from the Costa on the ground floor. I lifted the plastic lid and sipped the piping hot liquid, relishing tea that was both properly strong and properly hot. Even my fingers getting scorched through the cardboard sleeve felt amazing. I could hardly believe that one day these things would be normal again. That I would be making myself tea in my own kitchen. My new kitchen, I corrected myself.

'I can't wait to get out of here.'

'Do you know when?'

'They're being annoyingly vague about it,' I said. 'Not long, though. I hope.'

'Let me know. I can give you a lift.' I was floored, again, by the novelty of friendship. 'That's all right,' I said. 'Mark will do it.'

Parveen was blowing on the surface of her tea and didn't meet my eyes when she spoke. 'Are you sure?'

'Yeah, he said he can take time off whenever. He's been brilliant, actually. Nothing is too much trouble.'

'That's good,' Parveen said in a tone that said the opposite. 'I just wondered whether it was what you wanted.'

'What do you mean?'

'Nothing.' She took a sip of tea.

'He's bought us a house.' I hadn't planned on telling her, but it seemed important. Suddenly I wanted to prove to her that he was a good partner. A good choice.

'He did what?'

'Got a house. For us.'

'Oh my God.' She shook her head. 'That's huge. When did he even—'

'It was a bargain. He had to snap it up.'

'So, he bought it without you,' Parveen said and I hated the way it sounded. 'But you haven't even seen it.'

'I've seen pictures.' I didn't know why I was defending him, only that I felt embarrassed and wished I hadn't revealed anything. This, I remembered, was why I wasn't any good at relationships. They made you feel stupid and exposed. Things which seemed completely fine in the confines of your own mind sounded weird and wrong out in the open.

'And you're going to move in with him? Straight away?'

'He bought a house,' I said, irritated that I was repeating myself. It made me sound weak. 'It would be rude not to give it a try.'

'Yeah, that's a good reason for co-habitation.' Parveen looked away. 'Sorry. It's your life, of course. Just, that, you have other options. You have a flat. You don't have to move in with Mark.'

I didn't know how to explain to Parveen that I just wanted to get out of this ward, that I couldn't really think much further than that. 'I'm going to need help at first, it makes sense to live with someone.'

'What about family? Could your mum or dad or someone help out?'

I felt a knife twist in my stomach at the thought of Pat and Dylan. Parveen must've seen a trace of it in my expression as she added, hurriedly: 'I could pop in. Look out for you. You wouldn't be left totally on your own. And you'll be back at work soon. You're making a really good recovery.'

'Am I?' I was pleased, like it was an exam I was doing well in, not some stroke of luck. Then my oddly attired hallucination appeared at the end of the bed. She was wiping her hands on her white apron, as if to dry them, but she smiled at Parveen and for an irrational moment I thought about introducing them.

Parveen was still talking about Mark. Unsurprisingly, she hadn't noticed the non-existent nurse, who was watching our conversation. 'It just seems quite sudden . . . You and Mark, I mean.'

'We've been together for ages, though, haven't we?'

'Yeah, but you didn't seem "together, together" before.'

'How would you know?' It was hard to concentrate with the ghost-nurse there. I couldn't shake the feeling that she was really listening. 'It was a secret. We're very private people.'

Parveen held her hands up. 'Sorry. None of my business.'

'Look,' I started, trying to circumvent the urge to run away, to shut the conversation down. Perhaps it would help to say it out loud. 'I know that things weren't perfect with me and Mark before and you're right, I'm not sure I'm doing the right thing or how I feel about him or anything, but he's so invested in us, it seems cruel not to give it a go.'

'I didn't mean—'

The nurse was frowning now, she looked upset. So did Parveen. I was no good at this stuff, but I tried to reassure them both. 'I need to get myself sorted before I can really work out how I feel. Nothing's set in stone.'

'Absolutely,' Parveen said, determinedly upbeat. 'You need to concentrate on getting better.'

I had put a forkful of brownie into my mouth so I just nodded.

'And you'll still have your flat, won't you?'

☙

After Parveen had gone I tried calling Geraint again. I was messing around with the settings on the phone and didn't notice Mark come into the ward.

'Where did you get that?' He looked at the mobile as if it offended him.

'Parveen gave it to me.' For some reason I omitted to say that I'd asked her to buy it.

'Parveen?' Mark had been leaning in to kiss me but he paused. 'What was she doing here?'

'Visiting me,' I said. I felt annoyed. And a little upset. Was I really so awful that it was surprising colleagues would visit me? It wasn't exactly out of their way, after all.

'Sorry,' Mark said. He finished his 'hello' manoeuvre, kissing me on the lips in a definite, proprietorial way. 'It's just . . . you don't like her. And she doesn't like you. I never thought of you as two-faced.'

'Memory loss,' I said, stung. 'I didn't know I didn't like her. I knew we weren't close—'

'You said she was a gossip. Always talking about other people's business.'

'Did I?' The hollow feeling was back. I was standing on shifting sand and there was nothing to hold on to.

Mark shrugged and, although I thought there was something false about the move, I couldn't work out why. I was becoming paranoid.

I was letting Parveen's reservations about him bother me and that wasn't fair. He was my boyfriend. My partner. I had to trust him; it was as simple as that. What else could I do? He was all I had.

GRACE

race had never had a best friend. She used to wish she had a
sister, as that would be a ready-made confidante. Someone who
had to be on your side because you shared the same blood. Better yet, she wished for a twin. Another girl, just like her. In Grace's
imagination they would make up a secret language that only they
could understand, share everything, be best friends for life. In the
deepest part of herself, she also believed that if she'd had a sister she
would've been safe.

'Oh, go on. Be a darling.' Evie hadn't stopped asking for three
days and, Grace had to admit, the attention was rather pleasant.
There was something intoxicating about being wanted, even as a
spare body on a double date with an airman, who wouldn't meet
Evie unless his pal was set up, too. She could ask anybody, Grace
told herself, and she's chosen me. Still, she couldn't say 'yes'. What
had started as an automatic reaction (she had vowed to be a good
girl and who knew what trouble Evie would get them both into?)
had turned into something more like a test of her nerve. The longer
it went on, the more tempted Grace became, and the more she
said no, the more likely it became that Evie would get fed up and

ask somebody else. Grace both welcomed and dreaded this pros-
pect in such perfectly equal quantities that she couldn't force herself
to make any kind of new decision. 'Please,' Evie said at breakfast.
Opening her eyes very wide and dipping her chin to gaze up at
Grace.

'I couldn't possibly,' Grace said.

'Couldn't possibly do what?' Barnes asked, her bovine features
wide with confusion, as usual.

'Pass the butter,' Grace said smoothly. 'My wrists are too sore
from scrubbing the lino last night.'

Evie grinned at her, eyes shining, and Grace felt that unfamiliar
feeling in her stomach. Happiness, she supposed.

Later, Evie swooped past Grace on the ward, cheekily lifting
the cover on a steaming bedpan and treating her to a stinking
blast. 'We'll have a marvellous time,' she said. 'You're only young
once.'

'I can't be late back,' Grace said, and Evie lifted her head, sens-
ing a change in the wind. Grace expected her to say 'Of course we
won't be late', or something similar, but she just smiled beatifically
and continued to the sluice. The set of her shoulders and the way
she walked looked triumphant.

'I didn't say yes,' Grace called after her. Sister chose that moment
to appear and bellowed: 'No shouting in the ward, Nurse. You aren't
in the Navy.'

As they were getting ready for bed that night, both so tired they
were knocking into one another and Grace was fumbling with the
buttons on her dress and considering going to sleep fully clothed,
Evie said, 'Oh, go on. I promise it'll be fun,' and Grace found herself looking at the shape of Evie's mouth and the light in her eyes
that even exhaustion couldn't fully extinguish. She intended to say
'no' again and probably would have, but Evie's right shoulder lifted
a fraction and the light that danced in her eyes seemed to flicker out

for a single second. 'All right, then,' Grace found herself saying. 'But you have to promise you won't ditch me.'

Evie smiled and she looked like a movie star once again. She silently crossed her heart and then touched two fingers to her lips and pressed them to Grace's own.

The next day, Grace was so nervous and distracted she dropped a thermometer and had to hide the glass pieces before Sister saw. Like the parting of the seas, miraculously both Grace and Evie were granted their off-duty and Evie even managed to wangle a late pass that would let them come in at quarter past the hour.

Ever generous, Evie loaned her silk stockings and a fur capelet and when Grace looked down at herself she felt like a new person. She had already transformed her best dress by adding a couple of stitches to the darts above the waist and unpicking the fussy lace collar. Evie, of course, looked daringly chic in a white sequined number with a deep V at the back. She said it had been given to her by a viscount, but she had been smiling when she spoke and it was impossible to tell if she was teasing. Evie applied eyeliner and lipstick and made up Grace, telling her sharply to keep still and not to moan about the sharp point of the liner poking her eyelids. Grace wished that this part of the evening would never end.

The boys were picking them up outside the home at seven. Evie's airman had a motorcar he called 'Bessie', and a jawline pitted with acne scars. He had swarthy skin like a gypsy's and eyes that were almost black. Evie had described him as 'beautiful', but he seemed far too male for that word. Grace didn't want to stand near him, but he slung an arm around her shoulders and said to his friend, 'I told you the nurses in this town were the best.' Grace stepped away but he just laughed and offered her a cigarette. His friend was called Thomas and once they were loaded into the back of the car together he turned to Grace and introduced himself formally, which Grace found rather nice.

'Don't mind Old Thomas, he's not as dull as he appears,' the airman yelled over his shoulder.

Evie was snuggled against his shoulder, leaning in as he handled the steering wheel, and Grace tried not to think about the chances of them all dying in a fiery accident.

'Don't mind Robert,' Thomas said, imitating the airman. 'He's not as brash as he appears. Well, actually he is, but he's not so bad underneath it all.' He smiled at Grace in a way that suggested she was in on a private joke. Grace was too nervous to smile back, but she managed to glance at him, taking in the impression of light brown hair and neat ears.

The door to the town hall opened, letting out a blast of warm air and music. Inside, the hall was decorated with paper streamers and the floor was filled with couples dancing. The boys went to fetch drinks from the punch table and Evie turned to Grace. 'What do you think? Do you like him?'

'Too soon to say.' Grace was hoping she sounded bored and worldly, rather than stiff and ungrateful.

Evie laughed. 'That's my Grace, so cautious. I always know right away.' She clicked her fingers.

'Really?' Grace said, mainly to keep her talking.

'Oh, yes. If the spark isn't there straight away, there's no point.'

'And you're feeling sparky about your airman, I take it?'

Evie lowered her eyelids and smiled in a sleepy, sexy way. 'Maybe.'

Then she stopped vamping and gripped Grace's arm. 'They're coming back! Quick, is my face all right?'

'Of course.' Grace was thrown by the change in Evie's manner. She was so outwardly confident, her surface so bright and sparkling, that her flashes of insecurity made Grace's heart hurt.

'Laugh,' Evie said. 'Men like girls who are fun.'

Grace didn't see how laughing at nothing would show that they were fun, but she forced a smile anyway. It was difficult to maintain as Evie's fingers were digging into her upper arm quite painfully. Grace felt it turn into a grimace.

'Refresh yourselves, ladies,' said Robert, passing out cups. The band changed tune and he held out one hand to Evie. 'Shall we?'

She took a long sip of her punch and then gave the cup to Grace. She put her hand into Robert's and they took to the floor.

Thomas held out a paper cup to Grace and she took it with her spare hand. There was a moment of awkward silence. Grace held out Evie's drink. 'You don't have one.'

He took the cup and put it down on the window ledge behind them. 'I don't drink,' he said. 'Don't remind Robert, please.' And he gave her another of those sweet, conspiratorial smiles. He really did have a nice face. Open and honest like a farm boy's.

He leaned against the wall and dug out a pack of cigarettes from his trouser pocket and offered one to Grace.

'Please,' she said, and joined him against the wall. The silence felt companionable now that they were smoking together, now that Grace had the comforting routine of inhaling and exhaling and tapping ash to occupy her. It was loud anyway, not good for chit-chat. She watched the couples whirling around the floor and pretended that she was a normal girl out for a night out with a handsome man and her glamorous friend and that all was well with the world.

He leaned in to speak into her ear. It tickled and was faintly moist. 'How do you like the hospital, then? Bet they work you hard.'

Grace shrugged and smiled. She didn't want to lean in and shout into his ear.

After a while, their cigarettes finished and stubbed out, he took her hand and led her on to the dance floor. 'May as well,' he yelled. 'Since we're here.'

Grace didn't let herself think about whether she wanted to dance, didn't let herself panic at the thought of his hands on her waist, her shoulder. She shut that Grace Kemp in a box and let a different one out to play. Grace, the girl who was fun. Grace the dancing girl. With her handsome airman and the music playing.

Later Grace was glad Evie had shown her the dances. She'd managed a foxtrot and a waltz without incident. She'd drunk some lemonade and smoked another of Thomas's cigarettes. The whirling figures in the dusty hall had become, if not familiar, then less shocking.

When the band took a break, she sat with Thomas at a table overflowing with paper cups and found that he was just as pleasant a conversationalist as he was a dancer.

'Do you like your work?' he asked. Earnestly, as if he truly cared about her feelings.

Grace had been going to nod and say something bland about helping others. Instead she found herself being honest: 'I don't have enough time to read,' she said. 'Not as much as I would like. And my shifts often stop me from getting to the library.'

'I miss my books,' he said, leaning forwards slightly. 'I carry a few with me, but it's not the same.'

❧

Full of good feeling and excitement, Grace almost lost her dinner when she caught sight of the time. Evie had promised! Grace explained to Thomas that she had to leave and that she couldn't go without Evie. She found her sitting with Robert next to one of the little round tables. There were several cups on the table and they were all empty.

'It's almost quarter to,' Grace said, feeling the panic rising as she spoke.

'Hello, darling,' Evie said, loudly. Her cheeks were flushed and her perfect finger waves were beginning to flatten out; stray hairs had stuck to her flushed face.

'We're going to be late,' Grace said. 'I can't be late. I can't.'

Evie leaned across her airman and spoke quietly. 'Will you just relax? This isn't—'

'You promised.' Grace leaned across to face her, suddenly not even caring how close her body came to Robert's. He was leaning back, an amused expression on his dark face.

'Hey, if you need to get back, I can take you,' Thomas said, moving out from behind her. He stuck his hands in his pockets and rocked on his heels.

Grace looked at Evie, willing her eyes to convey everything she couldn't say out loud. *Please don't leave me alone with a man. Even this man, with his farm boy's face. Please.*

Evie must've seen something because she rose to her feet. 'Darling.' She held a hand out to Robert. 'Would you be a dear and run us home?'

'But it's early.' Robert was not impressed by the turn his evening was taking. He'd been drinking, too. Grace hoped Thomas was going to drive this time.

The air was cold now, and their breath fogged in it. Robert lit a cigarette and sucked it moodily as they walked to the car.

'Poor show, Evie,' he said.

'Why don't you love birds sit in the back?' Thomas said. 'I'll drive and you can say a proper goodnight to each other.'

Robert brightened instantly and opened the door for Evie.

'Don't worry,' Thomas said, as he slid into the driver's seat. 'We will be having a deep intellectual discussion and we shan't hear a thing.' He winked at Grace and, in her gratitude, she put a hand on his arm and squeezed.

However, the damage was already done. Thomas was a steady driver and they'd left the dance hall too late. There was no way they were going to make their specially extended curfew of quarter past ten. Grace checked her watch and saw that it was already almost twenty past and they were only at the bottom of the hill that led to the hospital.

Once the Morris Oxford had hauled up the slope, Grace asked Thomas to stop at the end of the road. She didn't want the night porter to see them getting out of a man's car.

'One second,' Evie said, still entangled with Robert.

'Now,' Grace said. Anxiety stripped her nerves and the word came out harshly.

'You'd better go or your friend will never let you see me again,' Robert said. He was smiling at Grace but there was no warmth in it.

'You girls run along now.' A challenge. There was something lupine and unpleasant about Robert. Grace didn't understand how Evie could be besotted with so odious a specimen. Of course, she hadn't always been the best judge of character herself.

Evie kissed him one last time and then swung her legs out of the car and pushed herself upright with one elegant movement. She spoiled it slightly by stumbling. Grace caught her and Evie leaned against her, surprisingly heavily.

Grace began walking along the pavement, half supporting her. 'You're going to have to sober up, sharpish.'

'You're mean tonight,' Evie said. She was pouting, trying to defuse things, but Grace felt fury wash over her.

'You promised we wouldn't be late and we are. If we get into more trouble because you've been drinking, I will never forgive you. Never.'

Evie was quiet for a few steps. Then, as they came in sight of the nurses' home and the night porter's cabin, a miracle occurred. Evie straightened up. Her arm was now linked with Grace's in a girlish manner, not in a leaning-on-her way.

The moon had slid out from behind the clouds and was shining mercilessly down as they walked up the driveway.

'We should go through the window,' Evie said, quietly.

'Too risky.' Grace had thought about it but, having obtained a late pass, the chance that the porter would remember them and be looking out for them was too great. If they didn't come back at all, the alarm might be raised. Grace had pictured sirens and searchlights, as if the home were a prison, the police running down cobbled streets waving batons, her imagination supplying the worst possible scenario with agonising ease.

The porter was a man called Miller. The same man who'd given them the late pass which, at least, confirmed that she'd been wise not to try climbing through the window. Miller was all right, too. Not as miserable as his colleague.

'What time do you call this?' Miller stepped out of his cabin, giving Grace a shock. He looked furious. 'I trusted you, Nurse, and look what you've done with it. Thrown it back in me face.'

'I'm sorry,' Grace said. She nudged Evie until she said 'sorry', too.

'It was the bus. It was late.'

'My backside it was,' Miller said. 'How come three girls just managed to hit the curfew, then? They got the bus all right.'

'It was a bit late, but Evie's hurt her ankle. We couldn't walk very quickly and she had to have a little rest.' The words were tumbling out now. She felt herself shift back to the old Grace. The one who could weave a story. The Grace who had spun tales to charm her father and his friends, making them laugh and call her a 'funny thing', back before things had gone wrong. She thought she'd buried that girl, but there she was. Waiting just under the surface. Grace could feel Evie shifting next to her; hoped she was shifting her stance to favour one leg, to look subservient and in pain. People in power liked that.

'We're sorry,' Evie said, her voice small. 'My ankle really is very sore.'

'Well . . .' Miller said. His voice was still gruff but Grace knew they were going to get away with it. She felt elated and she felt sick.

'Go on inside, girls. I'll let it go this time, but don't let me catch you out past curfew again.'

In their room, Evie was all admiration. 'Coo! I had no idea you had it in you, Gracie girl.'

'Lying?' Grace said. 'I'm not proud of it.' She was shaken. She knew that she was going to have to work harder to bury the old Grace, otherwise she'd rise up and ruin everything.

'Oh, don't be such a stick in the mud,' Evie said. 'You were wonderful. You could go on the stage.'

Grace was in no mood to be teased. 'I did what I had to do. You broke your word.'

'If I'd known you'd be such a bore about it, I wouldn't have bothered,' Evie said, finally. She collapsed on to her bed and, shortly afterwards, began to snore lightly.

MINA

Iwas asleep when I heard Pat's voice. It was a warbling sound, running up and down scales like an operatic thrush, the way it did when she was angry, and it pulled me out of my dreams with a violent tug. Instantly awake, I blinked furiously to clear the stickiness from my eyes and looked over to the doorway. It was light and bright in the ward with the sun streaming through the windows and I blinked again, trying to prepare myself. Pat's voice always went up an octave in pitch and at least a class in accent when she was angry. You could gauge the severity of the situation by her diction and, right now, she sounded like the Queen.

And there she was, framed momentarily in the entrance, her solid, rectangular body emphasised by her bulky coat and habit of clasping her handbag in front of her. The sight of Pat – here in this place – was surreal. And, to make matters worse, there was a siskin on her shoulder.

I struggled to sit up, feeling at a distinct disadvantage, but thanking God Mark had brought in a nightie so that I wasn't wearing a hospital gown. Yes, it was a vile peach item with a rosebud at the neck, more suited to my grandmother, but it was preferable to the sickly institutional green hospital issue. I had never realised how many choices I'd had until they were taken away.

I was barely vertical and my head was swimming dangerously when Pat reached the bed. She bent down and treated me to one of her brief, hard hugs.

Then she sat in the chair and dropped her handbag on the bed. 'I'm not putting it on that floor,' she said. 'It's probably filthy.'

I shushed her, feeling awkward in case one of the staff heard.

'Well,' Pat said, then she lapsed into silence, glaring around at the ward and not meeting my eye.

I waited, not saying anything either.

Pat sat with her back ramrod straight. She shook her head, lips compressed into a line as if she was keeping the words behind them locked up. Then, when I thought she might sit through the entire visit like that, she said a typical Pat thing. 'What did you do?'

I thought about turning my face to the wall. I thought about lying back down and closing my eyes until she left. But she was my family. The closest thing I had to a mother and, despite everything, she had travelled hours to check on me. Travelled to England, of all places.

However much I hadn't wanted her to come here; however much I kept my family in Wales firmly in place, and however straight and thin the line of Pat's mouth, I knew something in the secret place of my heart. I was glad to see her.

'I was in a car accident,' I said. My voice sounded croaky so I cleared it before adding, 'I don't remember anything.'

'So, how do you know?' Pat said.

I wasn't sure if she meant: how did I know I'd been in an accident, or how was I sure it had been an accident, that it wasn't my fault somehow? It wasn't something I particularly liked to think about so I just said: 'They told me.'

Pat's hair was up in a bun as always but her usually frizzy grey fringe was sleek and well tended. I imagined her getting up early and taking extra care with it, and felt prickles along my scalp. 'How did you know?' I said. 'That I was here.'

Pat's eyes narrowed to slits. 'Your boyfriend rang. Nice of you to tell us about him, by the way. Lovely for your family to find out like that.'

I closed my eyes. 'What did he tell you?'

'That you were in the hospital. Asleep, he said, but I assumed he was tiptoeing around. I thought you'd be in a coma.'

'Sorry to disappoint you.' I kept my eyes closed, couldn't cope with the sight of Pat in this place. She didn't belong here. She didn't belong anywhere except Gower.

I could feel something patting my hip through the blankets. I opened my eyes and saw Pat move her hand hurriedly, as if it had been acting against her will. Then she straightened the edge of my blanket and checked that the cord for my buzzer was lying straight.

When she leaned down underneath the bed, presumably to check the cleanliness of the floor, I said: 'It's okay. I'm fine. I promise.'

Pat popped back up and fixed me with a sour look. 'Apart from the fact that you're going to hell.'

'Apart from that,' I agreed, injecting as much cheer into my voice as I could manage. There was one thing that made me feel like myself again and that was irritating Pat. It was a reflex. Impossible to resist. 'Where are you staying?'

'I don't know yet,' she said. 'I just arrived.'

She looked uncharacteristically worried. Everything about her was less frightening than usual. Maybe it was because it felt like I hadn't seen her in years, or maybe it was because everything else was so strange and difficult, but taken out of her house she seemed smaller. 'You can stay at my flat, if you like,' I said, surprising myself. 'My keys must be around here somewhere. My bag was in the locker, I think.'

'I'm not sleeping in the same place as a strange man.'

Mark. I kept forgetting about him. 'He'll be at his house.' As soon as the words were out I realised I was wrong. We lived together. Mark lived in my flat. With me. And my purple sofa. I didn't remember him living with me, but I had to assume that the memory of it would come back eventually. Sooner or later I would remember his clothes in my wardrobe and his shaving stuff in my bathroom and perhaps even us in old clothes, painting the walls, like a scene from a romantic comedy.

'He has a house, too?' Pat sniffed. 'Is he made of money? Or is it just for when you two argue? When he needs a break from you?'

Despite myself, I was annoyed. It derailed me from thinking about Mark's house. 'Why do you assume that?' I said. 'Maybe I want him to go somewhere because I need my space.' Again, I had the strangest feeling. I knew what I was saying was true. I did need my space. I always had done. I'd sworn I'd never live with a man. Even if I loved him desperately, I was going to make us both keep our own homes. I was independent to a fault. But, apparently, I'd let Mark move in. The feeling of wrongness was back again. It sat on my chest and I felt as if it was a real live thing, staring at me, waiting for me to make a connection.

'So, does he have a house or not?'

'I don't know,' I said, frustrated. 'My memory—'

At that moment, Stephen made an appearance. He introduced himself and shook hands with Pat, speaking to her warmly. 'They told me Mina had family arrive and I wanted to be on hand in case you had any questions.'

'That's very good service,' Pat said. 'Is she being treated privately?'

'Excuse me,' I said, waving my hands. 'I'm right here.'

'But *you* don't even know where your man lives,' Pat said witheringly, turning immediately back to the doctor.

Stephen looked momentarily confused. Then he said: 'Good old NHS, I'm afraid. Although your daughter is a valued employee, so we're taking extra special care of her.'

If this was meant to be a joke, it fell on deaf ears. Pat had barrelled on, was asking searching questions about the accident, my injuries, my prognosis.

Once that fun portion was winding down and Stephen was making a move to leave, Pat homed in on the one fact I'd hoped had passed her by. 'Valued employee? You mean she works here? At the hospital?'

'Of course,' he said. I wanted to signal to him to shut up, but it was too late. 'Mina does wonderful work in therapeutic radiology.' He glanced at me. 'Research, too, right?'

'Yes,' I said.

'Wonderful,' Pat said. 'Isn't that wonderful?' She turned back to me. 'You can show me around once you're on your feet again.'

'Excuse me,' Stephen said, beating a retreat.

The siskin was still on Pat's shoulder. It had its head tilted, as if listening to her. Then it turned its head and seemed to chirp into her ear, although I couldn't hear any sound. I wondered if the bird was explaining radiology to her. I waited until Stephen had disappeared from view, then said: 'Please stay at my flat.' It was a peace offering. I knew Pat wouldn't like a bed and breakfast or a Premier Inn. And the plus side of not being able to remember my flat properly was that I didn't feel quite as panicked as I might have expected to at the thought of her being there unsupervised, though fear still clutched my heart. What if I had some horrible habits that I'd forgotten about? Pornography strewn around the living room? Or, worse yet, a dirty kitchen with an overflowing bin and rancid fridge? I didn't think being in hospital would completely absolve me in Pat's eyes. If she were ever incapacitated, you could be damn sure you'd find the house in perfect order, with laundry dry and ironed and the furniture freshly polished with that disgusting fake lavender spray she favoured.

Pat was looking at me oddly and I realised I was probably making faces. With too much time spent alone, I was losing what few social skills I'd previously possessed. Or might have possessed. Pat stopped staring long enough to locate my bag and then my keys. 'Address? Or is that a secret? Something else we'll have to find out from a complete stranger?'

'You have my address,' I protested. 'You must do.'

Pat shook her head slowly. 'No. We do not.'

I couldn't stop the word 'Why?' from coming out of my mouth. Then I wanted to punch myself in the head.

Pat smiled with no humour whatsoever. 'When you're feeling yourself again, no doubt you'll explain. It's probably something I've done wrong.'

'I'm sorry,' I said.

Her eyes widened. 'Well,' she said. 'You're in a worse state than I realised.'

I swallowed, not sure whether I was about to dump Geraint into trouble, break some confidence that he'd asked me to keep, but I couldn't stop the words that were demanding to be spoken: 'I had a phone message from Geraint.'

Pat's lips went very thin. 'That's impossible,' she said, her voice a shard of glass.

'I didn't know whether—' I began, but Pat was up and out of her chair. In that moment I remembered that you never could get Pat to sit still. Especially when she was upset.

'I'm going to speak to your doctor,' she threw over one shoulder. 'You get some rest.'

I watched her leave with a curious mixture of relief and terror. I was alone again. Fear clutched at my chest and I wanted to call her back. I wondered if it would be different if my mother were alive. I wondered if she would be by my side, stroking my forehead, and whether I'd feel pure comfort, rather than this strange clawing mix of emotions. I knew my mother through stories, photographs and her brightly coloured dreamcatchers. I'd always thought that she would understand me, that she'd be warm and open, and that I would have grown up to be an entirely different person had she been around.

ᔆᘓ

No matter how pleased I'd been to see Pat, I was still furious with Mark. I tried to calm myself down by flicking through the hospital book, looking at black-and-white images from the past as if they could give me some perspective. I was also hoping to see my ghostly nurse. There was a shot from some kind of event, with a field and runners. I looked for my nurse, but the quality of the reproduction wasn't good enough for me to see the faces properly. For a while I convinced myself that I recognised her amongst the cheering crowd, but I knew that I was kidding myself. The caption under the picture read: 'Nurses take part in sports day fun'. Instead of feeling calmed, I felt a new surge of energy. Angry energy. Something about those carefree figures, running full pelt, the material of their uniforms flapping, made me think of a flock of birds rising into the sky. My resentment towards Mark solidified and I imagined, just for a moment, that I could leave him. Have a fresh start.

When he arrived after work, I didn't waste any time. 'What the fucking hell?'

'What?' He put down his newspaper and coat on the end of my bed.

'You called Pat. She was here.' I waved my hands to indicate the ward. 'Here.'

'Of course I called your family. Why is that so terrible?'

'I don't—' I broke off, unable to continue. He'd made me speechless. I didn't think that was possible. Ger had always said that I talked in my sleep, that not even being unconscious could shut me up.

'Oh,' Mark said, drawing out the word as if comprehension was dawning upon him. 'You don't remember?'

'Remember what?' I was so bloody sick of playing that particular game. The 'what the fuck is going on' game. The 'big holes in my mind' game.

'Christmas? You went down to visit and when you came back you said you'd promised to keep in touch more.' A smug, sanctimonious expression took over his face. 'I promised to help you honour that. We were going to visit together next time.'

'I said we were going to Wales? Together?' Everything about that statement was wrong, I knew it. I knew it in a deep, true part of me. At that moment, Mark was a stranger. His face morphed into a robot face. An imposter. I could feel my heart racing, my breathing coming in shallow gasps.

He patted my hand. 'I know this might be a bit of a shock, but it's a good thing. You've been unhappy about your family for as long as I've known you.'

Unhappy. That wasn't right. The feelings I had about my family were too complex to slap a neat little label like 'unhappy' on the front. It was like labelling a war 'unfortunate'.

'Take some deep breaths, you're going to make yourself sick.'

That snapped me out of it. I really didn't want to throw up. Just the idea of it made my head pound. I forced slower breaths.

'It's time to move on with your life,' he was saying. 'Build bridges so that you can move forward. So that *we* can move forward.'

The man spoke like a management seminar. At that moment I had absolutely no idea why I was with him. The realisation that he was all I had knifed me in the gut. I didn't care that I didn't feel anything, I just didn't want to be left on my own. I forced my voice to behave, to speak calmly. 'I don't want Pat to see me here. I don't want her to worry.'

The smug look was back. 'That's what mothers do. It's part of the job description.'

And again, the urge to throw something at his head was back.

'Besides,' he said, 'it's done now. She survived. You survived. Now you can move on.'

'You don't understand,' I began, but then I realised I didn't want to finish that sentence.

Mark seemed to sense the fight draining out of me and he patted me on the leg. 'This will be for the best, you'll see. Something good to come out of your accident. You've got to learn to look for the bright side.'

◦◦◦

When Pat came back the next morning, she looked tired.

'I've spoken to Mark and he's willing to look after you,' she said. 'I'm going to move in for a week or so, to keep an eye on you while he's at work, and after that we'll reassess the situation. Hopefully, by then you'll be okay on your own during the day and I can go home.'

'That's—'

Pat held up one hand. 'No arguments. I'm not having people say that I don't look after my children.'

I wanted to say 'I'm not your child' but I knew it wouldn't do any good. Pat was an unstoppable force.

'He says the house purchase is moving quickly so hopefully you'll be recuperating there. If not, we'll have to make do in your flat. Mark says his place is mostly boxed up.'

'When did you speak to him?' My head was spinning and, for once, it was nothing to do with my injuries or the cocktail of medication.

'Last night, after I left here.' Pat pursed her lips. 'Can't say I'm pleased that you've been living in sin, but he's a doctor at least.'

'PhD, not medical. And why is that better anyway?' I said, knowing the answer, but unable to stop myself from needling Pat.

'I asked him to do the right thing by you, but mind you don't let on I told you that. Act surprised when he asks you or his pride will get hurt. You know how fragile men are.'

I felt cold horror. Embarrassment mixed with terror. 'You didn't?' Oh Christ, oh Christ, oh Christ.

Pat shook her head. 'Don't take on. You can't very well buy a house together without getting married. It's not sensible.'

This surprised me. Pat had always put the 'burning in hell' bit above any other concern.

'And it'll save you from eternal damnation,' she added, looking slightly flustered.

'I don't want to get married,' I said. 'It's never going to happen. And especially not with Mark.' The thought popped out of nowhere but I couldn't pretend I didn't mean it.

Pat smiled. 'Don't think you can push me away. I know you're trying to rile me but I'm not taking the bait. I'm going to stay with you when you get out of here and look after you while your future husband is at work. I'm not leaving you until you're healthy and settled.' She reached out and patted my hand. 'You don't need to worry about a thing.'

Pat was being far too calm and nice. I must've looked worse than I realised.

'Now that I know what's needed, I'm going to go home and pack properly. And I'll get some decent sleep before I'm to look after you. I never sleep well in England.'

'I don't think you can blame the entire country,' I said. 'You just don't like being away from home.'

Pat gave me a pitying look that spoke volumes and began unpacking things from a cloth shopping bag. 'Fizzy Vitamin C so you don't get the flu, goodness only knows what bugs they've got flying around in here. There's a couple of books in case you've run out – I know what you're like – you'll read until you go cross-eyed . . . and there's this.' She pulled out the soft toy rabbit with the long twisted, chewed ears I'd had as a child.

Rabbity was dead. Pat had killed him. It was one of the stories I told myself, one of the pieces of evidence for her uncaring, overly controlling, basically soulless nature. But here was Rabbity. Limp from lack of stuffing, riddled with holes and no longer the yellow I remembered but a dirty off-white from repeated cycles in the washing machine. I held him to my face and inhaled the scent of washing powder. Underneath that there was the faintest forgotten odour of childhood. I held Rabbity underneath my nose and twirled his long ears around my fingers in a motion I hadn't known about, hadn't thought about in years. His ears were crumpled, one severely twisted and both frayed at the tips, but the feel of the material was soothing and familiar. I blinked back tears. Rabbity was so very welcome. I felt that a talisman against evil had been given to me in a time of need.

'We had a new boiler put in and they took out the hot water tank in the airing cupboard. I know you thought I'd thrown him out but he really was lost, just like I told you. He'd slipped down the back, must have come off the tank or one of the shelves when he was drying one time. You know I was always drying your bedding.'

I knew. I'd wet the bed long past the age these things were supposed to stop. Despite my gratitude for Rabbity I felt a stab of resentment towards Pat for bringing it up. That was the problem with family; they never let you forget a single thing.

Pat wore a strange expression. I moved Rabbity away from my face. 'Thank you for coming,' I said. 'Give Uncle Dylan my love. Tell him I'm fine.'

Pat nodded. 'Of course.'

I wanted to ask about Ger, see if he'd rung Pat, too, but my heart was too full. If I felt a single other thing, part of me would break.

Pat's lips were compressed, like there was something trying to get out. She nodded again and gave me a quick dry kiss on the cheek.

After she'd gone, I held Rabbity back up to his rightful place, just underneath my nose and breathed deeply. As soon as I did, I was back in my childhood bedroom, sitting up in bed with the flu or measles or something. Bored and hot and out of sorts. Pat was on the edge of my bed, her back resting against the wall, and we were playing cards. Happy Families. I could picture the illustrations on the cards.

People say that twins aren't complete without one another and, speaking as a twin, it's deeply annoying. And insulting. When it comes to my mother and Pat, though, it's nothing but the truth. My mother was always everything Pat isn't: creative and free-spirited and bohemian. My whole life, I've heard stories about her wild nature and her creativity and, because she died when I was just a baby, I've never had to confront the reality. I've kept the fairy tale of my mother safely under glass but, as much as I'd like to deny it, without Pat I would've had a far less stable upbringing.

My mother is the elemental half of Pat. It's as if all the practical, solid stuff went into making Pat, and all the ephemeral soul stuff into making my mother.

That makes it sound as if Pat doesn't have a soul. I didn't think that. I might have done, once, but as I held Rabbity close to my face and breathed in, I knew that I didn't believe it any more.

GRACE

Grace skidded into the sluice with her arms so full she could hardly see where she was going, the stack of bedpans threatening to topple over at any moment.

'You shouldn't carry so many,' Barnes said, her back to the room as she bent over the sink, elbow-deep in soapy water.

'If I don't, I shan't get finished before rounds,' Grace said, breathless. 'I mightn't get finished anyway.' She broke off, suddenly aware that if she carried on speaking she'd dissolve into sobs. She was so tired. Her feet hurt, her legs ached, her back screamed.

'Sister Atkinson says, "More haste, less speed",' Barnes said, turning her bovine face briefly to Grace.

At once, she had the wild urge to say something shocking, something Evie-like. 'Sister Atkinson can jump off the roof for all I care.'

Barnes snorted and turned back to her task, washing up glass measuring flasks like a woman possessed.

Grace went to the sink on the opposite wall and began rinsing down the pans. The impossible list of jobs marched through her mind. She'd changed the sheets and remade all of the beds but she still had to finish the pans, tidy the linen, polish the castors on the beds and get the morning drinks done, and all before eleven.

'Oh!' Barnes let out a little cry. 'Damn and blast.'

Grace left her pans and turned to her. Barnes never swore. She was one of those wholesome girls, ruddy and outdoorsy. Grace sometimes pictured her in a farmhouse kitchen with a lamb tucked into her apron pocket and a mixing bowl in her hands. 'Are you hurt?'

Barnes lifted her hands out of the water and revealed a broken beaker. 'The glass will be everywhere now. What will I do?'

Grace was shocked to see that Barnes had gone pale. Her mouth quivered as if she might cry.

'It's all right,' Grace said, in as bright a tone as she could manage. 'We can sort this out in a jiffy.' Grace carefully put her hand into the sink and found the plug. She rescued as many beakers as she could while the water whirled away. After a moment, Barnes helped and they soon had a draining board full of beakers and a sink with some shards of glass and a few bubbles in it.

'Shall I get some newspaper?' Grace said.

'No time.' Barnes began gingerly picking the glass out. 'I'm behind already. I'll never get done and now this. Sister is going to kill me.'

To Grace's complete astonishment, Barnes stopped picking up pieces of glass and slid her back down the cabinet to sit on the floor. 'I can't do it. I'm a terrible mess and Matron will send me home.' She wasn't crying loudly but the tears were simply pouring and, soon, her nose was even redder than her cheeks and her eyes were swollen.

Grace crouched down and patted her shoulder. 'Come on, now. It's not that bad. We're all really busy; we're all getting things wrong . . .' What had started as something meant to be comforting had given Grace a lump in her own throat. She felt a prickling in her eyes and blinked rapidly. Now was not the time to dissolve. Barnes needed her. Besides, if Grace didn't get her mopped up and off the floor, Sister would catch them sitting down on shift and they'd both be on the rug.

'It's all right for you,' Barnes said between sniffs. 'You're a natural.'

Grace opened her mouth in astonishment. 'I most certainly am not,' she said, finally. 'I haven't a clue most of the time.'

Barnes produced an enormous handkerchief and mopped her face. The tears seemed to have stopped as suddenly as they'd started and Barnes just looked wrung out now, as if the storm of weeping had drained her. 'I don't believe you,' she said, so quietly that Grace almost didn't hear her.

'Believe what you like,' Grace said, 'but I've never been so exhausted in all my life. Sometimes I think I'm going to drop down dead from it all. And I'm frightened all the time.'

'What of?' Barnes was looking decidedly perkier. The news that Grace felt awful was obviously cheering.

Grace looked at her own hands. 'That I'll get something serious wrong and I'll hurt a patient.'

'Little chance of that, we don't get to do anything medical.' Barnes voiced the regular grumble of the juniors.

'Yes, well, that doesn't stop me from fretting about it,' Grace said. 'And I worry that I'll get a hundred little things wrong and Matron will get fed up of shouting at me and just send me home.'

'That's what I worry about!' Barnes spoke as though this was miraculous and entirely new information, as if she herself hadn't voiced the very same fear just a few minutes ago. Grace felt a surge of protectiveness towards her. Barnes barrelled around the place like a bull in a china shop and looked so sturdy and strong that everyone assumed she had a thick hide to match. Maybe that wasn't true after all.

'Come on.' Grace stood and took hold of Barnes's hands, hauling her upright. 'We'll be all right. We'll look out for each other.'

'What about this?' Barnes looked mournfully into the sink.

Grace took the lid off the bin and rummaged until she found some old socks which Sister had declared too disgusting and holey even for mending. She held them out and Barnes wrapped the shards. They buried them at the bottom of the bin and got back to work.

'I won't tell a soul,' Barnes said, glancing at the top of the bin. 'Even if Matron calls me in.'

Grace wondered if she'd forgotten that she'd been the one to break the glass in the first place. She crossed her heart, though, and nodded in a conspiratorial fashion.

'Nurse Kemp.' Sister Atkinson's voice could have peeled paint and for a terrifying moment Grace thought that Barnes and she had been heard talking. She felt every muscle in her body tense and turned to face the ward sister.

'Billy has gone downstairs,' she said, her tone softening slightly. 'I thought you might like to visit.'

Grace tried to process the words. Was Sister trying to tell her that Billy had died? He'd been doing so well, the paralysis in his legs had begun to wear off and word on the ward was that the worst of the polio had passed.

'He's been asking for you,' Sister said, peering over the top of her spectacles. 'You may go at quarter to four if you've completed all of your tasks.'

Once she had walked away, Barnes shook her head. 'Time off to visit a sick kid? I don't believe it. Sister's lost her mind.'

Grace wanted to explain that Billy was special – all of the nurses on the ward adored his good manners and kind nature – but she couldn't speak. Downstairs was where the hospital's new iron lung was kept; it meant his paralysis had grown worse. That his improvement had been a respite, not a recovery.

Barnes patted her arm. 'Cheer up. I'll give you a hand with the tea trolley.'

ᖇᘏ

The iron lung had its own room and it was very warm in comparison with the frigid corridor. There was a fire burning in the grate and the contrast between the homely sight of those orange flames and the cold grey metal tube was stark and strange.

Billy's head looked painfully small protruding from the massive machine and, although Grace had spent the last hour of her shift preparing herself for the sight, it still stabbed her between the ribs. 'Hello, young man,' she said, amazed at her jolly, nurse-like tone. 'Isn't this marvellous?' It was astonishing, Grace thought, how effectively you could lie when you cared enough about the person you were lying to.

'I couldn't get me breath,' Billy said, the words coming out in a rush.

The sight of his sweet face was too much for her to bear. Grace focused on a spot in the middle of his forehead to avoid bursting into tears.

'Sister Atkinson says I'm the luckiest boy in the hospital.' Billy's mouth turned up at the corners in an approximation of a smile. His voice was so quiet it was almost drowned out by the steady wheeze of the respirator.

'She's quite right,' Grace said. She knew that the machine was saving his life, manually forcing his lungs to work when the polio had robbed them of their function. Grace knew that, without the contraption, he would die. Billy knew it, too. But, Grace wondered, did he know that they called the lung a steel coffin because so many of the children who went into it did not come out? Not Billy, though. Billy was going to be one of the lucky ones. She simply would not allow any other possibility. Grace busied herself checking the dressing around the neck seal, making sure the nurse in attendance had used lanolin to stop his skin from chafing. 'I've been to the kitchens and you're having jam sponge today. Cook heard what a brave boy you're being and wanted to make you something nice.'

Billy smiled weakly. 'I wish I had my train. It got lost.'

Grace reached into her pocket and produced the toy with a flourish. She'd found it underneath the bed, next to the wall. 'I was keeping it safe for you while all the fuss was going on.'

Billy's eyes, red from crying, shone with their old light. 'Thank you, Nurse.'

'Call me Gracie,' she said as the door opened, letting in a blast of cold air.

๑๛๑

Dr Palmer took a sweeping look around the room, as if checking for other staff, and then said, 'Kemp. You look like the sturdy type. You'll do.'

'I'm sorry?'

'That's quite all right,' he said, in an unpleasant tone that suggested otherwise. 'We're short-handed in surgery and I've been looking everywhere for a spare body.'

Grace opened her mouth to say that she was off-duty but he clicked his fingers. 'Come along, Nurse, I haven't got all day.' Grace didn't dare disobey.

In theatre, she stood at his side for hours, light-headed with exhaustion. She passed instruments with hands that felt numb, and he didn't look at her once.

Barnes, who liked to read romances and had a dreamy disposition, said that Dr Palmer was 'sweet on' Grace but she knew differently. There was malice in his face. A current of danger in his voice. He was toying with her. Enjoying his power. Something in her called to him; maybe he could see the broken parts and, like a boy with a magnifying glass held over an insect, he wanted to see how long he could torture her before she burned away.

'Not that way,' he snapped as she handed him a scalpel. 'Do you want me to cut myself, Nurse?' Then, to the other surgeon, he said: 'I do wonder at the calibre of the girls they take in these days.'

Grace could feel her cheeks flaming and was glad of her face mask. She still felt dizzy, though, and swayed a little.

'If you're going to faint, you'd better get out,' Palmer said, without even glancing in her direction. Grace fled and went straight to her room to lie down.

'Where have you been? Weren't you off ages ago?' Evie said, unrolling a stocking and inspecting it.

Grace was too tired to answer. She pushed her face deep into her pillow and tried to block out the mocking sound of Palmer's voice.

⌒↩

The next week, Grace was walking to the dining hall when Barnes shot out from her room. 'I've been looking for you,' she said, in that slightly aggrieved tone he often used. Since the crying jag in the sluice, Barnes had been particularly friendly towards Grace, which was both gratifying and a little stifling.

Grace plastered on a smile. 'You found me.'

'Did you want to play table tennis later?'

'I can't, sorry,' Grace said, almost automatically. She and Evie had the same off-duty and had plans to visit the Blackbird for tea and scones.

'Why not?' Barnes said.

Grace hesitated. She ought to invite Barnes to join them, but she knew that Evie would be unimpressed with a third wheel. Plus, unkind as she felt admitting this to herself, Grace was in need of a break from everything hospital-related, including Barnes. 'I have other plans. Perhaps another time?'

'With Evie?' Barnes said. 'You two are thick as thieves.' And she walked away, back held very straight.

MINA

I had moved on from staring at the photographs in the book and was now reading the text. I uncapped my pen and opened a notebook, enjoying the familiar and comforting feeling that I was studying.

I heard the sound of magazine pages turning and glanced across the room. Queenie was peering at me over her copy of *Hello!* 'What've you got there? Book?'

'History of the hospital.'

Queenie wrinkled her nose. 'Don't you want to escape this place, not read about it?'

I gave a small shrug. Queenie couldn't bother me today; nothing was going to bother me today. Thankfully, the book was well written and I became so engrossed in it that I lost track of time. I didn't know if my brain was starved of facts, or whether the machinations of the hospital council during the 1960s really was a riveting read, but either way it kept me going all afternoon. I ate my chicken chasseur with one hand, holding the book open with the other. By the time Stephen appeared, my eyes felt gritty from reading. I put the book to one side and took in the sight of an off-duty Dr Adams.

It was peculiar. Even though I'd never seen him in a white coat and he hadn't taken off his staff security badge, there was something different about him. I checked to see if his tie was loosened, but it looked the same as always. Perhaps it was just the knowledge that he wasn't about to take my blood pressure or examine my joints, the knowledge that he was by my bedside out of choice, not duty.

'I love this.' I tapped the front cover of my new favourite thing. 'Thank you.'

'That's all right.'

Stephen looked a little bit embarrassed and I wondered if I'd calibrated my tone of gratitude too high. Or maybe he blushed easily, which would be incredibly endearing.

'How was work?'

'Not too bad. Lots of sick people.'

'Occupational hazard.'

He nodded, sitting in the high-backed chair next to my bed. 'Sometimes I forget what well people look like and I'm out somewhere and I start thinking about what's wrong with everyone.'

'Do you find yourself trying to diagnose strangers?'

He laughed. 'Sometimes. If I've been really busy I find it hard to switch off.'

'I used to see people's insides,' I said. 'I mean, not really, but I'd find myself picturing their X-rays, their MRIs, imagining them—' I stopped talking. 'I'd forgotten I did that.'

'I told you stuff would come back.'

'You didn't tell me I'd remember being such a weirdo, though.'

He held his hands up. 'You can't hold me responsible for that.'

There was a pause and I suddenly felt awkward, like I'd been looking at him for a second too long. He cleared his throat. 'So, is there anything else you're desperate for?'

The words hung there for a moment and I wondered if he was going to blush again, but he looked away instead.

'No,' I said. 'Just to go home. Get back to normal.'

'Your flat's nice.'

The reminder that he had seen my flat when he went to get my laptop made me anxious. It felt alarmingly intimate and I grew defensive. 'I suppose you're in a penthouse apartment overlooking the sea.'

He looked surprised for a moment but said, 'Oh, because of the massive NHS salary.'

'Consultant. Must be pretty good.' I didn't know why I was suddenly being arsey, but I couldn't seem to stop myself.

Stephen didn't appear put off by it, though. 'Not a consultant. Senior doctor. Too young for consultancy.'

'Is there a law?'

'You'd think so, the way the board talks.' He shrugged. 'I'm doing okay, though, if that's what you want to know.'

It was my turn to blush.

'So, that was your mum. Yesterday.'

'No, my aunt Pat.'

'Oh.' I could see he was momentarily stumped. 'Right. She really looks like you.'

I stiffened, about to deny it, before I realised how ridiculous that was. 'She's my mum's identical twin.' I waited for him to ask why my mother hadn't been with Pat, why neither of my parents had visited me.

'Was it okay?' he said, instead. 'The visit? She must've been really worried about you.'

'We're not all that close.'

Stephen looked confused. 'Why was she here, then?'

'She brought me up,' I said. 'My mum died when I was born.' I always hated saying that. Died in childbirth sounded Dickensian. The more honest 'I killed her coming out of her body' was a bit dramatic for everyday use. Plus, it encouraged people to reassure, to sympathise and make those sad faces with their heads on one side. I didn't deserve any of that. I knew it wasn't my fault. Not strictly speaking. If anything, I was a joint culprit with Geraint.

'We probably would have lived with Pat anyway. My mum had a few difficulties,' I found myself saying. 'She didn't get enough, I don't know, nourishment or blood while she was in the womb. It's called twin-to-twin syndrome.' I didn't know why I was telling him. Perhaps it was his white coat, it made me babble.

'Ah,' he said. 'I'm sorry.'

I waved a hand. 'It's fine. She was fine, apparently. Lucky. It can be really serious. Lots of twins don't survive. She was just born underweight and had a few issues.' The last words came out in a rush. 'Some cognitive impairment.' They're the same words they've been using about me since the coma and it hit me that I finally had something in common with my mother. It wasn't the stuff of greetings cards, but it was something.

'That must have been tough, growing up without a mum.'

I snapped back to the conversation. 'Not really. I had Pat. She's a force of nature.'

'Still—'

'I had Geraint, too. He's my twin.' I didn't know why I hadn't said 'brother' like I usually would. Why I'd mentioned him at all when my entire brain was screaming at me to change the subject. It was like my mouth was no longer taking orders.

'Are you two close?' Stephen hesitated and added, 'Is that a stupid question?'

I nodded, my mouth suddenly dry. 'I can't remember when I last saw him. I don't know if we had a fight or something.' I broke off before the tears came. I didn't want to be a sobbing mess in front of him.

'It will come back. It'll be okay.'

'But I remember my work, now, and Parveen, and living in Brighton, and Mark. It doesn't make sense I don't remember seeing Geraint.'

'Well, Mark is your boyfriend. And your day-to-day life is bound to be more ingrained in your memory.'

I pulled a tissue from the box on my bedside cabinet and scrubbed at my face. I couldn't explain it properly. I couldn't have forgotten Geraint; that would be like forgetting myself. 'So, lots of twins in your family, then?' Stephen was tactfully ignoring my red eyes and I appreciated it.

'It's always been weird to me that Mum and Aunt Pat were twins, too,' I said, after a deep breath. 'The proper sort.'

'Proper sort?'

'Identical. They were so different, though. Inside.' The stories about my mum were always about her creativity and constant movement; the way her hands were always fluttering. While Pat was immovable as a brick wall. 'Pat's always done the practical stuff, but I've always been in love with my mum. Or the idea of her, at any rate. She's still my mother, even if I never knew her.'

'Must be hard for her.'

'She's dead, so—'

'Not your mum. I mean, it must be hard for your aunt.'

'What do you mean?'

'From what I can tell, the practicalities are a big part of parenting. And she didn't have to take you on.'

I felt mildly rebuked. And cross as a result. I wanted him to leave. 'You have kids?'

He shook his head. 'God, no. I'm far too young.'

'My mother was twenty-one when she had me and Ger.'

'Well,' he looked away, 'it suits some people.'

'And you're not very young really, are you?' I was being downright unpleasant now. I was punishing him for sympathising with

Pat. I knew this and I knew I wasn't being fair but I couldn't stop myself.

I expected him to get up. To look cross. Instead, he laughed. 'I suppose not. I'd better get a move on, then.'

'Only if you want them.'

'Oh, I do.' His earnest tone surprised me. 'Definitely. Don't you?'

I opened my mouth to say 'No way, no how, no thank you', but the words stuck in my throat. I didn't know. I didn't think I was the sort of person who had children. I prodded around my mind for some maternal instinct.

'I'm sorry,' Stephen said. 'That was a bit personal, wasn't it?'

'I'm picturing babies. Cute ones with little hats and stuff.'

'Okay . . .'

'Trying to see if I feel anything,' I clarified. 'I don't know how I feel about things. Some things are really clear, like whether I like cheese or whatever, but other things . . .'

'Well, it's a more complex issue than cheese.'

'Is it, though? Don't you just know? In the same way? Isn't that what the instinct thing is all about?'

'Your instincts are fine. It's normal to be a bit muddled and I really don't think the question of parenthood is easy or simple for anyone. Especially not someone with—'

'Some cognitive impairment,' I finished his sentence.

'I'm sorry,' he said, again. 'I'm not making a good job of this conversation, am I?'

'Stop apologising. At least you've reminded me how much I like cheese. I'd kill for some mature cheddar right now.'

Stephen smiled then, but it wasn't a relaxed expression. There were shadows in his face and his eyes were watchful. 'Well, I'd better get on.' He paused before leaving. 'I'll see if I can find you some cheddar.'

∽

My mother and father were fated to be together. According to Pat, my mum described it as a great love affair. Admittedly short-lived, but a grand passion nonetheless. The way she told it, it was filmic, huge – nothing less than a 1970s Welsh *Casablanca*. She'd dressed the story up in finery so that when Pat passed it on, I'd thought it was like a fairy tale.

Our father's name was Howard. Mum had first seen him when she was fifteen. Seen his image, that is; she didn't actually meet him until she was twenty.

There's a giant lump of granite on top of the *bryn*. It's a Neolithic burial chamber called Maen Ceti or, for the tourists, Arthur's Stone. The tradition goes that at full moon the maidens of Gower would make an offering of honey cake, then crawl around the stone on their hands and knees to see a vision of their one true love.

Pat passed on the story to me and Geraint along with the photographs of Mum and a selection of her sketchbooks and dreamcatchers, but her mouth twisted as she told it. She couldn't help adding her own commentary. The story began with one magical moonlit night, when Mum drank her father's bramble wine and climbed the hill with half a packet of digestives and a torch. She ate most of the biscuits but left the broken ones in the space underneath the capstone. Then she crawled three times around Maen Ceti and, at the end of her final rotation, saw Howard Davis – or his image at any rate – shimmering in the night air in front of her. 'Your mother said that when he walked into the Spar shop five years later, she recognised him straight away,' Pat said, but she would always add that Mum was only in the Spar shop because she'd been driving Dai-the-Shop demented by rearranging his stock, and that the reason she'd seen a figure up the hill was because the bramble wine was twenty per cent proof. She also added that although Mum had been very happy to be pregnant with us, Howard Davis was a big mistake. Pat's face would get a sad closed-off look and then she'd say Mum 'paid too highly for it, too'.

When I hit my teens, I began asking Pat for more detail, but she would always find some job that needed doing urgently. The side garden needed weeding. The tomato plants were due to go in. The washing was waiting to be hung out on the rotary airer and those clothes weren't going to walk outside and peg themselves. One time I even asked Uncle Dylan. His lips went thin and his body very still. After a moment or two, he left the room and I heard the back door bang shut.

I asked Geraint, too, in case Pat had ever let anything slip to him. He repeated the same story that I knew or told me to shut up about it, depending on his mood. Once I asked Pat outright about my father and she said that he was from Llandaf in Cardiff. I waited, holding my breath for more, but Pat pursed her lips, just said that he'd been on holiday when he'd met Mum.

When I turned fourteen, Pat sat me down at the kitchen table. 'I know you wonder about your father and you've every right.'

I was in shock. She was bringing up a subject that I'd seen her turn up the radio, leave the house, get into the shower to avoid.

Pat's voice was quiet. 'And I suppose you're old enough now.' Pat, who was incapable of sitting still for more than sixty seconds without finding herself something useful to do, was leaning back in the wooden chair. A strand of hair had worked loose from the twist at the back of her head and was stuck to her cheek. 'Fact is, Howard Davis knew your mother wasn't a full bushel. He wasn't stupid and he could see it. More than that, our parents told him. When he came to the door, asking to take her out. My mam and dad, your *mamgu* and *tadgu*, told him straight.'

'It was love at first sight.' I wasn't ready to give up the fairy tale.

Pat looked at me sadly. 'Men and women are very different. A woman might feel love at first sight, but for a man it's biological.'

The kitchen was full of steam. Pat had been boiling bones for stock and the window was misted up. I concentrated on its opaque surface and prayed she didn't decide to give me The Talk.

'Boys have certain urges. When they say love, they usually mean lust. And lust doesn't last. Once it's burned out it's gone and so are they.' Pat shook her head. 'Howard Davis took advantage of your mother. He knew she didn't have the sense to say no. He took advantage and left her pregnant.'

'Did he visit when I was born?'

'Have you heard anything I've just said?' Pat said, frustrated. 'He was a bad sort. Tadgu wouldn't have let him into the hospital even if he had shown up.'

I straightened up.

'Which he didn't.'

But it was too late. I was convinced that my dad had travelled from Cardiff to visit Mum and me that day. I could see him. Not his face exactly, but a medium-height, dark-haired man with black eyes and a teddy bear under one arm. He would've been excited and hopeful and then heartbroken when Tadgu sent him away without so much as a glimpse of his beloved twin babies. Especially his daughter, his precious baby girl. My eyes filled with tears.

'Don't turn on the waterworks. It's ancient history. I'm only telling you so that you can leave the subject well alone.'

I shoved my chair back so that the legs scraped on the tile floor.

'Don't run off, I want you to top and tail the beans.'

I scarpered anyway. Went down the bottom of the garden to sulk and, for once, Pat left me to it.

The idea that my dad was out there, thinking about me, took hold and a couple of weeks after the conversation with Pat, I decided to find him.

I didn't tell Geraint what I was doing and I don't remember why. I think I must have assumed he wouldn't be interested; he never wanted to talk about our dad or join in my 'what if' flights of imagination.

I took the school stuff out of my backpack and replaced the books and folders with my purse, pyjamas, a change of underwear and a T-shirt. I added a paperback for the journey (although I knew I'd be too excited to read), but left my toothbrush in the holder in the bathroom. Pat would notice if it was missing and might come looking for me too quickly. I didn't mind being caught eventually, but I needed time to find my father and enjoy our tearful reunion first.

That morning, I got the bus to school, but instead of heading towards the main building to find my friends like every other morning, I slipped straight out of the front gates and walked towards the main road.

There were loads of kids coming towards me, heading in the other direction towards the school. I felt self-conscious, as though a big finger was pointing at my head and announcing to the world 'skiver'. I'd never cut school in my life and although, technically, I wasn't doing anything wrong at this point, and a casual observer might assume I lived locally and was popping home for some forgotten homework, I was sweating with nerves.

I'd never used the bus stop on the main road, although I'd passed it every day. I hoped that all of the teachers had already passed this way and parked in the staff car park. If not, then I was a sitting duck. I took my tie off and put it in the front pocket of my bag. I had a black T-shirt on underneath my school shirt but I felt too self-conscious to start undressing there, out in the open.

I saw the double decker come around the corner. It had the right number and 'City Centre' on the destination board. Just then, a familiar figure appeared from the side road that led to the school. My heart leaped into my mouth, but it was Geraint, not a teacher.

'Mitching?' Geraint said, as he reached me. 'Never thought I'd see the day.'

The bus pulled up and we boarded. I'd prepared my excuse for the driver – I was going to say that I had a dentist's appointment in town – but he didn't so much as glance at us.

'What are you doing?' I asked. Geraint was wearing a dark grey hoodie and wires snaked from the pocket to the ear buds around his neck. He didn't even have his school bag. At fourteen, he already towered above me.

Ger treated me to his favourite facial expression. The one that said, 'Stop asking stupid questions, you fool'. 'More pertinently,' he said, 'since when did you skive?'

'It's a special occasion,' I said, primly. 'I'm going to Cardiff.' I explained, as best I could, my plan to find our father.

'That's nuts,' Ger said. He settled back in his seat. 'I bet you won't get on the train,'

'Nope,' I said, gleeful with the rare opportunity to surprise Ger, to be the adventurous one for once. 'Costs too much. I'm getting the coach.'

He shook his head, but didn't argue. At the bus station in Swansea, I found the National Express office and bought a return. Geraint didn't say anything, but he bought one, too. I hadn't asked him to come with me, but I was secretly relieved. I didn't like the bus station. It smelled of cigarette smoke and bins, and there was a homeless man with a scary-looking dog.

I remember the coach ride as fun. I didn't let myself think about what I was going towards, or what I'd left behind. I knew Pat was most likely going to find out, and that I would be in a world of trouble, but that reality lay in the future. It was a long way from the fuzzy seat cover of my coach seat and the scenery rushing past the window, the sense of adventure and freedom.

Once we got to Cardiff, a bigger, busier bus station, with unfamiliar buildings crowded all around and a light drizzle falling, my sense of elation fled.

'Right, then. What now?' Ger said.

My heart sank further. I had no answer. I realised, then, that I hadn't really expected to go through with it. I'd thought that a teacher would stop me or the bus driver would refuse to let me on. I'd got caught up in the moment, and hadn't wanted to back out in front of Geraint. Now I had to admit I had no idea what to do. Howard Davis wasn't going to magically appear, just because I'd made the effort. I was an idiot and a child. I felt myself go red.

Geraint looked at me for a moment, then he said, casually, 'I'm starving. Have you got any money left?'

We pooled our resources and went to the nearest fast food place for burgers and milkshakes. At once, it was fun again. We were on a mini adventure. A trip to the big city, eating the kind of crap food Pat never gave us, in a restaurant on our own. I don't remember us discussing Howard again, or the original intention of the day. Ger just messed around, sticking straws up his nose and making me laugh, and then, later, we got the next coach back again.

We even made it in time for the school bus home and nobody was ever the wiser, but I never forgot how kind Ger was that day.

GRACE

In the weeks after an exceptionally wet and dreary March, people began to talk about the May Day concert. It was a hospital tradition and everybody from the janitors up to the senior house surgeons got involved. Dr Palmer was doing a magician's act and he required a girl to saw in half. He pointed at Grace. 'You'll do,' he said.

'Doctor, please,' Grace protested. Every part of her wanted to move away and, too late, she realised that this reaction was only going to encourage him. 'I can't.'

'Not can't,' Palmer said, smiling humourlessly. 'Won't.'

Grace gathered her strength. 'I won't,' she said.

'I'll do it,' Barnes said. 'I'll lie ever so still.'

Palmer barely glanced at her. 'I don't think you'll fit in the box, Nurse.'

Barnes blushed redder than usual and hurried away.

Grace made to follow her.

'I don't think I excused you, Nurse Kemp,' Dr Palmer said. 'You go when I say you can go.'

Grace froze.

'That's better,' he said, moving a little closer. 'Now, I want you to be my assistant in the show. I don't think that's too much to ask, do you?'

'No,' Grace managed.

He straightened up. 'A couple of rehearsals ought to do it,' he said, sounding business-like. His manner could change like that; one moment so threatening and wrong, and the next back to an entirely normal air of detached authority. It made Grace question whether she'd really glimpsed a monster, whether she was going quite mad.

'Don't look so worried, Nurse,' he said, putting a finger on her cheek. 'I'm not going to bite.'

❧

'I don't know why you don't want to do it,' Evie said that night. 'It'll be fun. And Dr Palmer isn't half bad.'

'He's all bad,' Grace said, without thinking. She did that more and more these days. Evie's friendship had made her less guarded.

Evie looked up in surprise. 'What do you mean?'

'Nothing.' Grace shook her head. 'I just don't like him.'

'You don't have to like him, just let him buy you a drink, take you out for dinner . . . He can afford to treat you.'

'I'm never going anywhere with that man,' Grace said. 'Not ever.'

'Very well.' Evie waved her hand. 'If you aren't going to take my wise and wonderful advice, at least come out with me and Robert tomorrow. You've been stuck in this place for too long. It's not healthy. Besides,' she added, 'Thomas would like to see you.'

They were both on off-duty and Grace had been wondering about whether to take the tram home or not. Grace felt the pull of temptation. She pictured Thomas's warm eyes, his sweet smile. A shutter came down in her mind. She could see her father standing above her, the black rage in his face. Grace swallowed the sudden lump in her throat.

Evie frowned. 'You've gone a peculiar colour. You keep doing that, you know. It's quite alarming.'

'I'm fine,' Grace said. She cast around for a subject to deflect Evie. 'You still like Robert, then?'

'Don't say it like that,' Evie said. 'Do at least try to be polite about him.'

Grace blushed. She hadn't realised she was so obvious. 'He's just a bit . . .'

'Strong. Handsome. Definite.' Evie arched an eyebrow. 'That's why I like him. Can't stand wet blankets.'

'He makes me nervous,' Grace managed.

Evie laughed. 'That's because you're a sweet little bird. He'd eat you for breakfast.'

Grace shuddered and, at once, Evie was at her side. 'What is it? I was only teasing, you know.'

Grace found she couldn't stop shaking. Her father was still there. Angry. She tried to blink him away, but it didn't work. 'I know,' she managed to say, her teeth clashing together. 'Ignore me, I'm being silly.'

Evie wrapped both arms around Grace and held her until she stopped shaking. Then she pulled back and looked into Grace's face. 'I wish you'd tell me what's wrong.'

'It's nothing. I'm just a nervous sort,' Grace said, forcing a smile. 'Tell me more about Robert. Perhaps if I hear about his virtues, I'll like him a little better.'

'Oh, he's not virtuous,' Evie said, flashing her most wicked smile. 'But then, neither am I.' She paused, considering. 'I like his get-up-and-go. He does things. He's not just sitting around waiting for the next thing to fall into his lap.'

It was freezing in the bedroom and Grace got into her bed, lifting the cover so that Evie could climb in beside her. She had a crocheted blanket – bright granny squares edged with navy blue – that she had spent the previous winter working on. Back when she was still a good girl, a good daughter. She ought to be grateful. It was so cold in the bedrooms that every scrap of extra covering was needed, but she didn't like this reminder of her old existence. It was so much easier if she pretended that none of it had happened, that she'd just hatched from an egg on her first day of training.

'He talks about the world. And ideas. And he really thinks. He says I'm jolly ignorant but he asks me questions that make me feel like there's something else out there. A life beyond this.'

'The hospital?'

Evie shrugged. 'The hospital, Brighton, England.'

'I don't like to think about that. Father used to read from the paper at breakfast and I hated it. Once you've heard the bad news you can't forget it and you can't do anything about it.'

'Robert doesn't think like that. He says that it's our duty to be informed. That the more we know, the better we can be prepared.'

'Prepared for what?' Grace said, snuggling down further under the blankets.

'Anything,' Evie said. 'That's the point, Gracie.'

Grace lived in constant dread that Dr Palmer was going to collar her for a rehearsal, but as May Day drew closer, she began to wonder if she was being silly. He changed his mind about his act and told everybody that he was going to do some card tricks and a 'five-ring illusion'. Grace wasn't certain that he still needed an assistant and began to let herself believe that he might have forgotten about her.

The concert included a motley variety of skits and songs and in the days before, the common room was in near-constant use. Grace was admiring a line of elaborate papier-mâché masks, which were lined up to dry on the table tennis table, when Dr Palmer crossed the room to speak to her. 'You'd look rather fetching in one of those, Nurse Kemp.' They were grotesque and twisted faces, painted in primary colours, and Grace didn't know how to respond. She tried to say 'thank you, Doctor' as politeness demanded, but her tongue felt stuck to the roof of her mouth, her jaw clamped tightly together.

'We'll have a run-through on the day,' he said. 'Not that you need it. I'm the one doing all the hard work, you just have to do as you're told and smile for the audience.'

Grace felt her stomach swoop at his words but he seemed distracted and walked away without adding anything else.

On the day, Grace woke up with such a knot in her stomach that she felt she would be sick. The thought that she was going to have to spend time alone with Dr Palmer for their rehearsal, and then perform with him in front of everyone, made her chest tighten. She could barely breathe.

'You can't be poorly today,' Evie said, pouting a little. 'You'll miss my song.'

Until that moment, Grace hadn't even considered the possibility. Hope shot through her, as Evie laid a hand on her forehead and frowned. 'You're disgustingly hot. I'll fetch Sister.'

Sister Bennett had a reputation for disbelieving in illness, at least when it came to the nurses. Barnes had once told Grace (somewhat proudly) that she'd had to work a full shift with a fever. Grace decided the only option was to lie so she told the sister that she'd already been sick three times. Miraculously, Sister Bennett told Evie to help Grace to the nurses' infirmary – a double room on the corridor below – and to tell the ward sister that they were a pair of hands short. 'Of all days,' Sister Bennett said, but the usual acerbity was missing. As she stumbled to the sick room, her head spinning, Grace realised that it hadn't occurred to Sister Bennett that she would fake illness on May Day. The idea that a nurse would willingly miss the concert, and the cider-with-dinner and the assistant matron's famous Simnel cake, was beyond her understanding.

In the infirmary, after a disgruntled Evie had gone to breakfast, Grace closed her eyes. Her skin was clammy and she felt as weak as a sparrow, but her soul was soaring high with relief.

MINA

I was definitely getting stronger. I could walk from one end of the corridor outside the ward to the top of the main staircase and back again. My next goal was to use the lift. If I used the lift, I'd be able to make it to the patients' garden. I'd heard there was such a thing and I was determined to see it. I'd fixated, you could say.

After Pat's visit, things felt more real. It had hit me that this wasn't some strange dream. I had really been bashed up in an accident. I was truly in hospital and, until I recuperated enough, I was stuck in the hospital. All the talk I'd heard about 'treat 'em and street 'em' didn't seem to apply once you'd had a coma. It seemed like a bit of an overreaction to me, but then my PhD was in physics, not medicine, so what did I know?

I felt a renewed sense of purpose, though. Dr Kanthe had said that I could go home as soon as I was mobile enough not to end up back in A&E. I wanted to see the house that Mark had bought and restart my life. At least I thought I did. All of that – life after hospital stuff – still seemed hazy and unreal. My immediate desires consumed me. I wanted a really good cup of tea. I wanted a full night's sleep in a bed that didn't have collapsible sides. But what I really wanted, most of all, was to make it to the patients' garden.

I was making a bid to get there. I had shuffled down the corridor and pressed the button for the lift. I knew that if it didn't come quickly enough, I was going to use up too much of my valuable strength standing and waiting. I considered leaning against the wall but I was worried I'd get too comfortable or not be able to move fast enough when the doors slid open. I stood as close to the doors as I dared. I didn't want to get knocked over if a group of fast-moving people came bowling out. There was no way I would be able to take evasive action. Picturing this scenario made me feel vulnerable and a little bit frightened. I straightened my spine. *You are not afraid*, I told myself. *You are fine.*

When the red light showed four and the doors opened, the lift was empty. I let out a breath of relief and stuck my hand in between the doors to stop them from closing while I shuffled inside. I needn't have worried, hospital lifts are calibrated for the infirm, but my heart was hammering as if danger was about to strike at any moment.

My heart didn't slow and I could feel sweat running down the back of my T-shirt. I had a hoodie on, in case it was cold outside. Outside! But it was sweltering hot inside the hospital even without the exertion of walking so far.

When I got out of the lift, I saw the sign straight away. It was at the end of the wide corridor and the green arrow pointed right. I wanted to follow that arrow. Green for grass. Green for open spaces and fresh air. I assumed there would be park benches. Patients needed seating, after all, but apart from that I couldn't imagine what I was going to find. A neatly kept lawn and a couple of flowerbeds? A giant oak tree with squirrels running amongst its spreading branches?

The pain in my knee, which had been manageable thus far, began to really complain halfway down the hall. People walking in the same direction as I was split their groupings and flowed around me, overtaking with ease. There was an old man, probably in his nineties, sitting on a plastic chair in a window recess. He was looking through the glass and I wondered if he'd been trying to make it to the garden, too. It strengthened my resolve and I managed to speed up a little. I wasn't an OAP. I was going to make it.

I turned right at the sign, hoping with all of my heart that the garden wasn't much further. I could see the next sign, it wasn't so far. For a healthy person it was probably twenty paces. For me, it suddenly might as well have been twenty miles. I thought about the long trek back to my bed and felt tears pricking my eyes.

'Miss Morgan, as I live and breathe.' It was Stephen with a paper cup that smelled of coffee and a smile that faltered as he took a closer look at me. 'Are you okay?'

'Garden,' I said. I took a couple of breaths and managed to elaborate. 'I wanted to see the garden but it's a bit further than I thought.'

'Shall I get you a chair?'

He meant a wheelchair. I shook my head.

He hesitated, assessing the situation, then transferred his cup to his other hand and offered me his arm. 'Shall we? I'd like to drink this in the sun.'

I leaned on him gratefully. My spine was on fire. Flames were licking outwards from the central strip of white-hot pain, sending lines of fresh agony down my legs, spiking up into my skull. I knew my knee was complaining but my back hurt so badly I didn't have enough brain space to process the separate feeling. I was dissolving in a mindless scream of 'it hurts'.

Stephen was walking very slowly and talking in a calm, but upbeat kind of way. I was leaning on him so heavily I was amazed he didn't fall over. I guessed he was a lot stronger than he looked. I distracted myself by trying to imagine his body from what I could feel through his shirt sleeve. Long-limbed. On the skinny side. But with a wiry strength. Strength, I had to admit, he needed as he bore me along the hallway. I hadn't been this close to a strange man for – well, I had no idea for how long – and it was distracting. I concentrated on the slight scent of his aftershave or deodorant, the male otherness of his skin and low voice, and used those details to push the pain down. I compressed it into something small, something I could carry.

When we got to the garden entrance it was a heavy door and I knew that on my own I would never have been able to open it. Even standing unsupported for the seconds it took Stephen to let go of me and pull it open was a gruelling test of my ability to stay upright. I knew that if I fell I would probably lose consciousness and that would mean a trip straight back to bed-land. Maybe even the ICU. I was so close to the outside now, I had to make it. I had to get into that garden and feel the fresh air on my face. Maybe hear some birdsong.

I was working so hard not to pass out that I didn't really take in the garden until I was sitting on one of the benches, Stephen next to me, casually laying his arm across the back of the bench and sipping his coffee in a manner that was clearly calculated to disguise the fact that he was professionally assessing my medical stability.

As the pain receded in the relief of sitting, the weight off my bad knee, I was able to focus on my surroundings. To say they were disappointing was an understatement. The garden was a small quad, guarded by the high walls of the hospital on all four sides. In my daydreams, there had been a view. Maybe not the rolling green of parkland, trees and pathways, but definitely a bush or two. Some flowerbeds, maybe a weeping willow.

Instead, there was a scrubby patch of bare earth and bins overflowing with cigarette butts. Stephen followed my gaze. 'You aren't supposed to smoke here, it's not one of the designated areas, but,' he shrugged, 'you know.'

'I don't know if I'm a smoker,' I said.

'Do you want one now?'

'A cigarette?' I inhaled deeply, catching the faintest whiff of old cigarette smoke from the bin. It smelled stale and unpleasant. I shook my head.

'Probably not a smoker then,' he said. 'Although, you've been cold turkey for weeks so that could've cured you.'

'Cured me?'

'Of the addiction,' he said. 'Although, most smokers I know say it never ever goes away. That's why I never started.'

'Sensible.'

He pulled a face that was hard to read. 'Yeah, sensible, but more like scared. Something that you could do a couple of times and then it has a permanent hold over you, an effect that lasts your entire life.' He looked momentarily embarrassed, like he'd revealed more of himself than he'd meant to. 'I don't like the idea of something having the upper hand, you know?'

I did know. At that moment I felt there was a connection between us, something hanging in the air like a silvery thread. I didn't want to break that thread but I wanted to tell another person what I'd been seeing even more. I knew it would rip apart the fragile respect, comradeship, whatever this was we both felt, but a part of me wanted to break it anyway. I liked Stephen and that made me feel vulnerable and I'd had more of that than I could take already. I shifted slightly on the bench, trying to find a more comfortable position.

Stephen moved, too, began shucking off his coat. 'Do you want to sit on this? These benches are a bit hard.'

'I'm fine,' I said. 'It's nice to be outside.' I waved a hand, encompassing the grim scarred benches, the bin that looked like it had been set on fire in the not-too-distant past and the scrubby bit of grass, flecked with rubbish. 'Maybe it's the coma, but I'm genuinely happy to be here.'

'You don't have to do that, you know.'

'Do what?'

'Assume that everything is different now. You're still the same person you always were, you've just got some gaps to fill in. You mustn't think that you're starting all over again.'

'Is that your professional opinion?'

'I suppose. Why? Do you want to start all over again?'

'It's a tempting notion, don't you think? A clean slate. That's why that born-again nonsense is so popular.'

He let out a startled laugh that could've been a snort.

'Sorry. You're not—'

'No.' He held up his hands. 'Are you always this outspoken?'

I gave him a crooked smile and tapped the side of my head. 'I have no idea. Gaps, remember?'

'You've got a few weeks' grace, you can play the coma card. You could really try it on.'

'Now you're thinking,' I said. 'And I want a T-shirt that reads "bona fide miracle" with your name signed on the bottom.'

'Oh, God, I didn't say that, did I?'

'There was something else I wanted to ask you about.'

He noticed the shift in tone. I could see the humour drain out of his face and the neutral professional expression appeared.

'I've been seeing things.'

He waited, not saying anything. Which was probably a technique they were taught at medical school. Or during their compulsory psych rotation.

I took a deep breath. 'Birds. I saw them when I was a kid, but then it stopped for years and now it's started again.'

'When you say you can see birds—'

'I mean birds that aren't there.' It was done. I'd crossed into crazy territory now. I'd said something so outlandish that the way back was going to be tricky.

'How do you know they're not there? Are they unusually large? Or are they frightening? Or do you just know, instinctively, that they aren't real?'

I silently thanked him for staying calm and speaking to me like a rational human being. 'Partly it's the latter – something I just know – but it's also the way they behave. Sitting on my bed or my shoulder. That kind of thing.'

'Can you feel them?' Stephen pointed to his own shoulder. 'When they're sitting there, can you feel it?'

'Sometimes,' I said. 'Little birds are really very light and if I've got a coat on then I wouldn't feel their feet or claws or anything so I don't. But if it's something big like a crow or a raven then I feel their weight.'

'So, it's very logical. Very real.'

'Apart from the fact that I know they're not, yes.'

'Could they be real? I mean, some birds are so used to us now, they can get really close to humans.' He indicated a pigeon, which had arrived since we'd sat down and was pecking at the ground near our feet.

'No,' I said. 'They're not real.'

'Okay. Do you see any now?'

I looked around. Apart from the real live pigeon, there weren't any birds here at all. It was one of the disappointing things about the garden. I'd been looking forward to hearing birds, at least. Chattering and calling. 'It's spring. Where are they all?'

'I guess this space just isn't that enticing.'

Having started, I didn't seem able to stop. Rather than taking the easy route and changing subjects, maybe moving on to garden planning in municipal spaces or the latest football scores, I said: 'I see ghost-birds when something bad is going to happen. They're a warning. I don't usually know what they're warning about, although sometimes I guess.'

'Do you really believe that?'

'I know it's impossible, if that's what you're asking. I also know seeing the birds is probably random and I've just ascribed cause and effect afterwards to try and explain it, give it some meaning.'

'It's not at all unusual for people to have hallucinations after a head injury.'

'You said that before. But I saw them when I was a kid. A long time before the accident.'

'Did you suffer any injuries as a child?'

'No.' I compressed my lips.

'Okay.' Stephen wasn't looking directly at me any more; he was gazing at the grey wall opposite, lips twisted while he thought. I watched his profile, glad of the break in eye contact and for the chance to look at him. He really had a nice face. It was the kind of face that made me want to open up, to trust, to over-share. All those mushy things I'd successfully been avoiding. His face was so nice, in fact, that I didn't even feel angry that I was acting all needy, like a baby bird coming out of a broken shell.

'What were you like as a kid?' he asked. 'Were you very . . .'

'If the next word out of your mouth is "imaginative" then this conversation is officially over.'

His mouth twisted further into a quick smile, but he didn't look at me. 'I was going to say "crazy" but that seemed rude.'

'No. I wasn't crazy. Not diagnosed crazy, anyway. And I know kids have imaginary friends and obsessive behaviours and all kinds of weird shit that's considered normal until they hit adulthood.'

'Normal-ish, perhaps,' he said, glancing at me.

'So,' I said. 'What do you think?'

He turned to face me fully. 'I think you've been through a hell of a lot and that a return to childhood thought patterns is a completely normal and understandable reaction to trauma.'

'Right,' I said, slumping a little. The disappointment was complete and I didn't even know what I'd hoped for, which made it worse.

'I also think you are one of the strongest people I've ever met and that if anybody can regain their sense of self and their physical strength, then it's you.'

So now I warranted a pep talk. It was sickening.

'And if seeing birds that aren't really there is part of who you were before, then I don't think it's necessarily a big deal that you're seeing them now. Unless they're linked to unhappiness in some way. Some people see dark shapes, black figures or birds, when they're depressed. Do you feel depressed?'

'I'm in hospital,' I said flatly. I wanted the conversation to be over. I wanted it never to have started.

'Are you sleeping? Has your appetite changed? Do you still take pleasure in things you used to enjoy?'

And now he was trotting out the Pfizer PHQ. Just in case I was in any danger of forgetting that I was a patient. 'I used to enjoy running, so I'll have to get back to you on that. I used to enjoy drinking cold beer and playing pool, I used to enjoy going out for a nice dinner and getting happily drunk on wine and then going home with my boyfriend and fucking my brains out.' I looked down. 'I'll have to get back to you on all of those things.'

'I'm sorry,' he said quietly. 'That was stupid of me.'

'No,' I said, taking a deep breath. 'I'm sorry. I just—'

'It's my fault,' Stephen said. 'I'm doing that annoying thing. Trying to make it all better rather than just listening.'

His earnest tone changed my mood. He was so delightfully serious; it made me want to be frivolous, magnanimous. 'Is that a problem of yours?'

'So I've been told,' Stephen said, visibly relaxing, although the ridges between his eyebrows remained. Stubborn little quote marks that I wanted to reach out and smooth away with my thumb.

'And you've got enough to deal with without me blundering around.'

'Honestly, it's fine,' I said. 'You're not blundering. And I like talking to you. I just feel kind of weird. Like I'm homesick but I don't know where for.'

He nodded, leaning towards me as if I was the most fascinating creature he'd ever laid eyes upon.

I was just about to say something else, to tell him that I missed my mum even though I couldn't remember her properly, when the door banged open. I twisted around, welcoming the fresh jolt of pain that rooted me in the present. It would serve as a reminder of how bloody close I was coming to cracking open like a walnut.

'Isn't this cosy?' Mark said, his voice heavy with sarcasm. 'Extra sessions?'

Stephen stood up and offered his hand. 'Hello, again.'

Mark ignored his outstretched hand. 'Do you do physio now, as well? Or is this a neuro-psych test I'm not aware of?'

'Mark, please,' I said.

Stephen straightened up. 'I'm not on duty, actually. Not here in my professional capacity at all.'

'I see,' Mark said.

'Just as a friend,' Stephen said.

'You should be careful,' Mark said, his voice mild.

I sat up straighter. When Mark's voice got gentle that was when you really knew he was furious.

'After all,' he continued, 'there are professional conduct rules, aren't there? Guidelines to protect vulnerable patients.'

'What are you getting at? Are you suggesting I'm some kind of predator?'

'I'm sorry,' I said to Stephen. I tried to stand up, to get in between the two men before things could get any worse. I misjudged how quickly I could move, though, and fell back against the bench, pain jolting through my spine. Mark was there, half catching me, and I leaned against him, straightening up.

'I'll get a chair,' Stephen said, moving towards the door.

'I think you've done quite enough,' Mark said. To me, he said: 'Bed.'

I was pretty sure I'd always hated being ordered around, but I hadn't got the energy to argue. Plus, and this wasn't something I was particularly proud of, there was something oddly comforting about being helpless. It removed the need to make decisions or to feel culpable. I was helpless so I was blameless. Pathetic but true.

As he pushed me along the corridor he said: 'I don't like that doctor.'

'Really,' I said, keeping my voice light and teasing, 'because you hid your feelings so well.'

He stopped wheeling me and came round in front, kneeling down to gaze into my eyes. He took my hand for extra effect and said: 'It's only because I love you so much. I almost lost you. And I know how much you hate being looked after, so the thought of that man taking advantage of you while you're in this state is terrible.'

'He's not taking advantage,' I said. 'Really. He's just being friendly.'

'Oh, please,' Mark sneered. 'Your brain isn't that damaged. He's sniffing around you.'

'Don't be disgusting.' I was so tired. I didn't want to argue with Mark and I didn't want to think badly of Stephen, but most of all, I felt ill. I hated Mark telling me I was vulnerable because I felt that way. I was scared and I was sick of being scared. I wanted to be back in my bed, the blankets pulled up high.

Mark shook his head a little, as if I was being silly, and then he smiled, humouring me. 'You look exhausted. Tell me next time you want to see the garden, won't you? I can take you. You'll set your recovery back if you keep trying to do too much.'

I closed my eyes and let my head fall back. The one good thing about being injured was that it gave me an excellent way to end conversations. I heard Mark sigh. *Drama queen.* But I couldn't stop hearing his crude phrase 'sniffing around you'. He'd used that before. I remembered a drunken argument after a night out, his face bright red and pushed up close to mine. The memory jolted me so hard I felt as if I was falling. I knew I ought to tell Mark he couldn't speak to me like that, not ever again, but I felt so tired. It was easier to push the memory aside. It was easier to pretend.

∾

Back in my bed and still exhausted, I went to the history book, scouring its pages for my ghost-nurse. I was more comfortable with birds that weren't there; this woman was unnerving me. I couldn't shake the feeling that she was real. Or had been real, at least. I turned the pages expecting her image to leap out at me, in a continuous state of hope and disbelief.

I woke up in an uncomfortable slumped position with a burning pain in my neck. It was night. The lights were low and Queenie was mumbling in her sleep. Her voice rose and became briefly clear: 'Put the bloody cat out.'

The ghost-nurse was next to my bed. 'Want to go for a walk?' Her voice was soft. So quiet, in fact, that I wasn't sure she had spoken at all.

'Who are you?' My voice was real enough.

'Grace,' the woman said. 'How d'you do?'

'Did I fall asleep?' I looked around at the ward. It didn't seem quite right and the light had become brighter.

'You've been reading about me,' Grace said. She pointed to the book on my nightstand.

'You're not in there,' I said. 'Because you're a figment of my imagination. Or a symptom of my mild cognitive impairment.'

Grace smiled. 'If you say so.'

Then I knew I was dreaming. We were in a hallway and I didn't remember getting out of bed. Plus, nothing was hurting.

One man was shuffling along, locked in a private battle with his body; another dressed in blue scrubs streaked past, on a mission.

'Where are we going?' My back began to hurt, as if I'd reminded myself that it should and the dream world was obliging.

Grace didn't answer.

'I can't walk far,' I said, hating the plaintive sound of my voice.

At the end of the corridor was a central stairway. Someone had commissioned stained glass for the windows, which suited the old, handsome carved wooden banisters. It was like stepping out of a hospital and into an art gallery or museum.

'This way,' Grace said, speeding up a little.

We turned left and into yet another corridor. This one was part of the old building. The proportions were different and there was the unmistakable odour of age, underlying the antiseptic. I could smell floor polish, and the doors leading off the corridor seemed burnished. There was a paper label attached to the nearest door and I stepped closer to see it. The handwriting was heavily sloped, the penmanship old-fashioned, but the paper was very thin and tinged blue: 'Kindly wash all cups and cutlery after use. This kitchen is for all and its use is a privilege not a right. Sister Atkins'.

I reached out to touch the note but Grace was already at the other end of the corridor. Besides, there was something about the paper that stopped me. My fingers hesitated just above its surface. I turned and followed Grace.

There was a sign hanging down from the ceiling, the kind I was used to seeing in the hospital with departments listed and directional arrows. The door at the end of the corridor had a modern sign which read 'Orthopaedics' but underneath that I could see another sign, an old one. I squinted, trying to read it, but the letters danced around and my eyes began to water.

'Smoking room,' my companion said. I tried the door, expecting it to be locked, but it swung open.

Grace, who had been just next to me, was suddenly in the middle of the room. I blinked, expecting her to disappear completely, but she remained. She turned slowly, looking around the plain little room, and, as she did, details became clear. Or, more accurately, things appeared. Where there had been a couple of chairs and a birch-effect conference table, there were several mismatched chairs including a wing-backed armchair covered in worn brocade. The wall that had been blank seconds earlier, was filled with a giant noticeboard, and the light fitting changed from recessed ceiling spots to a hanging central light with a strange metal shade.

'Badminton league,' Grace said. 'We had a sports day, too.' She looked wistful. 'Evie was brilliant in the three-legged. Nobody could catch us.'

'Evie?'

Grace walked to a wooden board and pointed. 'There.'

I went closer until I could read the names in gold type. Three names down, Nurse Grace Anne Kemp and, underneath, Nurse Evie Jones.

I reached out to touch the wooden sign, but something held my fingers back, a thickness in the air that warned me not to.

'I'm dreaming,' I said. 'I'm asleep.'

Grace shook her head. 'I don't know what this is, but you're not asleep.'

'Why are you here?'

'This is my hospital,' she said. 'I'm on duty.'

'Why do I see you?'

Grace shook her head. 'That's the wrong question.'

GRACE

Sunlight streamed through the windows. It hurt Grace's eyes. No matter how long she worked at the hospital, she still hadn't grown used to the early starts and her head buzzed with tiredness.

'Is anybody coming for you tomorrow?'

'Sorry?' Grace had been concentrating on getting as much food into her body as possible and she wasn't sure that she'd heard Barnes correctly.

'To cheer you on? Or aren't you going to race with us?' Barnes turned and sniffed. 'Are you too refined for that kind of carry on?'

'By your standards, the porter's a lord,' Evie said. 'Grace doesn't have to run if she doesn't want to, it doesn't make her stuck up.'

'My Terry's coming,' Barnes said. 'He might be a bit late, though, because it's all the way from Broadstairs.'

'Goodness,' Evie said, her voice dry. 'He is keen.'

'And why wouldn't he be?' Barnes said, her face turning even redder than usual.

'No reason at all,' Grace said, trying to diffuse the row before it got the attention of the assistant matron, who was delicately dissecting a boiled egg at the next table.

'I haven't anyone coming,' Evie announced. 'I didn't tell the ancestors, couldn't abide the fuss.'

'I didn't realise we could invite civilians,' Grace said.

'What on earth do you mean?' Barnes said, not looking mollified in the slightest.

'You know, people who don't belong to the hospital.'

'So, you haven't anyone coming either?' Evie said. 'That's good, we can keep each other company.'

Grace thought about her parents and wondered whether she would've invited them, had she realised it was a possibility. She pictured her mother with a napkin tucked neatly at her neck, eating her dinner as fastidiously as the assistant matron. *Perhaps not.* The fact was, she didn't miss her mother any more. She no longer felt homesick, no longer pressed her face into her pillow at night to stifle the sound of her tears. Her life as Grace Kemp, only daughter of Mr and Mrs Harold Kemp, seemed very far away. Almost as if it belonged to somebody else. It was a blessed relief.

'Haven't you got one of your men coming to see you?' Barnes said to Evie, her tone just shy of nasty.

'And see me puffing along the field in my gym shorts? No fear.' Evie gave a theatrical shudder that made Grace smile. She was glad Robert wasn't going to be there. Glad it would be just the girls.

Barnes pushed her chair back and stood up. 'Some of us have got work to do.'

As she turned and walked away, Grace glimpsed something on what Sister Bennett would've referred to as Barnes's 'lumbar area'. A black shadow. She closed her eyes, willing it to be a trick of the light. When she opened them again, Barnes was disappearing through the door, but the shadow shape was still there, like a hole in her back.

'Are those eggs off?' Evie said, nodding at Grace's plate.

She shook her head and pushed her plate towards Evie.

'Don't mind if I do.' Evie loaded her fork with scrambled egg and then paused with it halfway to her mouth. 'You've gone a queer colour.'

'I'm fine,' Grace managed. She stood up and followed Barnes but changed her mind halfway down the corridor. What could she say? 'I've seen a shadow and I think you might be ill.' No. She would simply pretend she hadn't seen it; that would be for the best.

She reversed direction and went to her bedroom to add an extra hairgrip to her cap, which was already slipping. Barnes was waiting outside. 'I wanted to catch you,' she said, looking nervous.

Irrationally, Grace assumed that she somehow knew about the shadow and was going to ask about it so she was doubly surprised when Barnes said, in a rush: 'Don't let Evie laugh at my Terry, will you? He's awfully shy.'

'Why would she laugh?'

'Oh, you know what she's like,' Barnes said.

Grace was going to say 'no' out of loyalty, but honesty compelled her to change the subject instead. 'Are you feeling quite all right?'

'He's not a handsome man,' Barnes said defiantly. 'I don't care about that sort of thing but some people do.' She sniffed, significantly, clearly referring to Evie.

'Who cares what anybody else thinks?' Grace said, trying to work out whether Barnes looked paler than usual or had any obvious signs of poorliness. She'd eaten well at breakfast, so her appetite hadn't altered and she didn't seem especially weak or feeble.

'Well,' Barnes said, 'I've got to get on.'

Grace went into her room to fetch her grips, rather than watch Barnes walk away. What was the point in seeing shadows if you couldn't do anything about them? The familiar feeling of helplessness wrapped around her and squeezed tight.

MINA

I was playing rummy with Parveen when a woman in uniform arrived. The first police officer had been in plain clothes, which I assumed meant a higher rank. I wondered if that meant the accident had been downgraded in importance or whether it meant nothing at all.

'Sorry to interrupt,' she said, smiling. 'My name is PC Coleman and I'm from the Sussex Collision Investigation Unit. There's a bit of follow-up to do on your case.'

I sat up straighter and Parveen began collecting the cards.

'Got a few blanks to fill in, still. I believe you were suffering from amnesia when my colleague visited you last. Is that correct?'

'Yes,' I said.

'Is there anything you can add to your statement, now?' The officer flipped open a notebook.

'I still don't remember the accident,' I said, feeling like a bad pupil, a failure. 'I don't know what happened.'

The constable nodded. Her expression stayed neutral and I couldn't tell whether she believed me or not. 'It's clear from examination of the scene that you veered sharply to the right while travelling at speed. If we discount a deliberate act, this suggests a loss of control of the vehicle. Your blood tests were clear.'

'Deliberate?' I said.

'You tested negative for controlled substances and your alcohol level was almost zero.'

'Right,' I said. 'I don't do drugs and I would never drive drunk. Never.'

The officer's mouth twisted a bit. 'I thought you had amnesia. How do you know what you would or wouldn't do?'

'That's not how post-traumatic memory loss works,' Parveen said, her voice sharp.

'I'm not a doctor, obviously,' Coleman said. 'Do you have a history of fainting or blackouts? Epilepsy?'

'No,' I said. I was pretty sure I was telling the truth. Ghost-birds didn't count. They didn't obscure my vision, couldn't make me crash a vehicle. At least, I didn't think so.

'Do you remember anything about the journey before the crash? Do you remember where you were going? It was almost two o'clock in the morning, not a usual time to be on the road.'

I shook my head, keeping my lips firmly closed. She was watching me carefully. 'Are you sure there's nothing you can tell me about that night? It's important that I get all the details down so that I can finish the report. You don't want any hold up with that, it could affect your insurance.'

'Isn't there CCTV footage?' Parveen said, standing up. 'I thought Britain was ninety-nine per cent covered by surveillance these days. You should be looking through that, not hassling someone who is in hospital.'

Parveen put emphasis on the last word but the officer didn't seem perturbed. 'Not on that particular stretch of the road,' she said. 'We do have footage of your car travelling at fifty-six miles per hour at an earlier point in your journey.'

'That's inside the speed limit,' I said, more relieved than I cared to admit.

'You're not being accused of anything here,' Coleman said, more gently than she had spoken before. Her eyes flickered to Parveen, who was standing up, her arms crossed. 'Our department is just concerned with working out the exact sequence of events. There might be information which is in the public interest, something that can help us to improve the safety of our roads.'

'But I can't remember,' I said, my throat closing up.

She pursed her lips a little, but I didn't know if she was frustrated by my lack of cooperation or worried that I was beginning to sound upset. 'I've spoken to Dr Kanthe and she assures me that long-term memory loss is unlikely. At some point this is going to come back to you and, when it does, I need you to give me a call.' She put a business card on to the bed.

'I didn't hurt anyone?' I couldn't shake the feeling that there was something they hadn't told me, something I was missing.

'No.' She looked confused. 'Just yourself.'

'Thank God. Thank God.' My chest had tightened up along with my throat and my thoughts were coming in staccato bursts. I heard my voice say 'Thank God' again and I pressed my lips together to force myself to stop babbling.

Parveen moved back and put an arm around my shoulders. 'You're upsetting her,' she said. 'She's answered your questions and I think you should leave.'

PC Coleman put her notebook away and gave a fake smile, which went nowhere near her eyes. 'Get well soon.'

'Bloody hell,' Parveen said as soon as the officer had gone. 'That was intense.'

'Thank you,' I managed. My chest was hurting and I couldn't take a full breath. 'I don't like thinking about it. Trying to think about it. I know I have to, but I don't want to.'

'It was an accident,' Parveen said. 'You didn't do anything wrong.'

I didn't know that, of course, and neither did she. It was nice of her to try, though. 'What if I didn't do something I was supposed to do, though; what if I was distracted? In a car you can kill someone because you didn't put your foot on the brake or turn the wheel at the right time. Not taking action can be just as bad as doing something.'

'But you didn't kill anyone. You only hurt yourself.'

I knew Parveen was right, but I didn't feel it. The guilt was weighing on my chest, crushing me, and I couldn't breathe. For a moment I felt a strap pulling across my shoulder. It was the sensation of a seatbelt, like I was in a car. Blackness came in from the edges, swift and sure. My mind shutting down the memory before it could take hold.

Parveen's arm was still around my shoulders; she gave me a squeeze and then got up to pour some water into a cup. 'Drink.'

After a few sips, I felt my heart rate begin to slow, the blackness receded and I came back to the moment. That was when I noticed that Parveen looked tense, her hands shaking. 'Are you all right?'

'Just the adrenaline. I hate confrontation.'

'You were amazing with her. Like a guard dog.'

'Cheers,' Parveen said, pulling a face.

'Not a dog. Something more flattering. A guardian angel.'

Parveen smiled weakly. 'Yeah, but . . . the police. You just get that instant sense of guilt. Like you've done something wrong even when you know you haven't.'

I let my head fall back on to the pillow and closed my eyes for a moment. 'I'm just so relieved I didn't hurt anybody. Mark said—' I broke off. If I repeated what he'd said it wouldn't sound good. It might sound like he'd been trying to make me feel bad. Parveen wouldn't understand that he was just freaking out.

Her expression closed down at the mention of his name. Now that memories from my life before were coming back, I knew that I'd thought she was very quiet and meek, almost unemotional. I didn't know, now, how I could ever have thought that. Everything she felt was written on her face.

'What?' she said.

'Just thinking about before. I wish we'd been friends earlier.'

Parveen smiled, as if to take the sting out of her words. 'You weren't very interested then.'

'Sorry,' I said. 'Was I really awful?'

'Not awful,' Parveen said. 'A bit scary.'

'I was not scary. Pat is scary,' I said, affronted. 'Self-possessed.'

'Closed off,' Parveen said. 'Aloof.' She stopped smiling. 'Actually, you really didn't seem very well. I kept wanting to ask you if you were all right but then—'

'I was scary and aloof,' I finished for her.

Parveen made a finger gun and shot me. 'Exactly. And then there was Mark, which was awkward. Especially since I wasn't supposed to have noticed that you two were getting hot and heavy in the stationery cupboard.'

'We did not!'

Parveen paused, smiling wickedly, and then she shrugged, letting me off the hook. 'I have no idea.'

'You shouldn't tease the amnesia patient,' I said, but I couldn't stop smiling.

❧

After the let down of the garden, I decided to explore the hospital in a more random fashion. If I wasn't setting my heart on a particular destination, then I couldn't be disappointed. I was practical, too; trips to the vending machine on the floor below meant chocolate, and salt and vinegar crisps. I gained strength by walking up and down the hallways closest to my ward, gradually increasing the distance, hour by hour, day by day.

The Viking took me for hydrotherapy sessions in the pool and was thrilled with my progress. It brought my release date ever closer and every time my back screamed at me, or my knee threatened to buckle, I reminded myself that this was my way out.

One of my forays took me past the hospital chapel. I hesitated outside the door for a moment, feeling a strange pull to go inside. Then I had one of my now-familiar conversations with myself. Was I religious? Was the fact that I was a person of faith another facet of my personality that I'd lost in the accident?

As I dithered, looking at the posters of doves and messages of hope that were pinned alongside the entrance, I realised that the feeling of connection I had experienced was just a jolt of recognition. I realised, in the way that every fact seemed to come back to me, in the manner of something always known and simply not acknowledged, that wild horses couldn't drag me into a place of worship.

I remembered, too, that Pat hadn't been brought up as Catholic, but had converted when she'd married Dylan. She had embraced Catholicism with the fervour of an ex-pat living abroad. While Dylan was lackadaisical about his faith, Pat acted as if the pope himself was planning a surprise visit to check up on us.

I leaned against the wall, my head brushing the 'God loves you' poster, and saw, instead of the blank beige wall opposite, the picture of Jesus that hung in our hallway. His slim handsome face and soft brown eyes. They were almost coquettish, inviting.

Pat wanted images of Mary around the place, but Geraint had argued with her. He'd fully embraced his position as black sheep by then and seemed actively to enjoy winding her up. Sometimes it was really funny, like the time Geraint said a picture of Jesus was beautiful and that he quite fancied the Son of God. Later that night, we couldn't stop reliving the moment Pat's face had gone purple as she'd tried to formulate a response. We argued over whether it was the suggestion of man-on-man attraction or casual blasphemy that had enraged her more. Once he'd obtained such a good reaction, Geraint couldn't resist baiting Pat. 'You'll go to hell for an eternity of pain and suffering,' she'd warn. 'Tell him,' she'd say to Dylan. She was always appealing to her husband in these matters. In nothing else, of course, but in these matters he was the original Catholic so she deferred to him. At first, at least. His moderate nature and quiet faith weren't enough and she'd end up talking instead. Ranting about sin and demanding that Geraint say the rosary with her.

Our church was Our Lady, Star of the Sea. Most of the people in the village were either agnostic or quietly Church of Wales. Protestant. Pat said we were doubly persecuted, historically speaking, both Welsh and Catholic. A double-whammy.

Leaning against the wall, my body hurting and my mind following each new memory hungrily, hoping the trail wouldn't end, I knew that the religious side to my upbringing had seeped into my soul. I wanted to ask God for help. I wanted to make a bargain with the deity I didn't even believe in. 'If you make my mind work properly again, if you bring back my memories,' I said silently, 'I'll do Good Works.'

I waited a moment, just to see if Dr Adams was right and I really was a miracle.

Pat said that life was about suffering. Or guilt over not suffering enough. Or not being good enough in the face of suffering. When your bedtime stories are of saints, you're royally screwed. How are you supposed to measure up to poor Lucy, patron saint of the blind, with her eyes on a plate? And, most annoying of all, I still felt the pull of those teachings. I still felt like a sinner, who was being right-eously punished.

ୡୄ

In stories about twins one is good and one is evil. Like lots of siblings, Ger and I had our labels early on. I was the good child and he was the naughty one. Ger was the child who couldn't stay neat and tidy for Sunday school. In fact, Ger was the child who couldn't even stay in Sunday school. The terrifying lady who ran it made him sit outside in the vestibule more often than she let him stay in the main hall. I would bend my head studiously over my colouring, shading in the basket with baby Moses or the donkey that carried Mary, feeling the stone in my gut that said Ger was in trouble again and was going to catch it from Pat when we got home. Worse than that, though, was the sense of disappointment in myself. If only I were braver, I could be out in the vestibule with Geraint and we'd be having fun. Instead I was trying to colour with stupid broken crayons. I didn't want to complete a picture neatly for the horrible teacher but I was too scared not to do so, and I hated myself for my cowardice and compliance.

Ger was the one who didn't do his work in primary school when he couldn't see the point of copying out words to practise handwrit-ing or learning phonetics when he'd been able to read since he was three. By the time we were both at the local comp, he was bored and rebellious and hardly ever turned up for lessons. I was even better, as if to make up for it. I don't remember him ever holding it against me, although the comparisons must've worn thin.

When the kids in the top year began picking on me, Ger set his jaw. I told him not to worry, that it wasn't anything I couldn't handle. Truth was, I didn't expect it to escalate. I was a girl. I didn't believe for a second that they would really do anything to me. All the trouble I'd seen was of two varieties: girls being mean to each other (with the occasional face slap or hair tug) and boys all-out fighting. Throwing punches and rolling around in the playground until a teacher broke it up. So when Justin and his fellow knuckle-draggers cornered me on the way to the buses after school, I was nervous but not properly frightened. I didn't know that I should've run. I thought I should take the advice of every grown up I'd ever heard on the subject and stand up to them. It hurts to think about it now. How close to disaster I came. Three large boy-men. Six-teen-year-olds with impressive acne and wide shoulders and newly developed jaws. One, unpopular even in this subset of society, was lookout.

I knew this was, in some way, about Ger. I flew under the radar at school and there wasn't much about me that seemed to offend anybody or garner attention. This group, though, hated Geraint and, when we'd first started at the comp, they'd bullied him. The last couple of years things had died down and I assumed they'd grown bored, or Ger had done the magic 'standing up' and they'd backed off.

Now Justin was standing far too close to me. I felt the first proper wave of fear as the smell of Lynx deodorant and testosterone hit my nostrils. The other guy, I didn't know his name, had moved behind me without me noticing and suddenly he grabbed my arms. He pulled them behind my back, jerking them from the sockets and making me yelp. I knew that there were tears in my eyes and I couldn't wipe them away. I felt exposed and the first tendrils of real fear wound their way around my body.

Justin leaned in; he had his head tilted like he was consider-ing something. I thought he was going to hit me, knew in some primeval part of my brain that that was what he had intended. In that moment, though, he changed his mind. I saw it. His intention shifted. Instead of smacking me in the mouth, his hands came up and began kneading my chest through my school jumper and shirt. It hurt, but I turned my face to the side and took shallow breaths through my mouth, trying not to panic, trying to seem unbothered. Like I could pretend this was a minor inconvenience and that would, somehow, make it less humiliating.

My twisted arms really hurt but when the pressure eased a little it was worse, because whoever was behind me was pushing me forwards, making me bend a little at the waist so that my chest was falling into Justin's horrible meaty hands and the guy behind me was pressing against my back. I felt something lumpy and hard against my backside and I realised what it was with a rush of pure embarrassment. That's what I remember most. Feeling ashamed and embarrassed. More so, even, than frightened. I don't think I fully realised the danger I was in. I thought Justin would eventually stop gripping my breasts like they were handholds on a climbing wall and he and his mates would saunter off. Part of me was even a little bit relieved that they weren't going to hit me. It was mortifying, but I'd been groped in the school hallways before and, once, on the bus by an old guy with a tent in his trousers, so it wasn't too much of a shock.

That's when I felt the hand on my thigh. Justin had stepped in really close now. He had his head bent towards my neck and I thought he was going to try and kiss me, which was a whole other level of weird. Instead he said, loud enough for the other guy to hear, 'Let's shag Ger's sister.'

The hand was pulling my skirt up and the shot of terror I felt then made me almost throw up. I started struggling, ignoring the pain in my arms, but I could hear the guy behind me laughing a little. He was breathing heavily and I felt him grip both of my wrists in one hand. He needed a hand free. I went completely cold. What if he needed a hand free to undo his fly?

I don't know whether Geraint knew I was in trouble or whether it was pure luck that he walked to the bus stands that way. We never talked about it. In fact, I don't even know if I ever thanked him.

I just remember seeing him appear around the corner. I was bathed, instantly, in a potent mixture of relief and terror. I didn't want Justin and his pals to turn on Geraint. It was three of them against one and I didn't want Ger to get hurt. But, Christ on a bike, I was glad to see him. My saviour.

The one who was on lookout duty took off running as soon as he saw Ger. He was that type, cowardly, and maybe things had gone further than he'd expected, and he was glad of the excuse to get away. I could easily imagine boys signing up to harass Ger's sister, to give her a little scare, but it was harder to believe they'd all signed up to do something so serious.

Ger wasn't distracted, he came bowling towards Justin. I'd seen Ger angry plenty of times. I'd seen him lose it when drunk. I'd seen him raging in his own room, punching and kicking the walls until his knuckles bled and there were holes in the plasterboard. I'd never seen him like this, though. It was another level of fury. I guessed the guy behind me hadn't either, because he let go of me instantly and had his hands in the air. 'We were just messing,' I heard him say. I'll never forget his voice. He sounded much younger than I expected and I felt a fresh rush of guilt for falling victim to such an unlikely attacker.

Ger was punching Justin. He got him a couple of times in the face before Justin got one back on Ger. A blow that sent him staggering before, fuelled by fury, he was back. Justin's nose was bleeding, then his lip, then a split opened on his cheek. I had gone from relief to terror all over again. I wanted Geraint to win, of course, but I didn't want him to get hurt, then or later when there were reprisals. His eyes were mindless with fury and I didn't want him to go so far that he actually killed someone and ended up in jail for life.

Fear. Then more fear and guilt. Worry and exasperation. Guilt and fear. And love. Don't forget love.

GRACE

There was a precious slice of time in the morning. Just before the rush of all the other girls but not so early that you felt like death warmed up before lunch. Well, that wasn't entirely true. Grace had never been a morning person and getting up before five was never anything less than painful, both at the time and at four o'clock in the afternoon when she was reliably struck down by a wave of black tiredness so powerful it threatened to drag her under.

Still, once a fortnight or so, Grace forced herself to get up before the morning nurse shook her awake. The shared bathrooms were blissfully empty and quiet. She could shower in water that was actually hot and not have to talk to anybody.

It was Evie, of course, who had let her in on the secret, but she was slumbering peacefully, her lavender silk eye mask perched on her face. Grace picked up her towel and wash bag and tiptoed down the corridor. This morning the bathrooms were not completely deserted. Sister Bennett was washing her face in the sink and it was peculiar to see her doing something so intimate. She caught Grace looking and said, mildly enough, 'My plumbing has gone funny.'

Grace bit her lip to keep herself from smiling.

Sister Bennett wore a plaid dressing gown and pink slippers. It was like seeing your father in his underpants. This random thought immediately quashed the urge to smile.

Sister Bennett patted her face dry with a towel and then, drawing herself up to her full height, said: 'Cleanliness is next to Godliness, Nurse.'

'Yes, Sister,' Grace said. She wondered if she was in for a lecture now. She could feel her precious minutes creeping away.

Sister Bennett was full of aphorisms. If she caught you buttering the bread in a manner she considered sloppy, she'd say, 'Make in haste, repent at leisure.' If, thinking you were alone, you dared to increase from a fast walk to a pace that verged recklessly on a slow run, she'd pop up from nowhere and yell: 'Running is for horses. Are you a horse, Nurse?' Privately, Grace longed to neigh loudly but, instead, she stopped, apologised and generally made herself late for whatever appointment or task she was hurrying towards.

With a final, disapproving glare that took in every inch of Grace's being from the top of her head to the ground beneath her toes, Sister Bennett swept out of the bathroom.

Grace nipped into the first cubicle and showered quickly in the blissfully hot water. Stepping out, into a room shrouded in water vapour, she caught sight of something pale moving in the mirror. She felt a moment of fear before realising it was her own reflection. She turned slowly from side to side, looking at her naked self in profile and front-on. It felt safe with the room all steamed up and, for once, she didn't reach for her combination right away. She felt as if she was becoming, being made, in the mirror. That was her image, that was her body, but as it turned in the glass Grace began to feel afraid. A silly thought crept across her mind that if she stopped turning the figure in the mirror would keep moving.

Left side, right side, left side, right. Then, on the last turn, she pivoted a little more and caught a glimpse of her back. It was just a flash, over so quickly that Grace wasn't entirely sure she'd really seen it. Was it even possible to see your own back? Was her mind playing tricks on her? Perhaps the tiredness had truly sent her around the bend. Deep down, though, she knew: there was a black shadow. She'd seen it. A ragged-edged starburst, so dark and terrible that it stopped Grace's breath.

MINA

There was a precious slice of time early in the morning, when the ward was relatively quiet and I could read in peace. I picked up the history book. It was like a comfort blanket to me, even though I'd given up hope of ever finding my nurse within its pages. And then, as I flicked through, just trying to stop my mind from following Geraint, I found her. I was looking at a picture of an iron lung – the poor kid trapped inside the thing had a mirror above his face, angled so that he could see some of the room, rather than just staring at the ceiling. I had been so captivated by the horrifying image that it took me a moment to realise that I recognised the nurse standing next to him. She was holding a toy train, as if the photograph had been taken in the middle of a game, and it was my nurse. Grace, if my dream could be believed. For a moment, I couldn't breathe. She was real.

The caption underneath the photograph read: 'The Royal Sussex's first life-saving iron lung, donated by philanthropist Lord Nuffield'.

No mention of the patient or the nurse, they were just set dressing for the enormous machine. A metal box, not entirely dissimilar to the scanners I used every day at work. Frightening to the patient, vital to the scientist, fascinating to all. It was definitely her, though. That oval face, so serene and pretty. Like a figure from a pre-Raphaelite painting.

I held the book up to my face and studied the picture. The way her fingers curled around the toy train, the expression on her face as she looked at the boy. His lips were slightly parted as if he was saying something and I had a fierce longing to know what they were talking about. I felt happy for him, though. If you were going to have polio and end up in an artificial respirator, then she was undoubtedly the nurse to have by your side.

I wondered whether the little boy in the picture had made a full recovery or whether he'd become one of the tragic polio statistics. I couldn't imagine anything worse that being trapped inside a machine like that for your last living moments. I tried to imagine lying on my back, my body encased in metal, being spoon-fed or having my face washed.

My stomach lurched dramatically and I felt, for a moment, as if I was falling. Then I was inside a different metal box. There was broken glass everywhere and bright lights were making it sparkle. A strap across my shoulder and waist pinned me tightly. I couldn't move. There was something viscous and warm running down my face and when I tried to open my eyes, I couldn't. My eyelashes were stuck together. I knew something really bad had happened. I knew I was hurt. I couldn't feel the pain but I had a dreadful, cold feeling inside and the words 'this is bad' running, unhelpfully, on a loop through my brain.

It was the accident. I was remembering being in the car. The little lift of excitement I got from remembering something was tempered by a wave of sickness. I had been so scared. Thinking had been like forcing my way through concrete, every disjointed realisation a marathon.

I forced myself back into the memory and breathed deeply to control the remembered panic. I couldn't see anything but I knew I was in the car. The windscreen must've been shattered because I could feel the night air on my skin and there was lots of noise. I could hear traffic moving on the wet road and bright lights were shining red through my closed eyelids. There had been a movement by my left hip. I felt my clothes shifting as if a small animal was burrowing underneath them, which didn't make any sense, and then I realised that something was being lifted from my jacket pocket. I wanted to speak but I couldn't make my mouth open or sound emerge. I might have moaned, but there was a shifting from beside me. Someone was moving and the passenger door opened and then slammed shut.

'I remembered something,' I said as soon as Mark arrived that evening. I had been desperate to tell him and couldn't keep it in for another second. Okay, that was a lie. I really wanted to tell Stephen, it felt like a victory for his medical skills, but I hadn't seen him all day. 'That's great,' Mark said. He kissed me on the cheek. 'I hope it's our first date, that was a cracker.'

I was momentarily derailed. The words 'first date' did bring back a memory. More and more, memories were coming back. Doors opening that I could simply step through. I remembered meeting Mark at work, and I knew that we'd had an ill-advised one- night fling after a couple of drinks, but that he'd refused to accept that it wasn't something more serious. I'd woken up the morning after our night together feeling faintly ridiculous, but he'd been in full romance mode, going out to buy breakfast and the papers and phoning me later that day to say how wonderful it had been. I remember that he'd kept on asking me out for dinner and that I'd agreed, finally, as a kind of salute to his persistence.

'I do,' I said, 'but that's not what I wanted to tell you. I remember being in the car.'

Mark had only just sat down, but he jumped up. 'Do you want a coffee? I need a coffee.'

'Did you hear what I said? I remember—'

'Not everything is about you, Mina,' Mark said. 'I didn't sleep well and I've had a very trying day and I need some coffee.' He walked away.

I was halfway through the laborious job of getting myself out of bed in order to follow him, when he returned, looking conciliatory. He had two paper cups and he put them on the bedside cabinet and swung my legs back on to the bed. My back screamed but I knew he was trying to be helpful so I didn't say anything. He must have seen my grimace, though, as he said 'sorry' a bit gruffly and plumped my pillows.

'Someone was there,' I said, not able to keep it inside any more.

'At the scene? Of course. The ambulance people. And the police. You had everyone up and out of their warm beds, I'm just glad you didn't hurt anybody.'

Guilt slammed me again. What if I'd been driving recklessly? I knew that I hadn't been over the limit with alcohol or drugs, but I might have been upset. An electric charge shot through me and another door opened: I *had* been upset. There wasn't any information to go with the realisation, but the feeling was true.

'Someone was next to me. But they left,' I said, trying to keep hold of my thoughts, trying to get back the clarity I'd felt when I'd remembered. 'The door shut. Not my door, the passenger door.'

Mark took a sip of his coffee and pulled a face. 'Disgusting.'

'You don't seem very interested.' Annoyance cut through my confusion. I didn't understand why he didn't care. I felt like I'd made a major breakthrough. I thought he'd be pleased.

'You're very jumbled still,' Mark said, shaking his head. 'You think you heard something but the car doors would have been opened by the emergency services, not to mention all the other vehicles nearby.'

'No, there was definitely someone there. In the car. I think they went through my pockets. Could some opportunistic bastard have robbed me?' The idea that someone had taken advantage while I sat there, halfway unconscious, bleeding and vulnerable, was like a punch in the stomach. 'That's awful. How could someone do that?'

'I think you probably had all kinds of strange dreams. You hit your head really hard. The doctors think you were unconscious, don't they? You can't remember being in the car. It's just not possible. I know you want to get your mind back, but you mustn't latch on to fantasy and dreams. You'll never get better if you give in to that.' He patted my hand. 'You've got to stay strong. You've got to stick with the facts.'

'But what if someone was there? Shouldn't I tell the police? If there was a witness, shouldn't the police speak to them?'

'You're not listening to me,' Mark said, his voice steely calm. 'You were driving alone and you crashed your car. Nobody stopped by to nick things from you. You said it yourself – what kind of person would do that? You're being paranoid.'

Paranoid. 'But—'

'Can we please talk about something else?' Mark's voice had an edge to it that made the hairs on my arms stand up. 'I've had a fucking awful day and I was looking forward to spending time with my girlfriend, not rehashing this all over again. I'd rather not think about that terrible accident, I'd rather look to the future.'

Mark ran a hand through his hair. He looked pale and tired and I felt a stab of guilt. 'Of course,' I said. 'Tell me about your day.'

He patted my hand and I resisted the urge to snatch it away. I took a sip from the coffee instead. It really was disgusting.

229

Mark began a blow-by-blow account of his day's meetings and I tried to pay attention. The word 'paranoid' kept repeating in my mind, though, and I couldn't make it stop.

After Mark had left and I was alone, I still couldn't get the word 'paranoid' out of my head. I missed Geraint so much. I had been worried about him, I'd been upset about my memory loss, and I'd been frightened, but now I just felt homesick. I wanted my brother. I wanted him to sling an arm around my shoulders and make me laugh. I wanted him to tell me what I should do about Mark, too.

I had a strong feeling that Mark knew something about the accident. Maybe, even, that he was the figure I remembered being in the car. His reaction had cemented this suspicion and, although I assumed he would have a sensible explanation for it, I still felt cast adrift.

I picked up my phone, thinking that I could try calling Geraint again. The sensation of the phone against my face brought something back – listening to a message on my landline phone. Suddenly I could see my flat clearly and the little table where I kept the telephone. The base unit was showing the steady red light of a saved message and it was achingly familiar. I knew that I'd pressed the button to listen to that message over and over, until every syllable and breath was scored deeply across my mind.

Geraint's voice: 'Mina? You've got to call me back. Right now. Or, like, five minutes ago—'

I dropped my mobile and it slipped off the bed, clattering on the floor. Geraint's voice continued, though, as distinct and clear as if it was happening now, not playing from my memory.

Why had I memorised that message?

I didn't want to know.

Why had I listened to it over and over again?

I didn't want to know.

I remembered plugging in my answer machine in the new flat and seeing the saved message light. The unit had a back-up battery, which had preserved the memory during the journey from London to Brighton. I remembered the feelings of relief and misery that had rushed through me. The little red light signalling so much pain and guilt and anger. Part of me had hoped the battery would fail, that the message would disappear into the ether, but I should have known that I didn't deserve any respite.

I didn't want to remember these things.

The door had opened and all I had to do was to walk through. Geraint was waiting for me on the other side, I was sure of it, but for some reason I didn't want to join him.

GRACE

race was rushing to fold and pin her cap and, as usual, it was
being obstinately uncooperative. She was thinking about one of
her patients and wondering how he'd spent the night so didn't
hear Evie the first time she spoke. 'Sorry. Miles away.'

'Thomas asked me to give you this.' Evie was holding out a
book. It was a hardback copy of *A Room with a View*. Bound in red
cloth with gold lettering on the spine. 'He said you'd mentioned
that you never had time to get to the library.'

'He shouldn't have bothered.' Grace turned away from Evie and
the beautiful book.

'Aren't you an ice maiden?' Evie said, approval in her voice.
'You're not as daft as you pretend.'

'It's not a game,' Grace said, more crossly than she intended.
'He ought to know better. If the sister sees that she'll have me on
the rug.'

'I hardly think she'll report you for reading,' Evie said. 'Although,
she is a peculiar one, so who knows?'

'I don't think it's worth the trouble,' Grace said. And she
didn't just mean the book. She couldn't stop thinking about the

black shadow. She could almost feel it sitting on her back, biding its time. It was a constant reminder that happiness was not hers to take, that everything she held dear could come crashing down at any moment.

Evie nudged her to one side, to get a spot in front of the mirror. 'Robert says that life isn't worth living without a little risk.' She bared her teeth and ran a tongue over them, like a cat.

Grace turned away from the mirror. Taking risks was a luxury she couldn't afford.

ᘖᘙ

As if to prove her philosophy, the ward was in a state of chaos when she arrived on duty. The ward sister shook her head as she hurried past. 'Barnes has gone and sprained her ankle. Just what I need.'

With one pair of hands short, the day flew by in a blur of activity. Grace rushed from one task to the next and didn't have a moment to think about mysterious shadows and fate.

As soon as her shift ended, she went to visit Barnes, who was sitting up in bed with her textbook on her lap.

'Oh, it's you,' she said, and slipped a magazine out from underneath the covers. 'Sister said I had to study if I was going to be lying around all day like Lady Muck.'

Grace felt the knot in her chest loosen a little. Barnes was her usual healthy colour, her usual cheerful self. 'Are you comfortable?' Grace reached for the pillows. Barnes leaned forward obligingly and Grace took the opportunity to check her back. No shadow. It had gone. She sat down heavily on the bed.

'Oof, watch out!' Barnes said, shifting her legs.

'You're all right,' Grace said. 'You're not dying.' Barnes wasn't terminally ill. The worry that it was Madame Clara happening all over again flew away.

'Bloomin' feels like it, I can tell you. Have you ever had a sprained ankle? It hurts something terrible. And I won't be able to run on sports day.'

'Yes, but—' Grace hesitated. She couldn't explain her urge to smile, to grab Barnes in a hug and dance her around the room. Not without seeming doolally, at any rate. Seeing a shadow wasn't a death sentence. It might just mean a little mishap. Grace didn't mind a sprained ankle, wouldn't mind sitting out of the races on sports day or not being able to play table tennis for a few weeks. She kissed Barnes on one rosy cheek. 'I'm just glad you didn't really hurt yourself.'

'Weren't you listening?' Barnes said, clearly offended. 'I've never felt anything like it. Red hot poker right in my bones it is.'

'Which bone?' Grace said, tapping the textbook. 'Sister Bennett is bound to ask.'

'Too true,' Barnes said, catching on. 'I'd better check.'

'Talus,' Grace said, standing up. 'But it's your ligaments you've damaged. Probably your anterior tibiofibular ligament to be precise.'

'Swot,' Barnes said, mildly enough, and turned her attention to her magazine.

Grace said goodnight and went to find Evie in the smoking room. Perhaps she might read that book from Thomas after all.

MINA

I got the card that the police officer had left and looked at it for a while, trying to decide what to do. If I called her with my memory of the car door closing, what would it really achieve? Except for a massive fight with Mark.

'Hello, you,' Stephen said, walking into the room. He brought the scent of outside with him and I breathed in deeply, resisting the urge to lean closer and get a proper lungful.

I was grateful for the distraction and slipped the card between the pages of the paperback on my lap.

'How are you feeling?'

The crease of concern between his eyebrows reminded me that the last time he'd seen me I'd done an impression of a delicate fainting Victorian lady and that Mark had been a massive knob. I tried to sound extra hearty when I replied, 'Good. Yes, thanks. How are you?'

He lifted his chin. 'No visitors today?'

'Mark will be in later,' I said.

'Ah.' Stephen looked away. 'I guess I shouldn't be here.'

'It's all right with me,' I said. 'And Mark is just a bit overprotective. I'm sorry about the way he was with you.'

'You've got nothing to apologise for,' Stephen said. His cheeks were quite pink and I wanted to reach out and squeeze his hand, show him that we were okay.

'How are things?' I said, trying to ease the tension. I was surprised by how badly I wanted to do that.

Stephen had folded his frame into a chair and was looking too intently at my face, as if trying to diagnose me.

'I heard you had a visit from the police. Did they have anything new to say?'

So many things were coming back to me now, and I remembered that I had kept everything in my life strictly separate. It felt strange to have every part of it laid open. I reminded myself that Stephen was a friend and that it wasn't a secret the police officer had visited me. 'How do you know that?' I asked.

Stephen smiled. 'Parveen told me.'

'You two talk? About me?'

'A bit,' he said. 'We bump into each other in the corridor sometimes and you're really all we have in common.'

'Oh,' I said. The thought of Parveen and Stephen talking about me, about my progress or health or whatever, wasn't as awful as I'd expected. The me from before the accident would have hated it so much she would have wanted to punch something. The post-coma me felt a glow of comfort, with just the tiniest touch of anxious nausea. Interesting.

'Nothing new,' I said. 'They've appealed for witnesses but no one has come forward and it wasn't on camera. I don't think it's high priority, and hopefully my insurance will cough up for any damage.' I swallowed, trying not to think about the wreckage, the things that could've happened. 'Thank God the road was empty.'

'It wasn't your fault,' Stephen said.

I didn't want to talk about the accident. The stuff that was coming back to me – stuff about my life and my family – was overwhelming enough. 'I'm remembering lots more,' I said. 'I remember you from before.'

He tilted his head. 'Had we met?'

'No,' I said, smiling at the memory. 'But I checked you out at the Black Dove.'

'At the Christmas drinks thing?' He smiled as if remembering a private joke. 'I love that bar.'

'Me, too,' I said, delighted by both the clear memory and the connection. 'I was going to introduce myself.'

'I wish you had,' Stephen said with feeling.

That was the night I'd got so drunk I'd ended up in bed with Mark. The one-night stand which hadn't ended the morning after, the way it was supposed to. 'Anyway, I wanted to thank you for keeping me company in here.'

The crease came back but Stephen's tone was light: 'That sounds suspiciously like a goodbye speech.'

'Things are going to be different when I get out. I'll be living in this place for starters.' I indicated the estate agent's details, which were resting on the bedside cabinet.

'Here?' He picked them up and whistled. 'Very nice.'

'Mark's organised it all. I'm lucky.'

Stephen picked up my mobile and began tapping. 'Just putting my number in. Home and mobile.' He paused and looked me straight in the eye. 'You're not alone, you know.'

I laughed to try and diffuse the seriousness of his tone. 'I know. I'm going to be with Mark and Pat's coming to look after me for a few days.' I pulled a face, trying to ignore the sudden tightness in my chest. 'I tried to put her off, but she's determined.'

'That's nice, though. Right?'

'You don't know Pat. She'll organise me until I don't know whether I'm coming or going.'

'She loves you, that's all.' I marvelled at the easy way he used the word. I knew he was right, though. I had thought that Pat was angry, disappointed in me for fucking up again, but her expression when she had visited had been one of relief. I had seen the worry etched on her face, and felt the force of her care in a way I'd never acknowledged before. 'Give me your phone,' I said. 'Fair's fair.'

I navigated to his contacts and put in my number and the address of Mark's house. My new house. I felt sick but I told myself I would just have to get used to it. I needed help and I was lucky to have Mark. We chatted a bit longer, but Stephen kept glancing at the door.

'Do you have somewhere to be?' I finally asked.

He looked away. 'I don't particularly want another scene.'

I felt irrationally disappointed. It was completely understandable, of course. We hardly knew each other. Our friendship was new, and it would probably wither and die as soon as real life intervened. Stephen had probably felt some kind of obligation to me as he knew I worked in the hospital and that he might see me around after I recovered. That responsibility didn't extend to dealing with a grumpy, suspicious boyfriend. And why should it? 'Fair enough,' I said, forcing a small smile.

'I don't mind,' Stephen said, 'but I don't want to make things worse for you.'

My old fire came back. 'What do you mean "worse"? You don't have to worry about me.'

'I know his type,' Stephen said calmly. 'And I don't particularly like it.'

I welcomed the old flames as they burned through the fear that Stephen's words brought. 'You don't know anything about him. About us,' I said.

He stood up. 'I'd better go.'

Stephen held out a hand and I shook it, quickly. Not fast enough, though. I still had time to enjoy the sensation of his skin on mine, time to notice that his hand felt as nice as it looked.

'Stay in touch,' he said. 'Call me if you need anything at all.'

And the fire burned out, just like that. I felt tears prickling my eyes and I blinked hard.

გ~Ⴢ

I was in the middle of my finals when I got the call. I saw the number on the screen and answered, 'To what do I owe the pleasure?' expecting to hear Pat but, for once, it was Dylan. He never called me and I was so surprised to hear his voice that it took me a moment to realise that it was my turn to say something. 'Okay,' I managed, but the line was already dead.

'Please,' Dylan had said. 'Go and see your brother. Pat's worried but she won't ask you to do it, she doesn't want to bother you.'

I lived in a shared student house then – a big old Victorian terrace with over ten bedrooms – and I stumbled down the multiple staircases, calling out to see who was home. I went from room to room until I found someone with a car who was willing to do me a favour. Sam didn't even live with us, he was the boyfriend of Lisa, who lived in the third room I'd tried.

I don't remember anything about the journey there, what we talked about or even if we talked. In that respect he was the perfect taxi driver. I didn't know Lisa well and had only ever exchanged small talk with Sam. It was perfect because I wasn't up to a conversation, all I could wonder was what had made Dylan call me. What had Pat said or done that had prompted him to pick up the phone? I had my phone in my lap and I kept hitting redial and Geraint kept on not picking up.

When we got to Cheltenham I directed Sam to Geraint's house. Once he found a space on the road outside, Sam unfolded himself from the car but in that time I was at the front entrance, finger pressed to the button marked 'G. Morgan'. The front garden was paved with slabs, weeds growing up between. I pressed the buzzer again and tilted my head, waiting to hear Geraint's voice fuzzy over the intercom, the click of the door unlocking. Without warning, it swung open and a woman appeared. She was middle-aged and tired-looking. She wore a navy polyester tabard over her clothes and an across-the-body handbag with a thin red strap. I was standing in her way and she looked none too pleased about that fact. 'Yes?'

'I'm visiting Geraint Morgan. Upstairs.'

The woman stood aside to let me pass.

'I'm his sister,' I added, unnecessarily.

The woman didn't look back and the door swung shut behind her. Geraint's flat was on the top floor and I was just about to start up the stairs when there was a pounding on the door. Sam. I had forgotten about Sam.

I opened the door, trying to work out whether it was better to go upstairs and have a near-stranger witness whatever . . . whatever I was about to witness. Or whether it was better for me to climb those stairs and bash down Geraint's door on my own. I didn't much like either scenario, but Sam decided it for me by starting on the stairs. 'You don't have to . . .' I began but he just shrugged his wide shoulders and carried on climbing.

At the top of the stairs there were two doors. I hadn't been here so wasn't sure which flat was Geraint's. I settled for banging on both doors and crossing my fingers he opened up first. The left-hand door opened a crack and a blast of warm fetid air wafted into the hall.

'Ger?'

The door opened a little further, revealing a slice of my brother, wearing a red hoodie. An arm shot out and pulled me in. Slamming the door behind me.

'Wait . . .' I stopped trying to talk. All thoughts of explaining that my ride home was grinding his teeth on the other side of the door fled from my mind as I took in the room. It was a standard bedsit, small and oddly proportioned, the ceilings too high, the bay window too big. What had once been a no-doubt stunning living room was now an oddly carved up living space with an unmade sofa bed taking up most of the floor space. There was a tiny kitchen area with a sink and about a foot and a half of grey counter top, and an orange curtain was half pulled open, revealing a diminutive hand-wash basin, toilet and beige-tiled shower cubicle.

What had me stopped in my tracks wasn't the bedsit chic or even the piles of dirty crockery, old takeaway cartons and the pervasive smell of unwashed man. What held one hundred per cent of my attention was the assortment of holes in the wall. The plasterboard was ripped in several places and bundles of wire had been pulled through.

'What happened?'

There was thumping on the door and Geraint flinched.

I moved to let Sam in and Ger stepped across to stand in my way. He put a hand on the door and looked at me with red-rimmed eyes and a wild look. 'It's not safe.'

'It's just Sam,' I said. 'He's a friend. He gave me a lift here.' I put my hand on Ger's arm. 'It's okay.'

Geraint didn't move immediately, but let me reach around his body to open the door.

'What the fuck?' Sam squeezed through the gap left by Geraint. He looked around and I watched compassion chase the annoyance from his face. When he spoke next, his voice was neutral. 'All right, mate?'

Geraint was locking the door. There was the standard Yale, a newly fitted deadbolt and sliding bolts top and bottom.

I started to bundle up the bedding so that I could re-fold the sofa bed. I was moving on automatic pilot. I needed to be moving, to be doing something. A cold dread had settled in my stomach and it was as if by keeping busy – the word 'bustling' came to mind – I could somehow outrun it.

Once we had somewhere to sit down I moved to the kitchen and filled the kettle. 'Tea?'

'No milk,' Geraint said. 'I haven't been out.'

'You're telling me.' Sam made to open the window.

'No!' Geraint jumped up from the sofa.

'Jesus. Calm down.' Sam had his hands in the air, was shaking his head and looking at Ger like he'd lost his mind.

Geraint made for the window and tweaked the curtains to close the tiny remaining gap. He turned to face us, his whole body shaking. Rushing with lack of sleep and caffeine or maybe something stronger. 'I'm being watched.'

I had moved dishes out of the tiny sink and was blasting hot water so I wasn't sure I had heard him correctly. I finished rinsing the sink, filled it with soapy water and washed up three mugs.

'Sit down. I'll make drinks and we can talk.' I sounded calm and in control. If I didn't look directly at the holes in the walls, I could feel my pulse returning to normal. I took the coffee (strong for me, weak for Geraint, medium for Sam as I had no idea if he even drank coffee) to the sofa and it hit me; I was acting like Pat. She never sat still in a crisis either and I suddenly understood why. She couldn't.

Sam had been talking in a low voice – a gentle tone that sounded professionally calm. I wondered if he was studying psychology or social work and thought that, if not, he ought to consider it – but now he and Geraint were sitting in silence. As I made to give Ger his drink, he jumped up. He took the mug of coffee but immediately put it down on the nearest available surface, where it merged with the general detritus. He paced up and down, running his hands over his scalp. His hair was all gone, shaved close to his head, and every bump and lump of his vulnerable scalp showed. He said something very quietly.

'What?' I leaned in.

'I'm in trouble.' He stopped pacing and hunkered down in front of the sofa, fixing me with a look so naked I felt my insides contract.

'What kind of trouble?'

'I'm being watched.'

'Who is watching you?' I said.

'Them. The same ones as always.'

'Who are they?' I was hanging on to my patience with a vice-like grip, but it was still slipping.

'Rival company. Maybe.' He shook his head. 'Defence people. I don't know.'

'Defence?' Sam said.

I took a sip of my coffee and burned my tongue. 'Have you been working on a military contract?' Geraint's work often had an eventual military or defence application. He solved problems, worked on software issues and logic problems. To him, they were like high-level, super-charged Sudoku puzzles. If I'd asked him a year earlier if his job could lead to his being watched, he'd have found the idea inconceivable. He'd have laughed in my face. Now, he'd apparently decided that he was a combination of John Dillinger and James Bond.

While most of me found the thought ludicrous, there was a small murmur of dissent. It whispered: MOD. Official Secrets Act. A half-remembered news story flashed through my mind. The computer coder who was found zipped inside a duffel bag in his bath.

'You work at GCHQ?' Sam said, but Geraint wasn't listening.
I took his hands. 'Your work is top secret, right?'

Geraint winced, then nodded.

'And you work in teams? You're not the only person who knows about any given aspect of the work?' I was talking myself out of paranoia as much as Ger, at this point.

Geraint shrugged but it turned into a shake of the head, which set off a fresh bout of jitters. I reached out and grabbed hold of his hand. 'Come and sit down.' He sank to the floor in front of me, sitting cross-legged as if we were in the story corner at primary school and I was Miss Webb about to wow him with a picture book.

'Why do you think you're being followed?' Sam asked the sensible question I had been dancing around and I realised something: I didn't want Geraint to say anything that sounded mad. I couldn't bear it.

'There was this thing. I did something—' Geraint broke off, looking around in sudden fright. 'Did you hear that?'

I pretended to listen, humouring him. 'Nope.'

'I don't want to say too much.' His voice dropped to a whisper. 'They might be listening.'

'When did you last go out?' Sam was all practicality, he really was coping with this weirdness very well.

'Not sure. Thursday maybe.'

'You've been inside for a week?'

'Maybe.' Geraint looked truculent at being asked questions by a complete stranger. 'Not sure.'

'Are you eating?' Sam said, which was exactly the question I wanted to ask.

'Some. Look. It's not important.' Geraint shot Sam a pissed off look that was so entirely normal I felt my heart swell slightly in my chest. 'I have to figure this out.'

'Let me help,' I said. 'When did this start? The feeling that you were being watched?'

Geraint lifted his finger to his lips. A moment later he said loudly: 'It's been lovely to see you. Do come again.' He got up from his position on the floor and, still making the international gesture for 'shut up', he went and opened and closed the door to the flat, calling a cheery ''Bye' as he did so. Next, he turned on the iPod in its sleek white docking station and dialled the volume up. The Super Furry Animals' 'Bad Behaviour' filled the room, so loud it made me wince.

Ger crossed back and took my hands, leading me closer to the speakers. It was deafening so when he began whispering into my ear, I only got about half of what he was saying and I wasn't too sure I'd heard that correctly.

'I've been working on a big contract—' I got that, along with an earful of spit. I tilted my head and frowned. I mimed turning the music down but Ger shook his head and mouthed: 'They might be listening.'

He leaned in again and said a load more stuff that I barely caught. Something about a project for MI5. And 'hush-hush'.

I pushed him away. I indicated that we should leave the room, but he shook his head violently. He got up and went to the bathroom, so quickly that I thought he might be going to be sick.

While he was gone, Sam turned the music down to a more acceptable level.

Ger walked back in and Sam said, perhaps to pre-empt any argument: 'This will be fine. It'll be enough to cover our voices.'

Geraint didn't seem to be listening to him, though. He sat down on the sofa, his leg jiggling up and down. His pupils had gone very large and I wondered what he'd taken.

'It's more than usually secret. Got to lock up documents every time I leave my desk, only deal with the company on-site. No email, no post, no telephone. That kind of deal.'

I could feel my own eyes grow wide. 'Does that happen often?'

Geraint shrugged. 'Yeah. Quite often. Then, couple of weeks back, I was followed home.'

'A car? Did you see a suspicious black sedan with tinted windows?' Sam's mouth was quirking up in the corners and I frowned at him.

'No.' Geraint ignored Sam. 'I saw the same cyclist, though. I mean, you tend to see the same faces when you bike. There's a bit of comradeship amongst riders. But this guy was new.'

'That doesn't mean anything. Just a new face. He probably lives around here.'

'And I heard beeping noises on the phone. I ditched my mobile. Got a new one, pre-paid.'

I remembered the text messages from the unknown number, Geraint asking about the man in the café. That was ten days ago. I had known something was wrong and I'd left him to go back to the flat alone, to descend into this state of paranoia.

'But why?' I kept my tone gentle. 'I mean, you're not very high up, are you? It doesn't make any sense—'

'That doesn't matter,' Geraint said. 'If the work is wanted by an outside agency or a terrorist group, then anyone on the team is a possible target.'

He was so certain, sounded so – momentarily – rational that the hairs on my arms stood up. 'Have you spoken to your team? To your boss?'

Ger shook his head so violently I felt my own neck twinge in sympathy. 'God, no. I don't know who to trust. It could be an inside thing. I mean, there could be a mole.'

'Very *Spooks*,' Sam said. Unhelpfully.

Geraint turned his gaze on to Sam, eyes widening still further. 'What the fuck do you think they based that stuff on?'

Sam held up his hands. 'I'm just saying. You don't expect this in the real world.'

Geraint shook his head. 'Not in your world perhaps. I've known it was a possibility since day one. Nature of the business.'

'You're not being serious?' Sam said.

'Okay.' Geraint pulled out a packet of cigarettes and lit up. 'When I first started, my line manager had just come off long-term sick leave. Stress, we were told. I didn't take a lot of notice. Breakdowns are common in coding. Obsessive people who can't leave work at work. You know the type?'

'Vaguely,' I said, raising an eyebrow. Ger didn't seem to notice.

'Well, it turned out that the stress wasn't just overwork. He'd had a wiretap on his phone. We caught on to it quite early on, but he had to carry on as normal. Not tip them off that we knew people were listening. The strain of it got to him.'

'What happened? Who was spying on him?'

Geraint shrugged. 'Militant group. Middle Eastern most likely although I didn't just say that.' He flashed a quick smile, the first I'd seen since we arrived. Talking was making Geraint seem more balanced. His leg was no longer jiggling and he sounded quite sane. On the other hand, my head was threatening to explode. I'd had no idea that his work could be properly dangerous. 'So . . . You've always known this was a possibility. Your bosses know it is a possibility. There must be some, I don't know, guidelines or something. Steps you're supposed to follow in the event. I mean, don't you get training on this?'

'Of course . . .' Geraint's voice trailed off. He was staring over our heads, seeing something in his mind. 'This project was a little bit different from the other stuff I've done, though. The security level was through the roof. I was working on a code.'

'For who?' Sam was leaning forward, caught up in his very own television episode. 'Government? Terrorists? Al-Qaeda?'

'I can't tell you,' Geraint said. The withering tone of voice was back. 'Obviously. So, I was working on this code—'

'Were you going to crack it? Is that it?' Sam said.

Geraint looked at him pityingly. 'I did that ages ago. And I had almost finished a program that would decipher it in real time, too, but that wasn't when the problems started.'

He looked around again. 'I remember the first morning I saw the cyclist. It was after I decoded a particular message.'

'So, what was the message?' Sam was on the edge of his seat. Literally. If he got any keener he'd fall off.

'It's better if I don't tell you. Safer for you.'

'Oh, for goodness' sake, Geraint. Get a grip. This is crazy.' My voice sounded shrill and I wished I could snatch the words back. I wanted Geraint to let me help him, not make him retreat.

Luckily, he didn't seem offended. 'I know how it sounds,' he said. He took a long drink of his coffee and pulled a face. 'Jesus fuck. What is this?'

'Coffee.'

'It tastes like piss.'

'Good,' I said briskly. 'You don't need any more caffeine.'

'I'm going to shower.' He lurched upright and disappeared into the bathroom. I wanted to get up and follow him, to check for blades and pills, although that was more because I felt it was the kind of thing I ought to do in the circumstances. I didn't think he was depressed or suicidal, more hyper. Possibly high. As always, I couldn't get the proper perspective when it came to my twin; his mix of charming bravado and stomach-churning vulnerability eroded my logic. I just wanted to wrap him up in a duvet and feed him soup. And, at the same time, I wanted to shake him stupid.

While he was gone, Sam and I sat in awkward silence for a moment or two. Then, Sam said: 'Jesus. Your brother . . .'

'He's just stressed,' I said, defensive. 'He's been working too hard, that's all. He does that. He's fine.'

Sam shook his head. 'I don't think he's fine.' He paused. 'Look, I'm not an expert and feel free to tell me to take my big nose elsewhere, but—'

'You're just seeing him on a bad day,' I cut in before he could finish. Sam seemed like a nice guy, but I didn't want to hear his opinion of my brother. 'He gets a bit fried when he works too much. He forgets to eat and sleep and then he gets a little strung out. That's all this is.'

'So, you think he's just paranoid?'

I took a deep breath. 'I don't know. I think so. But . . . his job. It's possible.'

'Jesus,' Sam said again.

I stood up, did a bit more tidying. The holes in the wall seemed to watch me; the patches of damp mould on the ceiling seemed to be creeping. I thought I saw something move from the corner of my eye. If Ger hadn't left this depressing place for a week, it was small wonder he was going peculiar. All I had to do was get him out, for some fresh air and a decent meal.

Once he was clean and dressed, he seemed even better. With plenty of coaxing from me and a blokey 'Come on, mate' from Sam, we convinced Ger to come out to eat. It wasn't a comfortable meal, especially since he insisted on sitting at an outside table as it would be 'harder to bug' and it wasn't a warm day.

Sam zipped up his coat and didn't complain. He made conversation, as if the situation was entirely normal, and joked with the confused waiting staff, who wanted to know why we didn't want the perfectly nice table they'd offered us inside.

It was a shame, I thought, that I would probably never speak to Sam again. Nothing beyond a 'hello', at any rate. Even if I could come to terms with the enforced intimacy of the day, his knowing my twin, seeing us in this vulnerable state, I knew that he'd remind me of it all. Whenever I saw Sam, I'd remember the fear and anxiety of this day.

After lunch we walked back to the flat and the exercise warmed me up. Geraint seemed almost normal and was even managing to make jokes. I asked him to take some time off work, to come and stay with me for a few days, but he refused. I wasn't surprised.

'What are you going to do then?' Sam said.

Geraint shrugged. He looked at me. 'I'll speak to my line manager. Work a bit less.'

He was just saying what I wanted to hear. I knew that, but I believed him anyway. 'You need to eat regularly,' I said. 'Three meals a day.'

'Yes, Mum,' he said, smiling a little.

'And call me,' I said.

'All right,' he said, although we both knew he probably wouldn't.

I hugged him. 'Email me,' I said, quietly. 'Email me every day.'

༄

I opened my eyes and cast around the ward for something to distract me. I didn't want to think about this. I didn't want to remember Ger this way. I wanted my brother back, my strong other self. The bulletproof version who never got scared.

I wanted Grace, my nurse, to appear. I wanted her comforting presence so badly I ached with it. I stared at the end of my bed, hoping she would magically materialise, that I could conjure her just by wishing. The curtains around my bed stayed resolutely still, though, and nobody appeared.

There was nothing to stop the memory from coming back even though I knew, now, that I didn't want to remember it.

GRACE

vie had a picture of Nancy Beaton torn from a copy of *Vogue*. She kept it tucked between the frame and the mirror of their shared dressing table. Nancy was a shooting star, with a cascade of shining foil for a dress and a peculiar spiked hat jutting out from her head. In one hand she held a spear-like pole with sparkling streamers dangling from the tip and, behind her, there was a burst of silvery light. Evie thought it was the most beautiful thing she'd ever seen. 'Imagine being Cecil Beaton's sister, the lucky thing! Fame, parties, all those clothes. And she's beautiful,' Evie said, sighing. 'Good thing, really. I don't suppose he'd have much time for an ugly girl.'

Grace wasn't so sure. She had become accustomed to the photograph, of course, seeing it every day, but she didn't envy Nancy Beaton. The girl looked sad, Grace thought, and all of that shining material bunched behind her looked heavy, as if it were weighing her down. She didn't look like a shooting star about to streak across a dark sky, she looked anchored to the earth. Trapped. Like a butterfly in a jar.

꩜

Dr Palmer wasn't going to stop. Grace knew that she wasn't especially worldly and that the things she knew about men could be written on the back of a postage stamp, but she understood that much. He was playing with her and the more she backed away, the better he liked it.

She looked into his eyes and saw something dark behind them. He looked at her the way a cat looks at a mouse. But also, sometimes, with a flash of recognition. That was the worst thing. Like there was something in her that had drawn him. A shadow self that called to him. That wanted him.

Grace didn't tell anyone. She couldn't tell anyone. The shame was too much and the shadow too dark. Palmer kept coming. He acted professionally in front of the other nurses, the sisters, his fellow house surgeons. When they were alone, or even when there was just a maid running a broom along the floor or sorting the linen, he showed her his real face.

He liked to find her in the sluice. More often than not she was immobilised before a sinkful of hot water, and if she had a companion, he would send the other nurse out with an errand.

He was good at pretending to be jovial. 'Ah, if it isn't my favourite washer-woman.'

Grace stared at the wall. There were tiny black cracks in the tile that were impossible to get really clean.

'Does your father know that he sent you away to become a maid?'

Grace lifted her head a fraction.

'Won't he be pleased when you bring home a surgeon? That's like winning the pools for a girl like you.'

'I'm not going home,' Grace said, realising the truth of it as she spoke. 'I live here now.'

'Don't be ridiculous, child,' Palmer said, lazily. 'Everyone goes home eventually. One way or another. Besides,' he smiled, 'I'll have to ask your father for your hand. The working classes are very traditional, in their way, I believe.'

Grace knew he was trying to get a rise out of her. He wanted her to hotly defend her family's lower-middle-class status. He wanted her to be offended and upset, but he had chosen the wrong target.

She took a calming breath and dried her hands and arms with a towel. Her cuffs were on the side and she took strength from the sight of them. She wasn't the girl Grace, not any more. She was Nurse Kemp. Unapproachable, unimpeachable. The words 'touch me and you'll lose a hand' jumped into her mind and she wished she had the guts to say them. Evie would say them. Evie wouldn't hesitate.

'Dr Palmer,' Grace said, 'please don't tease me. You're not going to propose to me and, if you did, we both know that my answer would be no.'

Grace picked up one of her cuffs and began to fix it, her fingers shaking slightly.

Palmer looked momentarily blank, but then he rallied. 'I could change your mind. A little romance, perhaps. I've been told I'm rather good at kissing.'

Grace's fingers slipped on the buttons and her linen cuff fell to the floor. 'I won't,' Grace said. 'I'm sorry, sir, but I won't kiss you.'

Palmer smiled as if he had anticipated this resistance, but that it meant exactly nothing. 'Not here, Kemp. We'd need the proper setting. I was thinking we could go out together, into town.'

'No, thank you,' Grace managed. She wanted to dip down to the floor, to retrieve her cuff, but she was frozen in place. Palmer had got much closer without her noticing him moving.

He reached out and touched her cheek. 'Dancing would be very good for you. It would help you to relax.'

'I'm sorry, sir,' Grace said. 'I won't go dancing with you.' She tried to edge past him. 'Or for dinner. Or to the pictures.'

That did it.

'Good.' Palmer spun her around then whispered into her ear: 'We both know what you really want.'

Grace felt as if she'd been slapped. She tried to pull away, but with one of his arms around her waist and another across her shoulders and neck, she was held fast. She could feel the length of him pressing against her back. Feel his damp breath on her neck. She pulled away harder and he let her go, so suddenly that she stumbled a little. She kept moving, though. Through the door and into the ward.

Barnes looked up from the tea trolley, raised her eyebrows and then carried on, stirring sugar into a cup. 'Cuffs,' she said, then moved off down the ward, the wheels on the trolley squeaking.

MINA

I'd started seeing birds that weren't there, that weren't real, when I was a child, but it tailed off throughout my teens. I was distracted by the twin discoveries of bourbon and sex, of course, but it was more than not paying attention. They just didn't seem to visit me any more and at eighteen, away from home and at university in England, they'd all but disappeared. Occasionally, a magpie would sit just a little too long on a wire above my head and, one Christmas, a robin sat outside the window of my student room like my own personal greetings card. Except it was sitting on a crushed lager can rather than a frost-coated tree branch, and it sat for too long in the same position to be real.

After his paranoia trip, Geraint emailed me (a gif of a baby owl which I stared at for ages, trying to parse the deeper meaning), but he didn't telephone. I had the feeling he was embarrassed, which was highly unusual. He was always so brazen, his ego bulletproof. I thought, in my ignorance, that it was a good sign. That no matter how brave the face he'd put on, no matter how sharp the spikes on his homemade armour, he realised that he had gone too far. I assumed that it had been a wake-up call and he'd understood he couldn't keep pushing himself so hard, that he had to cut down on his hours at work, and ease up on the drugs and whatever else he was doing. I decided he'd been on a collision course but had swerved at the last moment.

I was wrong.

I was studying hard at the time, stressed beyond belief by my exams, and when Geraint finally called, I let it go to voicemail. Part of me was angry with him for not calling sooner. I'd been so worried about him but that worry had morphed into frustration.

No matter how much I wanted to forget that fact, I couldn't deny it. I had been cross with him and took petty revenge by not calling him back. I'd planned to let him stew for a day or two, show him that I wasn't always going to drop everything and come running, that he couldn't keep playing the drama card.

It was an effort not to call him back that evening; our roles were so entrenched. I told myself that I would call him the next day or the day after that, and it would do him good to wait for a change.

That same night, I woke up sweating and terrified. I sat bolt upright, the way Ger used to when we shared a room, and, in that instant, I knew something terrible had happened. My face was wet with tears that had appeared while I slept and my throat felt raw and tight.

My phone began buzzing quietly and as I reached for it I became aware of a row of birds – black-eyed starlings – sitting on my duvet. There was no weight to them and they made no sound. They didn't shift their feet or twitch their feathers. They sat completely still and silent, watching me take the call.

I knew it would be Pat before I saw the number. The knowledge was a black weight in my stomach as I reached for the phone. 'Come to the hospital,' she said. 'It's Geraint.'

I listened to the name of the hospital, Pat's directions. Even in this, the ultimate crisis, she was calm and careful. She repeated the directions and the address of the hospital, made sure I knew where I was going. 'Take a taxi, we'll pay when you get here.'

I wanted to say that I didn't care about the cost and that, of course, I had spare cash ready for an emergency (a lie), but I was consumed with the knowledge that I was going to be too late. That I was never again going to see Geraint alive. I don't know if it was because he was my brother or because he was my twin or because of the birds sitting in a silent row on my bed, I just knew. No amount of therapy will convince me otherwise.

I can remember the hospital with startling clarity. I wish I didn't, but it's preserved like a museum diorama. I remember the green-grey walls and the harsh quality of the light. I know a male nurse spoke to me in a lilting Welsh accent of the kind I'd always found comforting and that when Uncle Dylan saw me, he stood up and pulled me to him. He called me *cariad* and I remember the pine resin and fresh air smell on his clothes. I remember, too, that Pat looked right through me as if I wasn't even there.

I know that I was too late and that when I went with Pat to see Geraint's body he wasn't there. It was just a waxwork figure lying in the bed, tubes springing from the back of one hand. I knew his face so well, better than I knew my own, but the face of the figure in the bed wasn't familiar. It wasn't him.

I know, too, that early the next morning, once we were home from the hospital and were tumbling, exhausted, from Dylan's car, Pat said, 'How did you let this happen?' and it didn't even hurt. I wasn't capable of feeling any more guilt than I already was. The guilt had consumed me. It was everything and I was it. I hadn't stopped him. I hadn't known (or wanted to know) how bad things had become. I'd ignored his dilated pupils the last time I'd seen him. I'd wanted to believe that he'd scared himself if not exactly straight, then something close to it, and then, for the sake of teaching him some kind of lesson, I'd not answered his call.

Time and time again Geraint had come to my rescue, and when it mattered most, I'd let him down. I didn't save him and I would never forgive myself for it. Compared to that, it didn't really matter that Pat thought the same thing.

GRACE

When the nurses socialised with the male staff in the communal living room, with its battered table tennis table and sagging armchairs, he watched her. The others thought a fine romance was blossoming, a myth he did nothing to dispel. Grace heard him telling the senior house surgeon that she had volunteered to work in the fever block just because she knew he was on duty. Together, they raised their eyes to heaven, bemoaning the trials of dealing with silly, smitten nurses.

Grace told Evie that the rumours were nonsense, but Evie didn't understand why she was upset. 'A doctor is taking an interest. That's no bad thing, you know.' She was putting lipstick on before going out and she pouted at herself in the mirror. 'And if you don't like him, he'll get bored and move on to someone else soon enough. Men are easily distracted.'

Grace wanted to say that she didn't think that was true in the case of Dr Palmer, but she didn't want to sound egotistical, as if she was suggesting that she was especially appealing.

'Tonight is going to be a special night,' Evie said, turning from her reflection and giving Grace a knowing smile.

Grace still didn't particularly like Robert but she knew that had more to do with her own mouse-like nature than any real failing in his character. Glad of the distraction, she sat closer to her friend. 'Is he taking you somewhere good?'

Evie named a restaurant with such a flourish that, even though Grace hadn't heard of it, she understood that it was something to gasp at. So she did.

'I think he's going to pop the question,' Evie said quietly. 'Don't say anything to the others, they'll be green with envy.'

'Of course not,' Grace began. She felt ill. Dr Palmer. Robert. They were all at it. Not that Palmer had meant it, of course. He'd just been trying to get a reaction from her.

'And I want to enjoy it,' Evie said, giving Grace a twirl before picking up her evening bag.

Evie skipped out in a cloud of perfume, a gift from Robert, and Grace tried hard to be happy for her friend's sake.

A moment later, Evie popped her head back around the door. 'Be a dear and walk me downstairs. I'm too giddy to be alone.'

Grace felt so bad about her own selfish thoughts that she stood up immediately and, ignoring the pain in her feet from the long day, went to Evie.

With linked arms, they left the nursing quarters and took the closest stairs. The back door of the hospital was the best way to avoid being seen by senior staff. Evie wasn't kidding about her giddiness; she chatted and laughed, hardly seeming to draw breath.

'I just know it,' she said for the hundredth time. 'He said he wanted to wait until things were settled in Europe, but the way he looks at me . . .'

'Europe?' Grace said. 'What's Europe got to do with marriage?' It was pitch black and freezing cold outside. She hoped Evie's Robert wouldn't be long.

Evie clutched at her. 'I haven't the faintest idea. To be perfectly honest, I only understand half of things he says and sometimes I don't even listen. I just watch his mouth as he's talking.'

'You are terrible,' Grace said, laughing. Their breath was fogging in the night air. Just then the clouds parted and the moon lit up the path and the hospital garden. The bulk of the glasshouse, the mysterious dark shapes growing inside, loomed up to their right and Grace was glad once they turned the corner and stood in front of the hospital. There were lamps at the front door and gates, and a light was on in the porter's little booth.

There, waiting by the entrance, as bold as brass, stood Evie's Robert. Nobody could accuse him of being shy, Grace thought. Not like Thomas. Who had no doubt forgotten about her by now. Which, she reminded herself sharply, was for the best. She wasn't going to have any of that nonsense.

'Good night, darling,' Evie said, loudly. She kissed Grace extravagantly on each cheek in the continental manner. Grace knew that it was a production entirely for Robert's benefit, but she didn't mind in the least.

'Be good,' she said to Evie, smiling and waving her off.

'Not going out tonight, miss?' the porter said, leaning on his elbows. He had a mug of something hot and the steam looked like smoke.

Once the car had pulled away, Grace said 'cheerio' to the porter and turned to go back inside.

'Hang on,' he said. 'Some of the lights are out around the side. Take this.' And he passed her a Bakelite torch.

'Thank you,' Grace said, touched. Whatever Evie said when she was complaining about curfew and the porters, Grace liked the feeling of being looked after. She liked that it mattered to the hospital what she did and where she went, it gave her a sense of belonging that was comforting.

The porter was right; without Evie by her side the gardens seemed ten times darker. She hefted her torch to cast a circle of yellow light on to the path and set off.

There was a noise to her right, a crunching on the gravel. 'Hello?' Grace said, the torch beam wobbling.

A figure peeled out of the shadows and lunged. Grace let out a shout of surprise that came out more as a gasp.

It was Dr Palmer. He wasn't wearing his white coat but she recognised him straight away. His figure and the way he moved were imprinted on her memory. Something silver glinted in the glow of the torch and Grace felt a surge of adrenaline rush through her body. She lifted the bulky torch and brought it down in an arc. The doctor sidestepped the blow, knocking the torch out of her hands with one movement.

Grace turned to run but she felt his hands on her, pulling her back. His voice in her ear was accompanied by drops of moisture and a waft of halitosis. 'Behave or I'll cut you.'

Grace went still. She thought about playing statues with her friends in the school playground. She thought about Evie's bright smile and Nancy Beaton's shining dress. She thought about the colour of the sky that morning and how the clouds had been tinged with red. She tried not to think about blood and sharp scalpels and the man holding her tightly. If she let any of that in she felt she would break apart with terror.

'You think you're above me,' Palmer said, spittle flying. 'Don't imagine I don't see it. I see you.'

The words didn't make any sense. Grace didn't think she was above anyone, let alone a doctor. That was the point. That was what was drummed into them from day one. There was a strict order, not just in hospital but in life. Grace never even came second, let alone first. She was below her teachers, her parents, matron and the sky. She was so low down she was lying in the mud.

He had a hand around her neck, the hand with the scalpel. He held the blade in front of her throat, next to the artery that ran there. Thanks to her lessons with Sister Bennett, Grace knew that it was called the carotid artery and that if it were cut she would become unconscious within seconds and bleed to death in under ten minutes. Grace tried not to think about this nugget of information, tried not to breathe either. His other hand roamed over the front of her body, undoing the buttons of her coat and feeling her chest, squeezing. Grace went as far inside her mind as she could. She kept very still and waited for it to be over, for the man to stop kneading her chest like it was bread dough.

Grace wished for someone to come. Barnes or Evie or even Sister. Especially Sister. She knew he'd stop if Sister walked by. Matron would be problematic. Palmer would definitely stop, but she'd probably send Grace home. Grace concentrated on these thoughts. She tried to stay on the path of rationality. She thought of her training, of the importance of remaining calm even in trying circumstances, of paying attention to details (his hands were struggling with other buttons, now) but not becoming overwhelmed by them.

She could feel his body pressing against hers and his excitement. He was breathing heavily as he pawed at her and the hand holding the scalpel moved with him. Grace was frightened of what he was going to do, but also frightened that he might slip and cut her throat by accident. She kept as still as she could, not to encourage or provoke. She wanted to ask him to stop but she thought that if she opened her mouth, tried to speak, she'd be sick.

His hand moved lower, over her clothes but squeezing and insistent, as if the material wasn't even there. 'This is just a warm up,' he said, and his words turned her stomach. 'Our first date.' The hand kept moving, touching every part of her as if marking his territory.

The most important thing was to keep taking action. That was what Sister Bennett always said. But the right action. Sometimes that action might be to ask somebody else if you weren't sure. Better to check a dosage than to give a patient too much. Grace felt tears leaking on to her cheeks. She didn't know which was the right action to take and there wasn't anybody to ask. It didn't matter how much she thought of Sister Bennett, she couldn't do anything at all.

Afterwards Grace went back to her room and got into bed fully dressed. She didn't unlace her shoes or move at all. She stared at the ceiling and kept her mind a perfect blank. When Evie arrived back from her date, Grace kept quiet and still. She didn't answer when Evie asked what was wrong. She thought that she was perfectly controlled and that her expression was proper. Didn't understand why Evie insisted on getting out of her own bed and into Grace's and why her arms went around her and squeezed.

'Stop it, Gracie, you're scaring me,' Evie said.

She had been speaking, Grace realised, for some time but the words hadn't penetrated before this. She felt wetness on her lip and tasted salt. Putting a hand to her face she realised that she was crying. Snot and tears mixed together and dripped over her mouth, off her chin. There was a noise, too, a low keening sort of noise. Like a wounded animal.

'Gracie, Gracie, Gracie!' Evie was chanting her name. 'Shush, now. You'll wake them up.'

That did it. Grace didn't want anybody to come into the room. She stopped keening and wiped her face on the rough top blanket.

'What's wrong, pet?' Evie said. She stroked hair away from Grace's brow, kissed the top of her head. 'Tell me.'

Grace shook her head. She didn't trust herself to speak. The shadow had found her again. Every squeeze and stroke from that hateful man had been a promise. Grace knew that Palmer wasn't going to stop, that he would find her again and finish what he had started. He had marked her as his own and he would catch her again. Next time it might be somewhere warm and quiet, somewhere he could hold her in his arms like a lover.

Grace must've fallen asleep because she woke up with her arm stiff from where it was lying half under Evie. She felt Evie's hair tickling her cheek and her soft breath. She felt hollowed out from crying but strangely clear, too. She shifted her arm, trying not to wake Evie, who smelled deliciously of herself; a combination of perfume, smoke and Evie-ness.

'Gracie?' Evie's voice was thick with sleep and Grace stayed quiet and still, seeing if she was really awake.

She felt Evie move and turned on to her side, so that they were facing one another.

'Are you going to tell me?' Evie said, sounding perfectly alert now. Her breath was slightly sour with sleep.

Grace decided she would. Evie was her friend. And it was dark and safe. She decided she would tell Evie about Dr Palmer and maybe get her advice. If anybody knew what to do about him, that person would be Evie. Maybe she'd even know a way to stop him. Grace opened her mouth and was surprised to find herself saying, instead: 'I lost my baby.' As soon as the words were out she felt their inadequacy. Like she'd left her baby on a train or outside a shop, forgotten to push the pram home. 'It died.'

'Oh, Gracie,' Evie said. She stroked Grace's shoulder, then her hair, smoothing it away from her face the way a mother might. 'I'm so sorry.'

Grace had expected her to be shocked. Disgusted, perhaps. 'He was so angry,' she whispered, meaning her father. 'He pushed me down the stairs and kicked me.' Her hands fluttered to her stomach.

Evie didn't say anything, she just stroked Grace's hair and let her cry.

MINA

When I woke up the next morning there was no blissful moment of not remembering, no golden reprieve. I'd been dreaming about Geraint and, as I surfaced from sleep, my subconscious feelings of loss were replaced by the conscious realisation of it. I opened my eyes and stared at the square ceiling tiles. He was gone. My brother was dead. I had been broken long before the steering column smashed into my body.

The time after we left the hospital was a blur. I was given compassionate leave by the university and I missed the rest of my exams. I slept in my old bedroom at home, and I remember Dylan gently encouraging me to join him on walks along the cliffs and, eventually, I did. His company was comforting, but I couldn't even look at Pat. The guilt was crushing. Eventually, I couldn't breathe and I went back to my student house. I hadn't been back to the house in Wales since.

Stephen visited, but I turned my face to the wall and pretended to be asleep. Parveen called my mobile but I didn't answer. The ghost-nurse sat on the end of my bed for a while but I put my fingers in my ears, like a child, and closed my eyes. Eventually, I felt the air move and, when I opened my eyes, she had gone.

That morning, as if I'd magically unstuck my life by remembering the end of Geraint's, Dr Kanthe came by with the news I'd been waiting for. I was being discharged.

I was going to start my new life. I was going to live with Mark. It no longer mattered that I thought he'd been in the car with me. I didn't even care if he'd lied to me about it. If he had, then I just assumed he had reasons. Probably good reasons. I was in no position to judge anybody else's actions. I had proved that.

Geraint was dead. I knew that I'd been through this horror before, but it felt just as fresh and cold as if I hadn't. I didn't know if that was thanks to the amnesia or whether it was simply the nature of grief. It didn't really matter; it hurt just as badly either way. I had no room to feel betrayed or angry with Mark. Everything felt unreal and, in the quiet corners that weren't filled with screaming grief, I was simply numb.

I tried to think about my new life. Pat was going to come and stay for a week or so and then I'd gently, but firmly, eject her. It wouldn't be difficult. I knew she would be desperate to get back to Wales, to her own home. And my Uncle Dylan would apply pressure in his own quiet way. I don't think he'd even need to say anything, Pat would just feel him calling to her across the Severn.

Thinking about Pat made me want to speak to her. I had to tell someone about Geraint. I knew it was no longer news, but I felt an overwhelming urge to say his name to somebody who understood, someone who felt the same way. My family were my partners in loss. Pat picked up on the third ring, her voice guarded. 'It's me,' I said. 'Mina.'

'What's wrong?'

For once, I didn't take her words badly. It was fair enough. I never called her. I never wrote. I never visited. My memory was back and I knew that the last five years had been an exercise in exorcism. I'd cut my small, imperfect family out of my life as cleanly as if I'd been performing surgery. First because seeing them amplified my guilt and then because the absence of Geraint was too obvious in their presence. And, finally, out of a kind of habit.

'I'm fine. I'm getting out today.'

'Oh, that's good.' Pat's voice receded and I heard her call to Uncle Dylan, 'They're letting her out of hospital.' Her voice came back. 'Do you need me to help you?'

'Mark's coming,' I said. 'He's taking me home.'

'To his house?' The tone of disapproval was back.

'Our house, he says.'

'Well—'

I interrupted Pat before she could say anything else on that particular subject. 'I'm sorry.'

'Well, it's not what I'd choose for you, of course, but there are worse things, and if you start to attend church again . . .' Her voice had a hopeful note.

'I don't mean I'm sorry about Mark. I'm sorry . . .' My voice cracked. I took a breath and tried again. 'About Geraint.'

There was a short silence. Then Pat said: 'Why are you sorry? It's not your fault.'

I couldn't speak. My throat closed up tight and my whole face felt stretched and weird.

'Mina, you listen to me,' Pat said, her own voice strong and clear, 'Geraint was a very troubled young man. We all loved him and we did the best we could, but there wasn't anything any of us could've done.'

The tears came, then. A sob escaped and I swallowed hard, wiping my eyes. I knew that if I let out another sob I'd be properly bawling, that I wouldn't be able to stop. I took a deep breath and then another. My hand gripping the phone was slick with sweat and Pat was still speaking. Her voice was more hesitant now. 'I know I looked for reasons at the time. For a long time really. I was angry.' She paused. 'Have you been worrying about this?'

I still couldn't say anything. I wanted to feel a weight lifting, a shift inside me that meant all my pieces were clicking back together, but it didn't happen. I still felt hollow and broken and alone. I knew that I couldn't keep blaming Pat for that, though.

'I know,' I said. 'I just wish I had done something or that there was something I could've done. I just wish—' I couldn't finish the sentence, my throat had closed.

'I know,' Pat said, gently. 'We all do.'

❦

When Mark came in, carrying an empty suitcase to pack the detritus I'd accumulated over the weeks, I told him to put it back into the car. 'I don't want any of it.'

He looked momentarily hurt and I remembered that he'd bought me new nightshirts and toiletries, books and chocolates.

I tried to explain: 'This has just been a nightmare. I want to leave it like that. I don't want any reminders that it was real.' I gestured around me at the ward, the bed, the horrible green curtains. 'This was just a temporary blip.'

'Right-oh,' Mark said, closing the case and putting it on the floor. 'Do you need help to get dressed?'

'No.' I had underwear on. Had wrestled myself into a bra for the first time since I'd arrived. It felt strange and restrictive, like when I'd first started wearing one as a flat-chested eleven-year-old. I had the stretchy yoga trousers I'd been wearing for physio laid out and a clean T-shirt. 'Give me a sec, though.'

'No problem. I'll go and see if there are any forms to fill out.'

When the curtain closed I took a couple of deep breaths. I could feel the panic rising.

The ghost-nurse, Grace, was back. She was standing in the corner of the cubicle, next to the bedside cabinet. She was more translucent than usual and it was apparent that she wasn't really there. I was glad to see her one last time. I wanted to say goodbye, to close the chapter. And to make it clear that she wasn't welcome in my new life.

'Goodbye,' I said. Loud and clear.

The ghost didn't turn her head. She didn't speak or give any sign that she'd heard me, but something told me she was listening.

'I don't want you to follow me,' I said, quieter this time.

I didn't want to take my nightshirt off and pull my T-shirt over my head. The thought of being momentarily blind in front of the apparition was suddenly terrifying. I'd never felt frightened of her before. Was it because I was so close to normality? Was it because I had finally got my mental faculties back? With startling clarity I realised that fear was the correct response. Why hadn't I felt it before? There was a ghost. Next to the drab green-beige wall, half turned away from me. I should be screaming. I should be running away.

'Hello?' I said, my voice cracking a little.

She didn't move. The ward was quiet. It was just me and two sleeping old dears.

I wanted the ghost to move, to stop being so scarily still.

For a moment I thought I heard a voice. It was nothing more than a mumble and I couldn't work out the words. Maybe I just heard the sounds in my head. Maybe it was my own panic speaking, or perhaps I'd developed another symptom. Tinnitus. Or schizophrenia.

The figure began shaking her head; she held out her arms as if she wanted to stop me from leaving.

The curtain swished and Mark appeared. The ghost blinked out of existence. Then appeared again, between me and Mark. She shook her head, her expression beseeching. She pushed her hands into Mark's chest, as if trying to shove him away.

I knew, looking at Mark, that I didn't love him. I'd probably conjured up the ghost as a way of warning myself that I didn't love the man I was going to live with, but it wasn't necessary. I didn't require it. I didn't deserve it. Geraint was dead. Nothing else mattered. I felt a tightness in my chest and tried to breathe more deeply.

'Pat is arriving tomorrow.' Mark was still chatting, seeming not to notice that I was having a panic attack. 'I'm picking her up from the station at six. So, we'll have the first night alone. It'll be like a mini honeymoon.'

Very mini, I thought. *And we're not married.* Then, I thought: *Touch me and you lose a hand.*

'I can't wait for you to see the house,' he was saying.

I made a vague noise of agreement. I couldn't wait to see the outside world. The hospital garden didn't count. I was going to see proper sky and roads and houses and gardens and trees.

It was overwhelming. Getting out of the building was fine, I'd done nothing but walk corridors for the previous week, but going through the main reception with the shop and the café concession and the central information desk was like being in an airport. It felt vast and was so crowded with people. I clung to Mark's arm, frightened of being knocked over.

He had parked right outside the entrance, in a short-term patient pick-up spot. He held the door open and I got into the passenger seat. I'd braced myself for an onslaught of bad memories. I assumed I'd have a traumatic flashback as soon as I was inside a vehicle, maybe even a panic attack, but it didn't happen. I was just in a car seat, the inside of Mark's Audi familiar and comfortable. Mark started the car and we pulled into the traffic and I felt nothing. I reasoned with myself. I'd been in a car perfectly safely far more often than I'd ever been in an accident. My psyche was clearly just being sensible and scientific, playing the odds.

The sun was out. It was hot through the glass and I leaned forwards to punch up the air conditioning. The strap tightened against my collarbone and shoulder and I felt sick for a second.

'You all right?' Mark glanced at me.

'Fine,' I said. Fine, fine, fine. Like a mantra.

I looked out of the window and marvelled at the world. It was as if I'd been shut away for years, not months. Everything was both strange and familiar and I felt unaccountably affectionate towards it all. I wanted to gather everything up: that lamp post, that drainage cover, that teenage boy with the skinny jeans and ridiculous scarf, even his frightening-looking dog. I wanted to hug them all tight to me. The world. I was back in the world.

'I was thinking we'd get takeaway tonight,' Mark was saying. 'I didn't think you'd be up to going out to eat, but I can make us a reservation if you like.'

'Chicken chow mein is perfect,' I said, loving the ease with which the words came back to me. A takeaway. I pictured foil dishes with cardboard lids, even though I knew that my local had switched to plastic microwaveable boxes ages ago. This comforting thought was immediately followed by a flash of panic. I wouldn't be going to my local. Mark and I would have a new local. I was going to live with him in a house I'd never seen. 'Can we go to my flat first?'

Mark didn't look pleased, but he agreed. 'I don't want you to get too tired before we go home.'

Home. I felt a shudder of fear, which I pressed down tight.

'I just want to say goodbye to it,' I said. 'Maybe pick up a few things.'

'There's nothing there,' he said. 'I moved all your clothes and make-up and stuff to the new place.'

'What about my books? My plants?'

'Those, too. There wasn't space for all of the books but they're boxed up ready.'

I wanted to ask 'Ready for what?' but I didn't.

It didn't take long to get to my building and, as we pulled up outside, a rush of familiarity hit me. I knew this place. I lived here. The front entrance and my own door were completely normal. I remembered them as soon as I saw them, even though seconds before I couldn't have recalled them if I'd had a gun to my head.

Inside, however, I didn't feel so good. The living room was filled with boxes and the purple sofa – the one I'd been trying to picture for the last couple of weeks – was a disappointment. It wasn't as nice as the one I'd imagined.

Mark was hovering, clearly hurrying me. 'What do you want? Let me get it for you.'

'I don't really know, I just wanted to be here.' I wandered into the bedroom. Mark hadn't taken the linen off the bed and I touched the duvet cover. It was mine. I knew it was mine. I recognised it. I didn't feel anything, though.

The book on the floor by the bed was very familiar. It was the same book – a history of the hospital – that Stephen had brought me. Not exactly the same, of course. This book was older, well read with a broken spine and scuffed pages. I picked it up and, like touching Rabbity, the feel of it in my hands brought things back. I remembered sitting up in bed – in this bed – and reading.

The numbness inside opened wider, sucking in every other feeling like a black hole. I had definitely imagined the ghost-nurse. I'd been reading about the hospital before the accident, looking at those old black-and-white photographs, the women in their funny starched uniforms. Then I'd conjured her up for comfort, a half-memory from my old life. I didn't know why but I felt like crying.

I put the book down on the bed and swallowed hard.

I'd seen that picture of the little boy in the iron lung; I must've liked the look of the nurse with him and her image had floated up out of my subconscious. She wasn't looking out for me; I'd just imagined she was because I'd felt so alone. Now I knew the truth. I really was alone.

Mark came into the room behind me. 'Our new bedroom is much bigger,' he said. 'I know you feel like you're leaving your home, but you are going to love your new one, I promise.'

Whatever else it was, this place didn't feel like home, though. I didn't have an urge to climb into that bed or to sit on that pale imitation of a purple sofa or even to go into the kitchen. I could picture it now without needing to see it. I'd had enough visual cues that the rest of the flat, the outside space, the place where I kept the wheelie bins, the bathroom with its underpowered shower, all came back. Just like Stephen had said, the information was there, it was just waiting for me to turn the page and look at it again.

'I'm ready to go,' I said. I picked up a handful of jewellery from the top of my chest of drawers and a pot of sparkly grey eyeshadow in order to justify the visit. I left the history book on top of the duvet. There was nothing there for me now.

GRACE

The morning after Grace had fallen asleep in Evie's embrace, she expected the matter not to be mentioned again. That was Evie's style, after all. Instead, Grace came back from the bathroom to find Evie sitting on her bed, her hands folded neatly in her lap. Her face was freshly scrubbed, meaning she must've been up for ages, which wasn't at all like Evie.

'You're up early. Are you feeling quite well?' Grace tried to inject a note of frivolity into her voice, but Evie's expression remained serious.

'Tell me what happened last night.'

Grace thought Evie meant the tears, the confession. She felt better for telling someone. Speaking the words had been cathartic, but she was still worried about Evie's reaction. What if she decided Grace was being too dramatic? Too tragic? She couldn't bear it if Evie cast her off. 'Oh, you know. Just a case of the blubs.' Grace couldn't meet Evie's gaze. 'I'm fine now. All better.'

'I don't mean that,' Evie said. 'Something must've happened to bring it on. You've never spoken about it before.'

'Oh . . .' Grace moved to the mirror and began trying to neaten her impossible hair. The words wanted to stick in her throat, but she forced them out. 'Just a scrape with Dr Palmer. You know I told you he was bothering me?'

'Explain,' Evie said, steel in her voice.

So Grace did. As quickly as possible. She avoided looking at Evie as she did so, couldn't bear it if she saw disgust or pity in her face. Then Grace began to put on her uniform.

'You're going on duty?' Evie said, her tone incredulous.

'Um . . .' Grace glanced at her watch. 'So are you. Better hurry if you don't want to be late.'

'I don't believe you, Gracie.' Evie shook her head.

Finally, Grace let herself glance at her friend's expression. It was unreadable.

Evie frog-marched Grace to Matron's office. She wouldn't hear any argument. When Grace pleaded with her to 'leave it be', she gave Grace such a terrifyingly grim smile that Grace's voice dried up. Suddenly, she wasn't frightened of Matron or even of Dr Palmer, she was frightened of Evie.

'You simply must do something,' Evie said crisply, and pulled on Grace's arm all the way to the office.

Grace was braced for the feelings of terror and worthlessness that always accompanied a trip to Matron's office, but she wasn't prepared for her inability to form a coherent sentence. When Matron peered at her over her glasses and said, 'What is this about, Nurse?' she only managed to stammer 'improper behaviour' before her voice disappeared.

Evie's voice was clear as she stepped in to describe the incident last night, her tone imperious enough to match Matron's. When she named Dr Palmer, Grace expected Matron to throw them out of the office there and then.

Grace had expected disbelief. She'd expected to be in trouble. She'd expected anger. So when Matron's nostrils flared and her eyebrows shot upwards, she felt tremors of fear. This was an enormous mistake. She was going to be dismissed. Sent home in disgrace, with no job, no qualification, no reference.

Matron seemed to be mastering her fury before Grace's very eyes. Grace's fingers had found her bluebird brooch, settled in her pocket, and she held it tight. It was her favourite thing and biggest source of comfort – besides Evie.

And then Matron said something surprising to Grace. 'Are you hurt?'

'No,' she said. It was such a simple and obvious question, but she had not expected to hear it. She blinked rapidly to stop herself from blubbing and squeezed the brooch harder, so that the pointed wings dug into her skin.

Matron was shaking her head but not, it seemed, at them. 'This was going to happen sooner or later. Like a time bomb, that one. I warned them . . .'

'He's got form?' Evie said.

Grace gaped. Matron might've been acting peculiarly, but that was unbelievable cheek.

Matron must've thought so, too, as she tilted her head back and regarded Evie without answering. Then, just when Grace thought that Evie was going to get her papers on the spot, Matron nodded slightly. 'There was an incident. Last year.'

Evie shrugged as if this was no surprise. 'I know the type,' she said. 'And his sort never give up.'

'I won't have it,' Matron said, straightening further in her seat so that she appeared to grow a couple of inches.

Grace took a step back, still waiting for the other shoe to drop, for Matron to explain that she meant she wouldn't have jumped-up nurses spreading malicious rumours about the doctors.

'I was given assurances that this would never happen again,' Matron said quietly. 'Promises were made—' She broke off. 'You two run along now. Nurse Kemp . . .' She took a piece of notepaper and wrote rapidly on it for a minute. 'Take this and give it to Sister Bennett. You're to have three days' compassionate leave. I'm sorry it's not longer, but we're stretched as always.'

Grace took the thin sheet of paper.

Then Matron Clark did something even more unexpected. She patted Grace's arm. 'I'm so sorry, my dear.'

Outside the office, Evie's grim smile was still in place. Grace re-read the note from Matron, gripping it tightly as evidence that she wasn't losing her mind, that the past ten minutes had, in fact, happened.

'Come on.' Evie was towing Grace behind her again. Outside, they walked in the garden, around the back of the glasshouse and as far away from the main building as possible. There was a low stone wall that ran along behind the vegetable garden and they sat on this while they talked over the meeting.

'As long as she does something about him.' Evie shook two cigarettes from a packet and lit them both, passing one to Grace.

'She said she would.' Grace's adrenaline was draining away, to be replaced by the more familiar feeling of dread. 'What if she doesn't? What if he's allowed to stay?' She shuddered. 'He'll kill me if he knows I've told.' She meant it only as an expression, but once the words were in the air they took on a horrible air of truth.

'I won't let him,' Evie said firmly.

'But he's a doctor,' Grace said, despair taking over, 'they won't make him leave.'

'They will. I promise.'

'How can you be sure, though?' Grace put her head in her hands. She had awful images of meetings in Matron's office, Dr Palmer on the other side of the desk, his mouth lifted at the corners in a parody of a smile. Dr Palmer lying through his teeth until Grace was branded a troublemaker and a liar.

Evie rubbed Grace's back in small circles as she puffed her cigarette. 'If they don't make him leave, I'll go to the papers,' she said.

'What?' Grace straightened up. Evie was always saying the most unexpected things.

'I know a newspaperman. I'll go to him and he'll do a piece on it.' Evie waved her hand airily as if it was as good as done. The trail of smoke formed the shape of a bird's wing and then disappeared. 'If there's one thing Matron hates more than nurses, it's gossip. I'll tell her the hospital's name will be splashed all over the dailies and she'll jump to it.'

'Can you really—'

'Not that it will come to that.' Evie rubbed Grace's back faster. 'You saw Matron. She's furious.'

'I can't believe it,' Grace said. 'I never expected . . .'

'I know.' Evie leaned down and stubbed out her cigarette on the path, pocketing the butt. 'The old dragon has a heart after all.'

❧

Grace thought about going home. Three days' leave gave her ample time, after all. In that moment, she realised that she'd been using her lack of off-duty as an excuse. She hadn't felt ready to face her parents or her old home, which was now and for ever tainted with the memory of that terrible night. Now, with the time to spare, she looked herself square in the mirror and admitted that she didn't want to see them. Not even with her starched cuffs and her new hospital vocabulary. Not even, she realised, if Matron gave her a certificate of merit and three badges to sew on her apron.

Months in the hospital had opened Grace's eyes. She had been brought face to face with the things she had been raised to believe were sins. Things that a nice girl from a good family should never even have heard of. There were syphilitics and unwed mothers, unwanted pregnancies that had ended in botched attempts at abortion with disastrous consequences for both mother and babe. There were men who'd been fighting and men who'd been caught in the machinery at the button factory. There were children who slept ten to a bed in their home and who came in with limbs deformed by rickets, the bowed stomachs and empty eyes of malnutrition. There was the baby who died of pneumonia because the parents couldn't afford the fare to take him to hospital in time, and the pale, doomed tuberculosis sufferers who lay in their beds on the terraces outside the general wards. So much suffering. So many deaths. As Grace strapped poultices to chests and washed out wounds, she'd begun to feel the tiniest shift.

Everything and everyone had told her that her misfortune was her fault, brought about by her own sluttish ways or the fact that she'd been over-friendly and, however inadvertently, 'given him the wrong idea'. The terrible thing that had happened was a result of her error, and the chastisement her father had imposed – while painful – had been for her own good. The only thing, really, he could do in the face of such a bad daughter.

Now, Grace wasn't so sure. When she nursed a woman who had clearly been punched several times in the head by her stocky and mean-looking husband, she felt that perhaps the fault didn't – couldn't – lie entirely at her feet.

Instead of going home to see her parents, she borrowed Evie's bicycle and a tent from Barnes's brother and spent the days riding along the coast and out into the countryside. She was strong from long days spent on her feet, and as her legs pumped the pedals and the air rushed through her hair, she felt the wings of happiness beating.

She found a nice spot to pitch her tent and lay quiet and perfectly alone, listening to the night creatures and the wind. She cried a little, but not as much as she had expected, and she didn't let herself think about going back to the wards, or worry about whether Dr Palmer would be there when she got back. Matron had said she would take care of things and Grace's belief in her power was absolute. If Matron said something would be so, then so it would be.

Best of all, Grace used a mirror in a public bathroom and gathered the courage to look at her back. The shadow had gone. She twisted from side to side, checking and rechecking, but it was true. There was no mark. It was as if the shadow had never been there in the first place.

Barnes and Evie welcomed Grace back as if she'd been gone a month. Evie kissing her extravagantly on each cheek and Barnes, for her part, shuffling forwards to press a bar of chocolate into Grace's hand.

'He's gone,' Barnes said. 'A hospital up York way, I think.'

'Good riddance,' Evie said.

'Poor York,' Grace said. She pictured the nurses there, girls like herself and Evie and Barnes, and Palmer stalking the corridors, his long fingers reaching out to touch them. But what could she do?

As if reading her mind, Evie patted her hand. 'You can't save everyone, Gracie. We can only look after our own hospital. York will have to look after themselves.'

'I suppose,' Grace said.

'If it makes you feel better, you're a good nurse,' Evie said.

'Thank you,' Grace said, snapping the bar and sharing it around.

'I never liked him,' Barnes said, her mouth full of chocolate.

Evie caught Grace's eye, and raised a brow.

Grace felt herself smiling and knew that the smile went right through her like lettering on a rock. Evie was right, she was only one nurse. She could look after her own hospital, her own patients, her own girls.

Before she went back on shift, Grace opened the book from Thomas. There was a piece of paper with his telephone number tucked at the back; something she had ignored, but hadn't quite felt able to throw away. She took the paper and went to the red telephone box at the end of the road. Her heart was hammering as she waited for him to answer and she almost lost her nerve.

'Hullo,' Thomas said, after what had felt like an age. 'I'm awfully glad you rang.' She could hear the smile in his voice.

'I wanted to thank you for the book.'

'I've got another one you might enjoy,' he said. 'The new Wodehouse. It's not a nice edition like the other, but—'

'Sounds perfect,' Grace said. There was a pause and she wasn't sure what to say next. She willed Thomas to fill in the silence, but the pause stretched on.

There was the sound of him clearing his throat and Grace wondered whether he was as nervous as she was.

'Um,' he managed. 'Are you well?'

Be Evie, Grace thought. What would Evie do? 'You can take me for tea, if you like. I finish at lunchtime on Saturday.'

'Splendid.' The relief in his voice was clear. 'I'll even throw in a cream cake . . . not literally throw, of course. I mean . . .'

'That sounds lovely,' Grace said. She walked back to the hospital in a dream.

ᘒᘎ

The following night, tidying their little room before one of the assistant matron's routine inspections, Grace realised that she thought of it as home. She pulled the blankets straight on her bed and tucked her hairbrush and comb into a drawer. Evie was humming a Cole Porter tune under her breath and, although humming usually drove Grace to distraction, she found she didn't mind in the least. 'I never asked,' Grace realised. 'Your big night out with Robert. How did it go?'

Evie's mouth turned down. 'Oh, that.' She waved a hand airily. 'Nothing to report.'

Grace stepped in front of her; she felt daring enough these days. A new confidence boosted her so that she felt more of an equal to Evie, even though she'd never be as elegant or as clever. 'It's me,' she said, looking into her friend's eyes. 'What happened?'

Evie turned away, picked up an earring from the dressing table and fiddled with it. 'He says he won't marry me. Not yet, anyway.'

'Why not yet? Money trouble?'

Evie gave a short laugh. 'Sort of. He says there's going to be a war.'

'Oh, he's not on about those blackshirts again, is he? They've been banned, haven't they?'

'At least he isn't one of them, I was starting to worry—' Evie broke off. She shook her head. 'Vile people. Good riddance to bad rubbish.'

Grace was amazed. She'd never thought of Evie as worrying about anything.

'But he has a mother, you see,' her friend said. 'No father. And if Robert marries then she won't get his RAF pension.'

'I don't understand.'

'If he is killed.'

'Oh.'

'Indeed,' Evie said. 'If he's killed while serving then as things stand his pension goes to his mother; if he's married it would go to his wife. And Robert says he can't let that happen. He wouldn't leave her in penury. It's very noble of him, really.'

'But wouldn't you look after his mother? I mean, in those circumstances.'

'I don't think he sees me as the caring type. Not when it comes to a mother-in-law.'

'Well, more fool him,' Grace said. 'You're splendid.'

'Thank you, darling,' Evie said. 'But he's right. I'm not much for family.'

'Well, there won't be a war and then he can marry you, it's simple enough.'

'Perhaps,' Evie said. 'But he might've missed his chance.' She smiled. 'I shall go out tonight and dance with whomever I please.'

'I might come, too,' Grace said. Perhaps Thomas would be there. She pictured his smile and imagined his hand on her waist.

Evie mimed a fainting fit. 'I'm sorry,' she said, violently fanning her face with one hand, 'I thought you said you were going to the dance?'

'I shall,' Grace said. 'There's no need to make such a fuss.'

'Well, this is a very queer day. Robert didn't present me with an enormous diamond ring and you're volunteering to have some fun.'

Grace shoved Evie in the arm and Evie pushed her in return and they both fell on the bed, tickling one another and laughing. Grace had a coughing fit and Evie pounded her on the back until she could breathe, and then they looked at each other's tear-stained faces and began laughing all over again.

MINA

Mark was chatting as we locked up and got back into the car, but he fell silent as we drove. There was tension between us. A history of intimacy and a strange distance.

We were taking the wide road that ran along the seafront and I was staring hungrily at the blue-grey expanse, so I didn't notice the street until we'd turned into it, away from the water. The house looked even more beautiful than it had done in the photos. I realised that my cynical brain had filled in all kinds of extra details – broken-down houses to either side, a drug-addicts' hostel across the road, a rubbish-filled garden that had been cunningly cut off by the estate agent when he took the snaps. There was none of that. Just beautiful houses with neat front gardens and freshly painted black railings. Clean steps led up from the pavement to front doors with polished brass fittings.

Mark was shifting from foot to foot, impatient to get inside, but I stood on the pavement and looked up and down the street. It didn't disappear, so I took the steps, leaning on him a little and trying not to feel like an invalid in a Victorian melodrama.

The entrance hall was wide, with white walls and a wooden floor. The light from the window above the door cast patterns on to the oak and the stairs were covered in beige wool carpeting. Everything was tasteful and expensive-looking.

'That's the old dining room, I thought I'd use it as a study,' Mark said, pointing to the right, 'and this is the living room.'

I didn't walk through the door he was pointing to. I knew the room beyond it would be perfect and that I'd want it, the same way that I wanted the green-blue front door and the beautifully restored sash windows.

'Wait until you see this . . .' Mark was still talking. I walked with him down the hallway and into a big kitchen. It had a table and chairs at one end and French doors through which I could see green lawn and a thick hedge. 'I think I need to sit down,' I said.

'Of course.' He was instantly attentive, pulling out a chair from the table.

'May I have a glass of water?' I said. Then: 'Do we have glasses?'

Mark's smile burst out again. 'Look.' He began opening cabinet doors, displaying glassware, plates, mugs, bowls.

'It's all white,' I said, wildly grateful that something wasn't perfect. 'Like a rental property.'

He shrugged. 'You can choose whatever you like. Once you're well again.'

I didn't say anything. Just concentrated on feeling something appropriate. My partner was showing me a beautiful house. It was my new home. I should be grateful. Excited.

'There are four bedrooms. The fourth is tiny, really, but it'll do as a study. Or a nursery.'

I looked up. 'A what?'

'Oh, come on, Mina,' Mark said. 'We don't need a house this size for the two of us. You were looking for a family home. I found us a family home.' He looked suddenly angry. 'Don't tell me you've forgotten that, too.'

'Show me the garden,' I said, hoping to avoid an argument. The fear was back again. The edge in his raised voice had felt like a slap. When had I become so delicate?

Mark's face cleared and he unlocked the French doors.

I walked into the sunshine, feeling its warmth and willing it to banish the cold that ran through me. I wished I'd answered the phone to Parveen, that I'd accepted her offer to take me home. The lawn was overgrown but there were borders that had obviously been well tended and a conifer at the end, which shielded them from the house behind. I tilted my face to the sun and closed my eyes. Without thinking, I slipped a hand into the pocket of my hoodie. My fingers wrapped around something squishy but textured. I ran my thumb over it, feeling the napped surface of the fabric until the pieces clicked into place and realised that it was Rabbity.

Mark took my other hand and was squeezing my fingers; his thumb stroked my palm and I wanted to pull away. I opened my eyes and looked around. 'It's lovely. Shall we look upstairs?'

Mark looked pleased. Like I'd suggested we should shag. Which, I realised with a horrible sinking feeling, he could well be thinking. We had bought a house. He had bought a house. For us. I wasn't in hospital any more. I was, medically speaking, well enough for sex.

He led the way and, as soon as his back was turned, I pulled Rabbity out of my pocket. I didn't remember putting the toy there. Mark had packed my stuff while I dressed. I regarded Rabbity. He lay in my hand, a remnant from my distant past.

Inside I gripped the rabbit in one hand and the banister with the other. The bedrooms were light and bright and spacious. The fourth room was tiny, as I'd been warned, but I could see a little desk in there with my laptop or a comfy armchair and a pile of books. The narrow window looked out on to the garden.

I didn't want to go into the master bedroom, after my recent realisation. I didn't want to confront the way I felt. I didn't want to be near Mark, much less naked with him.

I stood in the doorway to the room, looking at the bed that seemed to be growing in size and importance as Mark walked around the room pointing out features.

Rabbity felt both soft and rough against my fingertips. I was gripping him so hard that my hand had begun to hurt.

'There's lots of space in the triple wardrobe,' Mark said. 'But we can always get a double, too, if we need one. There's plenty of room.'

I held Rabbity up to my face and inhaled, trying to shake the feeling that my old soft toy was here to tell me something. I had to stop expecting things to be looking out for me. Geraint had looked out for me but he was dead. The ghost-birds seemed to have gone and the ghost-nurse in the hospital was a figment of my imagination, brought on by my reading too much local history and suffering a head injury. I had to accept that I was alone. Completely and utterly alone.

Rabbity's right ear was folded down, producing a quizzical appearance. His remaining eye bored into me with an intensity that was surprising in a soft toy. I knew that Mark had been with me when I'd crashed the car. I knew that I had been driving, though. Not only had the emergency services cut me out of the driver's side, but I remembered it. I could feel the steering wheel in my hands, see the rain-soaked windscreen, feel the vibrations of the engine.

'Meen?' Mark was still waiting.

'Don't call me that,' I said, playing for time. The words made something catch hold. Another click. A cog turned in my mind, locked into place and, suddenly, I knew. 'We broke up.'

Mark looked serious. 'Once. Ages ago.'

'No,' I said, the feeling of certainty already slipping away. 'Before the accident. That day. We argued and—'

'We argued.' Mark nodded. 'One of our humdingers, but we didn't break up. That's crazy.'

I frowned, trying to hold on to the memory. It had been so bright and clear a moment ago. 'But we did. We argued and we broke up. You left. You went drinking and then—' I faltered. I could see Mark as a white blurry shape, standing in the garden of my flat outside the French doors. The French doors that were like an older, scabbier version of the ones in this new and shiny house.

Mark plucked Rabbity out of my grasp and took hold of my hands. He stared deep into my eyes. 'Try to hold on to reality, Mina. Stay with me.'

'What?'

'You know what Dr Kanthe said. You are going to struggle to adjust. Your memories are still very scrambled and then there's false memory syndrome, post-traumatic stress disorder, cognitive impairment—'

I couldn't stand to meet his eyes, focused on his forehead instead. On the lines that crossed his skin, on the place where his hairline met his face.

'I love you,' Mark was saying. 'We're finally in a good place. We can put the past behind us.' He was pulling on my hand, gently leading me into the room and towards the bed.

I walked with him while my mind whirled. 'But we broke up. I finished things, I . . .' I stopped talking. I had been going to say 'I was relieved' but that was cruel.

'We didn't,' he said, fierce now. 'You have to stop saying these things. You'll ruin everything.'

There was a siskin on his shoulder and I felt a rush of joy at the sight. I felt like something I had lost had come back to me and, as I focused on the little yellow bird, the memory came back, sharp and clear. I remembered that I saw a siskin on the morning of the accident, the first ghost-bird I'd seen since Geraint's suicide. I remembered the argument. I remembered that I broke up with Mark then. I knew that I didn't love him before the accident either. That I had never actually loved him. I knew it in every part of me, in every cell. The strange feelings of detachment and irritation weren't symptoms at all.

I moved back and his grip tightened. Suddenly I was afraid. I knew that something bad had happened in the car. The feel of his hand gripping my arm brought it back. It was as if Mark remembered it, too, at the same moment. Our eyes locked.

After a pause in which my relief at remembering something so completely was replaced by both sadness and panic, Mark's eyes widened slightly. His expression softened and his grip relaxed enough for me to step away.

'I'm sorry,' he said, apparently determined to close the door on our discussion. 'Did I hurt you?'

'Not now,' I said. 'Before, though. It was you. In the car.'

He sat down abruptly.

'We were fighting. You were really drunk.'

'Don't,' he said, hands over his face.

'You grabbed my arm, pulled me.'

'I'm sorry. I didn't mean to hurt you.'

I looked down at myself. The blue neoprene knee support and its attendant strapping, the mottled red skin underneath scarred and burned. I didn't feel angry. I didn't feel anything. I just wanted to get away from him.

'Have you got my bag?'

Mark looked up. 'What?'

'My bag. May I have it?' I kept my voice carefully polite and neutral.

'It's in the hall,' he said. 'Wait here and I'll get it for you.'

I moved with him, wanting to get my bag and be out of the house and away from Mark as quickly as possible. Once I was outside, I'd be able to think. I could call Stephen and he'd come and pick me up.

Mark was too quick, though, and he was on the other side of the door and closing it on me before I'd realised what was happening. It slammed shut and there was a scratching sound. I tried to open it, but the original period-feature lock was clearly fully operational. 'Mark?'

His voice, startlingly close, reached me through the wood. 'Don't panic. I just want to talk.'

'Let me out,' I said, trying to sound calm and a little bit amused, as if this was just some momentary lapse of social etiquette and not a terrifying abuse of my civil liberties.

'I want you to understand,' he said, from the other side of the door. 'You need to understand. I didn't do anything wrong.'

Anger momentarily overtook my fear. 'You made me crash the car! You could've killed me. You could've killed us both.'

'I made a mistake. I was upset.' Mark sounded distressed but his voice was measured, it still had that even tone that suggested a career in politics. It made me more frightened even than the locked door.

I took a deep breath. 'Okay, fine. I hear you. A mistake. It's fine, it's over.' I just wanted him to open the door, I just wanted to get out.

I heard a scraping sound and pictured Mark sliding down against the other side of the door to sit on the floor. I tried the handle again but it didn't budge. I looked around but there wasn't a phone.

'Mark,' I said, 'this is crazy. You have to let me out.'

Silence. I tried the door again.

'You're frightening me.'

'I wanted to stay with you. It all happened really fast.'

'It's okay,' I lied. 'I don't care. I understand.'

'I mean, I was really disorientated.'

Drunk, Mark. You were really drunk. Then the full implication of his words hit home. He'd left me in the car, bleeding and unconscious. 'You left me for dead.'

'That's not true. That's not how it happened. I think I passed out or something, and then I was on a kind of autopilot. I don't really remember anything about the accident. I was out of the car and on the other side of the road.'

Nice for you. They had to cut me out of the car. I didn't say it, though. I pressed my lips together and moved, as quietly as I could, to the other side of the room. I checked the bay window, but the sashes were locked down and I couldn't see a key. Not that I'd be able to climb down the outside of the house, anyway. I looked out, hoping to see a passer-by who might be able to help, prepared to bang on the glass and wave my arms, but the street was deserted.

I limped back just in time to hear Mark saying, 'Mina? Meen?' He opened the door and pushed past me, grabbing my arm and pulling me over. I fell heavily to the floor, my knee screaming and pain blooming behind my eyes.

'What were you doing?' He was practically screaming into my face, spittle flying.

'Nothing, I'm just listening.'

He lay on top of me, crushing my ribs. 'You were trying to get out, don't lie.'

'You're hurting me, I can't breathe.' I felt the pressure ease as he took some of his weight on his arms. His face was an inch from mine and I considered spitting at him. But what then? I might distract him for a split second but I couldn't do anything with that advantage. He was bigger than me, stronger than me and far, far healthier. I was five feet tall and could barely walk. I had to calm him down. I had to be ingratiating.

'I'm listening,' I said. 'I still don't understand why you left me. You say you love me—'

'You weren't alone. A car had already stopped, there was someone leaning in, checking on you, and some guy was on his phone. I knew they were calling for help. There wasn't any need for me to get involved.'

'You *were* involved.'

'But I didn't have to be, that's the point. What would that have solved? And I had to think of my position. I could lose my job over something like this and I was thinking of our future. I couldn't buy us a house like this if I lost my job. Don't you see? I did it for us.'

Suddenly, I realised what this was all about. It wasn't about my understanding or about love; it was about silence. Mark Fairchild was terrified I was going to break mine. 'Let me out,' I said. 'I'm not going to say anything. I'm not going to the police or the papers or anyone. I just want you to let me go.'

'You're just saying that,' Mark said.

He was right, of course, I'd say anything to make him let me out. The tightness in my chest was worse and there was a band of pain around my skull. I was angry and I was scared.

'I need you to understand.' The calm note in his voice had gone now. He sounded the way he did back in the car. I remembered the windscreen wipers going manically, the way he had swung from drunk angry to bat-shit insane. The way I had been truly scared of him.

'Mark, I do understand,' I tried. 'It must've been a really scary experience.'

There was a short silence, as if he was weighing up my words, deciding which direction to take next. Finally, he said: 'I walked along the verge but when I tried to climb the bank, I fell down. I woke up hours later in a ditch. The traffic had built up by then and it was getting light. I hitched a ride and cleaned myself up, then I went to the hospital to find you but you were asleep.'

'I was in a coma.' I clamped my lips together. When would I learn to shut up? I had to stop antagonising him.

'I took one look at you and I knew that this whole experience had been a sign.'

'A sign?'

'To stop messing around. To get serious. We have another shot at happiness, Meen. We need to grab it with both hands.'

He sounded evangelical now, and all I could think of was the image of him grabbing me with both hands, wrapping them around my neck and squeezing.

'I need to think,' Mark said. Before I knew what was happening he had pulled me upright and into the hall. A door loomed in front of me and Mark wrenched it open. A moment later I was inside a cupboard and the door was slamming shut. I lurched forwards but was too late. The door clicked shut. I pushed against it with all my weight but it didn't budge. Mark was leaning against the other side. 'Mark!' I yelled through the door. 'Stop messing around.' I tried to take a step back in order to give myself more leverage to push the door, but my heel struck something hard. I put my hands out and felt the walls of the cupboard and, behind me, the pitted metal surface of a water tank.

'Just let me think for a moment.' Mark sounded panicked. His usual calm demeanour had cracked open and I had absolutely no idea what was lurking inside.

It was so dark in the cupboard, I felt the air pushing in on me. The panic making colours flash through the blackness. Or was it the sensory deprivation? Hadn't I read that somewhere? That if you deprived your eyes of light, the receptors started randomly firing. As if they couldn't bear the absence of colour and had to start producing their own.

Why hadn't I kept hold of my bag? My mobile was in the front pocket. If I had my mobile I could phone 999. I could get help. Without it I was lost and alone and there was no hope. Mark had gone too far. He knew it; I could hear it in his voice. I knew how logical he could be. The tone of his voice had changed. He didn't sound angry or desperate any more, he sounded thoughtful. Calm. He would follow this situation to its logical conclusion and, as always, seek to minimise his risk. I was the risk now. I remembered the accident and his part in it. I was certainly going to remember that he'd frightened me and grabbed me and locked me in a cupboard. What would he do to keep it quiet? To stop me from telling anybody?

'Let's just forget about all this,' I said. 'I don't care about the car. It was an accident. It's over. Let's just start again.'

A big sigh. 'I wish I could believe you meant that.'

Oh, God. Oh, God. He was going to kill me. He could push me down the stone steps, he could hold a pillow over my face. I was weak and I was alone and I was utterly trapped. I felt something brush my cheek in the dark and let out a short, startled yelp.

'All I wanted was for us to be together, to have a life together. It was going to be so perfect.' Mark's voice, on the other side of the door. He sounded robotic, like he was going through a little speech but saying somebody else's words.

I swiped frantically at my face and neck, checking for the spider or whatever bug had landed on me. There was something soft on my T-shirt, I recognised the texture and shape immediately. A small feather.

Another brush, this time to the other side of my face, and then, something landing lightly on my head. I felt tiny claws tightening on my scalp. I was about to open my mouth, possibly to scream for help, possibly to try and startle the birds away, but feathered bodies pressed against my face and I squeezed my lips shut. Tiny feathers were sneaking up my nose, wings beating around my head, bodies pressing in from every angle. I've never been frightened of my birds but right there, in the suffocating dark, I thought: *They're going to kill me.*

Then, just as quickly as they'd appeared, the birds were gone. All except one. I felt it jump from my head, the air moving as it half hopped, half flew in the cramped space. Then it was burrowing into my jacket, a wriggling warm body trying to insinuate itself between the denim outer and the cloth of my T-shirt. The sensation was unbearable and, in the darkness, horrifying. I couldn't stop thinking that the bird was trying to get to my skin. To peck at me, to rip at my flesh. I wanted to grab it but I was too scared so instead I frantically unbuttoned my jacket and opened it wide, flapping it to dislodge the bird. I gritted my teeth and brushed my hand over the inside of my jacket, waiting for the sharp pain of beak or claw. Instead, there was just clear air. The bird had gone. I patted myself quickly, checking for it, and found something else. A rectangular lump in my inside jacket pocket. My phone.

I slipped it out of the pocket. Mark wasn't talking any more and now, with rescue a possibility, I was frightened he would open the door, snatch the phone before I could do anything. I pressed the screen, hoping it wouldn't make a sound as it woke up. 'Mark?' I spoke loudly, wanting to cover any possible noises. 'We can work this out,' I said.

Nothing.

The phone was on, the screen glowing so brightly that it made my eyes water to look at it. I wanted to phone 999 straight away, but I knew that Mark was listening and that he'd hear me do it.

I didn't know whether you could text the emergency services, so instead I scrolled to Stephen's number and typed a quick text. I asked for help, not knowing if he'd realise how seriously I meant it, and pressed send. Next, I dialled 999, my fingers fumbling and making mistakes. I had the phone up to my ear and had just started to say 'police' and 'help', the panic overtaking again with the adrenaline surge of calling, when light flooded the cupboard.

Mark was there, roaring. I couldn't hear his words or the words of the emergency operator. I just kept talking. Mark knocked the phone out of my hand, but I carried on talking, I thought I was giving the address as fast as I could, but I could hear my voice and it was just garbled sounds.

I wanted to pick up the phone and say 'Come quickly'. I wanted to say 'He's going to kill me', because in that moment I believed it, but I didn't get the chance.

My terror was so complete I couldn't really see Mark any more. He was just a dark bulky shape, then his arms were around me, hugging me tightly. My face was pressed into the place between his chest and his armpit. In the past, that had been a pleasant place to be, but now I struggled against him.

To my surprise, he let me go. 'I'm sorry,' he said, shaking his head as if to clear it. 'I'm sorry. I'm sorry. Don't be afraid.'

My muscles were trembling and my bad leg was throbbing horribly. 'I need to—' I started to say, but then felt my head swimming.

Mark caught me before I hit the ground and I was vaguely aware of him helping me down the stairs and into the kitchen. Once I was sitting on a chair, he went to the sink and got one of the pristine glasses from the cupboard, filled it with tap water.

He passed it to me without saying anything, his eyes sad and beseeching.

After a few sips, I felt my head clear. 'You can't do things like that,' I said. 'You scared me.'

'I know,' Mark said. He sounded wretched. 'I'm sorry, Meen. It'll never happen again.'

I drank some more water, keeping hold of the glass and thinking of how I could use it as a weapon if Mark lost control again. I didn't feel scared, though. Perhaps I'd passed through and come out the other side, used up all my adrenaline or something, but I felt weirdly calm.

Mark got down on to his knees next to my chair, an arm's length away. 'Mina, please.'

'I don't think we're good for each other,' I said, keeping my voice level. 'I'm not angry with you. And I really don't care about what happened in the car. I meant what I said, it's in the past.'

He tipped his head to one side. 'Why would you forgive me so easily?'

I shrugged. 'I'm not going to tell anybody about it. I've got no interest in ruining your life or getting you into trouble.'

Mark shook his head. 'I wish I could believe you. I want to believe you, but after . . .' He gestured helplessly, seeming to encompass the house he'd bought, my strapped up leg, the cupboard he'd recently used to imprison me.

'I wasn't very fair to you,' I said. 'Now that my memories are back, I'm quite ashamed of a lot of them. All you ever did was love me and I pushed you away. I was cruel. I should have broken up with you ages ago, but I didn't. Being with you made me feel safe.'

Mark winced.

'And it was convenient. I made you think there was something more between us when there wasn't, when I knew it was never going to work long-term.' I took a breath. 'I didn't love you and I shouldn't have kept you hoping. I'm sorry for that.'

'You did love me,' Mark said. 'Once. I saw it.'

I wanted to say 'I really didn't' but he was close to tears. 'I'm sorry,' I said, instead.

'So, what happens now?'

'You need to get a new job.'

'I beg your pardon?' Mark looked instantly more his usual self.

'London's nice, you could try there.'

'I just bought this house,' he said. 'And I have a good position at work, I'm not looking for a change.'

'And I'm not looking to make trouble, but I can't see you every day at the hospital. I can't work for you. I forgive you and I don't want to punish you, but I don't think I should have to leave my job in order to protect you. That doesn't seem fair.'

Mark opened his mouth but no sound came out.

'You get a job in another hospital, sell this place or rent it out, I don't care. Then we can both put this behind us and nobody gets hurt.'

'And if I don't agree?'

I shook my head. 'You do agree. Really. Just have a little think about it and you'll see that it's for the best all round.'

The doorbell rang and Mark jumped. 'Oh, Christ. Oh, Christ.'

I felt a surge of panic. I didn't want the truce to break, for Mark to flip out. 'It's okay. If it's the police, I'll tell them everything's fine.'

It wasn't the police. It was Stephen. I heard his voice and stood up in time to see him push past Mark in the hall. 'Mina!' he called through. 'Where are you?'

'I'm okay,' I called back and then he was there, his hands on my shoulders, his sweet concerned face peering down at me.

'What the hell is going on?' Mark had gone from placating to furious in one, frighteningly easy, step. 'I knew something was going on between you.'

'Do shut up,' I said to him. 'You're not in any position to make accusations.'

Mark shut his mouth.

'I'm fine,' I said to Stephen, keeping my voice carefully calm. 'I just need a lift home.'

His forehead wrinkled and he looked around at Mark, who'd followed him into the kitchen. 'What's going on?' He turned back to me. 'Mina, you said—'

'I know,' I said quickly. 'But it's fine. We were having a bit of an argument but it's over now. I just want to go.' I had the strongest feeling that I had to keep everything as calm and normal as possible. That this was the only possible way we would all get out alive.

'Okay,' Stephen said. He still looked worried, like he wanted to give me a quick physical exam, shine his little torch into my eyes and ears.

I held on to him, leaning against his body and letting him step around so that I was shielded from view.

Mark had visibly calmed himself. I could see him calculating the new situation. There was a witness now, another player. The situation had changed and he altered his demeanour to suit it. He was already remaking the last twenty minutes over to suit himself. 'Here are your keys,' he said, passing across the keys to my flat.

'Thank you,' I said. I was careful not to touch his fingers as I took them, as if the slightest contact would set him off again, change the rules of this fragile truce.

'I don't know where the spares are, but I'll pop them round.' Mark's voice was reasonable. The mask had slipped back over his face. I could almost convince myself I heard the 'click' as it locked into place.

I was going to change the locks that afternoon, but I nodded. 'Thanks.'

Once I was outside and Stephen had helped me to navigate the steps to the pavement, I began to shake. 'Quicker than an ambulance,' I said to him, to cover my weakness. 'Very impressive.'

'I was on my way before I got your text. Are you sure you're all right?' Stephen was ignoring Mark, which felt strange. I was used to his hyper-polite professionalism. But then I realised that he wasn't so much ignoring Mark as remaining completely focused on me.

'We're outside,' I said, stupidly. 'I'm used to seeing you inside. In the hospital.'

'I've seen you outside,' he said, smiling a little. 'In the garden that time.'

'I forgot about that.' I felt disconnected. Like nothing was real. We were chatting about the crappy patients' garden while the man who'd put me in the hospital was hovering behind us.

Stephen stayed close to me, looking at me very carefully with a professional, assessing gaze. 'Let me get the car door.' He opened the passenger door and pushed the seat back before helping me inside. He didn't look in Mark's direction once. Neither did I.

When the car was moving and I could look around without fear of seeing Mark or the house, reality seemed to slip back. 'Thank you,' I said.

'No problem.' Stephen was concentrating on the road and didn't look at me. I was grateful for it and watched him drive.

As my thoughts began to stop tumbling, something Stephen had said caught up with me. 'You said you were already on your way.'

He nodded, not looking at me. 'I just had a bad feeling.'

'About me?'

'About Mark. I wasn't even meant to be in today. Day off. But I was visiting one of my old dears and then Natalie told me you'd gone home. She assumed I was in to see you.'

Before I could digest that, he added: 'Should I take you to the hospital?'

'No,' I said quickly. 'I'm fine. I swear. I just want to go home.'

'No problem,' Stephen said, and went all the way around the next roundabout, doubling back to take the road leading to my flat.

After a few minutes, I said: 'You haven't asked me what happened.'

'I thought you'd tell me if you wanted to,' he said. 'You're safe and that's all that matters.'

Safe. I liked the sound of that and, better yet, I realised that was exactly how I felt. Safe enough to talk. 'I've remembered the accident.' I pulled the seat belt so that it wasn't pressing against my sore shoulder. 'Mark was in the car with me,' I said. 'When I crashed.'

'Oh, Christ,' Stephen said. 'And he hadn't told you?'

'No.' I let the bitterness take over. It was easier than all the other feelings. 'He omitted to mention it.'

I could feel the questions that Stephen wanted to ask, floating in the air between us. I tried to sort out my thoughts. I couldn't articulate the way I felt because it was so mutable. Just when I thought I had hold of a feeling, it slipped away.

'Bastard,' Stephen said. 'Why didn't he tell you?'

'We were arguing,' I said. 'He grabbed me. Pulled my arm and the car swerved out of the lane. I know I hit the barrier, but I still don't remember doing that. Probably for the best.'

Stephen's jaw went tight. After a moment he said: 'He made you crash. How the hell did he walk away from that?'

'I don't know,' I said. 'I guess he was just lucky. He's that kind of guy.'

'Are you going to tell the police?'

I liked the way he asked me what I was going to do. Mark would've said, 'You've got to tell the police.' Pat would've said, 'You've got to keep your mouth shut and marry the doctor.' Or, I realised, maybe she wouldn't. I couldn't keep assuming the worst about her, it wasn't fair. I wasn't a teenager any more.

'He could've killed you,' Stephen said, his voice small. Upset.

'He could've killed us both,' I said.

'That doesn't make it okay.'

I didn't reply and we made the rest of the journey in uneasy silence. I half expected Stephen to turn the car around yet again, drive me to the police station and force me to make a statement. Of course, then I remembered – he wasn't Mark. Or Pat. Or even Ger. He had never done anything except exactly what I'd asked of him. He'd never pushed. Never forced. He was the kind of man I'd always dismissed as weak. Certainly as 'too nice' for me. But now, suffused with gratitude at the sight of my building, and the quiet calm of Stephen's presence, I realised I'd been an idiot. More of an idiot than I had ever previously realised.

Stephen opened the door and helped me out. 'What can I do? Do you need anything?'

'Come inside? I don't want to be alone.'

'Of course,' he said. 'Although, as your doctor, I think I should check you over.'

'You're not my doctor any more.'

'Good thing, too,' he said, grinning suddenly. 'I'd be struck off.'

I stared at him for a moment before saying in my best Pat impression: 'Dr Adams, are you flirting with a woman who has just come out of hospital?'

He flipped the switches in the hallway and took my arm to help me inside. 'That depends on how you feel about it.'

'Pretty good,' I said quickly.

'Well, then. Answer's yes.'

The afternoon sunlight was coming through the French doors, casting squares of golden light on to the floor in the living room. I limped to the purple couch and sat down. It might not have looked as good as the one I'd imagined, but in that moment it felt like heaven. The adrenaline was leaving my body and I felt slightly sick.

Stephen was giving me his worried look again. 'Flirting aside, I would actually like to check your vitals. May I?'

'Be my guest,' I said, lying back and closing my eyes. I felt his fingers gently grip my wrist and even though I knew he was just taking my pulse, I let myself believe he was holding me.

GRACE

When Grace was admitted into the Royal Sussex with a broken hip, aged ninety-seven, she wasn't surprised. As she explained to the slip of a girl who was inexpertly washing her face, 'I always knew I'd end up back here eventually.'

The girl didn't seem to understand or perhaps she didn't want to make conversation. Or, and this was entirely possible, Grace's words hadn't come out clearly. They did that these days. She opened her mouth and a terrible jumble fell out. Grace didn't mind; she was very tired and her hip was sore. She slept.

While she slept she dreamed of her nursing days. The days before she'd telephoned Thomas and told him he could take her out to the Blackbird Tearoom. The days before they'd married and she'd become a housewife and a mother. Days that, in truth, she seemed to think about more and more. She couldn't seem to keep the names of her grandchildren and great-grandchildren straight in her mind, but she could remember conversations with Evie word for word.

It was a sign of being very old, she knew. She'd cared for enough old dears in her time to know that. People always regressed to their earlier memories. Sometimes, these days, she found it hard even to picture her lovely Thomas, and had to look at his photograph on the sideboard. He had been so handsome. There had been fun with the children and lemon cake and tea out of the good cups, but for some reason her mind kept going back to scrubbing the floor and those bally bedpans.

She was remembering patients, too. A parade of the sick and injured. So many that she nursed to health and so many that she lost. Like Billy. She could see the toy train running over his bedclothes and his sweet face as he watched it, just as if it was happening right in front of her. It wasn't though, Grace reminded herself. That was a long time ago. Besides, Billy had succumbed to a chest infection and had never gone home. 'You can't save them all,' Grace whispered. Somebody had said that. Grace couldn't remember who.

Her breathing didn't feel quite the thing. There was a gurgling in her chest. 'Pneumonia?' she asked the doctor (who, in truth, looked no older than a schoolchild – how had she ever been so frightened of them?). He patted her hand. ''Fraid so.'

'Well, that's me done for,' Grace said. She wasn't sure whether she'd said the words out loud – little things like that kept slipping past her now – but her doctor smiled. 'Nonsense. Antibiotics will sort that in no time.' He was a nice man. Sometimes she mixed him up with one of her grandsons and he had to say 'No, Grace. I'm Dr Adams', and then she felt foolish.

Grace looked around at the ward. It was very different, of course, but she recognised the worn black strip running around the room. It was simply covered in scuff marks and, she hated to admit it, Sister had been right. 'It looked better polished,' she said, and almost choked. She had forgotten that a girl with lots of little plaits all over her head was trying to spoon soup into her mouth and she spat some on to the table. The girl tutted and got another spoonful, but Grace closed her lips tight.

She couldn't taste anything and she just wanted to go back to sleep. Her dreams were so much more interesting than being awake although, quite honestly, she could no longer be entirely sure which was which. She was tired, though, so she let her heavy eyelids shut.

She'd had the feeling that there was something she was meant to do, one last thing. There was always one last thing. Just when you thought your shift was over and your legs were aching like the devil and you were so tired you thought you would faint at any moment. Always the way at the end of your shift. You've got one foot out of the door and plans for your off-duty and that's when someone decides to sick up some blood or Sister is just being awkward for the sake of it and calls you back to refold the bandages.

'Bandages?'

The girl's voice seemed to come from far away.

Not bandages. But a girl. Young thing. Grace felt a stab of fear for her. There were so many awful things that could happen to a young girl. You had to be so careful. Be so good. One slip and everything unravelled. Like a load of ironed bandages falling out of the linen cupboard and rolling over the floor. What a mess.

Sister was shouting at Grace. She'd forgotten something again. Not her cuffs. Not the bedpans or the drinks round. There was a girl lying in a bed. Grace watched her sleeping, wondering what she was supposed to do for her, wondering what she'd forgotten.

'Sister will have my guts for garters,' she said to Evie.

'Don't worry, old stick,' Evie said. 'I'll cover for you.' It was Evie as she was then. Young and beautiful and full of mischief. Not the old lady who'd exchanged letters with Grace right up until she died.

Grace felt her breath rattling in her chest. It was like trying to breathe the soup that girl had been feeding her. Thick, gelatinous mushroom soup. She'd never liked the stuff, but she didn't feel in the slightest bit frightened . . . At once, she knew that she didn't have to be frightened of anything at all.

She was wearing a dress made of silver and she knew she was beautiful. She thought she was in the mirror, wearing a hat with funny spikes and a lance-thing with streamers pouring from the top. She smiled at herself and Evie's lipsticked smile shone back at her.

MINA

There was a buzzard over the field on the left. As we flashed past, I caught just a glimpse of the bird hanging on an air current, surveying the ground for prey. I half expected to see it a moment later on the bonnet or, perhaps, sitting on the back seat amongst our coats, but when I turned to check, there was nothing there.

'You okay?' Stephen glanced at me then looked back at the road. I still liked how careful he was, how measured.

'Perfect,' I said. The buzzard hadn't appeared in the car because it had been a real bird, not a ghost. I had a feeling that they had gone for good. I'd told Parveen about them over lunch at the Blackbird, a vintage-style tearoom, and had been amazed by her matter-of-fact acceptance. 'The dead watch over us,' she said. Like it was something everybody knew, as self-evident as the pretty china teacups on the table or the scone she was busy demolishing.

It took Stephen and me almost five hours to get to the village. We argued amicably about music and listened to comedy podcasts and didn't talk about Mark or Geraint or my accident or any of it.

I watched his face as we put Swansea behind us and drove on to the peninsula. The roads narrowed and the sea appeared on our left, glittering and vast. To the right, we passed the long ridge of Cefn Bryn and I looked up at it, remembering the cairns and standing stones, the secret hollows and the endless bracken and prickly gorse of summers past.

Stephen switched off the iPod as we got closer and I gave him directions. The roads narrowed further, the thick foliage raking against the sides of the car, and Stephen slowed to a crawl. Then, like bursting out from a tunnel, we dropped down a twisting road and into the village. The shop on the main street looked the same, the post box was the same and the old red telephone box, one of the originals that hadn't yet been upgraded or carted away, still stood on the corner.

'Bloody hell,' Stephen said, looking around. 'I didn't know you'd grown up in the nineteen fifties.'

'Down here,' I said, indicating a side road. I was tense now, couldn't really cope with the overload of memory and familiarity, coupled with the terror of bringing Stephen home. I'd never brought anybody home. I'd remembered the arguments with Mark about it. I'd refused to go home, let alone take him there. The shame and the guilt and the fear I'd felt had coalesced. The mass of it had weighed me down, anchored me to London and then Brighton. I felt lighter now, even with the heavy strapping on my leg and the ache in my back. I was still terrified, though.

The village was a blink-and-you'll-miss-it cluster of houses and ours was further down the road. We turned the oh-so-familiar corner, caught the slice of green leading down to the hidden bay and the sea beyond, before the view was obscured by trees, and then there it was. The whitewashed house I grew up in.

I had a photograph of my mother standing in that same front garden. She was heavily pregnant and had one hand up, shading her eyes from the sun. For a moment I could see her there with her long blonde hair piled up on top of her head. Pat was in the photograph, too, squinting painfully but keeping her hands demurely crossed in front of her body. Although I'd always thought of them as wildly different, they looked in that picture like true identical twins. They were the same height, they had the same features and the same colouring. I was the same height as Pat now, and if Mum were still alive we'd make a little cluster of short, slight women with messy hair.

I added Grace, my ghost-nurse, to the little group. She would have the neatest hair of any of us, and the sweetest smile. I couldn't help but picture her in black and white, even though she'd appeared to me in colour. I knew that she'd been trying to warn me about Mark; she had watched over me as if I was worth saving and I would never forget that kindness.

Stephen was next to me, looming as always. It wasn't as if he could help it, the poor guy, and he wasn't in the slightest bit intimidating. He seemed uncertain, leaning backwards in his efforts not to impose. I grabbed his hand and pulled him forwards, through the little gate and to the front door. 'Thank you,' I said. 'For bringing me home. For coming with me.'

'No problem,' Stephen said, his cheeks flaming red. He was a blusher and I found it completely adorable.

I lifted my hand to ring the bell but the door swung open.

'All right there, *bach*?' Dylan was on his way out. He had his gun hanging by his side and for a moment my heart skipped a beat. He looked Stephen up (and up and up) and, for a split second, I thought he was going to shoulder his weapon.

'This is Stephen,' I said.

'Good to meet you.' Stephen held out his hand.

'The doctor,' Dylan commented. He nodded slightly and said, 'Stay for dinner.'

Stephen nodded politely. He was probably thinking that he had had no intention of driving back to Brighton without eating, but he didn't show any sign of it.

Dylan walked down the path, patting my shoulder as he passed. He set off towards the beach and, once he was a good distance away, Stephen leaned down and whispered in my ear: 'Does your uncle always greet people with a shotgun in his hands?'

'Only the boys,' I said.

'It won't help,' he said, normal volume.

'What do you mean?' I turned to face him, tilting my head so that I could look into his eyes.

He smiled down at me with such fondness that I felt my heart squeeze almost painfully. 'I couldn't stop loving you if I tried.'

'Have you tried?' I managed.

'Not particularly. Why? Did you want me to?'

I paused. There had been so much pain in the last few months. So much fear and so much uncertainty. He was part of all of that. It wasn't his fault, but he was always going to be mixed up with the hospital and the accident and the fresh grief over Geraint. The good feeling I had around him was always going to be rooted in pain and loss. 'No,' I said. 'I think I can live with it.'

He put his arms around me then, and touched his lips to my cheeks, my forehead, until I shifted my head and caught him in a proper kiss. We stayed like that until I heard Pat's voice from the hallway, carrying through the open front door.

'Mina Morgan! Are you canoodling on my front step in front of God and all the village?'

I smiled against Stephen's mouth and let my body relax against his for a moment. He tightened his arms and then let me go, settling me securely, checking that I was balanced.

Pat appeared, wiping her hands on a checked tea towel. 'Well, at least I know you're feeling better. Back to your usual shameless self.' Then I turned to face the house and, with Stephen's hand clasped tightly in my own, I went home.

ACKNOWLEDGEMENTS

Thank you to Keris Stainton and my lovely mum for reading the opening chapters and encouraging me to carry on. Also to Sally-anne Sweeney, for her editorial guidance and support, and the team at Lake Union for their belief in this book.

Dr Rachel Bodey was kind enough to let me steal details of her job for Mina, and to talk me through the technicalities. Any mistakes are my own.

I am also indebted to the excellent and comprehensive history of the Royal Sussex County Hospital by Harry Gaston, *Brighton's County Hospital, 1828–2007*.

The first scribblings of this story were begun during my MLitt studies at St Andrews and I'd like to express my gratitude to my tutors and fellow students, especially Nadine Kirzinger for her kindness and friendship.

To my brother, Matthew, and my dearest friend, Cath: thank you for always having my back.

Thank you to my wonderful children, Holly and James, for inspiring me every day; and, as always, to my Dave: I could not do this without you.

ABOUT THE AUTHOR

Sarah Painter writes contemporary fiction with a touch of magic. Her debut novel, *The Language of Spells*, became a Kindle bestseller. The follow-up, *The Secrets of Ghosts*, is also available now. Sarah lives in rural Scotland with her children, husband and a grey tabby called Zelda Kitzgerald. She drinks too much tea, loves the work of Joss Whedon and is the proud owner of a writing shed.